# JASPAR TRISTRAM

Edward Ashley Walrond Clarke was born in 1860. From 1876 to 1879, he was a pupil at Radley College, experiences which would later serve as the basis for his only novel, *Jaspar Tristram* (1899). This book inspired mixed reviews: some critics thought it a masterpiece and compared it favourably with the works of Henry James, while others considered it dull and morbid. Though the novel did not sell well enough to run into a second edition, it gained a cult popularity in gay literary circles, being avidly read by Oscar Wilde, Edward Carpenter, and Marc-André Raffalovich among others, and may well have been an influence on E. M. Forster's *Maurice* and Evelyn Waugh's *Brideshead Revisited*. Little is known about Clarke's life, except that he joined the Foreign Office in 1881 and by 1909 was stationed in Zanzibar, where he died of heart failure in 1913.

A. D. Harvey read history at St. John's College, Oxford and obtained a Ph.D. at Cambridge University in 1972. He taught English briefly at Cambridge, and later at Italian, French and German universities. His books include *Sex in Georgian England: Attitudes and Prejudices from the 1720s to the 1820s* (1994) and *Body Politic: Political Metaphor and Political Violence* (2007), and the novels *Warriors of the Rainbow* (2000) and *Mind-Sprung* (2015). He has also contributed to the *Times Literary Supplement* and *London Magazine*.

# JASPAR TRISTRAM

## 𝔄 𝔖𝔱𝔬𝔯𝔶

### A. W. CLARKE

*'Sans l'advertissement d'aultruy je veois assez
le peu que tout ceci vault et poise.'*

With a new introduction by
A. D. HARVEY

VALANCOURT BOOKS

*Jaspar Tristram* by A. W. Clarke
First published London: Heinemann, 1899
First Valancourt Books edition 2015

Published by Valancourt Books, Richmond, Virginia
http://www.valancourtbooks.com

ISBN 978-1-941147-48-1 (trade paperback)
Also available as an electronic book.

All Valancourt Books publications are printed on acid free paper that meets all ANSI standards for archival quality paper.

Set in Dante MT 10.5/12.8

# INTRODUCTION

When A. W. Clarke's only novel *Jaspar Tristram* was published in the late summer of 1899 it quickly found an admirer in Oscar Wilde ('The early part – half Hellenic – is charming'); Edward Carpenter, author of *Homogenic Love*, asked a friend for a loan of a copy; André Raffalovich, apostle of 'unisexualité', had his own copy specially bound in mauve morocco. The book was widely reviewed in the press, though there was considerable disagreement regarding its merits. *The Times* (4 Oct. 1899) thought it 'a study of character in the manner of Henry James,' presented 'with such delicate art, with so sure a knowledge of human nature, that we have read it from beginning to end with keen interest,' and *The Liverpool Mercury* (22 Nov. 1899) judged the book to be written in 'a style little removed from distinguished,' but *The Publishers' Circular* (21 Oct. 1899, p. 442) thought 'it would still have been laboriously dull' even if it had been shortened by at least half, and *The Glasgow Herald* (10 Aug. 1899) dismissed it as 'a very tedious record.' The problem for many reviewers was the novel's protagonist, the Jaspar Tristram of the title. *The Graphic* (14 Oct. 1899), for example, complained:

> The notes of his character from first to last – for it never changes – are morbid imaginativeness; a limitless vanity which he mistakes for ambition and genius alternating, very occasionally, with abject self-contempt; sensuality; jealousy; and a craving for sympathy which compels him invariably to say or do the most foolish possible thing at the worst possible time.

Only *The Morning Post* (10 Sept. 1899) gave much attention to the aspect of the book that had attracted Oscar Wilde, Edward Carpenter and André Raffalovich, and it did so in sneeringly dismissive terms:

> We hear little of the outdoor and breezy side of school life, of the cricket and the football, the athletic sports and the paperchase, but a good deal of the sentimental aspect, of the broken heart of Jones Major when Robinson supplants him in the affections of Smith Minor . . . .

*Jaspar Tristram*'s status as the first novel ever to deal with the psychological and almost physical torment of homoerotic passion was simply not noticed – at least not in public.

The first novels in English to depict a homosexual involvement were probably A. C. Benson's pseudo-biography *Memoirs of Arthur Hamilton, B.A.* of 1886, and Howard Sturgis's *Tim* of 1891, though the homoerotic aspect was as far as possible veiled and euphemized and apart from some surreptitiously circulated volumes of pornography such as the anonymous (and bisexual) *Teleny, or, The Reverse of the Medal: A Physiological Romance of Today* (1893), unreliably attributed to Oscar Wilde, the sexual aspect of homosexuality was not given emphasis till *Imre* (privately printed, Naples 1906) by 'Xavier Mayne' (i.e., Edward Prime-Stevenson) and, within Britain, not till the publication (and prosecution) in 1918 of a relatively circumspect work, *Despised & Rejected* by 'A. T. Fitzroy' (i. e., Rose Laure Allatini). The homosexual element in *Jaspar Tristram* was evidently rendered acceptable to most of its first readers (even if seeming rather soppy to *The Morning Post*) by the fact that it related to a school-boy 'friendship', and a more conventional love interest is introduced after the protagonist leaves school and transfers his passion to his beloved's younger sister.

It was the school-boy section of *Jaspar Tristram*, and the account A. W. Clarke gave in the novel of life at an English Public School (i.e. private boarding school) that claimed the attention of most of the early reviewers, and rereading the book after an interval of some years it is something of a surprise to find that the second part, dealing with Jaspar's love for Nita Southwood, is just as long as the first part dealing with his schoolboy infatuation for her brother Els. Certain passages dealing with Nita after she had grown up and 'come out' have a physical relish that was unusual in Victorian fiction:

> he grudged to lose before he must the pleasure of feeling her young body alive under the stiff sheath of whalebone and silk in which it was laced. (*JT* p. 227)

> Other beauties too there were now for the first time visible: the rounded satin-smooth shoulders whose dazzling whiteness he had never seen anything to match, and the firm small breasts. (*JT* p. 228)

But for the most part the Nita half of the novel is as unmemorable as the first half, focused on her brother, is unforgettable. It may be that in the conditions of upper-class social life that prevailed circa 1880 young ladies really did appear indistinct and elusive to the young men who courted them, but one cannot help noticing that Nita seems a good deal less distinct and vividly realised when she becomes a marriageable young miss than when she had been a pubescent tomboy who constantly reminded Jaspar of her brother.

A similar switch between siblings occurs more than a generation later in Evelyn Waugh's *Brideshead Revisited*. Though Lord Sebastian Flyte is involved in a homosexual relationship later in *Brideshead Revisited*, and had evidently been at least a target for erotic longings earlier when still at school, he is never portrayed as an essentially sexual being; Charles Ryder's relationship with Lord Sebastian's sister isn't less poignantly realized because Charles Ryder – or Evelyn Waugh himself – was a homosexual and couldn't portray heterosexuality convincingly but because the relationship with the sister, as both she and Charles Ryder came to recognize, was a false start, a deviation from the truth of who they were, or at best a necessary stage in a process of discovery, of facing up to eternal verities, that begins at Oxford with Lord Sebastian appearing at Charles Ryder's window and vomiting into his college room and ends in the chapel at Brideshead. The employment of a female 'twin' or 'double' to explore a homosexual, or at least homoerotic, relationship had also been attempted by two contemporaries of the author of *Jaspar Tristram*. In 1913 A. C. Benson, author of the very mutedly homoerotic *Memoirs of Arthur Hamilton, B.A.*, published a novel entitled *Watersprings* which took the author's delicacy with regard to saying what he really wanted to say a stage further. A Cambridge don (i.e. someone in the same profession as Benson himself) finds himself attracted to one of his pupils:

> his own feeling for the boy surprised Howard. He did not think him very interesting nor had they much in common except a perfect goodwill. It was to Howard as if Jack represented something beyond and further than himself, for which Howard cared – as one might love a house for the sake of someone who had inhabited it.

This sounds like a purely physical attraction if ever there was one. Then the don meets Jack's sister:

Maud had an extraordinary likeness to her brother, but with what a difference! Howard saw in an instant what it was that had haunted him in the aspect of Jack. This was what he seemed to have discerned all the time, and what had been baffling him.

Needless to say Howard and Maud get married, though this being 1913 and Benson being the son of an Archbishop we never learn if Howard fantasized about making love to Jack while performing his marital obligations with Jack's sister. Another approach to the same theme appears in *The Desire and Pursuit of the Whole* by the actively pederastic Frederick Rolfe, aka Baron Corvo, published posthumously in 1934. In this work Nicholas Crabbe becomes involved with a perfectly sexless girl called Zildo who customarily passes as a boy, and they eventually fall in love and marry. One may very well doubt whether Rolfe's Zildo, or A. C. Benson's Maud, ever had a real-life counterpart in these authors' lives, and one guesses that the same is true for Nita Southwood in A. W. Clarke's *Jaspar Tristram*.

The meagre details printed in *Who's Who* and the *Register* of St. Peter's College Radley constitute most of the facts we know about Clarke. His full name was Edward Ashley Walrond Clarke and though he dropped the 'Edward', or rather the initial 'E', from the title page of *Jaspar Tristram* he was later known to his subordinates in Zanzibar as Mr Edward Clarke. He was born in 1860, and was a pupil at Radley between 1876 and 1879. His father was a cavalry officer, and it is possible that both he and Clarke's mother died young and that the uncomfortable life during school holidays with an unsympathetic guardian described in the novel is based on real experience. Like his protagonist (*JT* p. 188), Clarke probably lived in Germany to study the language before joining the Foreign Office in 1881. He became head of the African department in 1904 and Agent and Consul General in Zanzibar in 1909. He died of heart failure in Zanzibar on 14 February 1913. The only clue we have regarding his sexuality is that in 1908 he married a general's blue-stocking daughter – a friend of George Moore's and contributor to *The Yellow Book* – who, aged in her mid-forties, was almost as old as himself. We may hypothesize a man emotionally ravaged in youth who eventually found some sort of closure in staid companionship in middle age: but we would be equally justified, with the minimal evidence available, in guessing at a man who after twenty years of frantically coupling with a prodigious succession of goodness knows what sort of sexual partners decided to settle down when the doctors began telling him he had overstrained his heart. The likelihood that he, like Benson and Rolfe, distorted the truth of his account of the emotional state of his novel's protagonist by intruding a female love-object suggests also the possibility that he edited, if not radically misrepresented, part of the truth behind his portrayal of the relationship of Jaspar and Els. The latter is far different from the wholesome and squeaky-clean love objects of Benson's and Sturgis's fiction. He is an archetypal example of what is, or at least over a period of a hundred years *used* to be, a familiar type at England's Public Schools: what is called a tart. His nickname, originally Elsie, is ostensibly derived from his initials L. C., standing for Lancelot Charles. Or is it? In his *Recollections of School Days at Harrow* (1890), H. J. Torre, who was at Harrow – one of the most famous English Public Schools – in the 1830s, recorded that 'boys with a very fair complexion usually received a feminine name, e.g. Polly, Sukey, Fanny, Dolly. . . . ,' and the implications of this were brought out in the *Memoirs* of John Addington Symonds, who was at Harrow twenty years later: 'Every boy of good looks had a female name, and was recognised either as a public prostitute or as some bigger fellow's "bitch".' Els cheerfully flaunts 'his slim and shapely' legs and arms (*JT* p. 86) His body language and facial expressions are what in a girl would be called flirtatious. (*JT* p. 67) He is constantly receiving notes, i.e. love letters, from other boys. (*JT* p. 71) His tussle with an older boy who has been doing his homework for him, which Jaspar overhears while hesitating outside the older boy's door, sounds distinctly erotic, if not sado-masochistic:

> 'Yes!' gurgled Els, who was seemingly being half choked.
> [. . .] there was a great noise of scuffling, and the wooden partition began to shake violently.
> 'Oh, you're hurting!' cried Els in muffled tones, and then there came a crash. (*JT* p. 62-63)

When Orr, the Senior Prefect and Captain of Boats, returns belatedly to the school some time after the beginning of term he immediately takes Els out of circulation: 'you're not likely to see much of him again!' (*JT* p. 66). In *A Tale of Halminster College* (1861) the Rev. Henry Cadwallader Adams, who had been both a pupil and a master at another of the older-established Public Schools, Winchester, explained:

Occasionally it will happen that some special quality in a boy, such as a pleasant and gentlemanly appearance, amusing wit and cleverness, precocious adroitness at football, cricket, or the like, will induce another much older than himself to 'take him up' as it is called, and bestow on him privileges which set him above those of his own position.

What else might be involved in being 'taken up' by an older boy is suggested by Adams in the remainder of the paragraph, where he describes one of those boys who

in every generation . . . become the centres of vice received from their forerunners, and who hand them on to their successors in the same unholy priesthood . . . A very high priest in this Devilish Succession was Charles Howard; to whom, as has before been said, Johnson, and it may be added many others also, had owed their ruin. A more dangerous associate for the younger boys of a public school cannot be imagined.

For some this was merely a matter of course: in later life Oscar Wilde's lover Lord Alfred Douglas dismissed their relationship with the offhand acknowledgement, 'I did with him and allowed him to do what was done among boys at Winchester and Oxford.'

According to John Addington Symonds's recollections of Harrow in the 1850s, 'Here and there one could not avoid seeing acts of onanism, mutual masturbation, the sport of naked boys in bed together.' In fact we have no way of assessing the incidence of such goings on at any one school, or the variations of incidence at different schools. It is not completely unlikely that these things were commoner at older-established public schools like Harrow and Winchester than at new foundations like Clarke's school, St. Peter's College, Radley (today Radley College), which needed to market themselves as nurseries of gentlemanly conduct and Christian principles: on the other hand, according to a history of Radley by Christopher Hibbert published in 1997, discipline was notably slack there throughout the 1870s. One way or another we just don't know what the schoolboy Clarke did or didn't do with a real-life prototype of the fictional Els Southwood. Nevertheless the convincingness of the tortured feelings set down in the novel suggests the painful recollection of real agonies, and the probability that the fictional Els did indeed have a real-life prototype is deducible from another publication in which Clarke occasionally featured.

There was a school magazine at St. Peter's College, Radley, appropriately named *The Radleian*, and Clarke appeared a number of times in its pages while a pupil. He was secretary of the Chess Club when it was established at the beginning of 1878 but was beaten in the first round of the chess tournament held during the summer time. Thereafter he evidently gave up chess, not being listed either as a member of the club in October 1878 or as a competitor in the chess tournament of that academic year. The protagonist of *Jaspar Tristram* seems the sort of youth who would resign in pique after failing to cut a dash, and this is what Clarke seems to have done. During the spring of 1878 he played Hermione in the Shakespeare Society's production of *The Winter's Tale*, but seems to have withdrawn from the society before the final night's performance, and when, during the same school term, he proposed the motion 'The Execution of Charles I was totally unjustifiable' at the Debating Society it was remarked how few members were present. He does not figure in any of the sports reports, which is also consistent with the characterization of Jaspar. It is tempting to assume that Clarke was the 'C.' addressed by the editor in a couple of notes in *The Radleian*: in April 1878, 'C. – Your poetry is a little too personal for insertion in the "Radleian". We shall, however, be glad to hear from you again', and in November 1878, more brutally, 'C. – Your poetry was pointless.'

The chief value of *The Radleian* to the biography of Clarke is that it suggests the possibility of identifying Jaspar Tristram's beloved. In the novel he is L. C. Southwood, later Lord Tremlett, the grandson of a duke and, after leaving school, a subaltern in Britain's most exclusive cavalry regiment, The Royal Horse Guards (Blues). There were no peers at Radley in Clarke's day and only a couple of peers' sons, though in other respects there is no doubt that the school called 'Bridwell' in *Jaspar Tristram* is a faithful portrait of Radley. The novel was reviewed in *The Radleian* when it came out and the reviewer, presumably one of the masters, had absolutely no doubts in the matter:

It deals with Radley in the times of the Wardenship of the Rev. C. Martin. Here we get all the phrases which must be peculiar to this place introduced without any apologies or explanation, as: – Upper

Octagon, Lower Octagon, Music Room, Bear Garden, Market Place, Upper Dormitory, &c., &c., and even the motto 'Sicut columbae'. This must make the book rather unintelligible to any one who does not know Radley. The book is rather morbid in tone, and is chiefly interesting as a character study. We believe that all the characters in the book have been identified by 'those who know'. (*The Radleian*, Dec. 1899.)

(There are in fact a number of detailed evocations of the school in the novel, e.g. p. 64, p. 111 and, especially, p. 131 where it is described none too fondly as 'a fine old country house . . . spoilt by the sham Gothic galleries, jerrybuilt chapels, tin passages, and all the other nondescript erections that had been put up.')

In the novel 'Els' is referred to as a favourite for the Junior Steeple Chase in the school sports, and winner of the Junior Hurdles (*JT* p. 80, 93) The winner of these two events at Radley in 1877 was William Griffith Forster, a boy roughly a year younger than Clarke who had joined the school in 1874 and left at the same time as Clarke in 1879. It is true that *The Radleian* does not enable us to identify another key character, Orr, Jaspar's rival for the affections of both 'Els' and his sister. In the novel Orr is somewhat older than Clarke, having bullied him mercilessly at prep school and having become Senior Prefect and Captain of Boats at Bridwell by the time Jaspar arrives there. In real life the three successive Captains of Boats of Clarke's school days were, respectively, a year older than, the same age as, and a year younger than Clarke. However the clue in the novel linking the real-life W. G. Forster to the fictional 'Els' seems convincing, for we find that the real-life W. G. Forster, a brewery manager rather than an officer in an elite regiment, died on 26 October 1898, eleven months before *Jaspar Tristram* was published.

Taken on its own *Jaspar Tristram* is an odd book for a successful Foreign Office official nearing forty to publish. It seems unlikely that he would have wished to publish it during the lifetime of 'Els's' original in any case. But if W. G. Forster really was the original of 'Els', it would be reasonable to suppose that news of his death, reactivating old agonies, provided Clarke with the stimulus he needed to make his belated attempt to use the novel format to exorcise the ghosts of his youth. It may be no coincidence that *Jaspar Tristram* ends with a funeral: that of Els's sister. This funeral was one of the things about which the reviewers were unable to agree: *The Publishers' Circular* thought 'the graveside scene at the end is genuinely pathetic', but *The Graphic* considered 'his efforts to lash himself into the proper poetic state of mind at the funeral of a girl with whom he had deliberately worked himself up into a grand passion are described with a remarkable insight into a character not worth the trouble of serious study.' One part at least of the account of Nita's burial seems completely and rather horribly genuine. When the girl's coffin scrapes on the bottom of the grave Jaspar feels as if 'now that he knew it to be where it would never again be moved, he needed not further to concern himself with it and what it held' (*JT* p. 273) This is not inappropriate for the obsequies of a girl with whom one had deliberately worked oneself up into a grand passion: but it also sounds fresh and personal enough to be the recollection of a recent impression.

If we accept that at least the first part of the novel is a record, or reminiscence, of a genuine passion for another person, it becomes easier to recognize the stature of the novel as a whole. Jaspar's love for Els and later, less convincingly, for Els's sister Nita, is always in the context of, virtually the outcome of, Jaspar's awareness of himself. It is Jaspar's relationship with himself rather than his feelings for others, that is the essential theme of the novel. *The Times*'s summary can hardly be bettered:

> Jaspar is an imaginative, unhappy child who thinks far too much. He grows up to be a proud, morbid school boy, full of absurd conceit, envying and at the same time despising all who are more fortunate than himself. As a man he is feverishly ambitious, a prig, and a social as well as an intellectual snob, without the force to achieve his vague dreams of *gloire*.

In short the book is one of the most painfully convincing portrayals of adolescence ever written, replete with gaucheries, humiliations and pretensions that for many of us, I think, are all too reminiscent of our own teenage years:

> he used to return from his walk, with his pockets stuffed full of what he tried to believe were interesting plants, but he really looked on them as dirty weeds. But the occupation of gathering them at least saved him from his thoughts. Sometimes however he would betake himself after dinner straight to his desk in school, and there sit and read till at last interrupted by Roll. Often it was Shakespeare that

he chose, for though it bored him hugely, his vanity was pleased to have fellows coming up, and crying out, 'What's this!' and to see the astonishment and disgust with which they read the name. (*JT* pp. 78-79)

When Young tells him that Orr has returned to the school and resumed his relationship with Els, he merely responds, 'Thanks, I know,' but:

He felt indeed, as always at such times, as if somehow a mask had fallen from his face and left the workings of his inmost thoughts bare to view, but still he pretended indifference, and presently, as no one remarked on his looking odd, began to hope that by the cold tones in which he had spoken he had thrown Young off the scent. (*JT* p. 66)

He finds himself increasingly unpopular:

He had only to sit down, to see those on either side with affectation slide away along the form as from something unclean, and however loudly three or four might be laughing and talking together, as he came up they would fall silent, and so remain, ostentatiously waiting till he should be once more out of hearing. (*JT* p. 102)

Later, when he had re-established himself to a certain extent,

he was far too anxious to avoid placing himself at a disadvantage with regard to others to allow of his attempting anything he could not do as well at least as they. He would much indeed have liked to have been able to descend into the arena, and there have shown himself as all at once immeasurably the superior of the rest; but since this might not be, he would hold altogether aloof. He even tried to persuade himself such things were unworthy his regard; yet he never really ceased to regret the inactivity to which, as he thought, he was condemned. (*JT* p. 123)

One recalls Clarke's dropping out of the Chess Club and the Shakespeare Society's production of *The Winter's Tale* in 1878.

Though the handful of references to Clarke in *The Radleian* are consistent with Jaspar in *Jaspar Tristram* being a self-portrait, the only other material relating to his personality dates from his final days in Zanzibar. His assistant, writing to inform the Foreign Office of his death in February 1913, referred to his 'possession of a highly-strung nervous temperament and an unbounded energy' and *The Zanzibar Gazette* (17 Feb. 1913) claimed: 'His extraordinary energy of mind was only rivalled by the pluck which led him we fear frequently to place too great a strain upon his physical powers.' He was obviously good at his job but his death at a relatively early age may indicate that he had kept himself going by drinking too much. His doctor noted the development of angina, and a recurrence of asthma 'which he had been free from for some years.' During the day before his death he had attended the government offices but had felt unfit for work. The doctor saw him at 6 p.m. and noted 'slight pains again suggestive of angina, a tendency to asthma, and a temperature of 100.' The doctor visited again just before 8 p.m. and 10 p.m., and on the latter occasion, finding his breathing 'distinctly asthmatic,' gave him a morphine injection. At midnight, when the doctor visited again, Clarke was asleep:

> Towards 3 a.m. he was found on the floor dead. He had, apparently shortly before got out of bed to get a remedy he was in the habit of using for asthma: rising quickly probably produced sudden heart failure and he fell and died almost immediately. (The National Archives, Kew, London FO 367/348)

*The Zanzibar Gazette* wrote a couple days later of how Clarke's 'ready and keen sense of humour . . . was often cleverly used to smooth ruffled feelings', and no doubt his years as a Foreign Office official enabled him to comport himself with a degree of professional emollience, though the thin-skinned and acerbic boy he seems to have been in his Radley years came out occasionally in his correspondence even with so grand a personage as the Foreign Secretary, the bird-watching Knight of the Garter Sir Edward Grey:

> Sir,
> I have the honour to acknowledge the receipt of your despatch No. 339 of the 15th ultimo in which you decline to sanction the issue of my proposed N'goma Regulations (Amendment) Decree on the ground that you do not consider it 'advisable or necessary to interfere to the extent contemplated with what takes place in private houses.'
> I fear this expression 'private houses' shows that you cannot be aware of the local conditions here: it might be imagined from its

employment that what I wanted was to stop a little pleasant musical party in a quiet respectable home and not, as is really the case,
to prevent a number of childish savages from wasting their money
and their very small stock of energy in a demoralising dance. . . .

Of course if entertainments which consisted of an intolerable
and maddening din and lasting for days together, took place constantly in an English town, the neighbours, in the more respectable
quarters, would find some means of preventing life being rendered
thus hideous and the good order of the place endangered by indict-
ing the offenders for a nuisance; while I imagine that in the poorer
parts the police would take action. (FO 367/345, 11 Dec. 1912)

As for Clarke's novel, it may be that *Jaspar Tristram* was mostly or
even entirely written in the author's youth and only revamped or res-
cued from an attic about the time of W. G. Forster's death. It does
however suggest long hours of painful introspection and self-analysis
over an extended period. And it is difficult to think of any other piece
of writing that exhibits more strikingly the way love (or infatuation)
takes form and strength from the peculiarities of one's personality,
rather than transcending or transforming them. It is from the per-
spective of the novel's handling of love as an expression, almost an
externalization, of personality that we can see that the second half of
*Jaspar Tristram*, dealing with the uninteresting and presumably imaginary Nita is simply an elaboration of the first half and its account of
Jaspar's relationship with her brother. When, realizing he is in love
with Nita in a more or less grown-up way, Jaspar reflects that 'as once
he loved the sister for her brother's sake, so now he felt he loved the
brother for the sister's' (*JT* p. 215), one suspects that this is mere eye-
wash, or a strange idealization of the feelings appropriate for prospec-
tive in-laws. The key passage associating Els and Nita comes earlier,
when Nita is still very much a child:

> And all at once it struck him, as she sat in front of him, that she was
> quite as much boy as girl. And as one of Els's greatest charms had
> been that he had something in his dress and manner and looks and
> limbs of the delicacy and grace of a girl, so now he took delight in
> finding in her a delicious flavour of the roughness of a boy. (*JT* p.
> 165)

It is not the eminently nubile Nita of the 'rounded satin-smooth shoul-

ders' and 'the firm small breasts' that Jaspar falls for, but the androgynous pubescent Nita of a few years earlier who is physically almost
the identical twin of her androgynous brother. His relationship with
Nita is not merely a re-run of his relationship with Els, it is evidently
the *same* relationship, except that it has been rewritten with a more
innocent, less compromised love-object who, precisely because she
is a girl who is being educated at home, has not passed through the
rough and tumble and possibly unmentionable night-time activities of
a boys' boarding school. His rambles with her in the Chase at Tremlett, the Southwoods' ancestral seat, with the innocent physical contact of the pick-a-back rides he gives her and their occasional holding
hands, are rambles he might have fantasized about having with Els, or
the prototype of Els. (*JT* pp. 171-176, 187) That it is the same person,
Orr, who comes between Jaspar and both Els and Nita may not simply
be a clumsy Dickensian coincidence perpetrated by an inexperienced
writer but a deliberate underlining of the way the two relationships,
with brother and with sister, are actually one and the same relationship. The novel is not about Jaspar and Els, or about Jaspar and Els presented first as a boy then as a girl, however: it is essentially about Jaspar
– a Jaspar most of the time quite on his own and, as in the chapter
describing his walks on the South Downs (*JT* pp. 114-121) sometimes
not even thinking of either Els or Nita. His feelings for Els are part of
the whole tangled web of his feelings. This may seem appropriate in
the case of unreciprocated love, where the rejected lover falls back on
himself, so to speak – but where has it been done better than in *Jaspar
Tristram*? – but it may be that this is basically the case with all great
loves. Clarke's former reviewers were not wrong in failing – or refusing – to recognize *Jaspar Tristram* as a 'gay' novel. It is a love novel,
and a very unusual one – not because of the love object but because it
faces up to the truth that, in love, the lover is always very much what
he is in himself.

A. D. HARVEY

*I am most grateful to Simon Stern for supplying me with copies of reviews
of* Jaspar Tristram *published at the time of the novel's first appearance.*

# JASPAR TRISTRAM

To Her
Whom the Happiest might count themselves
Still more Happy to have known
Jaspar Tristram's parent after the Spirit
Makes bold to offer
This History of the Boy's early Years
Not so much thinking it in anywise worthy
So honoured an Invocation
As in Hope to show
That the Dear Past at any rate
Can never be forgotten

# JASPAR TRISTRAM

## CHAPTER I

It was late in the afternoon of a desolate and cold January day when Jaspar Tristram arrived at Scarisbrick on his way to Dr. Tower's school as a new boy. The journey had been long; at every stage that he had left behind his heart had sunk more and more, and now, as the fly began heavily to lumber off, he leant out of the window, still, if he might, to keep the station to the last in view as the one remaining link by which he could fancy himself yet bound to home. So when at length it was hidden from his eyes by an envious turn of the road, he drew in his head and flinging himself back, burst into a passion of tears. Doubtless it was true that what he was obliged to call his home was very far from being happy; and true too that for weeks he had been looking forward to this going for the first time to school as to an entrance into a life in which those about him would not, as at Telscombe Rectory, be for ever finding fault. Yet now somehow the worst of home seemed as if it could not but be better than the best of that unknown world towards which he was thus irresistibly being forced. And then suddenly it occurred to him – and at the thought he sat upright and alert and looked out – that after all it was possible to escape. It would be easily enough done: the horse now, as they mounted a hill, was only walking, and it needed but to open the door and slip out and he would be safe from pursuit amidst the thick furze of the common that now spread as far as he could see on either side of the way. But it was only for the briefest of moments that he was thus dazzled by a flash of hope; in another it had disappeared and he was in darkness still darker than before. No, he was helpless; for he could only have gone home; and where would have been the good of that? Whatever there might be before him, he must bear it as best he could; and the fly, as it imperturbably rolled on, seemed to be the instrument of some mysterious force against which it was useless to fight. And as, with a glooming gaze, he continued to stare out of window,

3

in the gathering dark the heath appeared so inexpressibly forlorn and ghostly that his melancholy grew yet more intense. He wondered if in the whole world there was any one half so wretched as he. How happy and contented they must be, the people who were clustering round the fires which glowed so comfortably through the red blinds of the little cottages by the roadside! How cheerful they looked, the labourers he met trudging by! But could any one be otherwise, who was not being carried off to school?

A few moments more and the fly turned in at a gate and running smoothly and softly over the gravel of a drive, stopped at last before a portico of which the pillars glimmered white in the shades of the winter evening now fast drawing in. The driver clambered down and pulled out the bell; the echoes it awoke appeared to speak of an end-less series of great empty rooms and passages. He tried to make out what the place was like; but it was now too dark to be able to see more than that the house was big and high and looked singularly mysteri-ous and forbidding; to the left there seemed to be a sort of shrub-bery beyond which again was another building with one long range of lighted windows; across their uncurtained panes from time to time moved dark figures which must surely be those of the boys. But at that moment the door was opened by a maid-servant who with much bantering the while – everybody but himself had some one to speak to – helped the man to carry in his box; and he himself got slowly out and went indoors: – just to his fancy, it seemed, like one of those State prisoners he had read of, who, when he descended from his coach at the foot of the scaffold, was still left free, but only to mount to the block.

And presently he was with the Doctor and being 'put through his facings' as the old gentleman called it with a laugh. He, for his part, could see no particular cause for merriment in the remark at which however he did his best to smile; but he was sadly conscious that his nervousness only allowed him to do so after rather a sickly fashion. And then he became absorbed in the task of trying to answer the vari-ous questions put to him in such a way as would, he thought, be most likely to please. Yet, anxious though he was to impress his new master with the extent of his attainments, he was even more so to gain his good-will, whose power over him was to be so great, and whom at any rate he would have given much to have made well-disposed towards him, so that he might have had at least one person in that all-strange world of whom he could have thought as a friend; and he was therefore at no little pains to throw into his voice such inflections of humility and deprecation as were, he conceived, best suited to gain this end. But the effort was such a strain that his examination seemed already to have lasted hours, when the Doctor suddenly came to a stop. If only something would interrupt them and so allow him to get off without further danger to the good impression he flattered himself he had already made!

And even as he wished a bell began to ring. With an obvious movement of satisfaction, the Doctor let his coat-tails drop and, leaving the fire before which he had all this while been standing:

'Ah, tea!' he said, 'come with me!' and he was already moving towards the door, when, stopping and half-turning round:

'You must remember, Tristram, to say "sir," when you speak to me, do you hear?'

'Yes – sir!' he said, and not without some difficulty; for indeed this was an express acknowledgment of those new conditions of life, which since he could not altogether escape, it was his effort still if possible to differentiate from those imposed on the rest. He had indeed been told that he would have to call the masters 'sir,' but, having so far got out of using the word, he had begun to hope that they would accept instead such a tone of deference as that in which he had been careful to speak. It was disappointing to find himself mistaken; and then too this being addressed by his surname seemed as if it had made him lose in a moment every inch of the ground he had been at such pains to win, and set a gulf between the Doctor and himself, which he was sure that he would never succeed in crossing.

Presently, as they drew near the end of a low narrow passage, against one wall of which there hung a long row of curiously-shaped boards whose use it was quite beyond him to guess at, he caught a muffled sound of talk that, as the door was opened, became a hubbub of chatter, and then, as the Doctor was perceived, sank into silence, but only to be immediately succeeded by a hum of 'New boy' which went buzzing round the room from form to form. Meanwhile the Doctor, stopping, had put a hand upon his shoulder with a gesture which for a moment Jaspar almost took for one of kindly protection, and had begun a little speech about new playfellows, and how you should treat them. He for his part the while stood still, looking indeed intently at the floor, but conscious all the time that many pairs – how many he could not tell – of curious eyes were bent on him: and that the boys were nudging each other and pointing at him; and some one said:

'See how he's been blubbing!'

And his ears tingled as they used to do when boxed by his Guardian's wife, and his cheeks burned so hotly as to make him blink. Somehow too he felt that he and the others already understood each other quite well; and that he was saying to them as plain as if he had used words:

'I'm awfully sorry, but it's really not my fault, all the rot he's talking about being kind to a new-comer!'

While they on their side were making answer:

'Oh, that's all jolly fine, but just you wait until we get you alone!'

But once he had dropped into a seat, no one seemed to pay him any further heed, and he began to look about. How ever could they laugh and talk as they were doing? And how, above all, could they find such an appetite for those stodgy blocks of bread and scrape? He supposed – though it was hard to realise – that he would by and by be one of them, and feeling towards some new chap as doubtless they were then doing towards him; but he was sure that no one ever would see him helping with anything like the heartiness which they displayed to clear of their contents those high-piled dishes they were pushing about the clothless table, up and down and from side to side. But he thought he would like a little tea; and very shyly and politely he asked his neighbour on the form to give him some.

'What is it you want? Tea?' inquired the boy whom he had thus addressed, stopping in the midst of an animated conversation with some one on his other side; and then in an assured voice that, as Jaspar felt, contrasted curiously with his own diffident tones:

'I say, Piggy,' he cried, 'shove us over the jug, will you?'

'It's made out of the fellows' old slate-pencil ends, you know!' he added, as he saw the look of dismay wherewith the other considered the greyish-coloured fluid to which he was being helped. Jaspar felt vaguely there was something very winning and pleasant in the way he spoke and laughed. But he had scarce set his lips to the mug, when there was a great scuffling of feet and a scraping of forms pushed back and everybody stood up for Grace. Some little distance off at the farther end of the room, over the heads of the boys, he could see the Doctor who, his eyes fast shut, and waggling to and fro his old white poll, was mumbling out some form of thanks to which, hardly waiting for the last word – 'carter' it appeared to be – they all sang out 'Amen!' and began to troop tumultuously out; he could hear the foremost noisily hurrying upstairs, and hulloing and whooping as they went.

He let them one after another jostle past, being busy watching the Doctor as, slowly and with care, he stepped down from off the platform, and followed the other masters out. With a sort of fascination, he looked at the door as it swung slowly to, and the bang with which at last it shut seemed to announce that now indeed he was cut off from every possibility of help and left to sink or swim by himself. So turning dolefully in the opposite direction, he went out by the double-doors through which the others had disappeared. In the little stone-flagged passage just outside there was no one to be seen, but through a brick archway on the left was a steep dark staircase which must be that up which he had heard them go clattering a few minutes before. He was already sorry he had stayed behind; had he not done so he would not now have had to face them all at once, but going with the rest might perhaps have escaped notice altogether. However he could not stay where he was:

'I think I'll go up here!' he said out loud, and so began to mount the stairs, groping and stumbling as he went, for the steps were evidently much worn, nor was there any light to show you where you ought to tread.

At the top was a small landing, and on the farther side a door; this he pushed open and then stopped short, dazed by the sudden change from darkness into light and taken aback by the general shout with which his appearance was greeted by the rest of the boys. He hesitated however but for a moment and then, moving forward half-mechanically, he saw himself in an instant surrounded by a crowd all hustling up about him, and all at the top of their voices asking questions of all sorts and kinds. Unable to distinguish a single voice amidst the din or a single face amongst the many which were pressing in on him at once, he was trying to think of what to say, when, with a sort of laugh that he had never heard before, one of them gave a companion a quick shove and sent him cannoning against him with a force so great as almost to bring them both to the ground; at the same instant he heard a cry:

'Here's Orr!' and every one fell back.

Through the opening thus made he saw come lazily swaggering along, his hands deep in his trouser-pockets, a boy, who was taller by the whole of his bullet-head and broad shoulders than him or indeed, as it seemed, anybody there; at his side he recognised the little chap who had poured out the tea. For a moment or so Orr looked him in silence up and down; then, turning to one of those who were standing round:

'What's his name?' he asked.

'Tristram, Orr! Jaspar Tristram!' they all shouted out. 'Did you ever hear such a name?'

'Oh, well,' said Orr, 'of course we can't have such a rotten name as that here! What shall we call him?'

'I votes we call him "Rosy" as he blushes so!' observed the good-looking small boy who stood by Orr; and even as he was speaking Jaspar noticed what a curious charm there was in his voice. Everybody began to applaud:

'Rosy, Rosy!' they cried.

'I say,' suddenly said a voice in his ear; it came from a boy who was sprawling across the desk, up against which he had been gradually pressed: 'I say, do you know why your tie's like a telescope?' and at the same instant an arm was slipped quickly under his, and his tie was jerked so sharply out of his waistcoat that its sailor's-knot was drawn into a wisp unpleasantly close about his throat. And in the midst of the general laugh that followed, he saw one of them hitch his leg up on to the desk behind, evidently preparatory to scrambling up in order to get a better view of what was going forward.

'I say!' began another; but he did not answer, being busy tucking back his tie.

'I say!' repeated the other who had now elbowed his way to the front.

'What?' he asked in an impatient voice; he felt his temper beginning to give way. Never before had any one laid hands upon him after such a fashion; and, besides, it was very irritating to see Orr standing there looking on as if the whole thing were being done for his amusement.

'Squat! You're an ass an' I'm not!' the other gabbled out, evidently delighted at having got the answer he wanted; and there was a fresh roar of laughter.

'Well, I call it a beastly chouse, humbugging a new chap like that his very first night!' interrupted Orr's small friend; and then added: 'But, I say, tell us, do you smoke?'

The question appeared odd, but not only was it put in a simple kindly way that contrasted with that in which the others had spoken, but it was asked besides by the only boy who had been the least nice to him, and so he answered 'No' in such a tone as might, he hoped, be understood to mean that if it would give his questioner any pleasure he would certainly try and learn. Nor did he the least understand what was meant by the general shout of:

'Oh, what a beastly bung! why you're doing it now!' with which his reply was greeted.

But the small boy looked round with a pained and reproving air, and then, as silence ensued, went on:

'Well, are you up to snuff?'

By now, however, Jaspar had begun to have a dim suspicion that he was being made fun of, and he was thus still considering within himself what answer he had better make to this second inquiry, which seemed still more extraordinary and unintelligible than the first, when Orr broke in with:

'Oh, come along, Els, do! I'll give you a ride!' and hitching him up on his back, he ran lightly off, followed by the rest, whooping and shouting, just, so Jaspar thought, like a lot of savages.

Scarcely had they vanished through the doorway when the master entered who was that evening to keep school. By him he was appointed a desk at which to sit and furnished with such books as he wanted for the next day's work. So for a while he did his best to keep his thoughts fixed on the lesson he had been given to prepare. But presently, do what he would, they began to stray off towards the home he had that morning left, and soon the page was swimming before him in a mist of tears. Raising his head he threw a despairing look round the room; it was quiet enough now; the only sounds he heard were the creaking of the master's boots as he walked slowly up and down; the dreamily-mournful flaring of the gas burning in uncovered jets high up on bare cross-bars; and the low murmur of a boy two places off upon his right, who was softly repeating something to himself, now raising his head and looking about, now again consulting his book. Through the sort of haze with which the place seemed filled, he saw and noted the cracked and dirty yellow maps hanging awry against the dingy walls; the uncurtained windows, through the steam on which you could just perceive the close blackness of the winter's night that seemed, as it were, to be pressing against them on the other side; and the deal boards of the floor all splotched with ink. Everything was very strange: there was not so much as a fire whose cheerful blaze he could have welcomed as a friend.

And then, in the course of his rounds, the master went into the farther room: as he disappeared through the narrow doorway there was a general sigh of relief, and everybody began to take their ease. Just opposite him, side by side, were Orr and Els; the former, leaning back against the wall, was looking with a smile at his companion; the latter, alert and full of life, was sitting up, his hands already clenched and stretched out towards the big boy in readiness for the playful attack upon him which he was obviously intending, his eyes sparkling with fun, as now they followed the master's retreating back, and now returned to Orr on whom, the moment that the coast was clear, he began to bear rapidly down. The other, pretending to be afraid, put up his arm to shelter himself and went edging off along the form. And what a savage look he gave the boy next him, who was a little slow in making room! At last, driven back as far as he could go:

'Southwood, Southwood!' he said in a loud whisper, as if he wished to make the master hear – 'Southwood, go on with your work!'

Then the kitchen-clock over the door struck nine, the school-bell began to clang – he could hear the rope as it rushed up and down – desk-lids banged and bed-time, it appeared, was come.

His neighbour on the form – the boy he had heard called Piggy – had already told him he was to sleep in the 'Long Room,' and now was good enough, not only to show him the way but even, when they got there, to point out which of the many beds was his. So, falling upon his knees on the narrow strip of gaudy drugget which covered the bare and well-scrubbed boards at the side, he buried his face and hands in the hollow of the knot-patterned counterpane, and began to say his prayers. He found no little comfort in the thought that at any rate the God he was praying to was the same whom he had had at home; yet after the consolation was exhausted, which he had at first derived from this reflection, he still knelt; for the longer he so remained, the longer, he felt, he was putting off the moment, the steady approach of which he had now for some while past been considering with dread, when, for the first time in his life, he would have to undress in public. However, at last he got up and, seating himself

upon the edge of his bed, began slowly to take off his things. But
having pulled off his jacket and waistcoat and undone his tie and
shirt-collar, he stopped; under pretence of looking about he could still
perhaps gain a few minutes. As for the rest, they were already most
of them in bed; but five or six, including Orr, were looking on and
applauding Els who, mounted upon his bed, was apparently trying to
see how high by jumping he could send his nightshirt fluttering above
his head.

'I back you won't do that, Dick!' he cried to his friend, as, breathless, for a moment he paused. And then Jaspar after a last hesitation
– for once he had taken it off he would never again be able to say of
anything: 'This was put on at home!' – pulled his jersey over his head.
As he did so he heard a low hurried cry of 'Cavé, cavé!' and when
once more he was able to see, the Doctor was in the room on which
a sudden quiet had fallen. As for Els, he was lying on his back in bed,
quite still and with the clothes drawn demurely up under his chin.
Stopping for a moment by Orr as he went along, the Doctor said:

'You had better tell Tristram of our rules as to not talking and so
forth! And remember it is on you that I rely for their being kept!'

'Yes, sir!' answered Orr.

'Good-night, boys!' said the Doctor as he passed on.

'Good-night, sir!' they chorused in reply.

Scarcely, however, had the sound of his footsteps died away than
they began to talk; but though for a while Jaspar tried to listen, he was
so tired with all he had gone through since that morning he had left
home, that very soon the different voices began to mingle drowsily
one with another and he sank into a doze. He was woke by a noise
as of some one jumping violently out of bed and darting across the
room, and then there came muffled sounds as of a body being violently bethumped, and then a choking cry:

'Look here!' he heard Orr say, 'the next time you wake me with
your beastly snoring, I'll just jolly well stick my soap down your
throat!'

Then, turning round, he put his hand under his pillow, and drew
out his watch which he had tucked there with his handkerchief – now
but a limp and sorry rag though that morning new and stiff – and, as
it grew gradually warm in his clasp, once more fell asleep.

# CHAPTER II

And as the exercise of Orr's power was thus the last thing of which he was conscious on this, his first night at Rose Hill, so afterwards did he find himself reminded of it every hour of his life, from the moment when he was roused in the morning at half-past six – still, as it always seemed, in the middle of the night – to that when, long after they had gone up to bed, he was able once more to fall asleep. In the Playground of course it was only natural this should be so, but even up in form, under the very eyes of the masters, it was still the same. For suddenly he would feel himself sharply nipped in some tender part – the inside of the thigh seemed a favourite place – and when he turned angrily upon the boy who had thus attacked him, would be met by an apologetic:

'I'm awfully sorry! I couldn't help it really! I had to pass it on from Orr!'

Now and again when thus attacked he would be unable to restrain a cry, or perhaps would drop his book, and then, before he could so much as think of making any reprisals, the master would tell him to go to the bottom of the class and for the rest of the time stand up upon the form. But it was worse at night, at least for him and such as slept in the Long Room. For then they were quite at Orr's mercy, and without even such slight protection as in the day-time was lent them by their clothes; besides, his punishments seemed at such times to have about them something of a formal air they lacked by day, which made it as much out of the question to resist as if you had been going to be swished by Old Tom.

However for some little time after he had come he found himself still allowed to get into bed and remain there without being disturbed; but every evening he made sure his turn would come to get one of the lickings of which Orr scarce ever failed to administer two or three; for nobody escaped altogether except the small boy whom everybody called Els from his initials, so Piggy said, L.C.; though perhaps the one who suffered most was Piggy; and it was easy to see why, for even he himself recognised how very tempting it must be to try the effect upon such a chubby chap as him of the various instruments of punishment, slipper-heels and buckle-ends of braces, backs of brushes, fives-bats, ground-ashes and canes, of all which impartially Orr made use. But he had not been forgotten, for one night after he had been watching Orr lick his Minor and had seen the boy look round and, trying to take it all in good part, exclaim: 'Oh, please, Major!' and then at an impatient sign from his brother, turn again, he heard his own name called. He got out of bed and so for a moment stood, feeling very shy and awkward, as not knowing exactly what he ought to do and as being about for the first time to have to let the others see him naked. However he was soon kneeling down – just where a few minutes before he had knelt to say his prayers – and Orr was pulling up his nightshirt and arranging him delicately in the position in which he could be got at best; and then he felt that some one was balancing a book on the small of his back; it was the rule, he knew, that if you wriggled enough to throw it down, Orr always began all over again. Then followed a dreadful pause, and then the leathern brace descended, making him draw in his breath with a sort of hiss, and convulsively straighten his body up against the edge of the bed; he heard the book fall on the floor; somebody laughed; it was replaced, and Orr began again. But this time, not only did he keep himself bravely stuck out, but by dint of biting his nightshirt hard between his teeth, he managed to last to the end without uttering a single sound. It didn't really hurt so very much when it had once begun; the worst of it was that Orr always waited a little between his strokes, so that each had its full effect and you were kept wondering where the next was coming down. So, his licking over, he got stiffly up and with his eyes full of tears but still with a smile, went back to bed. At any rate he knew now exactly what one had to do and exactly how much it hurt.

So, the punishments of the evening finished, they began to talk. But as ten and half-past ten and eleven chimed from the neighbouring church, one after another dropped off, while even the three or four who still remained awake, would speak at intervals which grew longer and longer every time until the last, finding he could get no better answer to what he said than a drowsy grunt, would give it up as a bad job, turn on his side and address himself also to sleep. It was quite a new pleasure for Jaspar, this, of lying in bed and listening to voices whose owners were as invisible as if they had not existed at all, coming now from this corner of the room and now from that; and then, too, the darkness somehow appeared to him to suit the things they said and to give them a curious and delightfully troubling effect that was altogether wanting by day. At first, of course, he had never ventured to interrupt, but by and by, as he began to feel himself more at home, from time to time he would stop them to ask for an explanation of some word or other, at whose meaning his ignorance could do no more than dimly guess. But instead of answering they only laughed at him for being so green or perhaps – and that was worse – would make some reply which, at the moment accepted in good faith, he would discover afterwards to have been intended merely to stuff him up.

'But you said it was!' he would cry.

'Did I?' the other would answer with a careless air. 'Oh, well, I suppose it must have been over the left!'

And all this time he was deriving no little satisfaction from the thought that not only did he take his lickings better than any of the rest, but that the fact of his doing so was recognised, and had indeed already won him quite a reputation for endurance and pluck. He only hoped that Orr had noticed it too. He would gladly have suffered a hundred times more to have gained the approval of one who was so tall and strong and had such stern imperious ways. He would no doubt have preferred doing so after some other fashion, but, since this could not be, there was nothing for it but to try and surpass the others in the quickness with which he got out of bed when called, and in the steadiness and silence with which, his small body bared, he knelt while Orr lammed into him. But one day he overheard a few stray words that led him to fancy Orr looked upon him in a light quite other than that in which he was so anxious to be regarded; and it made him furious to think that, while he had been admiring Orr and flattering himself he was making way in his esteem, this latter had been entertaining for him nothing but dislike and contempt; and his feeling towards him became on the instant one of hate; and hate which appeared all the more bitter as he knew that not only had it tried to be something very different, but would gladly, had it been possible, have been so still. So his thoughts, which for a while had been quite content to stop with him, now for a moment went back to home; and he tried to find consolation in the thought that the holidays would soon be come. But the comfort he was able to obtain from this reflection was very small, and, driven back, as it were, again to school, he fell to questioning within himself Orr's right to the power he exercised. Would it not be possible to resist? Of course alone he wouldn't have a chance, but how would it be if he could get the other chaps to join? So very soon he was holding forth to any who would listen on the wrongs both he and they were always suffering at the hands of their tyrant. And as he talked he would feel himself carried away and his eyes would brighten and his voice grow firm. Sooner or later of course the things he said would be carried to Orr's ears; but, far from giving him pause, this consideration seemed only to make him even more audacious in his speech; an effect that was much increased by the mingled feelings with which he saw himself listened to by his audience. Such as it was indeed, the delicious thrill it gave him, talking after this fashion, was, he soon perceived, all he would ever get; it was hopeless to try and raise a revolt. And then, when left alone, he would think that perhaps if he could but *wish* hard enough he might change himself into some one quite different; perhaps even – who could tell? – into Orr.

The following Wednesday it rained, and so, instead of being taken out for a walk over the Common, as always on half-holiday afternoons had up till then been the case, they were obliged to stop indoors and amuse themselves as best they could, either in the Schoolroom or in the Playroom below. Jaspar at any rate was by no means sorry thus unexpectedly to have a whole long afternoon to spend in reading *The History of the Plague*, an old copy of which he had got from the Library the last time books had been given out. The story by itself was interesting, but there was besides something in its old withered binding and in the smell of the curiously blotched pages which made him almost see the red crosses on the doors and hear, approaching down the deserted grass-grown street, the ringing of a bell, and then the cry: 'Bring out your dead!' And so deeply was he soon immersed in his reading that, although he by and by became aware of some movement going on among the others in the room, it was not till the sudden and absolute cessation of every noise had caused him to look up that he found himself quite alone. He knew at once where everybody must be gone: to the Playroom. Two or three times already, when the weather had prevented their going out, he had been driven in there with the rest by Orr who had then proceeded to pick out a couple of them and make them fight. He himself had never so far been chosen though, unlike the others, he had on each occasion done his best to be so, for he had longed to let Orr see how, without a notion of managing his fists, he yet by sheer endurance would end by licking whoever it was he was opposed to. Now of course it was altogether different and he only hoped he had been forgotten: for while firmly resolved he would refuse to fight, he was by no means averse to having the actual moment of revolt still a little longer delayed. And then, with its usual preliminary whirr, the clock over the door struck five and, tired with having so long sat still, he stretched himself and, getting up, crossed over to the window. So, leaning his forehead against the woodwork of the frame which, scored and hatched over by many a knife, looked almost as if it had never been painted, dreamily he began to gaze out through the blurred panes into the yard. The round-backed cobble-stones with which it was paved were glistening with the wet, and with a hopeless and melancholy air the one forlorn tree that grew in the farther corner raised its leafless branches against the grey and streaming sky; from where he stood he could see down into the Doctor's study on the farther side, all ruddy-warm with the glow of the huge fire that was roaring up the chimney. Nothing surely could be amiss in his life, who had so comfortable, so quiet, so cosy a room! To the right was the boundary-wall, the impassable barrier that stood between him and liberty; over the top of the wooden gates which, though still too high to climb, were yet a little lower than the wall itself, he caught a rapid glance of some tradesman's cart rattling past, the driver bent nearly double in his effort to shelter himself from the rain which came furiously pelting in his face; in another moment even the sound of the wheels had died away, but in imagination he still followed the man to the home where presently he would be as safe from any molestation of his fellows as from that of the weather.

But suddenly he was called back to the realities of his prison-life by a shout from the door of:

'Rosy!'

And involuntarily he gave a start as if to answer to the name. He stopped short, however, in time and merely went on looking out of window. With his eyes at any rate he was resolved he would still be free.

'Rosy!' cried again the boy at the door; and then still as he could get no answer:

'Hi, Tristram!' he shouted. 'Do you hear?'

'Well, what is it?' Jaspar asked without however turning round.

'Orr says everybody's to come down into the Playroom!' was the answer.

'I don't want to!' Jaspar observed sulkily; and he began to pick at a corner of the window-frame.

'Oh, all right!' returned the other. 'Please yourself! But I should advise you to come! All the other chaps are there!' To this however he made no reply, and then, as with his back still towards the other, he worked away at trying altogether to detach from the frame the little splinter of wood he had begun to loosen, he heard the boy go racing back down the room; the door at the farther end slammed-to and once more he was by himself. The only sounds that broke the silence were the dashing of the rain in intermittent gusts against the windows, the gurgling of a gutter-pipe as the water came spurting out in jerks and, very faint, a noise of talking and moving in the Playroom underneath.

In a few minutes however he began to think that on the whole perhaps it might be wiser to go down, and so, muttering to himself the while, he went slowly off.

Downstairs he found nearly the whole school, but without the least attempt to interchange a word with any one, he edged his way to the back, and then, bent on continuing, so far as he could, to do what he had been doing before, he leant his elbows on the sill of a window and went on gazing out into the yard. But still out of the corner of his eye he could see how, while a few of the chaps were whispering among themselves, the greater part stood silent and only looked towards the open door. Presently in the passage just outside there were cries and a noise as of scuffling and then he caught sight of Piggy, clinging desperately to the door-post from which Orr, his arms about his waist, was trying to lug him by main force. So tightly however did he hold on, that it was not until a friend of Orr's came up and began grinding his knuckles that he let go. Up to then the boy's face had indeed been working curiously but he had never uttered a sound; now, as his fingers involuntarily unclosed, and he felt himself being torn away, he uttered a long and despairing squeal. Orr began to re-arrange his tie which had been somewhat disordered in the struggle.

'Who are you going to have?' asked the boy who had forced Piggy to leave go.

Orr hesitated and looked round; and as he did so, Jaspar somehow felt sure that it was he who would be taken: as indeed it was, for the next moment he heard his name called out and found himself, he scarce knew how, standing in front of Orr.

'Now then,' this latter cried, 'off with your things!'

'I don't want to fight!' he said. He spoke in a low voice and kept his eyes fixed on the ground.

'What?' cried Orr. 'Speak up! What do you say?'

'I don't want to fight!' he repeated in a louder tone.

But he was already beginning to be rather sorry he had not given in at once and was angry too at the notion that by being thus obliged to repeat what he had said he was being made ridiculous in the eyes of the others. And indeed there was a murmur in which he distinguished the word 'Funk!' and Piggy, in the very act of taking off his waistcoat, paused to stare at him in great surprise.

'Oh, well!' said Orr to his friend, 'perhaps we'd better take some one else. Rosy don't look as if he was up to much. What do you say to Tub?'

So Jaspar turned sullenly upon his heel and went back to his place. 'Funk, funk!' murmured the boys as he passed through, and there were even two or three who hissed. Such a reception seemed to intensify the feeling which once or twice already he had experienced, that somehow or other, he could not tell how or why, he stood apart and was different from the rest; and his vanity was hurt at the reflections that had been thrown on his powers and his pluck and at the very small importance Orr's easiness plainly showed was attached to what he did.

Meanwhile Piggy and Tub, with jackets and waistcoats off, were standing facing each other, and Orr and his companion, taking their places, each behind his man, a ring was formed and the fight began. What chiefly struck him, knowing that there was no quarrel between the two, was the hearty way in which they were exchanging blows; neither of them, it was evident, remembered anything, but that there was some one in front of him who was trying to hit him and whom he must try to hit back again as hard as he could. Between each round Orr pulled Piggy back on to his knee, and would whisper to him and point out, if you could judge at least from his manner, how best Tub's play was to be met. Piggy, however, seemed to pay but little heed and only sat there breathing hard and, with a fixed fierce stare such as was quite new to Jaspar, glared across at Tub through eyes which were already more than half bunged-up. And round him he overheard one or two of the other chaps bragging of what they would have done had they been fighting; but the most kept silence; they were afraid no doubt lest, if they made any rash promise of the kind, when their turn came, it should be brought up against them. And so the fight went on until at last it was interrupted by the sound of the bell ringing for tea and then Orr gave the signal to stop and told them to go and make themselves as tidy as they could in the Lavatory just outside; and the rest too began to hurry off, evidently not a little relieved at having at least for this time escaped. Jaspar would have followed them, but there was Orr standing in the middle of the room and only too plainly waiting for him.

'Come here!' he cried, as the last of the others disappeared through the doorway.

With an effort he broke the sort of spell that had kept him rooted, as it were, to that one spot and slowly, without a word, began to obey.

'Come closer!' cried Orr again, as he stopped a few paces off; and he did as he was told. So, for what seemed quite a long time, he stood in front of the other, his eyes fixed on the floor, his arms by his side, experiencing the same curious but not unpleasant sensations he had often had before when waiting to see what Orr would do to him.

'Look here, my young gentleman!' he began at last, 'what I wanted to say to you was just this. You're getting a precious sight too coxy! I——' but here he was interrupted by Elsie's voice shouting after him somewhere outside.

'I tell you fairly,' he went on, 'the next time——': and then again his name was called.

'The next time,' he continued, 'you don't do what you're told and pretty sharp too, I'll give you the jolliest licking you ever had in your life!'

At this moment Els, tired of shouting, appeared in the doorway.

'Oh, there you are!' he cried. 'What ever are you doing here?'

'I'll be ready in half a sec.,' said Orr, 'Rosy and I have been having a little talk, but we've nearly done!'

Then turning once more to Jaspar:

'Do you hear, you young cub?' he cried.

From his jacket-pocket meanwhile Jaspar saw Els take a ball and begin a little game of fives by himself. It was galling enough that one, who was smaller and younger than he, should thus be standing by, happy and at ease, while he was being bullied by that small boy's friend; but the case was made much worse by the fact that this same

small boy was a successful rival in his affections, who was now treating him with such indignity.

'Yes, I hear!' he said in a sullen voice.

'Well, then,' remarked Orr, 'I should advise you to attend. Come
along, Els!' and, putting his arm round the other's neck, he went off.
For a few minutes still Jaspar stood where he had been left, gazing
after them with a lowering glance; and then slowly followed them
out.

# CHAPTER III

Scarce a week after this he was one afternoon in the Playground to
which on whole days they were always kept; there were a dozen or
so others there, but he had gone off as far as he could and, talking to
himself and with eyes bent upon the ground, was mooning on along
the gutter, kicking aimlessly at such loose pebbles as chanced in his
path. Suddenly, just as he had bent a little out of his way for the sake
of treading on the edge of an inviting heap of sand, he heard a noise
and, raising his head, saw Orr and a friend advancing down, shouting
imperiously and making signs as they came on. He knew at once what
was going to happen; he had several times already been caught. Orr
and his chum would stand at the farther end and, having first driven
them all into a corner, buzz at them with fives-balls which from time
to time they would have to bring back, so as to be shot at over again;
and the game would end by the two big boys taking a running jump
on to their backs and bringing them in a confused and struggling heap
to the ground. So now, as he perceived the two coming his way, he
looked about in the hope of discovering some means of escape; yet he
knew perfectly well there were none. For the Playground was a great
bare rectangular gravel space without so much as a projecting corner
or a single nook behind which you might hope to hide; while as to getting away altogether, the very notion was absurd. On one side was a
high brick wall he felt sure he could never have climbed even though
with hours before him in which to make the attempt; on the other,
some palings nearly as high and with all the cross-pieces on the farther
side; while at the bottom, close to where he had stopped, some more
of the same sort divided off the Cricket-Field, the gate into which was,
as he knew, always kept locked. Across the top stretched the school-

buildings, in the centre of which was the archway he had come out by; but between this and him was the enemy. For the moment then there was nothing to be done but to take his place among the rest. However he was resolved not at any rate to condescend to struggle to get to the inside where alone it was that one could put a rampart of others' bodies between the stingers and oneself; and so thinking he advanced at a pace he made ostentatiously as slow as possible.

Nor, though thus left on the outside and so more exposed than any of the others, did he for an instant deign to do like them and stoop; but, as the balls came thudding hard and fast against his back and legs, remained standing as upright as when being drilled, now half fancying himself a martyr of the olden time, now filled with a sense of pride at seeing himself unmoved, erect, whilst every one else was crouching down, and now again essaying to distract his thoughts by gazing up at a tiny fleecy cloud which was slowly floating across the blue sky above his head; and once his eye was caught by Old Tom's garden of which he had a much interrupted view through the long pitched lattice of the paling close by. What a curiously remote look of peace it had and how the birds were singing! Only once he moved; it was when a ball struck him more than usually hard, and involuntarily his hands half-started from his trousers-pockets into which with so much resolution he had plunged them as deep as he could. But presently Orr, his ammunition being spent, sang out for the balls to be brought back, and at the word the boys scattered and began looking busily about upon the ground; he alone remained where he was, considering with no small contempt and self-satisfaction the evident anxiety of each to pick up a larger number in a shorter time than any one else. And then suddenly Orr shouted: 'Stop!' and on the instant they all pulled-up short and began to look about, evidently in much surprise as to what could be wanted now. What exactly it was of course he knew no more than the rest, but he was sure it had something to do with him. And indeed it had, for the next moment Orr went on:

'Let Rosy bring them here!'

But he did not move.

Then Orr, addressing himself to Piggy who happened to be by, and speaking in a tone of careful politeness, which was really far more alarming than would have been any loud violence:

'Would you mind fetching me my fives-bat?' he said. 'You know which it is.'

And even at such a moment Jaspar smiled to himself. Know it indeed! He should rather think Piggy did!

Meanwhile the others were drawing together, but quietly, and by almost imperceptible degrees, as if, he thought, afraid lest the slightest noise might attract Orr's attention and divert to them a portion of the storm just going to burst on him. Nor was it in anything but the lowest of whispers they conversed, as with faces of excitement and awe they thus stood and looked on. He for his part had not stirred; indeed he had a sort of feeling he could not have done so had he tried. But there was something even yet more strange; the sense of quiet that had come on him; he could almost have fancied he was waiting for some performance to begin, with which he personally had no concern. And at one moment he was glad that he was going to see what a real licking was like and would be quite impatient for it to commence, and the next would think that everything was over and that he was miles and miles away. And then in a sort of vacancy he fell to counting the fives-balls that were lying about on the gravel just as they had dropped from the chaps' hands: one – two – three – four – five – six – seven – eight: and there was Orr, still, he too, in the same place. And now there was a noise of trampling, and from beneath the archway began to stream – why, surely the whole school. Only not shouting and running and pushing as when they came out after lessons, but quietly and in silence. A little on the farther side of Orr with one accord they halted and so stood and looked on, while Piggy went forward alone to give the bat. He saw Orr take it with that careless air, as of one accustomed to be served, which he always admired, make it whistle in two or three preliminary cuts and then advance towards him. And yet he never moved; only in the effort of bracing himself to meet what was coming, he clenched his hands so hard as to hurt the palms, and, eyeing him as he came down, began to speculate vaguely as to where he would be hit first. But how tall he was, and big, and strong! How splendidly confident! He thought he would have liked to cry:

'Lick me as much as you please: the more the better: only let me feel it is still in the same way as I used to think it was!'

Then suddenly Orr gave a spring and, catching him by his collar, began to lamm into him as hard as he could; and so swiftly did the blows descend, they seemed to be falling everywhere at once and indeed his breath was almost taken away. But in a moment or two more he grew, as it were, used to it, and commenced wriggling and twisting and doing too his best to kick and hit, the while he kept on calling Orr all the names he could think of; the satisfaction of being thus able to speak his mind made him nearly unconscious of any pain. At last, stopping for a moment:

'Now, you young hound,' cried Orr, 'have you had enough?'

'Let me go!' was all he said, 'let me go!'

And, half-choked by the grip in which he was still held tight, his voice, even to himself, had a curious sound, as it evidently had too to others, for he heard some of them laugh. No sooner, however, was he free than he flew at Orr, and so suddenly that, before he could be stopped, he had succeeded in giving him at any rate one good hack on the shin; and then he was caught again and once more, but now with double quickness and weight, the fives-bat was coming down. Tired at length and somewhat out of breath, Orr flung him off.

'There,' he said, 'I back you've had enough to last you for some time!' and turning on his heel went off, followed by all the rest.

Still for a little he lay motionless where he had fallen, but presently, hearing nothing, cautiously he raised his head and seeing that the archway had once more swallowed everybody up and that the coast was clear, he scrambled to his feet and ran off towards the house. He wanted to hide, and that he could best do in the lobby. Here, curling himself up between two playboxes in the darkest corner he could find, he burst into a passion of tears. For a while he could think of nothing but crying, though even then he still retained a soothing consciousness that he had called Orr names and given him at any rate one good hack; but by-and-by, as snuffles and hiccoughs and sobs came at longer and longer intervals, he sat up; every inch of his body was throbbing and aching and burning; but it was his leg hurt most; he only hoped it was broken, so that Orr might get into a row, and he pulled up his trousers to see. The sight of that dark purple semi-circular weal somehow made him pity himself still more and he was just beginning to cry afresh when he heard Orr's voice:

'Well, I hope you're sorry,' he was saying, 'I should think another time you'll do what you're told!'

And scarce were the words spoken than, jumping up, from its pigeon-hole close by he snatched a boot and with all his force sent it whirling at the other's head. But he was in too much of a hurry to take good aim and then, besides, his muscles were still all unstrung from his licking and so, whizzing past Orr's ear, his missile only went banging against a box on the opposite side. His hand was already on another when his wrist was caught in an irresistible grip and his arm twisted so violently as almost to throw him backwards off his feet. He gave a sharp cry:

'You beastly cad!' he said in a voice full of tears and with his left hand he tried to strike Orr in the face; and then his other wrist was seized.

'You are a proper little devil!' Orr exclaimed. There was a something of admiration in his tone at which he thrilled with pleasure; but the time was now, he felt, gone by when a word from the whilom object of his devotion could have made him put up with any amount of ill-usage.

'You're a beastly cad!' he repeated.

'Am I?' inquired Orr and began twisting both his arms at once, preventing his falling backward by every now and again leaving go with one hand and giving him a punch in the stomach. It was at one of these moments that by a sudden and violent jerk he succeeded in wrenching himself free, but he was almost instantly caught again; there was a brief scuffle and then both fell to the ground, he underneath. Several of the chaps who, on their way up to form, had stopped to look on, now came nearer.

'Just see what faces he's making!' he heard one say, gazing curiously down at him as, panting, he lay there on his back on the stones. But he, arching himself up, made a convulsive effort to throw his rider whom however he scarcely moved and Orr, getting now well astride of him, put a heavy knee upon each outcrossed arm and settled himself as in a saddle on his chest.

'What shall I do to you?' he asked, looking down at him breathing with difficulty under so heavy a weight. Then:

'Am I a beastly cad?' he inquired once more.

'Yes!' Jaspar gasped out, and the next instant there fell about his ears, now on one side, now on the other, such a storm of cuffs as knocked him almost silly. Yet still he would not give in, but, shutting his eyes and screwing up his face, only rolled his head to and fro as if in a mechanical endeavour to avoid Orr's heavy hands. At that moment the bell began to ring for school and Orr, getting up, gave him a last parting kick in the ribs and so went off, leaving him still lying there.

'You're a beastly cad!' he shouted after him and, turning over, hid his face in his arms. Then one of those who had been looking on, approaching, tried to pull him over on his back so as to get a look at him, but, stiffening himself in his position, he let fly so savage a kick as made the other jump hastily back and now, afraid lest they might be late for school, they left him at last to himself.

And presently he too got up and went off to the Schoolroom, but only to find when he arrived his class already up in form.

'What ever have you been doing to yourself, you little scarecrow?' exclaimed young Nick, as he came in; and all the chaps began to laugh.

'Upon my word,' he continued, 'upon my word, it's really a little too bad. Not only do you come late, but, when you do condescend to put in an appearance, it's in that plight! I only wish there was a glass here so that you might see yourself! You're all covered with dirt, and your hair looks as if it hadn't been brushed for a week, and your collar's crumpled and unbuttoned, and as to your jacket, why, somebody must have been trying to tear it off your back! If you will bear-fight, you might at any rate have the decency to make yourself tidy before coming here!'

To all which he answered not a word, but only busied himself in getting his books out of his locker; he was pleased at the notion that by thus pretending not to hear what was being said to him he was irritating Nick. So when at length he came up and would have taken his place in the semi-circle that was standing round the master's elevated desk:

'Oh, dear no,' Nick observed; 'don't for a moment think we're going to have you here! Go and stand up on the form and when we've done, you can write out the lesson by yourself!'

Yet still he attempted no reply, but, turning on his heel, went back to his seat and flung his books down upon the desk with a bang.

'You can write out the lesson twice!' said Nick.

'Why?' he asked.

'Write it out three times!' said Nick again.

'What a beastly chouse!' he muttered under his breath, but still loud enough, as he intended, to be heard.

'You will do it in double lines,' said Nick, 'and stop in till it's done! And let me tell you,' he added, 'that you had really better take care what you're doing! I can assure you your conduct is very far from giving satisfaction! The Doctor has spoken to me about you more than once. It isn't only that your work in school is not at all what it should be – for you're clever enough, if you only choose to try – but you're sulky and quarrelsome with your companions. Go on, Ashworth!'

By this time however he thought he had paid enough for the gratification of his pride and, without saying anything more, got up on the form. Yet still, although aware he would by so doing have saved himself no little trouble, he would by no means condescend to listen to the others construe, but with a sullen cloud on his face and eyes that saw nothing, gazed fixedly at the book he held open in his hands. So for an hour or more he stood until, school being at last over, he stepped stiffly down and, taking paper, ink and pen, prepared to set to work on his long impot. But it was some time yet before he was able to begin. It had been bad enough to find himself driven into rebellion against one whom he only desired to obey and to know that the other chaps from whom he should have had sympathy at least, if nothing more, were all against him; but up to then he had, at any rate, been able to think that the authorities were, if not with him, certainly not upon the other side. And now this comfort must be given up and he must for the future resign himself to being alone. If only he could have felt that one was with him of the three sets with whom he lived, the Rectory family at home, and here the masters and the boys, he would, he thought, have asked no more, but in that knowledge have found enough support to render him perfectly indifferent to what the other two might choose to do. And then, as through the open windows came the distant sounds of the other chaps at play, a furious sense of injustice took possession of him. Why should they be happy, and he not? He had every bit as much right to be so as they! If only his father, the colonel, had been alive! And he pictured to himself how, in the hussar-uniform he wore in the portrait of him that hung over the table in the Rectory entrance-hall, he would suddenly have appeared, blazing with medals and ribbons and gold lace, and utterly confounded those who were behaving so ill to his son!

# CHAPTER IV

A fortnight afterwards the school broke up for the Easter holidays and Jaspar went back for a while to his home among the Sussex downs.

At first indeed he had been by no means in a hurry to return, but the eagerness to be off that every one else appeared to feel had little by little infected him as well, and when at length the last day came he found himself to the full as anxious as anybody there to be in the fashion and leave by the very earliest possible train. So, instead of arriving at the Rectory, as the Binneys had made out he would, just in time for high-tea at six, it was but a few minutes after one when, as they sat in the dining-room at their mid-day meal, they heard a ring at the bell and the next moment Jaspar burst into the room. Not one of them however moved; each of the five, his Guardian and Mrs. Binney, Violet and Rose and James merely greeting him as if, he thought, he had just come in from a walk.

'What ever made you come by the early train instead of the later one?' Mrs. Binney asked. 'You could then have driven back in the pony-carriage instead of having to take a fly. How much did you pay?'

He began in some confusion to explain that not only had he not paid but that he had no means of doing so.

'Upon my word,' she cried, 'you seem to think we're made of money! However, I suppose the man must be paid somehow or other!' and with that she got up and went off to the front door to try – he knew her so well – to beat down the driver.

'What have you done,' she asked, when a few moments afterwards she returned, 'with all you took with you to school?'

'And didn't he have an allowance as well, mamma?' asked James: 'a shilling a week, wasn't it?'

'If I were you, dear,' said the Rev^d. Orlando, 'I should deduct the amount from what you give him when he goes back!'

'Oh, well,' cried his wife with a good-nature for which yet somehow Jaspar disliked her as much as for the opposite he did the others: 'we won't say anything about that! And now,' she went on, as she helped him to a large plateful of carrots, suet-pudding, and boiled beef: 'And now let's hear about your school! Who's your greatest friend? What game do you like best?'

But to these and many other questions of a similar kind he could return no more satisfactory reply than: 'Oh, I don't know!' Indeed he himself was not a little surprised and discomposed to find how tongue-tied he was suddenly become when but a short while ago it had seemed as if he were nearly bursting with all the things he had to tell. His appetite too had gone.

'I suppose,' said Violet, noticing his plate, 'you've been eating good-
ies ever since you started? I think you might have kept a few for us!'

He sat up and, taking his knife and fork, made a feeble pretence of
once more attacking his food. But his guardian interposed.

'There, that will do! If you can't eat it, leave it! Don't mess it about!'

None of the family were indeed best pleased at thus having back
the ward whose presence they only put up with because the sum
allowed by Chancery for his support was of great assistance in the
house. It had been tiresome enough that his health should have been
too delicate to allow of his being sent to school at the usual age; but
they had hoped that this once done, not only would they have less
of him at home but that when he was there he would be more tolerable. But this was evidently not to be the case. And though still for a
little while Mrs. Binney made excuses for him, even she by the end of
the first week confessed that, though indeed he was changed since he
had gone to school, it was not, except in the matter of health, for the
better. He had been difficult to understand before; he was still more
so now. But to this her husband demurred.

'I flatter myself,' he said, 'that I can understand any boy's character in ten minutes and so I really think I ought to understand his!
Sulks, my dear, are what's the matter with him; and I'm surprised
they haven't been knocked out of him by the other boys!'

And that very afternoon at tea he took occasion to remark what
a pity it was that no bullying now went on at school. 'A little of that
sort of thing,' he added, turning to Jaspar, 'would do you all the good
in the world!'

But the most serious ground of complaint they had against him
was that he was always going off by himself. And so much was this
the case that Rose even complained about it to her father.

'It's quite hopeless now,' she said, 'ever trying to get hold of him to
go out with us in the pony-carriage!'

'And you know, papa,' added Violet, 'how useful he is for opening
gates!'

'Only this very afternoon,' continued Rose, 'we met him just a
little way out of Rottingdean, mooning along by the hedge and talking to himself like a mad thing!'

And as at this moment Jaspar came into the room, Mr. Binney proceeded to announce to him his firm determination not to suffer any
one who dwelt beneath his roof to separate himself from the others.

'While you are here,' he observed in his usual decisive tones, 'you will have the goodness to live with us and not treat the place as if it were merely a hotel where you were provided with board and lodging!'

But the end of the holidays was presently at hand and within the week he was on his way once more to school, quite as delighted to be going back as, but a little while before, he had been to get away. One thing at any rate he had learnt, which was, that if he could not be happy at Rose Hill, he had certainly not much chance of being so at home. And after all, from what he had heard, the summer-term could not really be half bad. For one thing, they were not kept so much to the Playground but regularly every afternoon went out to play cricket on the Common. And though somehow he hardly thought this was a thing he would ever care much about, what he greatly looked forward to was the exploring of that inviting stretch of country, which, as seen through the Playground palings, looked a land of the most fascinating freedom and adventure. At any rate from what he had seen of it when they had been taken for walks, it was really not so much a common as a whole country in little, with lakes and woods and rocks, hills, valleys and wide plains.

But he found himself disappointed of his hopes. For though it was true that they went on to the Common, yet, for all the exploring he was able to do, he might just as well, so, bitterly, he thought, have been still in the Playground; while as to cricket, he didn't care for it at all. What could be more dull than always running after balls that others hit? For of the batting and bowling Orr allowed only himself and a few of the bigger chaps and Els to have a share; who, when they were tired, would go and lie on the grass under the shade of the big walnut-tree just by the gate. From where he was standing out in the hot sun, he could see them stretched at ease, laughing and talking, eating cherries out of paper-bags and, with heads thrown back, tilting up those shiny brown stone-bottles of ginger-beer. Why should they have all the nice part, and he only the fagging-out? And then, while nobody ever took any notice of him except to abuse him and laugh at him when he did anything wrong, the whole time Els was playing, you heard nothing but: 'Caught indeed!' or 'Go it!' or 'Bravo!' Even when he muffed a catch or missed a ball – which certainly was not often – some one or other would be sure to cry: 'Well tried!' If only they had acted in the same way by him, he might have done as well. As it was, he would not even make an effort and, instead of attending to the game, on the contrary did his best to forget where he was and occupy his thoughts on something else. Then Orr, catching up a stump, would steal swiftly a-tiptoe over the grass and, coming up from behind, suddenly wake him with a sharp cut across his calves.

'What on earth good do you think you'll ever be,' he would exclaim angrily, 'if you won't learn to throw a ball like a boy and not like a silly girl?'

For the most part he would make no answer but only think to himself what after all was the use of this cricket. Neither the Romans nor the Greeks, about whom they were always making such a fuss, had ever played it. But sometimes he would turn fiercely round with a:

'What's that for, I should like to know?'

'Ah,' said Orr, 'I thought I'd make you jump!'

'What's it for?' he cried again.

'What's it for?' echoed the other mockingly. 'Oh, we should never get on if we had to tell you young squits what everything was for! Besides you know well enough!'

'No, I don't, you——' he began.

'Yes?' said Orr, with an air of polite inquiry. And then as he remained silent:

'Look here!' he went on, 'you really ought to take better care of that tongue of yours! It's already got you into trouble more than once! You're like a young blackbird, nothing but jabber!' and, turning on his heel, he went off.

Jaspar was still standing in the same place, looking after him with an expression of sulky hate, when he heard a shout and, raising his head, perceived that Els had bowled out the last man on the opposite side. Then all at once as he saw that, in the confusion, nobody was any longer paying heed to him, it flashed across him that if once he could reach, unseen, the furze which really there could not be more than twenty yards away, for the rest of the afternoon he would be free to explore the Common as much as he liked. The next moment, quitting his post, he had darted across the intervening space and, as fast as he could lay leg to the ground, was making for a certain little knoll perhaps a mile away, at whose two pines with their layers of foliage dark against the sky, he had often looked with longing eyes. Nor did he so much as stop to glance behind, but still tore on, now plunging breast-high through some scrub, now taking a low bush in

his stride, now ducking to avoid a branch. Once on the farther side of
the hillock, he sat down for a while to get his wind and then at length
slowly descended the sandy slope. And as, his arm put up to shield his
face, he went pushing his way through the furze that here grew far
above his head, he found himself at last in a sort of cave big enough to
shelter a dozen chaps and roofed by overarching boughs. And here he
stopped until he heard the faint sounds of the school-bell beginning
to ring for lock-up. On the edge of the Cricket-Field for a moment he
paused and, keeping still within the shelter of the furze, looked out
to see what the others were doing. Most of them by threes and fours
were already straggling towards the Playground gate, but half-way
between them and him, Orr and Els and a chap called 'Paddy' were
having a game of catch among themselves. It would in any case have
been hopeless to try and get across without being taken, but as that
evening at any rate, if not sooner, Orr would be able to punish him
in whatever way he chose for thus having shirked, it was really not
worth while even to make the attempt. So, coming out into the open
with an elaborate air of unconcern, he began to walk slowly towards
the gate on the farther side.

'Hullo!' cried Orr, 'you're just the chap I wanted! Where have you
been all the afternoon?'

At hearing himself thus spoken to he stopped, but made no effort
to reply.

'Oh, that's your game is it, my beauty?' cried Orr. 'I'll soon make
you speak! I say, Paddy, come and catch hold of him, will you?'

He waited for them to come up, when, taking each an arm, they
began to walk him across towards some furze. He wondered what
they were going to do to him.

'Now,' asked Orr again, as they arrived at the edge, 'where have
you been?'

And then as he still kept silence, Paddy suddenly whipt his feet
from under him, Orr caught his arms, and swinging him to and fro
with a 'One, two, three!' at the 'Three' they sent him flying into the
middle of the bush.

The delights of thus playing truant would, he conceived, have been
enough to have made him ready to pay any price if only they might be
his; but really for this being thrown into the furze, as now he was regularly every day, he came not to care a bit; and while he would rather,
he thought, have died than given a sign he was hurt, however severe

had been his punishment, still there was surely no need to explain to
Orr that the particular form in which he applied it was not in the least
painful. Nor was it likely the boy would discover his mistake, since,
when he saw him naked in the Long Room, his legs appeared quite
speckled with the prickles with which they had already got thickly
stuck. And very soon several chaps of his own age were worrying him
to let them into the secret of where he went and what he did when he
thus shirked fagging out. But it was not till they had begged very hard,
and then only under the most tremendous vows of secrecy, that he
could be prevailed upon to tell when, making them swear obedience,
he proceeded to organise them into a regular band of which of course
he was the captain. And sometimes he would set them upon enlarg-
ing the original cave, or contriving other hiding-places in connection
with it, or breaking all sorts of winding-passages through the furze
in order to facilitate escape; and sometimes he would put himself at
their head and start out upon a reconnaissance of the enemy, moving
with advanced guard, rear-guard, scouts, main-body, in imitation, so
far as his means would allow, of real troops on the march. And he
would fancy himself a general and the way between two hillocks a
pass, the pond a lake, and a piece of scrub, a wood. Then once more
back in the cave, they would spread over the brown dead prickles of
the furze with which the ground was thickly carpeted, an old green
plaid of his that he had contrived to smuggle out and, lying in a circle
at his feet, the while they munched their squashed flies or sucked their
silver-papered butter-scotch, listen to the interminable tales of adventure with which he had suddenly found the art to fire their imagina-
tions.

Then all at once as they talked, they would hear the sounds of the
chase.

'Sh!' he would say and hold up his hand and they would listen to
hear which way it was coming. So long as there appeared to be no
risk of their hiding-place being discovered, they would continue to
lie close, but the moment that in its castings the pack drew near, he
would dart away down one of the long tunnels he had contrived and
come out to view some fifty yards or so off. The first who caught
sight of him would give a view-halloo and the pack would break into
a run. Somehow it was always he whose part it was to try and draw
the enemy away from their hiding-place. He had chosen it at first as
that which, being of the greatest danger, it was clearly the captain's

duty and privilege to take; and he had kept it since, although, as he had found that he was far swifter of foot than any of them who were after him, it was no longer one of risk. However he did his best to make up for the want of that excitement by letting the foremost of his pursuers approach within a few paces of him and then suddenly dashing off again and, full of an intoxicating sense of confidence in his powers, leading them over the roughest and most broken ground he could find. And as, puffing and blowing and with dragging feet, the hunt toiled after him, he would go jumping from hillock to hillock, scrambling at break-neck speed down the crumbling red-sandstone cliffs and plunging through bracken and gorse. Indeed, there were not difficulties enough for him; and he was for ever trying though for ever without success, to lead the chase to the Canal, in order that, while they would be thinking they had got him, he might plunge in and, floundering across – he could not swim – stand and scoff at them from the opposite bank.

Yet he was always under the necessity of going back and falling at last into Orr's hands and so, when he had had enough and had made it plain he need never be caught unless he chose, he would suddenly stop and wait till the foremost of his pursuers came up. It was gener-ally Els, the only one of them who could run and jump anywhere near as well as he.

'I surrender!' he would cry as, panting, the other would catch hold of him and then he would try to maintain his dignity as well as he could in the midst of the lot of chaps who now came straggling up and were for hauling him off to Orr.

'Let me go!' he cried, 'I needn't have been taken unless I'd wanted!'

Once however having given himself up he ceased to struggle. Nor, however severe his subsequent punishment, would he ever so much as ask Orr to stay his hand. It was by no means sufficient to stand bravely; he would also fall so. Had he been a gladiator of old, van-quished, he would, he thought, have scorned to shrink his head when the insolent conqueror came to lift it from his shoulders. And though he felt sure that he had only to say he had had enough and Orr would have stopped, he was so far from doing this by word, that he would not even imply as much either by gesture, cry, or look, sustained by the sense of pride with which he saw himself, weak as he was, still rise superior to one so much stronger than he; and by the reflection that, as captain, it behoved him to show his men how to bear themselves when they fell into their enemies' hands. Nor was it merely by example that he taught; but often and often when some follower of his, aching and bruised from his licking, would swear he could stand it no longer, he would turn into a help, what was threatening to be a hindrance to the illusion of the characters they played by pointing out that cavaliers, robbers, early Christians and the like were always tortured when made prisoners.

## CHAPTER V

Presently somehow it came to Elsie's ears that Rosy could tell the most delightful tales and, full of the news, he went off at once to Orr to let him know that they could now again have that pleasure of listening to stories at night after the lights were out, which they had not enjoyed since Vicars had left two terms ago. But Orr showed no surprise; the little beast had always had the gift of the gab. He was afraid however it would be very hard to get anything out of him: he was as obstinate as he could stick. Of course for his part he was quite ready to try what a fives-bat would do, but he should advise Els first to see whether *his* coaxing, which was always so successful, would have the desired effect.

'I'll go at once!' the boy cried and away he ran. Jaspar caught sight of him while still he was some little way off and, halting, waited with a defiant air for his coming up: no doubt he was the bearer of some message from Orr. But when he found it was a favour that the boy had come to ask, with a sudden thrill of exultation, he caught at this unexpected chance of humiliating, if not his enemy, at least his enemy's greatest friend; whom of the two indeed he hated the worse, incited, curiously, by the very qualities that, as he felt, should rather have moved him to liking. So he met his cajoleries with the roughest rebuffs and to all he said returned but this one answer: if Orr chose to ask him, he would see what he could do. And there was an added pleasure in Elsie's obvious astonishment at not immediately getting his way. But the boy was evidently more successful with Orr, for that very evening hardly was the gas turned out when this latter began:

'I say, Tristram, will you tell us one of your stories? I hear they're spiffin'!'

And the rest, and among them he heard Elsie's voice, joined in:

'Oh yes, do, there's a good chap!'

It was already something quite new in his experience, and as pleasant as new, thus to be begged to do a favour; and when, complying, he found his first tale received with an applause as great as that which any of them had ever met with from the members of his band, it was all he could do to hide under a pretence of indifference the extraordinary sense of exhilaration with which he was suddenly filled.

And when each evening all appeared as anxious as upon the first he should go on, it was soon quite a recognised thing that the moment the lights were out he was to begin.

So for a while he remained content with the immunity he now enjoyed from being bullied by Orr and went about feeling much, he fancied, as must have done a herald in an enemy's camp, who knew himself safe but also knew the foe would only be too glad to kill him if they had but dared. Yet presently this ceased to be enough to console him for the loss of what now for some time past had been the chief interest of his life, his band to which ever since the first evening of the story-telling he had scarce given a thought; and he began to wish again to enjoy that sensation of being a leader which he had found so pleasant. And then as every night he saw his hearers grow more and more excited at his tales, and pound their pillows with their fists and sometimes even fling them in an ecstasy at one another's heads, he bethought him of proposing that they should have a regular bolster-fight with some of their neighbours along the passage. The suggestion was acclaimed with delight; and he proceeded to enlarge on it with an enthusiasm which was quickened by the fancy that he was thus in some sort usurping Orr's functions as head of the room; and he thrilled with excitement as he expected every word would rouse his enemy from the silence in which he remained in his dark corner. He ended by proposing that they should send a challenge in due form to the New Room. But just as he thought he was going to enjoy the triumph of getting the point carried on his own motion alone, some one cried:

'But what does Orr say? We can't do anything without him!'

And when this latter declared that so far as he was concerned they might jolly well do as they pleased, he was as much annoyed at hearing his scheme referred to so contemptuously as but a moment before he had been at finding the other chaps appealing to an authority he had almost begun to hope was shaken.

The next morning early the challenge was drawn up and delivered, and for the rest of the day he did scarcely anything but talk and think of the battle that was to come off that evening. It seemed much too on the others' minds, and when bed-time arrived and at prayers the hymn was 'Onward, Christian soldiers!' they all sang out as if, he thought, they had been exchanging defiances. But he did no more than just move his lips enough to make any one who might chance to look his way believe he was singing like the rest. Somehow he never could bring himself to shout or hurrah as he so often saw the others do; besides, on this occasion, he wanted to think that he who had set everybody on was the only one to remain unmoved.

And so it came at last the time when they could feel safe from inter-ruption for the night and, scrambling out of bed – into which they had got for a moment just to take in Old Tom as he went through – they pulled off each his bolster and so stood, ready waiting to start. He meanwhile was looking about cautiously in the hope of discover-ing without that having to ask which he so much disliked how one ought to manage one's weapon. Then the door was opened with all possible care not to make a noise and, having posted a sentry to keep *cavé* on the side from which any surprise from the masters must nec-essarily come, in Indian file, stepping a-tiptoe, holding in their breath, they went stealing down the moonlit passage. They found the door of the New Room temptingly ajar while within not a sound was to be heard. Els was for dashing in at once, but Orr, grasping him by the shoulder, held him back.

'Listen!' he whispered; but all was still.

'They're asleep, fast enough!' murmured the boy and as he spoke from out the darkness of the room there came a snore.

'Are they?' said Orr. 'That's all you know about it!'

And Jaspar noticed, and not without surprise, that he spoke with some contempt, just as he might have done to one of them. And then he saw him motion them all away to right and left and, sheltering the while behind the corner, push the door briskly in with his out-stretched hand. There was a rushing noise – a smack – a splash as a paper box, filled with water, fell bursting like a shell on the floor and a volley of slippers and sponges whizzed out and went banging, thanks to Orr's foresight, harmlessly against the opposite wall. And 'Now!' cried Orr and moved to one side. Jaspar thought he was like Napo-leon at Waterloo, who had led his Old Guard to the foot of the hill and then let them charge up alone; and burning to distinguish himself in his leader's eyes and to show him he was every bit as good as his favourite Els, while the others still hesitated and hung back: 'Let's come!' he cried and dashed into the room. Scarcely however was he inside the door than a bolster descended with such a swing upon his head as nearly to bring him to the ground; but, recovering himself, with a rush he was up on to the bed whence the blow had been dealt and catching his enemy round the waist – who it was, it was too dark to see – was trying to get him down. Then suddenly amidst the different sounds of the battle going on all round – dull bangs and thumps and muffled 'ohs!' – he thought he heard a cry for help that, stifled though it was again at once, he yet recognised as being in Elsie's voice. With a sudden crook of his leg he sent his adversary tottering back and, wrenching himself free, made a desperate jump for the next bed and thence threw himself down with all his weight upon a group by whom Els, kicking and plunging might and main, was just being borne off. And so unexpected was his onslaught, and so furious, so swift the recklessness with which he flung himself among them, that the enemy gave way and in a few moments more victory had declared itself on the side of the Long Room. Most of the vanquished scrambled higgledy-piggledy into the first beds they came across and, diving beneath the clothes, curled themselves up tightly in order to escape as much as they could the pummellings and bethumpings of their triumphant foes, the force of which however was not only deadened by the amount of wrappings through which they had to be dealt, but by the fact that they were only given at random and in the dark. But the three leaders were seized, their night-shirts whipped over their heads and so, at once blindfolded and bound, led off, their captors following round about and jeering and laughing at them, as with hesitating steps, they felt their way, bending double and only involuntarily straightening themselves as on their bare and defenceless bodies suddenly they felt the stinging smack of a slipper-heel or hand.

The first camisade, as Jaspar called it, having thus met with success, he had soon planned and carried out others and, immediately becoming puffed with ambition, began to aim at nothing less than the reduction of the whole school under what, borrowing the term from that portion of the *History of Greece* which he was then reading up in form, he styled the 'hegemony' of the Long Room. But it was only to others that he used the expression, for he himself was quite aware that it was his own aggrandisement he aimed at and not in the least that of the body to which he belonged. Of course, as he saw, if Orr had chosen to take the part he might in these night-games, he for his part could never have hoped for this place of leader, which he had somehow contrived to seize; he could only suppose that, as the chap was going to leave at the end of the term, now close at hand, he already looked on himself as a public-school boy and disdained any longer to be mixed up more than he could help with what they did. And while at home, as it were, the circumstances of his own room thus allowed Jaspar to take a place he could otherwise never have aspired to; abroad, he maintained his ascendency over his followers and imposed it on the rest of the school, not only by the vehemence with which he charged, as he phrased it, at the head of his troops: – which it seemed to him was such as must surely strike the enemy with something that was almost fear: – but by the powers of strategy and organisation which he had begun to think were his when captaining his band and which he was now able to display on a wider field.

At first in these altered circumstances he had been diffident and, affecting modesty, had seemed to ask for no respect; such a course of behaviour had more than once obtained him the pleasure of being pressed to take the place he pretended to think too high for him; besides in claiming nothing he left open a road by which to retreat should the others ever tire of their new game. But presently, as he saw that the more he took the more they gave, abandoning prudence, he began to let himself go. Even towards Orr his manner changed though but a short while back he had looked on him as one who, however much to be hated, was still somehow of a superior order to himself. He even tried to force himself as a third into the friendship that united him and Els. He was anxious not to omit anything that might show he was now on equal terms with one who had, he felt, so long looked down on him; and then he thought he saw in the pair just two such friends as he wanted: in Orr, ever-ready courage, firm-lipped determination, and dark brute strength; in Els, softness and prettiness and coaxing ways; while between the two he would be, as it were, the directing mind. By the former he would do what the Greeks had done by the Romans and, recovering through the superiority of his wits what the weakness of his body had lost, use as instruments for the securing and improving his position the very arms which had thrashed him once and might, if he were not careful, still do so again: for Els, not only would he be a means of indirectly getting at Orr but the assumption towards him of the part which he would have liked this latter to have played towards himself, would be rendered agreeable by the knowledge that the boy had both the greater influence over Orr and that, had it come to an actual fight between them, younger and smaller though Els was, it would probably have been he who would have come off conqueror, thanks to the careful way in which he had been taught to box by his big friend. But all his advances were rejected by Orr with a contempt he found the harder to bear as, though they had never been expressed in actual words, he was sure they had been understood; and this consciousness robbed him of the consolation that formerly had served him in such good stead, the knowledge that nobody but himself had had any notion what had been his feelings towards Orr; while with regard to Els it was even worse, since, though he was quite friendly, it evidently never occurred to him that anybody could be trying to take Orr's place. So, rebuffed, Jaspar began to assume towards both of them such a manner as might, he hoped, show them they had been much mistaken if they had ever supposed he had wished to be to either anything more than the most ordinary friend. Particularly did he affect to look coldly on the thousand and one outward evidences of their friendship; and this though there was not one but gave him the more pain as he suffered from a double jealousy, since he would have liked to have been in Orr's place and in that of Els.

Besides they ought to have been thinking of more serious things; of helping him, for instance, in the design he now had formed of turning the Long Room from the head of a confederacy of more or less equal powers into a kingdom with a number of subject provinces. He himself would have liked to have been king; but, since this could hardly be, he tried to think that he would really rather have the substance of power without its show than both and that he would greatly prefer playing *maire du palais* to Orr's *roi fainéant* to ruling in his own name alone. For Els, he made him Armour-Bearer; it was just the post that suited him since, with a title the picturesqueness of which fitted his good looks, it implied duties of a kind that seemed to accord with the relationship he stood in to Orr. And on this new kingdom of his he proceeded to bestow an entire constitution, even descending to such particulars as patents of nobility, flags, passports, and coats of arms, designs for all which he got from one of the chaps who could draw a little, and then pasted in the fly-leaf of a copy of those *Tales of a Grandfather* from which he had so often drawn inspiration for his own. And, last of all, he established an order of knighthood of which, of course, along with Orr and Els, he made himself a member and decreed that all who should be entitled to wear its blue ribbon should be exempt from the operation of the ordinary laws of the room. Meanwhile however he could not but perceive that all this not only rather bored the others, but even the pair on whose goodwill the whole fabric of his power rested. Yet, far from beginning upon this account to draw back, or at least to go no further, it seemed to him as if there were something forcing him on against his will and obliging him to choose just this most inopportune moment to press Orr to sanction the further scheme he had conceived of making the laws that obtained in dormitory of force in the day as well. Nor even when Orr roughly refused, did he take the hint, but, furious at being denied what he had considered it had only been a form to ask, began to consider how he might seize the crown for himself. He was tired of always having to consult some one else whenever he wanted to do anything; he must reign alone. Of course, a revolt would be attended with some danger, but even the prospect of failure was not without its charms when he could picture himself as the central figure in some great state trial.

But first he must reduce to subjection one of the rooms that not only had declined to accept its new position, but had even dared to make fun of him and his kingdoms. And that evening he gave the order to his troops to prepare to march and, while they were gathering, himself got out of bed and walked across the room towards them, fitting over his shoulder as he went the broad blue ribbon of his Order, that, comparing himself to Nelson, he always put on when going out to fight. Then suddenly they all fell on him at once, and so much at unawares as to bear him to the ground before he had fully realised what was happening. Had he had time, he would have fought to the last gasp, but, being down, it was surely, he thought, more dignified to give in at once and so there he lay and let them do what they liked; luckily he had come down face forwards and so escaped at any rate the actual sight of his shame. And they tore his nightshirt over his head and with slipper-heels, brush-backs and anything that they could lay their hands upon, belaboured the bare body that was stretched unresisting on the floor before them. But at last they let him get up and, avoiding their regards and with burning cheeks, without a word, he went back to bed. It was long, however, before he fell asleep; and in all the tumult of his mind what distressed him perhaps the most was the thought that when morning came he would have to face not only those who had so put him to shame but the rest of the school who of course would now be told of his overthrow and disgrace.

Yet when the time arrived it was with firm step, with head erect, and with what he conceived was a general air of proud defiance that he walked up the whole length of the Big Schoolroom to his seat, looking the while neither to right nor left but feeling nevertheless that the eyes of everybody there were fixed on his face. It was a terrible moment, too, when one of those belonging to the room he had intended to reduce came up to ask him how it was that he had never appeared. But he answered not a word and, pushing out of the little circle that had gathered round, went off to his desk. And all that day he kept to himself as much as he could, feeling as if, after the indignity that had been put on him, he would never again be able to look any of them in the face. In the solemnly exacted penalty that he had fancied he would have to pay had he failed in his rebellion against Orr, there would have been something not altogether displeasing, but the punishment that had actually been inflicted on him had excited not so much awe as ridicule; the way in which some of them had laughed was a thing he would surely never either forgive or forget. Els especially he tried to avoid.

And then they were all once more in the Long Room and scarce were the lights put out than:

'I say, Rosy!' cried a boy who but a little while ago, as he bitterly felt, would only have addressed him by his proper name, and with the greatest respect: 'I say, Rosy! how's your Order getting on?'

Some one gave a horrid laugh but he said never a word.

'Rosy, I say, Rosy, are you deaf?' the other cried again; and into those two short syllables that had not been heard for a good while past, there seemed to his ears to have been put such an amount of insult as caused him to have some ado not to jump out of bed and fly at the speaker there and then. The next moment he heard him, angry no doubt at finding his taunts thus remain without effect, get out of bed and make towards him, upon which he too sprang up and prepared to defend himself; mere words he had decided he would take no notice of but he was quite resolved that any one who should attempt to proceed to acts should have cause to repent. But Orr called out:

'What are you going to do? Let the chap alone, can't you! You've got what you wanted! I should think that ought to be enough!'

And then the other stopped and, grumbling, went back to bed. So presently they began to talk, while he for his part lay still and only listened to the conversation that, but a few hours ago, he would have led; nor was it the least disagreeable of his reflections that even for being let alone it was to Orr that he ought to give thanks.

But luckily the term was now nearly at an end, and some ten days afterwards he was once more back at the Rectory. He had not how-ever been there a week when, as he was sitting one evening in the drawing-room, he was suddenly addressed by Rose:

'What on earth are all these things for, Jaspar,' she asked, 'stuck in your *Tales of a Grandfather?*'

'What?' he said, though he had known at once what she had meant and, getting up, he crossed over to her chair.

'How very curious!' he went on, considering the designs as if he had never seen them before, 'I wonder what they can be?'

'Let me look!' the Rev^d. Orlando interposed, and then with what Jaspar fancied was a sharp glance of suspicion:

'Don't you know?' he inquired.

But feeling that he had already gone too far to be able to draw back with safety, he still professed ignorance of how the sketches had got there.

'You don't deserve to have nice things if you can't look after them better than that!' his Guardian said. 'I hope when you go back you'll find out who did it!' And so Jaspar returned to his seat; he had an uncomfortable suspicion that his lie had been divined.

Thus was he reminded of that downfall of his power, which for the last three weeks he had been doing his best to forget. But now, going over everything again, he tried to discover what it was that he had done to bring about such a catastrophe. One thing at any rate was clear; for the future he must take more care and not let himself go; he must never, as it were, advance so far out of his own ground as to give any one a second chance of inflicting on him such a disgrace. He was glad, at least, that it had happened at the end of a term, for now when he went back he would be able to start afresh.

# CHAPTER VI

Yet when at length he succeeded to the position of head-boy, he did not hesitate to exercise to the full all its rights and privileges. And though he could not think of it as he had loved to do of that that had been his in the days of his kingdoms, as due to himself alone, yet was it so far to be preferred as its occupant was recognised and supported by Old Tom; besides, the fact of its having once been filled by Orr enabled him to be always measuring himself against his former enemy. He was only sorry to find his rule not nearly so popular as, to the best of his recollection, had been his predecessor's. But he was quite convinced that his disappointment was not so much upon his own account as for those towards whom he was sure that, could he but have got a chance, he would have played the gracious prince to admiration. By rights of course he should, he felt, have been better liked than Orr, not less: *he* took no pleasure in making others wretched; *he* could enjoy his power without needing to see its evidence in small boys' tears; *he* never thought that because he had been bullied in his day he ought to bully others now. Why, even when there was a real occasion to lick a little chap, he would often hold his hand, restrained by this consideration, that he would not have dared to touch him had he been big and strong; and yet the others, he could see, believed it all was due to his being a funk. And equally disappointed and hurt at the manner in which he was treated by those towards whom he had none but the kindest intentions, though by no means abandoning any of his claims, he resolved for the future so far at least to avoid giving offence as not to talk of them quite so much as he had done at first: he must certainly not play James I. to Orr's Elizabeth. It might not either be a bad thing to show himself somewhat reserved and so, by letting them see what they would lose in losing him, bring them perhaps to an allegiance they seemed curiously unwilling to give.

But of all the various prerogatives of his place, it was perhaps the leadership of games to which he most zealously asserted his right; and it was precisely this which the others seemed least willing to accord; nor could he really blame them when he recollected how in old days he had muffed and shirked at cricket. It gave him a delicious thrill

of satisfaction to see how surprised they were now to find him playing football so well. And while his resolve to oblige them to admire
him in their own despite and acknowledge him as good as Orr would
have been enough to make him go on playing as he had done at first,
there was besides the constant irritation of Elsie's presence. The boy
was always captain of the other side, and it made him mad to see
that, while even his own men grudged *him his* post, the entire school
appeared to be of one mind in thinking Els as a leader to be only in
his proper place, and in considering that whatever he might want in
the way of age and strength and size was more than compensated for
by his swiftness of foot and pluck and skill. So singling him out as his
especial foe, Jaspar never, if he could help it, lost a chance of charging him with a savage viciousness which hardly grew less when he
perceived that, while all the others had observed this conduct upon
his part, Els alone seemed not to notice it; only, with a never-failing
good-humour, he would dodge aside and so dash on, leaving him to
recover himself as best he might and come tearing after in furious
pursuit to avenge the check. Nor could he at such times have told
whether he disliked or admired the boy the more for thus excelling
him, or whether he were content or no that such should be the case.

But it was not only because it afforded him so many opportunities
of acting at Els that he found football so greatly to his taste; he liked it
too because it furnished him with as much food for his imagination as
had done even his kingdoms or his band. Sometimes instead of leading the van, as he called it, he would take up his position in the rear,
and then sauntering up and down, would for a while affect to be careless how the battle went as proudly conscious of his power to turn the
tide at any moment he pleased, and only anxious that when at last it
was time for him to sweep to the rescue, his interference should have
the greatest effect; and he would fancy himself at once Napoleon
rejoining the Grand Army, and the Old Guard at the last charge of
Waterloo. On such occasions as Young Nick came to play with them
he would imagine he was leading a forlorn hope, and would fling
himself in the master's path in a desperate effort to stop him as, drib-
bling the ball rapidly in front of him, he bore down; the mere impact
of that strong thick-set form was enough to fling him some way off
with violence to the ground, but more than once as, shaken and dizzy
and smeared with mud, he picked himself up, he had not only the
intoxicating satisfaction of knowing he had done what nobody else

dared – that at any rate was always his – but of finding that he had also saved a goal. But whatever it was that he might be about, he still kept an eye on Els for whom it was that everything he did was done.

Nor when the game was over and they were making their way back did he cease to play before the theatre of that one boy. With brightened eyes and faces all aglow, laughing and talking, the chaps streamed away towards the Playground gate; dotted here and there down the straggling line the gay-coloured calico flags of the marking-posts fluttered as they were carried along like the pennoncels of lances; Els in the middle bore the mud-smirched ball swinging to and fro upon its thong. Jaspar for his part was nearly always to be found at his side, to secure which place he would manœuvre with all the art he could, though from his behaviour when there he felt it must have seemed to be one he cared for but little; for whenever Els spoke to him he would answer so shortly and in such a tone that the boy, looking at him for a moment in surprise, would turn away to one of the others and pay him no further heed. And so he walked on in silence, angry with Els for appearing to care so little what his humour might be, and with himself no less for having thus lost all chance of enjoying, as meant for him, the boy's voice and smiles. But even in the sensation of almost physical pain it gave him to see others having what he might have had himself, there was something pleasurable; and anyhow he had felt as if it had been out of his power to act otherwise than he had done. Meanwhile he listened to the talk that went on, nor even when he overheard his own play being praised did he say a word, although his heart swelled high with such a rush of exultation that it seemed to him almost more than he could do to keep from leaping and shouting for very joy; a joy which however would presently be dashed by a reference to the prowess that in days of old had been shown by Orr; and straightway he would fall to doubting whether his play was after all to be compared with his who, though now gone, was still at once his enemy and a standard by which he emulously measured all he did. He even fancied that Els who was surely in some sort a part of Orr, was laughing in his sleeve at the notion of its being possible to draw any comparison between them. But from this mood he would presently pass to one of firm resolve that he would – and he clenched his hands and pressed his lips hard together and strained with his whole body – that he *would* do something which should make every one confess that not only was he the greatest boy there now, but that he

was far greater than had ever been his departed rival. He had a confused notion that a year or so hence when he was gone, he would still
be able to listen to them speaking of him as they now spoke of Orr,
and thus, while yet living, enjoy a sort of posthumous fame. In the
meantime, pleased that the manner of his answers when spoken to,
no less than his present ostentatious silence, had already drawn the
general attention his way, with a dozen little tricks of behaviour he
tried, since he could not engross it all, at least to go shares with Els.

And while it was a feeling of opposition to the boy that football
roused, at prisoners'-base, which they played every morning between
breakfast and first-school, it was rather the notion of protection
that seemed uppermost in his mind, his one object being apparently
to rescue him. He loved to see how the moment that his erstwhile
enemy, his lieutenant now, was caught and sent to the prison right
away at the bottom of the playground down by the gate, three or
four of the best runners on the other side, as knowing what he would
presently be at, would instantly make ready to start off after him so
soon as he should leave his base and now, standing sideways, one foot
outside the line, the other in, serious, every nerve braced up, were
keeping their eyes intently fixed upon him. For a while, laughing, he
would amuse himself by making feints, until at length, when least
they seemed to be ready for him, out he would dash. But even then,
instead of making straight for the prison, he could never resist at once
tantalizing those who had thus come out after him, and giving his
own men a chance of making a few captures; and he would let his
pursuers get quite close, confident that even when they were already
reaching out to touch him, with a dexterous twist or dive, he could
elude their outstretched hands, and in an instant be yards away. And
so at last he would really go off; the wind would whistle past his ears
and flutter the outstreaming ribbons of his Scotch cap. He never
dreamt of rescuing any one but Els, whether or no the boy happened
to be at the end of the line; and he was only pleased when the others
grumbled at such a breach of the rules. So side by side at a jog-trot
they made their way back, safe in the midst of all the criss-crossing
of pursuers and pursued. And if there was anything he more enjoyed
than releasing Els, it was being himself released by him.

And finding it much to his taste, this treating him with special
favour, he now was always looking out for chances of doing what
luckily was easy enough, since, as head of the school, he had, in his

way, no little power. Nor was it only that he allowed him to do things he was strict to refuse to others, but again and again he let him off when by rights he should have been reported to Old Tom. He found a curious pleasure in the thought that, by thus partially exercising the authority intrusted to him, he was staining his honour for his friend's sake. But the mode of exhibiting his partiality that he most often practised was to help him in his work, and though not one with anything in the way of injustice to others to recommend it, it had at least the practical object of aiming at getting him promoted into a form where they would be together. And very soon he found Els taking it as a matter of course to come and sit by him every evening. He would always begin by refusing to do as he was asked, liking above all things to be pressed; and Els, sliding back along the form, so for a moment would sit and pout; but presently, turning his head, he would look at him out of the corners of his eyes, wrinkling up, according to his wont, the outer end of the brow where the arch was broken and the hairs grew sparse. The expression that this gave the boy was one which, by the charm of its mingled fun and pathos, never failed to make him feel that, not even to prolong the pleasure of seeing it, could he any longer withstand him; and Els, who had been watching for the signs of giving way that he knew would by and by appear, would come snuggling up, and put his arm round his neck and look up into his face, and coo in his ear:

'Oh, do, Raven! There's a good chap!'

Raven was the pet name by which Els had taken of late to calling him whenever in a specially gracious mood or more than usually anxious to get something out of him, and Jaspar loved it the more as it was the only outward sign of their friendship that had come of the boy's own motion. But in the meantime, Els, seeing him begin to smile, would give his arm a little squeeze and glance from him to the book already spread open on the desk and from the book again up to him, with eyes so bright and with such a vivacity of movement as made it seem more difficult than ever to resist him. Then, when the construe had been given, with a careless:

'Thanks awfully, old chap!' he would gather his books together and get up.

'You'd do the same for me!' Jaspar said with a simple air he considered rather fine; for he always affected to believe their friendship was conducted upon equal terms though indeed quite aware it was not; nor could he ever help feeling a little disappointed when Els said nothing; and the next moment he saw him amusing himself with two or three of the other chaps in some one or other of the many ways by which he was so ingenious at distracting the tediousness of prepara- tion, having evidently altogether forgotten the friend now swotting away like anything in the hope of making up for the time lost in ena- bling him thus to idle.

But this was hard to do, and very soon the imposition-book grew filled with such entries as: 'Tristram: Greek verbs: six times: Tristram: Cæsar: parsing: Tristram: texts of Catechism: twelve times.' And the after- noons that, up to then, he had always spent with Els, he now not seldom had to pass trying to work off these sentences. So while the rest ran off to the football-field, he, gathering together his books, would go slowly downstairs towards the dining-room where such as had impots to do used to be shut up. But still as long as he could he would hang about in the passage outside in the hope of exchanging a word with Els as he went through; only when at last the boy appeared he was always too much in a hurry to stop and talk, but, shouting something as he ran, in another moment was half-way down the Play- ground. So Jaspar with a sigh would turn and go in.

Dinner had already been cleared away, but the air, still heavy with the fumes of cabbage and suet-pudding, made him presently begin to nod; and then hour after hour, as it appeared to him, went by, and he was alternately falling drowsily forward over his paper, and recover- ing himself with a start and again for a while forcing his stiffening hand along line after line; but his clouded brain never lost the vague pleasant consciousness of its being all for Elsie's sake. Then as the long weary afternoon began at last to close in, and it drew toward tea- time, he would hear them all coming back from their game, one leaf of the double-doors would be opened, and he would see him once more. For a moment still, just as he was on the point of coming in, the boy would stop to speak to one of those who were making such a noise trampling through the passage, and so would stand, his hand upon the knob, his head bent back; while Jaspar for his part, unclasp- ing his cramped and inky fingers from his pen, would lean against the wainscot, and, looking towards him with a smile, so sit and wait. And then there was Els in front of him. For a moment still he considered him in silence. There was not a single detail of his costume, from the thin jersey drawn down outside his tight-shrunk flannel shorts all smirched with mud to the thick-ribbed stockings and his muddy knees, and his boots with their high insteps and pointed toes and brass hooks and leather thongs – so useful for chestnut-fights – that did not seem to give to his trim-built figure a charm quite different from what it had at other times, and to be almost indeed as much a part of him as the laughter that was dancing in his bright eyes or the dimples that played about the corners of his mouth. Then suddenly a cloud would cross his face:

'When you've done staring!' he would cry.

'Tell us about your game!' said Jaspar. And, complying, Els would put his foot up upon the table and pull down first one stocking and then the other and show the grazed skin and bruises all blue and green of his hacks. And as Jaspar listened and looked he almost fancied he was actually charging across the wet slippery smudged grass of the field, and breathing its keen damp air, the while, in the words of the hymn that they had learnt a few Sundays before, the brief November days fell chill and dun on the misty common. As for Els himself, he was the very essence of the boisterous life and health and spirits and strength and pluck of those who played. Then all at once:

'But I say, Ra!' the boy would cry, 'can't I help you?' and he would send his cap shooting along the table, and with a great show of zeal sit down on the form and draw the book towards him with a 'Where's your place?'

But Jaspar never failed to insist on Els continuing his account of the game, for, as he listened, he could think it was owing solely to him that his friend had been able to play. And then the bell would begin to ring, and he would gather up his things and arm in arm they would go off to get ready for tea. Of course the result of his not finishing his impot was its being doubled, but the very price that he paid for the pleasure of this talk only made him value it the more.

And indeed he was even rather glad than otherwise when, finding that whatever impositions they gave him remained without effect, the masters took to sentencing him to punishment-drill as well. And two or three mornings a week at least, instead of being able to play his favourite prisoners'-base, he had to go down into the yard and there, along with half a dozen or so others, do exercises with backboards. He remembered how when first he had come he had seen a lot of them hanging up against the wall as he had followed Old Tom along the passage, and had wondered what they were for. So with a 'Left!

Right! Left! Right!' round and round he marched, now in slow time and now in quick, at the word of command from a tough old sergeant. From the Playground on the other side of the house came the distant shouts of the boys. Close at hand through the study window he could see a huge fire roaring up the chimney, and Old Tom himself, who with a single word could have set him free, with hunched-up shoulders moving slowly about the room; at the end of the yard, just by the gate into the road, the groom, hissing cheerfully, was rubbing down the old white cob; above was the blue and cloudless sky of a fine winter's day, against which the lines of the roofs and every smallest twig of the bare trees stood out sharply; it was very cold, and at last, neither great-coat nor gloves being allowed, his hands grew numb and purple and he could scarcely tell where finger ended and board began; some of the smaller boys were whimpering.

# CHAPTER VII

Nor was it only at school that Jaspar thus suffered for Elsie's sake. For when the holidays came and he returned to the Rectory, he found himself received by the family there even more coldly than usual, and before he had been back many hours, with immense content and pride, discovered that this behaviour on their part was due solely to what he had done for his friend. For immediately after breakfast the next day, his Guardian called him into the study, and without a word, but with an air he understood as meaning, 'There! What have you got to say to that?' gave him his school-report. He saw at a glance it was as bad as bad could be, but, still holding it in his hand, he neither spoke nor looked up; not that really he was in the least ashamed, but he felt that excuses were expected of him, and, not knowing what to give, just stood and wished that his guardian would help him out of his perplexity by beginning the pi-jaw he was sure must be coming. Nor had he long to wait, for the next moment there burst on him a storm of abuse and warnings and threats. What a monster of ingratitude and folly and wickedness he was! How certainly he would come to a bad end! And through it all, with hot cheeks and tingling ears, he stood there hanging his head, but made not the slightest attempt to defend himself. He hoped that his silence and his humble attitude would make his Guardian think that he was taking it all to heart, the while, by keeping his mind fixed on Els, he was in reality merely trying to turn this thunder of words into so much unmeaning sound. At last, however, he was dismissed, and as, still hanging his head, he went slowly out of the room, he made a face of triumphant contempt, and muttered under his breath, 'If you only knew!' But yet it was hard to find that, as time went on, he was still to be considered as in disgrace. That none of them should ever put themselves out for him was only what he was accustomed to, and he had long ago arrived at the conclusion that the more they left him to himself, the better he would always be pleased; but it was a different thing when there was not one of them but by word and look was for ever showing him, and in the plainest way, how little in their opinion he deserved, not only his few poor amusements, but even the clothes he wore, the food he ate, and the very lean-to attic in which he slept. And so, when at last the holidays came to an end – their three weeks had seemed an age – it was with more than ordinary feelings of relief that he went back to school.

There the first news he heard was that Els had got his Remove. His delight was presently, however, somewhat dashed by finding that, so far from sharing it, the boy was more than half-inclined to be angry with him; for in Harry's form you had to grind like anything. But on the following day it was given out that Harry had left, and that Old Tom would take his class, and all Elsie's fears were set at once at rest, since now of course he would be able in perfect safety to do just as little as he pleased. And indeed from that moment he abandoned almost the pretence of work. Even when Jaspar had looked out all the words, and puzzled together a meaning, it still was more than he could do to get him to listen to their translation. With the knife he had brought back that term, he would be carving his initials on the lid of his desk or cutting coffins.

'Oh, I say, Els,' cried Jaspar, 'you might attend!'

For a moment yet the boy's whole attention would remain with the point of his blade, but at last he would turn his head a little, and glance at the page off which Jaspar was reading, and this latter, half-satisfied, would go on, but only to find, when he again looked up, that Els had returned to his carving, or perhaps had pulled a ball out of his pocket, and started a game of catch with some of the chaps on the opposite side of the room. So for the first two or three weeks after they had come back, Jaspar was always urging him to work, and

reproaching him for wasting his time. He found in so doing the same
sort of delightful contrast between what he said and what he felt as,
when he had charged him at football, between what he felt and what
he did; but little by little his efforts relaxed, and at last he was if anything the idler of the two. He liked to fancy that he was following
where he should have led, and was yielding himself up to the influence of one who was neither so old nor so clever nor so strong as he,
nor yet head of the school.

Nor was it only in this particular that he showed a disposition to
resign himself into Elsie's hands. He would indeed, he fancied, have
gladly become his slave, and, except at his bidding, scarce have dared
to stir hand or foot. If only he could have found some heroic opportunity of showing how absolutely he was his! Without a moment's
hesitation he would, he conceived, have laid down his life, not to save
his or do him some great service – that of course was understood –
but merely to gratify a passing whim; and he would have held himself
the more favoured in such an opportunity of devotion, as the price
he paid exceeded in value what it bought. But no such luck was ever
his, and Els – it was his only fault – could scarcely ever be persuaded
to help him to gratify this passion for self-sacrifice. So, while he on his
part stood ready to suffer anything that should be imposed on him,
not only willingly, but gratefully, it was not without the utmost difficulty that he could persuade the boy to command him a task at all.
Then, when at last successful, he was quite as fond of disobeying as
of obeying the orders he had been at such pains to have given him,
especially as by so doing he could get himself treated as though he
had really been what he pretended. Once indeed Els had cried:

'I've a great mind to box your ears! And——'

'You may if you like!' he had said in a low voice, and he had put
down his hands, as, in old days, and with something of the same sort
of feeling, he had done for Orr, and so, with eyes upon the ground,
had stood submissively before him. Sometimes, when he could in no
other way get orders given him, he would wait till some one came
with a request, when he would answer: 'If Els will let me! You must
ask him!' And of this plan of gaining his end he was especially fond,
as he considered it showed everybody the curious inversion he had
effected of the parts which he and Els naturally should have played.
He would compare himself to one of those Highland clansmen of
old days, who rendered absolute obedience not only to their natural

chief, but to any one to whom for the moment he chose to delegate his authority.

Yet even this was not enough, and to obtain the excitement he still wanted, he would proceed to quarrel, being the more pleased as he had less excuse. And often the only ground that he could find would be Elsie's laughing and talking with others besides him. Not, indeed, that this was an altogether empty excuse; for though he tried to believe the boy's doing so was really but another proof of how certain their friendship was, he could never see him thus engaged without a pang of jealousy; besides the sight recalled the fact that, even if he were faithful now to him, he had once been friends with the hated Orr whose shadow, though he had so long been gone, seemed still to interpose between them. Nor was he either without a certain awkward feeling when he remembered how the boy had been a witness of all the humiliations he had suffered at different times, from Orr at first, and later on, when his kingdoms had been overthrown. And so having left him as a slave, when next they met he would roughly turn his back. Then Els would put his arm about his neck:

'Why, what's the matter, Raven?' he said. 'What ever have I done to offend you?'

But Jaspar would shake him off, desiring to prolong as much as possible the unwonted pleasure of Els supplicating *him*, instead, as was usually the case, of he Els; whereupon the boy, getting angry, with an: 'Oh, very well!' would turn away, only for him to follow, pleading humbly to be forgiven.

Then, once more reconciled, for a while he was content to try to make his thoughts as much after the boy's mind as in his slavish mood he had desired should be his actions. But presently he began to want something which should be at once a visible sign of their union and a sort of palladium, with his safe custody of which he could believe the duration of that union to be mysteriously bound up. It must of course be something given him by Els, and he pitched at last upon a certain silver pencil-case with a cornelian top that the boy always carried. Now whenever *he* had had anything Els chose to express the slightest wish for, he had always given it up at once, and not as if surrendering something of his own, but rather as resigning what had merely been lent him for a time; but now, though he threw out the strongest hints of what he wanted, he found the boy so obstinate in declining to take them that at last, in very despair, he bought the thing for about four times what it was worth. Yet still for a while he tried to make believe his bad bargain was a gift, and indeed did not give up till he had begun to find that, so far from serving the purpose he had hoped, it only inspired him with doubts as to whether his theory of everything he and Els possessed being common to both did not in this latter's mind assume the form of: What's yours is mine, What's mine's my own. Then luckily he bethought him of that school tradition which pre-scribed that those who considered themselves really friends should interchange a few drops of each other's blood, and within a very few hours he had persuaded Els, and they had gone through the rite. He could not help feeling that to Els it was merely a lark, while in his eyes it was a sort of ceremony binding them indissolubly together.

But one thing at any rate was as it should be; the life they led was such as to enable him to be nearly always with Els. Their places were next each other at meals, their desks in school; they learned the same lessons, and out of the same books; they played in the same games, and at night, in the Long Room their beds were close together. And so at the end of a day, throughout the whole of which he had scarce lost sight of his friend or been out of the sound of his voice, the last thing he heard before at length he fell asleep was Elsie's soft regular breathing just a few feet off.

But it was Sunday he liked best of all. It was perfect from his very waking; for, for the hour that on week-days they had to spend in school, they were on that morning allowed to lie in bed, and in a dreamy state, such as of all things he enjoyed, outstretched at his ease he would lie and think of the long summer-day before him that, un-broken either by lesson or game, seemed to promise an almost end-less number of happy hours, of which there would not be one single moment when he would not be with Els, whose attention besides there would be nothing to draw off. Then, breakfast over, dressed in their best, each with a blue cloth bag in his hand to hold his books, two and two, they all set out under Young Nick's convoy down the straggling village street for the church at the farther end; and as they went along they would pass groups of people all in their smartest clothes; and louder and louder grew the sound of the bells, until at last the whole air seemed to vibrate with their rejoicing chimes in which he always found something curiously in accord with his mood as he walked at the head of the procession with Els who was wear-ing his Sunday-best of tall hat, broad turned-down collar of speckless white, black Eton jacket and trousers of light grey in which he always looked so well. Jaspar liked to see people turning round to stare; and sometimes he would catch an exclamation: 'What an extraordinarily handsome boy!' So, passing up the churchyard-path sunk low between two banks of grass stuck with old headstones half-buried in the ground and leaning this way and that, they would presently be trampling up the aisle towards their pew. His place was right at the end, and next him of course was Els; at his back was a little window, the stained glass of which represented two women going towards each other with outstretched arms; in front he was screened by five or six benches full of boys, and he was thus able in perfect safety to receive from the lad who blew the bellows, who was only separated from him by a foliated iron railing, the grub bought with the money he had handed through the Sunday before. The eating however he and Els would always put off till the Litany, when, by bowing their heads upon their arms, it was easy to munch without being caught; now and again, just to divert suspicion should Young Nick be looking their way, one or other would raise his head and chime in with a loud, 'We beseech Thee to hear us, good Lord!' a petition into which he for his part threw no little feeling.

After dinner he and Els, their arms over each other's shoulders, would saunter round the Sabbath-peaceful Playground until it was time to start again for church which generally the bigger boys were allowed to attend at a village some three miles off. And presently they were descending the last broad and gentle grassy slope of the Common, on the farther edge of which Ashtead lay; before them as they went down, appearing from among its elms, was the low embattled church-tower with its clock and gilded vane; the bells were ringing, and the chimes came floating softly up with a very different sound to his ears from that which in the morning those of Scarisbrick Church had borne; *they* had made his heart swell within him for very happiness, now *these* filled him with a vague yearning for he knew not what; for, happy as was the rest of the week, about just those few hours there was a something melancholy of a peculiar charm that seemed to him to find its completest expression in the *Nunc Dimittis*. Then, service over, they went back the other way by the fields, following the winding footpath through swing-gates and over stiles, now traversing a copse, now crossing an open meadow where the cows were grazing, and again, in single file, passing, waist-deep, through the poppied corn.

And Els would chatter of all the wonderful things he did when he went to stay with his grandfather, Lord Tremlett, at the place which was one day to be his; and every now and again, as a slight rustle would catch his ear, or he thought he saw something move in the hedge, he would break away; but Jaspar would stay where he was upon the path, affecting interest indeed, but all the time only anxious to have him back at his side.

In the evening after tea they would go into the Little Schoolroom, and climb up into the Doctor's seat where, squeezed together on the kitchen-chair at which Els had so often knelt to be swished, their heads touching, their arms round each other's necks, they would read out of one book. The doing so appeared to him to complete, by including the mind, that community of life which already extended to everything besides. So at length it would grow too dark to see; for the gas there was never used on Sunday evenings, and the only light they had was from the faint upward rays of a lamp outside that projected on an iron arm from the corner of the Doctor's stable, and that which streamed through the doorway from the outer room, from which too there came a low hum of many voices; and every quarter of an hour, soft and faint, sounded the chimes from the distant church. So in a far-away and dreamy voice he began to talk of what he would do when he should be grown-up; not that he had any very distinct notions on the point beyond a pleasant assurance that he was destined to be something great; but he was as fond of these vague speculations as to the future as of wondering what would have been his station in life had he been born into the tale of history he was for the moment reading. And then the bell began to ring for evening-prayers, and they would climb down from their seat and go out into the Big Schoolroom, blinking a little as they passed from darkness into light.

'Tristram and Els as usual!' some one would be sure to cry, for the other chaps were never tired of making fun of him and his friendship for the boy, and composing rhymes; and, though he never failed to affect anger when he heard them, at heart he was greatly pleased.

And now, to his delight, the term was almost at an end, and on the almanac he had ruled and pasted up on the inside of the lid of his desk there were actually but two squares more to be inked out: to-morrow – Swell-Tie Sunday – and Monday – Pay Day: – on the Tuesday the school broke up. Usually of course it was with nothing but regret that he saw the holidays coming nearer and nearer; but this time, instead of losing Els, he was going to have him altogether to himself, for the boy was to accompany him home. His father was ill, and with his mother had gone abroad, and the Rev^d. Orlando had actually consented to his coming to the Rectory. It was true that Jaspar's pleasure at the prospect was not absolutely without alloy, for though he could hardly be said to care what Els might think of the Binneys and the way they lived – they weren't really his people – he had many qualms with regard to the stories he had told of the adventures he had had there, the exaggerations of which Els would certainly soon find out. But after all this couldn't be helped now, and in the meantime he had not only his anticipations, but the pleasure of making continual references when others were by to what they were going to do together.

That afternoon every one had gone down to the Cricket-Field to watch a match. Jaspar had spread his old green plaid upon the grass, and now, half-sitting, half-lying, was holding forth to Brooke about the way in which when first he came he had been bullied; and as from time to time he dipped his hand into the paper of cherries by his side, or took a pull at his bottle of ginger-beer, he told again the story of the great licking, now almost a tradition, that he had been given long ago by Orr. The contrast between then and now was delightful. Suddenly there was a shout, and, looking up, they saw that Els had been bowled; and the next moment, all white in his flannels against the green of the smooth-mown turf, he was coming towards them, walking rather stiffly because of his pads, and trailing his bat in his hand. In the whole long line of boys, who, lying and standing in all sorts of attitudes, stretched away on either side of him up and down the edge of the ground, Jaspar was the only one who was neither cheering nor clapping his hands. He had always a curious dislike to doing either, but when Els was the object he thought he might really almost as well have applauded himself; just as, when the boy had asked him why he never played, he had answered it was quite enough for one of them to do so. Then as he made room for him upon the rug, Els sat down cross-legged and, laying his much-pegged well-oiled bat over his knees, was just dipping his hand into the bag of cherries which Jaspar pushed towards him without a word – what need of speech was there between them? – when his attention was caught by a good stroke made by young Farnall who now was in.

'I say,' he cried, turning round, 'did you see that?' and then: 'Go it!'

he shouted, 'run another! A fiver, by Jove! Well done indeed!' and he clapped his hands.

Then behind them they heard some one calling 'Southwood! Southwood!' and they both looked round. It was Mother Tower, who was standing on the terrace-walk that overlooks the field.

'Bother the old woman!' said Els, and, scrambling to his feet, he ran up the steps to speak to her, as she stopped at the low wicket-gate in the privet-hedge; then after a moment Jaspar saw her undo the latch, and let him in, and they both disappeared down the long path that led to the house. He was still wondering what on earth Els could be wanted for, when he was told that Old Tom wished to see him at once.

'Hullo!' cried Brooke, 'what have you been up to now?'

And 'You'll catch it!' said Strachey. But he pretended to be quite at ease. No one of course would have ventured to take his place, so with a careless 'I shall be back in a sec.!' he went off.

But for all this affected indifference, it was with a most uncomfortable sinking of the heart that he walked slowly up the playground. As he went he tried to think which of their many peccadilloes had been now found out. The worst of it was he could not tell how much Els might have already confessed, and he was thus, as he thought very much in the position of a commander preparing to defend the outworks of a fort of which the citadel, for all he knows, has been given up. Finally however he decided that there was nothing to be done but to act as the moment when it came should suggest, and so, composing his face as best he could into an expression of mingled deference and surprise and innocence, he pushed back the baize door of the Study and went in. There was no one in the room but Els who was standing at the window looking out into the yard. Hearing the door open he turned round, and, before Jaspar could get out a word, for he was taken terribly aback at seeing him there alone, hat and gloves and ash-plant stick – a present of his – in hand, evidently prepared for a journey, the boy began to explain how his father was very ill, how he was to start that night for Paris, and how he had asked to be allowed to see him to say goodbye. And then they heard Old Tom outside calling to him to come along, and in another moment Jaspar was standing among the wire flower-stands in the portico, staring blankly up the empty drive, still feeling the clasp of his hand, and looking into his eyes, and hearing the sound of that 'Goodbye, Ra!' in which there had surely been a tenderness of intonation such as the boy had never used before, and such as now almost consoled him for their having had to part.

When, two days after, he went home, he found things much pleasanter than they had been the holidays before, his guardian being disposed to look favourably on one who had the future Lord Tremlett for his friend, whose report besides was this time most satisfactory.

'I'm glad to see you took my warning to heart,' said the Rev^d. Orlando one day, 'and have been working hard!'

And he had had no little ado to prevent himself laughing out loud. If only his Guardian had known that, so far from doing more this last term, he had done much less! And so he went back to those thoughts of Els, from which he had for a moment been roused. To think of him was now, alas, pretty nearly all he was able to do, though indeed he wrote him three or four letters in the warmest terms of affection he could; only he was left quite in the dark as to their effect, for no answer ever came back.

But one morning he saw in the paper that old Lord Tremlett was dead. His grandson, it was added, succeeded him, his own son having died abroad the week before. And a fortnight later he received a letter from Els himself, telling him what had happened, and saying that he was to go to Bridwell at the beginning of the Easter Half, until which time he would stop at home. Jaspar could not help feeling that it was written very coldly, and this impression was not a little strengthened by the fact of its being signed 'Tremlett,' instead of with the familiar 'L. C. Southwood.' But, of course, if Els was going to Bridwell he must do so too. He had expected he would have had great difficulty in bringing his Guardian round to the same view, and he was pleasantly surprised to find this not the case; but the school was full, and the only way he could get in would be by obtaining a scholarship for which luckily there was to be an examination soon after Christmas.

So from the very evening that he went back to Rose Hill he began to work as he had never worked before, not only in school hours, but at every moment he could spare as well. In the morning, so soon as it was light enough to see, with resolute effort he would jump out of bed, and, wrapping himself up in counterpane and rug, would take his books and go and stand under the window; and at night would kneel and read by the fire. The rest of the boys, pulling up their nightshirts to warm themselves, would crowd round and talk; it was often rather difficult to prevent himself listening to what they were saying, but nobody ever directly disturbed him; they saw that to all intents he had ceased to be of their number. And indeed he no longer lived in the present, but in his hopes of a future that was going to be even still happier than the past. And when at length the fire, sinking down, drove the others to bed by the increasing cold, as him by the waning of its light, still for a while he would lie and look at the bare iron framework of the bed upon which Els had so lately slept, and think with satisfaction of what he had that day done to bring him nearer his friend, and so with a smile on his lips would fall asleep.

And he had his reward, for towards the end of January he was elected to the scholarship he had worked so hard for, and three days afterwards was on his way to his new school.

## CHAPTER VIII

The first evening after Jaspar and Els had once more met they were sitting side by side at their desks in school. But, though in the respect of being next his friend the former's life was thus still the same, in everything besides it had changed. Even from where he was he could have counted, he thought, three times as many chaps as there had been at Rose Hill in all, and in the various studies there were, so he had heard, half as many again. And then the place itself seemed less a room than such an old feudal hall as he had had in his mind when long ago he had told his stories. High up above his head the steep-pitched roof was lost in gloom; mid-way down, four dark and rough-hewn beams crossing at intervals from side to side, girded together the whole fabric; for the walls, one was hung with large black-painted boards covered with columns of names and dates; the other, that which as he sat he faced, was wainscoted up to about a man's height with some sombre wood, while above again was a long range of tall narrow diamond-paned windows. At one end was a lofty archway boarded-up, at the other a daïs, on which stood a table and a high-backed chair of state. Endless rows of forms and desks occupied the floor, but just under the windows was left a clear narrow space that, running the whole length of the room, served as a sort of gangway, up and down which was just then walking, cap upon head and sway-ing gown on back, the Senior Inferior who was that evening keep-

ing school. Yet, strange as were all his surroundings, he did not feel
lonely; rather was he happier than he had been since that summer
afternoon, six months ago, when he and Els had parted. It was true
that he would now no longer be able to read with him out of the same
book – for he had been put into the Upper, Els into the Lower Fourth;
but this apart, he had won everything for which he had been working so hard, and was, he conceived, quite justified in thinking that he
was about to enter on a period of even greater happiness than had
been his at Rose Hill. And as there was no danger of their being again
separated, except just during the holidays, for years to come, the time
during which he need have no care except how best to enjoy himself
in Elsie's company seemed, as he looked forward, almost an eternity.

It would now no doubt have been easy for him to have given his
mind to his work, since he was by his side, the thought of whom
had so often made his attention wander, but there was no longer
any need; what could swotting give him more which he would care
to have? So, his left arm lying loosely stretched out along the form,
as Els from under it had slipped his shoulder, he would now lazily
read a line or two of the lesson he had to prepare for to-morrow's
early school, and now look round at his companion, as if never tired
of assuring himself that they were really once more together. And
always he found him either gazing about with bright-eyed vivacity, or
addressing some whispered question to his neighbour on the other
side; and he would interchange a glance of what he thought was the
completest understanding with those laughing eyes, and so, with an
ever-fresh thrill of happiness, go back to his book. Presently however,
he saw the boy's curly head bending over the desk with that demure
air he knew always meant mischief, and stooping a little sideways so
as to get a peep at his face, had just perceived that his cheeks were
dimpling with smiles, when he came sliding swiftly along the form,
shoved a book in front of him, and, pointing with his finger at a
line, had already begun: 'I say——' when a chill voice broke in with:
'What is it you want to know?' and, startled, Jaspar looked up: it was
the Senior Inferior who had spoken, who now was standing gazing
severely down at them from the other side of the desk. For a moment
he waited to see if Els were going to answer, as he naturally expected
he would, a question in which, after all, it was he who was the more
concerned; but when still he gave no sign, he himself stood up and,
blushing, as he always did, leant over to show the passage of which a

translation was wanted. Then the big boy, taking the book, apparently began to consider how to render the phrase, but almost immediately broke off to steal a glance at Els over the edge of the page. As he did so however he met this latter's eyes in which it seemed to Jaspar cheeky amusement was peeping out from behind respect; and obviously discomposed, looked hastily down again, and took quite a long time before beginning his explanation. Even then, though he did his best to hide it under an affectation of great distance and haughtiness, his manner still showed traces of confusion. But Elsie's eyes were now obstinately bent down; and even when he presently asked if he might go and have his voice tried for the Choir, as he said he had been told to do, it was only for an instant that he raised his head; though as soon as his request had received a cold assent, and he was huddling his books, higgledy-piggledy, into his desk, from under the shelter of the upraised lid he shot a laughing glance of intelligence at Jaspar, and then stuck out his under-lip in the direction of the big boy.

On the following Saturday, having been asked by Els to go out jumping that afternoon with him and some other fellows, as soon as dinner was over and he had flannelised, Jaspar left his cubicle in Upper Dormitory to look for him. But not having found him, as he had thought for, at once, he had already for some time been wandering about, when a chap who was lounging in the Market-Place asked him what he wanted, and, on being told, advised him to try Lower Octagon. He wondered vaguely why he spoke in such a curious tone, but merely asking his way, was presently standing in a low small lobby, seven of the eight sides of which consisted each of a door, while the eighth was taken up with the passage he had come in by. He was not without some fear that Lower Boys had no business there at all; and without a notion as to behind which of the many doors he saw he was most likely to discover Els, there he stood in the middle, hesitating as to what he had better do next, and half inclined to steal away at once as noiselessly and quietly as he could. Suddenly he heard Elsie's voice:

'It's awfully jolly having you to do my work!' it said.

'Why?' inquired a second voice it seemed to him he knew.

'Well,' explained Els, 'you see you don't do it too well! Now' – but here there came the sound of a chair pushed hastily back.

'Do you mean that?' asked the other.

'Yes!' gurgled Els, who was seemingly being half choked.

'Do you?' he heard again. And the answer still was yes.

'Oh, very well!' cried the other, whoever he was, apparently releasing the boy, 'you just wait and see what I'll do!'

'What'll you do?' inquired Els.

'Never you mind!' was the retort, 'you'll see.' To this, seemingly, he made some cheeky reply, for there was a great noise of scuffling, and the wooden partition began to shake violently.

'Oh, you're hurting!' cried Els in muffled tones, and then there came a crash. For a moment there was perfect quiet; but presently the other voice went on:

'Well, you have done it now, and no mistake!'

'Oh, yes, I daresay! retorted Els, 'I like that! Why——'

But here Jaspar tapped at the door, and without waiting for an answer, went in.

In the middle of the tiny slice-of-cake-shaped room, already dressed for their excursion in a thick dark-blue football jersey and shorts, stood Els, looking toused and moused, and rubbing one elbow with that expression of mingled fun and pathos which he knew so well; his companion, who was the Senior Inferior who had spoken to them that first night in School, as he appeared, rose with flushed face from examining the wreck of the table which in the struggle had been upset and tilted everything on it – cloth, inkstand, candlesticks, papers, books – on to the floor where they were lying now in a heap. Els was the first to recover from his surprise, and before either of them had time to say a word, had shoved him into the passage outside, when, loosing his hold and crying out 'Come on!' he started off running as hard as he could. And away Jaspar went after him. So they raced across the Fives-Courts where the chimes from the Clock-Tower mingled with the successive echoes of their feet upon the flags, past the tin penthouse of Shop, over the long grass of the Bear Garden where Els gained a little by banging the wicket-gate behind him with a clang as he dashed through, and on into the path that skirts the Cricket-Ground rails until at last, just under the old red-brick wall of the Home Farm, they came up with the rest of the party who, tired, as it seemed, of waiting, had gone on before, but now greeted their appearance with a shout. It was one intended, Jaspar knew, for Els, not for him; but jealousy of the boy's popularity was a feeling he certainly had never experienced; on the contrary, looking upon him as a dearer self, he had far rather pleasant things should fall to his share than to his own. Nor was he ever uneasy lest his affections should be led astray, but, confident of being regarded as a sort of home to which to return, was only glad that now and again the boy should seek amusement abroad. And when, sometimes, as he was going down Covered Passage – the long barrel-vaulted tin gallery which strings together, as it were, the various scattered buildings of the school – he was startled by a sudden cry of 'Whoosh!' and looking up found it had come from Els, who, soundless in his canvas shoes, had stolen on him unawares; with eyes of affection, pleasure and pride, he would gaze after him who, as he still flew on, would turn his head and gaily laugh; he was evidently on his way to some one or other of those many games he was always being begged to take a part in – for indeed he had more invitations than his play-time, though it had been twice as long, could have allowed him to accept, and had already made more friends than he, Jaspar, knew names.

Especially did his company seem in request for the half-hour that came between breakfast and Chapel, which it was a general custom among the fellows to spend in strolling round the garden in twos and threes. For when he and Els appeared in the doorway that opens out of Covered Passage on to the terrace in front of the House, there was always a little crowd standing waiting just outside. There would be a general cry of 'Here he is!' and, 'It was me, Els, you know you promised!' one would call out, trying to attract attention by stretching out his arm; and then another, shoving the last speaker aside, would laugh and say, 'Don't you believe him, Els! it was me!'

And while the boy stopped for a moment on the threshold, looking about from side to side, shaking his head, and to this one and to that laughingly replying 'No!' and 'No!' Jaspar would be standing just behind in the doorway, with such an expression as seemed appropriate to one who is waiting for a friend whom he knows to be coming soon, but who is meanwhile being detained against his will; his feelings indeed were divided between impatience at seeing the already short time they could spend together thus further curtailed and contemptuous pity for the folly of those who could not perceive how useless and unwelcome were their attentions. But at last Els would break away, slip his hand through his arm and go off, though not without throwing a gay backward glance over his shoulder at the disappointed crowd now slowly dispersing; and then he would glance up into Jaspar's face, and when this latter affected not to see, would give his arm a little squeeze and look up again with dancing eyes under whose influence the other could not but presently laugh too.

But one of the fellows there was – the same who had advised him to go and look for Els in Lower Octagon – who now and again altogether refused to be put off. But while Els never seemed so bright as when Young was on the other side, Jaspar for his part walked on in glum silence; and the more Els chattered and laughed, the heavier grew the cloud on his face. He was angry of course that their walk was being spoilt, and angry because Els did not appear to mind; but angrier still because he found himself without the pluck to put a stop to what he so greatly disliked. He tried indeed to think that the best way of getting rid of the intruder was to make believe he did not mind his being there, and yet he could not but feel that in reality it was cowardice, not policy, which dictated his conduct, and that what his honour required was that he should throw himself, as it were, in the aggressor's path and, careless how much bigger and stronger this latter happened to be, at all hazards try to get rid of him. Once indeed he said something to Els about not liking Young coming with them, as now he so often did.

'Why don't you make him go away then?' asked the boy; and he said no more, for though he already had an uncomfortable notion that Els was aware of the real state of the case, he shrank from anything that might confirm his suspicions and oblige him either to fight or – which he was sure he would rather die than do – openly to confess himself a funk. And then one morning Young told them that the Senior Prefect and Captain of Boats – the greatest personage in the school – was coming back on the following day, some cause or another, he was ignorant what, having prevented his doing so at the proper time. Orr, he said, was his name. It was certainly a shock to Jaspar to hear that he was once more to meet his old enemy; yet he assured himself that he was quite indifferent in the matter; he was too old now to be bullied, and as for Elsie's affections, of those he was perfectly certain. Yet for all this, he could not help as they walked along stealing a glance at the boy out of the corner of his eye to see how he was taking the news; and more than once he led the conversation round again to the subject of Orr, for the purpose of noting what effect it would produce, this name which to them both meant so much. But Elsie's air was quite inscrutable.

# CHAPTER IX

Hitherto he had had Els next him in Hall as well as in School, and when therefore some few days after he had thus heard of Orr's approaching return, dinner was now half over and the place beside him on the oak form was still empty, he began to wonder what could be keeping him. Then Young from the opposite side of the table inquired if it was Els he was expecting. 'For if so,' said he, 'you're not likely to see much of him again!' And he went on to explain that Orr having come back that morning and found him there, had promptly made him his fag and carried him off to his own table in Middle Hall. For a moment Jaspar had thought his heart must have stopped beating, so great had been the shock given him by Young's first words, and it was almost with a sense of relief that he now learnt how matters really stood. Yet they were surely bad enough. Before he was even aware that the campaign had begun, the enemy had made two moves, and Els – and it was this that, so soon as he was assured no harm had come to him, he took most ill – had left him to learn the news by chance. But all he said was, 'Thanks, I know!' and so went on with his meal. He felt indeed, as always at such times, as if somehow a mask had fallen from his face and left the workings of his inmost thoughts bare to view; but still he pretended indifference, and presently, as no one remarked on his looking odd, began to hope that by the cold tones in which he had spoken he had thrown Young off the scent, and disappointed him of the pleasure he had doubtless expected to derive from the communication of such a piece of intelligence.

And even when he next met Els, he only said: 'I think you might have told me, old chap!' And then presently he took an opportunity of pointing out how small a thing after all it was that Orr had done; for it was as well not to let him be too grateful. Nor was he quite without a feeling of the grapes being sour; for though he was not such an ass as to pretend to put himself in any way in competition with his friend, still he really thought that Orr might have taken some notice of an old schoolfellow. At the same time, wishing to persuade both Els and himself beforehand that, however in the future the former might behave to Orr it would only be from motives of interest; and not unwilling either thus to establish a friend at court; he went on to say that it would certainly be silly to offend one who had so much in his power.

Yet, whatever importance he attached to Elsie's standing well with Orr, he had no notion of allowing himself to be neglected; and when therefore two days afterwards the boy came late for their walk, and had no better excuse to give than that he had been with Orr, he told himself that the sooner he made his stand the better; and the very next morning kept Els waiting for him. Now since they had ceased to sit next each other in Hall, and could therefore no longer go out together as soon as breakfast was over, they had chosen the Music School for their place of meeting; and there accordingly it was that, while Jaspar dawdled on purpose outside, Els was now wandering about, wishing he would be quick and come, and quite determined not to wait for him much longer. He had just indeed made up his mind to go, when Orr, passing through on his way from the Common Room, where he had been to see some don, recognised him as he stood idly looking out on to the drive, and turning aside: 'Well, young 'un, who is it *you're* waiting for?' he asked.

'What do you want to know for?' inquired Els with a charmingly pert air.

'Oh, nothing particular!' said Orr, and made as if to go.

'I'm waiting for Rosy!' Els observed, and out of the corner of his eye archly he watched to see what effect the name would produce.

'Oh, indeed!' ejaculated Orr.

So they began to talk, and were still together when Jaspar at last came in. Els, leaning back and resting on his hands on the edge of a low oak cupboard, was watching his foot as slowly he swung it to and fro over the floor, the while his face wore the pout which, as Jaspar knew, he always put on when, not liking what was being said, he wanted to make the speaker relent; Orr was standing just in front, and, to judge from his low voice and earnest air, was saying something very serious. It was the first time Jaspar had met him since they had been together at Scarisbrick, but, though taken by surprise, he was already advancing to shake hands with an air as suitable to the occasion as on the spur of the moment he could contrive, when: 'Don't forget!' the big boy cried, and turning abruptly on his heel went off, without appearing so much as to see he was there.

'What is it you're not to forget?' he asked in a tone he tried to make light and unconcerned, as he followed Els out through the glass-doors on to the steps in front of the house.

'What?' cried Els peevishly. 'Oh, nothing!' And Jaspar made no further attempt to talk. He had been angry with Orr for having met his advances after such an insolent fashion, and with himself even more for having risked a rebuff; now he was so with Els.

'Oh, I say,' presently cried this latter, 'do say something or other!'

'I thought you didn't want to talk!' he observed coldly.

For a moment neither spoke; then, as they came to a place where a side-path branched off from the drive, along which up to then they had been walking, Els stopped short and in his usual voice: 'Which way shall we go?' he asked.

'Whichever you like!' answered Jaspar in the iciest possible tones.

Els said nothing, and side by side they went on in silence. And as they walked slowly round the spacious garden that with its broad terrace-walks, and smooth wide lawns lies round the House, it made Jaspar crosser than ever to see how there was scarce a group they passed that did not stop and look back in evident surprise at such a cloud upon the handsome face which already every one had come to associate with fun and the most musical laugh you ever heard.

Now more than once already Jaspar had felt inclined to take it ill that he, who at Scarisbrick had been a great personage, should here have suddenly become of absolutely no consequence; and the change had grown doubly distasteful since Orr had appeared, and at every turn he saw him treated as well by dons as boys with a respect which made his own insignificance still harder to bear than before. Nor did his old enemy act generously and try to break his fall, as, had their positions been reversed, he felt sure he would have done himself. He did nothing certainly to make it worse, but this, far from mending matters, was only an additional aggravation. At their old school he had bullied him, it was true, but that he did so showed at least that he considered him as one with whom it was necessary to count; while here, for all that appeared to the contrary, he was not even aware of his existence. But Jaspar's chief reason for hating him was that he had dared to come between him and Els, having already altered the course of their outward life, and even, it might be, diverted some small portion of the boy's affections: for several times of late it had struck him that there had been a certain constraint in the other's manner, such as he did not remember to have previously noticed. It was clearly then

no more than prudent at once to do what he could to render his position too strong to be assailed with any hope of success; for even if Orr
had no intention of trying to supplant him with Els, it would still be
not amiss to make his hold over him even more secure if possible than
it was already, and so render it a matter of indifference whether or no
any attack was delivered from without. And the wisest plan to attain
this end would surely be to assume the part of mentor; so best would
he at once relieve that feeling of anger he could not choose but enter-
tain at seeing himself left without the smallest share in the attentions
lavished upon Els, and perhaps even prevail on this latter to be more
chary of accepting them. Besides, by so doing he would both humili-
ate Elsie's new friends by showing on what terms of intimacy he lived
with one, even a few minutes of whose conversation *they* had to look
on as a favour; and afford such a demonstration of his ascendency as
must certainly discourage any attempt to put him from his place; and
lastly, by thus warning Els of the dangers attending association with
Orr and his set, it would enable him to deal his enemy a blow all the
more effective because delivered on such disinterested grounds.

Yet so far was he all this time from entertaining any serious fears
on the subject of his friendship, that he was rather afraid lest, in thus
acting, he might be falling into the mistake of an excess of precaution;
and so for a while gave less of his thoughts to Els and Orr than to
Young. It really seemed as if this latter were trying to revenge himself
on him for being on such easy terms with one towards whom his own
attitude had to be that of sucking up. Not that he actually bullied him;
that of course he would not have stood for a moment; but he never
let slip a chance of worrying him in some petty fashion or another,
shoving against him roughly when they met, or knocking off his cap
or catching hold of him by his gown or standing in his way when he
wanted to pass through a door; all which was not only in itself irritating, but kept him in a perpetual state of trying to make up his mind as
to whether or no it was worth while to resist.

But his attention was soon recalled to Els by the way in which he
saw him advancing in general favour. For not only was he extraordinarily popular with the set – *the* set of the school – he had been
introduced into by Orr; but those of his own age and standing were,
if possible still more devoted to him, blindly following in whatever
his high spirits and daring suggested; though indeed, when he was
leader of the escapade, being caught by no means entailed such con-

sequences as you might think in the way of punishment; for on such rare occasions as his quick wits and ready resource were not enough to get him and his companions out of the scrape he had led them into, there were very few dons and fewer prefects, who had the heart to punish him, when he looked up into your face with that gaze which, as the story ran, when it had been tried on him, had made even the austere Cator in angry surprise at his own weakness, ask what he meant by having such eyes; and of course those with him had necessarily to be let off as well. And in proportion as he thus daily became more popular with the rest of the school, so did Jaspar, by the increasing severity of his remarks, seek to defend himself against charms which to him also appeared to be constantly growing more difficult to resist. It was partly too to the same end, and in part to be beforehand with the ridicule he was always so ready to expect, that, he now adopted a depreciatory tone in speaking of him, and all the more if, as was usually the case, he heard him referred to in terms of the most exaggerated praise. He never indeed could help looking on it as a liberty that any one but himself should venture to talk of him at all. Besides, he found a curious pleasure in the fact that what with his lips he blamed that in his heart he most approved. And all the time he was observing him with great attention, and pondering the inner significance, not only of what he said, but of his looks and tones and gestures.

So still for a while he persevered in the plan on which he had originally decided; but at length growing frightened, as it seemed to him that Elsie's manner insensibly altered, he resolved to try whether a change might not be productive of good effect. Hitherto, while his one anxiety had been to secure a firmer foothold, he had only slipped the more; now he would see what would be the result of stopping still. Besides it was altogether beneath him to force his affection upon any one, be he who he might. If Els chose to remain friends, why, well and good; if not, he would certainly never engage in any scuffle for his affections. His dearest wish, no doubt, was to be all in all for his friend, but he must be so of the boy's own free will, and not as a result of anything he himself might do or leave undone. And while he conceived that he would be best consulting his own dignity by adopting this method of letting alone; he was not without hope that after all in other respects as well it would turn out the best. It would give Els a foretaste of what he would lose in losing him, and might perhaps beget in him a desire to merit a trust so nobly given. Only a few days ago up in form he had read in his Livy: *'habita fides ipsam plerumque fidem obligat.'* Why should not the maxim serve him? And not only would he release Els from all claims upon his time, but he would show him that he was free to do as he liked. So, whenever they met in Covered Passage or Hall, in School or Dormitory, he was careful not to say a word which could lead him to suspect that anything he did was known, much less either blamed or approved. But all the while he kept his eyes open, and flattered himself there was not much the boy did of which he remained long in ignorance.

So matters continued for a while. But presently, despite the resolves he had made that he would wait for the first advances to come from Els, he found he could hold out no longer; and that evening at tea sent a servitor with a note – the boy was always receiving them – to ask if the next morning after breakfast he would once more come for a walk. With this step, however, jealousy, he assured himself, had nothing to do; he had certainly no such feeling towards Elsie's friends and least of all towards Orr; he would never condescend to bestow so much as a single thought on one to whom he himself was of such little concern: and, besides, he had already gained his object, since Els by this time must surely have seen that he was far from being so indispensable as no doubt he had thought. But he presently discovered that it was easier to drop than to pick up the thread. It was not altogether without difficulty that he persuaded him again to take him as his companion in the morning stroll; and even then they had now no subjects of conversation in common, since he could hardly speak of amusements with which he had nothing to do, or of those with whom Els shared them, who, he felt, were either loftily ignorant of his very existence, or knew him merely as one of that crowd of Lower Boys whom with a few exceptions, such as Els himself, they disdainfully lumped all together in their minds as smugs. Indeed, in every way Els seemed to have greatly changed. Even his clothes were now of a number and sort, and worn with such an air that he who had only one every-day suit and one for Sunday-best – made at the little village tailor's corner-shop in Rottingdean – could not help feeling as if he were suddenly become one of an inferior class. As for the boy's manners, winning as they had always been, they had now, so Jaspar thought, acquired 'a sovereign and radiant grace,' which seemed, however, after all no more than the complement of his altered life and ways and finer clothes.

Thus irritated at once and pleased; anxious to assert himself as being on equal terms, and yet at the same time more than ever convinced that Els was of different and superior clay; but, above all, eager to maintain that place in his affections which he grew the more desirous of keeping as the possibility of losing it increased; his memory fondly went back to the day when he was not as yet distracted by all these conflicting emotions, and he began to talk of the life they had led together at Scarisbrick; he was half afraid that never again would he be so happy as he had been then. Meanwhile, the recollection gave him courage in face of Elsie's new greatness and charms by assuring him that once they had been friends, and by letting him fancy he was showing him that nothing now could ever get over the fact of their having had a common past. Then, when he saw him obviously bored, he would ask what was the matter:

'Oh, nothing!' Els would answer. 'Why?'

Or would burst out with a 'Do you care for me?'

'Oh, yes, of course!' responded Els.

'As much as you used to?' he persisted, trying to get the other to look him in the face.

'Oh yes, I suppose so!' said Els, and for a moment raised his eyes, but only to turn away again and move a little aside so as to shake off the hand laid upon his shoulder. And then for a little while Jaspar would let himself sink into a fit of despair; it seemed as if just as his affection for Els grew, so Elsie's for him waned, while every effort he made to secure his position only resulted in his losing ground. But by and by, and often while they were still together, he would begin to hope for better luck next time, and so would leave him but to count the moments till they met again, and he should have another chance. The worst of it was that whenever he essayed to express his feelings, if he did not simply weary Els, it appeared as if there were something in him stronger than himself that either forced him to speak in so vague a way there was no understanding what he meant, or else gave such an air of irony to what he said that even to himself it sounded as though he were laughing in his sleeve. For a while, indeed, he tried what making him presents would do; but though he ran into debt for every sort of thing from tuck at Shop to a pair of silver and coral links from the jeweller's in the neighbouring town, it did not take him long to see that not only did Els himself not care for all these offerings, but that, even had he done so, it was little good for him with his small means to try and rent, as it were, the affections of one, to whom there were half a dozen big chaps at least who would have been only too glad to have given anything he wanted – not to mention that he himself had always any amount of tin.

Thus was it Els who was the first to break through the custom they had only of late resumed of walking together after breakfast. But when Chapel bells began to ring, and Jaspar saw it was no use waiting any longer, angry though he was at being thus thrown over, it was by no means without pleasure that he found himself able to look forward to another quarrel; he only hoped that when next he met Els it would be in public, that so he might astonish such as happened to be by by insulting one to whom he was known to be attached, and whom, as he was well aware, he still held dearer than anybody in the world. Nor was it long before he got the chance he asked. That very afternoon he was going down Covered Passage, talking as he went to his form-master Toady Maude, when Els with another chap passed by, half-walking, half-running, yet still not so fast but that this latter had time to shoot at him a laughing glance. This he, upon his side, succeeded in meeting with a stare of cold surprise, though he was very glad the other's eyes had been so quickly taken off, for in another moment they would have overcome him; as it was, his legs felt as if they were giving way. For a little he walked bravely on, but they had scarce gone a dozen yards before he found it so much more than he could bear, thus to be going at every step farther and farther from Els, that he plucked up courage enough to break through etiquette and suggest to Toady Maude they should turn back. There was, he recognised, little or no chance of catching Els up, but still there would be some comfort in following the road he had taken.

'Why?' asked Toady Maude in some surprise.

'Oh, I don't know, sir!' he murmured; 'I only thought——' and so stopped, confused.

But at last he managed to get free, and hurried back to the spot where he had seen that swift-passing vision of laughing eyes, hoping indeed against all hope that there would Els still be found. But no such luck was his. And so he began aimlessly to wander about, not going far, but staying always near the place where they had met; it was just where Covered Passage proper ends and the round arch that supports the Infirmary vaults the way; and from Covered Passage he would go out on to the path that, running past Hades with its low terracotta battlements and shrubs, forms an outdoor communication between the Market Place and Hall, and through the porch into the Big Schoolroom, out by the little side door and so back into Covered Passage once again. Sometimes, thinking that the longer he was away, the greater would be his chance of finding Els when he returned, he would go all round by Mother Collins's old garden, the shrubbery, and Chapel, and so back once more by the entrance close to Hall, which he and Els had always used when first they had gone for their after-breakfast walks. Then, as he came near, he would resolutely keep his eyes fixed on the ground, raising them suddenly again at the last with a sort of hope that they would meet what so ardently they desired to see. At length however, tired out, he let himself drop into a window-seat close to the spot he found it impossible to get away from, and taking a book out of his pocket began to read. And there he remained till the bell commenced ringing for Roll, though during the hour that intervened, each time he heard footsteps he would jump up to see if by good luck it was Els.

# CHAPTER X

The next morning after breakfast as Jaspar was passing through Middle Hall he stopped for a moment to speak to a chap who was standing, one of a group, by the marble mantelpiece, warming himself at the great fire roaring up from its huge basket-grate. And presently, as he lingered, appeared Els; and at once he grew so self-conscious there was nothing he did from the attitude in which he stood to the way he talked – but he scarce knew what he said – that was not done with an eye to his friend. Yet he flattered himself that to all outward seeming he was still the same, and even affected not to know the boy was there. Suddenly, as, leaning back against the jamb, he was opening one hand to the blaze, he felt it touched, and, looking round, met Elsie's eyes, and in that instant it seemed to him, not so much that they were reconciled, as that their friendship somehow passed into a different stage. Yet even then, as he caught sight of the boy's hands, he recognised, with a curious pleasure at the incongruity of such a reflection at such a time, that they were large and coarse; in particular was he unpleasantly affected by what yet he had seen countless times before – the swelling on the top of the forefinger of the right, which, as he knew, was due to an accident that he had had years ago as a child. Then, as they went away, with a gesture that filled him with pleasure, Els slipped his hand affectionately through his arm and began to talk; he even proposed that they should go for a long walk that afternoon. And presently he referred to Bagley Wood.

'Where's that?' asked Jaspar; but 'Where you and I are going this afternoon!' was all the answer he got.

So they separated on the best of terms, and after dinner, as soon as he was flannelised, he made haste down to the Market-Place where they had arranged to meet. But time went on and still there was no Els, until at last, his patience gone, he went off to his place in School, using all the little devices he was master of to hide, as well from himself as from any by whom he might have been seen, the fact that he had been waiting, and waiting in vain. But his suspicions were so quick that when in the distance he saw a group of loudly-laughing boys, he thought it could only be at him they were mocking, and he even fancied that among them he recognised Els. And as he sat alone at his desk there rang in his ears, 'Where you and I are going this afternoon! Where you and I are going this afternoon!' Yet some little consolation there was to be found in promising himself that he would be revenged. But when on the following morning he came out of the Library, where, since breakfast, he had been keeping out of the way in the hope that Els all the time was waiting for him in the Music School, he had the mortification of overhearing some one say that the boy had been with Orr in his study.

So resolved that none should ever have a chance of saying that he had begged for love, and least of all that he had begged in vain; and equally determined that he would never stoop to remind Els of what he had done for him in days gone by, and so seek to obtain from gratitude what affection denied; he made up his mind once more that, happen what might, the first offer at reconciliation should not come from him; and this time he would keep his word. Meanwhile he would so act as to show the boy, what perhaps it was partly his own fault had been forgotten – that he had no notion of being friends unless upon equal terms; and again he murmured to himself the old refrain – if Els did not care for him, he did not care for Els. And he took every opportunity of putting himself in his way, and letting him see by his loud laughter and talk that at any rate it was not he who was pining to have their quarrel made up. He even tried to excite his jealousy by taking up with young Clavering, but dropped him again when he saw that Els was not even aware of what he was about; besides, though he wasn't going to push and scuffle for a share in any one's affections, he found it equally little to his taste to appear as wanting what scarce any one else desired. However, he was quite content so long as, constantly meeting Els, he was able by his demeanour to prove to him in a way it was impossible to mistake, not only that he had ceased to care for him, but, if that might be, that he had never done so at all. He would doubtless have been happier could he have perceived in him any signs of being sorry for what he had done; but, unfortunately, far from this being the case, he more than once had actually seen him laugh, and having felt sure it had been at him, had replied in the only way he could, by assuming as he passed an air of killing scorn and dignity. More especially did he put this on when, as was generally the case, he met him in company with Orr, when he would give the pair a rapid look of as much insolence as he judged safe, and so continue on his way without even a pause that anybody but himself could perceive. Yet every time a pang shot through his heart as he plunged on into the darkness – such was his phrase – now only made more dense by the glimpse he had obtained of light. He had often thought it was that black devil, who was chiefly responsible for the way he and Els had quarrelled, and the hate he had borne him so long was now increased. What would he not gladly have done and suffered, could he only have had revenge! And yet he was powerless, it seemed, and must console himself with nursing his vengeance till they should meet in after-life. And then it would be his turn! Then *he* would be the greater of the two! For *he* when he came of age would have, if not a large fortune, one at least which would allow of his choosing his own profession, while as for Orr, he would be a nobody – a city clerk perhaps, or something of that sort. Yet while hatred and contempt were what alone he would have liked to feel, he could not choose but recognise that for the present they were largely mixed with envy and admiration; and the knowledge this was so intensified a hate, which was still further increased by his enemy's obstinate affectation of ignoring his very existence. But worse than all was the curious sense of physical submission that ever since old Scarisbrick days, not only Orr's actual presence, but even the mere thought of him never failed of producing; for while in all other respects his passions proceeded outwards, in this they appeared to return against himself.

Meanwhile, instead of trying to avoid Young, or at the least to keep him at arm's-length, suddenly he veered about, and did everything that he was asked. Partly he wanted to be free to give his entire thoughts to Els, and partly he was inclined to think that once out of the boy's favour, it really was no matter what he did. But he had never expected as the first result of his new complaisance that he would be treated with contempt. However, he only smiled, and was pleased to think that in so doing he showed that his real self could remain unaffected by any slight put upon it from outside: indeed he considered that he was even more superior to Young than ever in that, while this latter was doubtless of opinion that he was now still more to be despised, he knew that in his own eyes his surrender was a matter of no account.

A few days after this he was on his way to the French master's room to leave a piece of translation he had had to do, and, pushing back the red baize swing-door, which opens out of Covered Passage, was already about to mount the small dark staircase, when he saw his path was blocked by two chaps scuffling violently together. So, stopping short, he began to watch for a chance of slipping past, when suddenly the smaller gasped out:

'Oh, I say, Raven, pull him off!'

And recognising Elsie's voice, he darted up the stairs, and throwing himself unexpectedly from behind on the bigger boy, created a diversion which, momentary as it was, was yet enough to give Els time to scramble to his feet, bound up the remaining steps and vanish. The next moment the big boy turned round, and with so savage an air that he was not a little relieved to find it was only Young, who, seeing how their relations had changed, would surely make a joke of the whole thing. He was therefore unpleasantly surprised when, far from calming down on recognising who it was that had thus interfered, he only seemed the angrier; and indeed for an anxious second or so, Jaspar was half afraid that the patience with which he had put up with so much at the other's hands would turn out to have been wasted, and that he would have then and there to fight. Trying, however, not to let his voice shake, he spoke him fair, and had at last the satisfaction of seeing him fling sulkily away, go downstairs, and disappear behind the door as it swung-to. He himself waited until he thought the coast was clear, and then slowly followed. And as he went along, and little by little once more grew calm, he reflected with much pleasure on

the success with which he had avoided a row; but though he was glad
to see his belief in his own powers of persuasion thus strikingly confirmed, he was obliged to confess that it was only with some little loss
of honour that he had achieved such a result, in that he had so far
stooped as to say that had he but known who it was, he would never
have interfered. Yet on the whole he was not ill-satisfied: he had per-
formed a generous action in rescuing one who had behaved very ill to
him, and that too at no small peril to himself. How lucky he had not
stayed to see who it was he had flown to attack! For had he recognised
Young he would have conceived that he ran no risk, and though, as a
matter of fact, he would have been quite wrong, yet the mere calculation would have robbed his act of all its merit. And then he went off
dreaming of the delights of the reconciliation Els could not now fail
to seek. He pictured it all: how the boy would look as he came up, and
what he would say, and the noble generosity with which he himself
would behave.

Only Els never came near him at all; a piece of neglect on his part,
at which indeed at first he was highly indignant, though he presently
succeeded in convincing himself that in such conduct he should only
see a proof of how unworthy the boy was of any regard. And he
was very glad when he could have this opinion confirmed by hearing anybody abuse him. But to be angry at anything he had done, or
still might do, would be to pay him a compliment altogether beyond
his deserts; while as for revenge, the only kind it was not below his
dignity to take was to pay him no further attention. Yet he could find
no heart to join in the general games, but would instead, whenever
possible, go off for long solitary walks on the Netherton Road, or
sometimes only moon about the park. But he could think of nothing
except Els.

'And I felt sure,' he would cry, 'and I felt sure we were going to be
so happy together!' But it was all over now. This was an end. This
was the end! though indeed he did not really believe it was anything
of the kind. But anxious to divert his mind if he could from such
dismal reflections, and casting about for something to serve his turn,
he bethought him of the botanizing expeditions on which at home
he had sometimes had to accompany his Guardian's eldest daughter,
Violet. He would gather such flowers as he saw in the hedgerows or
along the banks of the little stream that runs through the park, and
send them home and learn their names. So presently he used to return

from his walk, with his pockets stuffed full of what he tried to believe
were interesting plants; but he really looked on them as dirty weeds.
But the occupation of gathering them at least saved him from his
thoughts. Sometimes however he would betake himself after dinner
straight to his desk in School, and there sit and read till at last interrupted by Roll. Often it was Shakespeare that he chose, for though it
bored him hugely, his vanity was pleased to have fellows coming up,
and crying out, 'What's this!' and to see the astonishment and disgust
with which they read the name. Yet somehow he could never feel as
superior as he knew he might well have done. Moreover, by and by
Young, discovering where he went, would leave the field and, coming
in to him while he was all alone, would sit himself down by his side
and shove up against him, and shut his book or put upon him some
one or other of the thousand and one tricks he was so ingenious to
play. And he, with a sort of weary indifferent air, let him do as he
would, nor ever said a word; he even found a certain relief in the
cessation of any necessity for defence; and all the time he would be
thinking that he was suffering thus for Elsie's sake, who, not content
with being ungrateful, was besides, as he saw, on the best of terms
with the very chap whose fresh enmity he had incurred on his behalf.

And now the day that had been fixed for the Athletic Sports was
drawing near. Several times lately, as starting for one of his solitary
walks, he had been crossing the Cricket Ground, he had caught sight
of Els, now, as he waited his turn at practising for the high-jump,
laughingly insisting on sharing a railway-rug with another boy – for
the wind blew cold – or again actually jumping. What a difference
there was between the way the others did so and the easy grace and
neatness with which he took his run and, drawing his bare legs up
under him, cleared the lath, and so, arched backwards, came lightly
down on to the loose brown earth! His were the lissom continuous
movements of a kitten compared with those of a lot of great clumsy
dogs. Or perhaps the boy would be running round the track, while
Orr, encouraging, swearing, and finding fault, with great loose strides
would be slinging along a few paces away. For himself though, in deference to custom, he had put down his name on several of the lists
that fluttered on the Prefect's Study door, he was resolved that nothing should make him compete; not even would he go and look on.

Yet when the day at last arrived he found himself somehow compelled to add to his unhappiness by seeing the friend he had lost made

still more desirable by all the triumphs which were to fall to his share. Was he not the general favourite for several events, and of the Junior Steeple-Chase and Junior High-Jump at any rate considered cock-sure? So, as a sort of compromise, by which he could at once have his wish and keep his word, he determined to betake himself to the Library, from the window of which you really got not half a bad view of the field. So, while everybody else was hurrying away and out of doors, he, for his part, slipped down by Turret Stairs, and reached his destination, not a little to his content, without being seen. But, still fearing that possibly there might be some one inside, he stopped for a moment before going in to put off the air he felt he wore of having at last arrived where he wished. Yet, after all, he found he need not have been at any pains upon this score, for the room was empty. It was always dark and chill, for, low and of great size, and completely lined from floor to ceiling with sombrely-bound books, its only window was obscured by heavy stone mullions and a wire netting outside; but now, with a bench lying overturned on the floor, crumpled newspapers littering the tables and the large stove in the middle, its fire gone out, merely an openwork case of cold black iron, it had besides such a look of neglect and desolation that, even as he came in, his spirits sank lower than ever. But, making at once for the window, he hid himself behind the folds of its ragged curtain of faded red baize and looked out. The sun was shining brightly down out of the pale-blue March sky, against which the tall elms of Dormitory Clump raised their bare branches and countless twigs in a curiously delicate tracery; the carriage-drive and the grass on either side was covered with a moving crowd of boys. And then, as he looked, close to him there opened a gap, and he saw Els. He was wearing a long 'deerstalker,' of some soft and dark-grey stuff, with ever so many buttons and pockets, capes and flaps, from beneath which, as he walked, peeped out the tiny shining tips of his pumps; his cricket cap was of silk, brilliant with his Social-Colours of chocolate and sky-blue; at his side was Young, carrying his spiked running-shoes. His eyes were sparkling with a light which almost transfigured his face; and in his whole attitude, from the turn of his well-shaped head with its thick-clustering curls, to the way in which his feet seemed scarce to press the turf, there was altogether such an air of radiant triumph as Jaspar did not remember to have ever seen before. The next moment Orr appeared, scattering the crowd to right and left, the flaps of his old yellow ulster alternately opening as he came rapidly on, and showing glimpses of his bare legs which were already those of a big strong man, and, taking Els by the arm, he led him off, seeming from his earnest gestures as they went to be imparting some last advice. And the crowd closing up behind and following after, the pair were lost to view.

Jaspar knew however that in Chapel that evening he would see the boy again, and hear him too, since it was he who was to take the solo in the anthem. He had already grown to like the fashion after which it was the custom at Bridwell to celebrate the various festivals of the Church, and never failed to display the utmost seriousness and dignity in acting such part in them as fell to his share. He was only sorry it was always so small, being indeed but to mount to his place, but he tried to forget that he was nothing more than a boy with the rest, and loved to conceit himself rather a king at his coronation, the central figure in the eyes of God and man in some great pageant of religion and state. And so now, as proud and erect, he stood and waited in his stall, the organ in the gallery above began to play, and while the full notes were rolling tumultuously down, filling his ears with the magnificent thunder of their music, in two long undulating white lines, their surplices swelling and rustling about them, he saw the Choir come streaming down Ante-Chapel steps. Els led the Cantoris side, and as he advanced, not so much walking as borne in a sort of floating pace over the soft crimson carpet, the level rays of the setting sun shot through the west window and, taking the gorgeous colours of its saints' robes as they passed, flamed like a halo round his fair head and dyed his wide turn-down collar and the spotless folds of his surplice in all the colours of the rainbow. But a few hours before, as he had watched him at the Sports, he had appeared extraordinarily good-looking no doubt, but still a boy; now he was an angel descending from the clouds.

So while the last notes of the organ were still rumbling among the dark timbers of the roof, Jaspar knelt down and, bending over the desk, pressed the palms of his hands hard against his eyes. It was only for a moment that he so remained, but when, at the general rustling with which the others regained their feet, he also rose and, with a half-dazed glance, looked round, it seemed as if the place had undergone some sudden and mysterious change. From out the blackness that brooded heavily overhead and even shrouded the aspiring finials of the tabernacle-work above the stalls, there loomed the great carved stone angels who bore up the roof; only walled-in up to the waist, with half their bodies they hung in air above, and their arms devoutly crossed on their breasts, their mighty wings outstretched behind them, sphinx-like and unmoved, they fulfilled their eternal task. Below, on his own level, ranged in three tiers, motionless and dazzling, there stretched away on either hand long lines of surpliced boys, his schoolfellows now no more, but rather part of that great multitude he had read of as standing, clothed with white robes, before the Throne of God. And the throne was the altar, upraised on its marble steps and shut off in mystic seclusion alone within its low gilt rails. From among the strange tropic flowers and innumerable twinkling candles with which at the back it was banked high, there rose aloft, solemn and awful, a great cross of polished brass that seemed not so much to reflect as to radiate light, and to be, if not a deity itself, at least a symbol on which some effluence of the Divinity had been poured out. And while from his lofty canopied stall the Warden read, his musical full voice giving an expression to his words of sonorous grace and stately magnificence; and while the Choir in alternate strophe and antistrophe chanted the Psalms; Jaspar clasped his hands together in an agony of supplication and, turning his eyes in passionate appeal toward the Holy of Holies, brilliant now, as he thought, with a more than earthly light, prayed, yet not in words, for he knew not what, to he knew not whom.

Presently, as once more they were standing waiting, the organ began its prelude, now exulting as if in triumph, and pealing forth louder and yet more loud till the massive framework of the roof seemed to be actually quivering in response; and now letting its notes, tender and pathetic, go floating gently down until at last, growing fainter by degrees and more remote, they trembled for a moment, and then softly died away upon the air, and everything was absolutely still. Then suddenly there stole on his expectant ears, familiar at once and strange, a voice that somehow appeared as if it came from far away, from out heaven's gates themselves. Low at the first and soft, it quickly gathered strength, as higher and higher it went, now for an instant held in pause, now soaring fresh and clear once more, as if every rest but served for a foothold from which to spring each time to loftier flight. And as he listened, all the solemn-burning lights melted together into one dazzling and unearthly blaze, chapel and boys disappeared, and, rapt on high, he grew faint with desire for a happiness he had never had, home-sick for a heaven he had never known. And all the time he derived a curious sensation of pleasure from the thought that it was none other than Elsie's, this voice which was so strangely moving him, and from the contrast between what the boy really was and what his looks and function would have had him be, with a soul as white as the spotless robe of innocence that he was wearing. He resolved he would lose no time in seeking reconciliation with one who, already endowed with every mortal charm, was proving now that he had those of the angels as well. Then, while he was still half on earth and half in heaven, the rest of the Choir took up the tale, and with one triumphant burst of melody the anthem ended.

As he came out of Chapel, still under the influence of all the various emotions which, one after another, he had gone through within its walls, he seemed suddenly to have been raised so high above all mean and petty things that he found it hard to conceive how he had ever given a moment's consideration to such foolish trifles as those upon account of which he had quarrelled with Els. Indeed, it required some little effort of thought to persuade him that their reconciliation was so far from being already completed that, if it was to be at all, it must be brought about before they separated for the holidays on the following day. What a pity it was that the last Sunday of the half had gone by; otherwise, they could have celebrated their *reintegratio amoris* by taking the Communion together, and so marked its final character by uniting themselves after a fashion which, while not unlike that of their interchange of blood at Rose Hill, would, by its being really sacramental, have better responded to the manner in which since then his notions had grown.

But bed-time came, and though more than once he had seen Els, on not one of these occasions had they been alone. He was just behind him indeed as they went upstairs, yet could not speak, for standing in the arched doorway of Upper Dormitory was a noisy group of exactly such of Elsie's friends as he hated most. And as the boy would have passed, he saw one of them stretch out a hand and ruffle over his hair, while another called out: 'Goodnight, sweet re——' but he heard no more, for, seeing his enemies' attention thus taken up, he thought he had better not let slip so good a chance of getting past unperceived. Yet still he refused to give up, and, having undressed, stood shivering, partly with excitement and partly with cold, listening with all his ears to what was going on on the other side of his cubicle-curtain, but

not daring even to peep out. And now the various noises of the other
fellows undressing had nearly ceased when, by the darkness that suddenly fell upon Recess, he knew that the servitor had begun to put out
the lights. And nearer and nearer the blackness came and swallowed
up the two gas-jets opposite his own cubicle, and went on until at last,
as that which burned over the entrance disappeared and the heavy
door clanged-to, from end to end it shrouded the whole place. And
still he stood and waited. Presently here and there away on the right
and on the opposite side sounds of snoring arose, a sign, he thought,
that now at last he might venture forth upon the perilous expedition
he had resolved to undertake to Elsie's cubicle. Slowly and cautiously
he slipped out, taking especial care not to disarrange his curtain, so
that should any one pass, there might appear no reason to suspect
him not to be in bed, and as he went he kept as close in to the side as
he could. He had already reached his journey's end when suddenly,
lightly as he stepped, a board creaked under his tread. His heart was
in his mouth; it seemed as if the entire dormitory must have been
woke by such a noise; and for a few moments he remained poised on
one foot and holding his breath. But when the precipitate thumping
of his own heart was still the only sound to be heard; and when the
only light that could be seen was still that of the watch-lamp glim-
mering, solitary and mournful, in the midst of the vast black waste;
and when the long rows of cubicle-curtains which stretched away on
either hand into the thick darkness, remained motionless and mysterious, his courage returned and he slipped in.

'Who's that?' asked Els in a whisper, and sat up in bed.

'It's me!' he answered, and began to move cautiously forward.

'I'm very sorry!' he said, and, as he heard himself speak, he was
struck with the noble simplicity of his own tone and words: 'I'm very
sorry! It's been my fault!'

'Oh, all right, old chap!' answered Els. 'It doesn't matter!'

For a moment he was so taken aback at the small success of his
magnanimous confession that he found himself actually wishing he
had never come, but soon recovering, he began to talk; he hoped every
moment to arrive at that perfect understanding they surely once had
lived in, to return to which had but a short while ago seemed so easy.
But so far he had got nothing from Els beyond the vaguest answers,
when suddenly he heard him whisper: 'Sh! what's that?' and in an
instant was outside the curtain; behind him, he heard the rings rattle

slightly on their pole as, with long strides, a-tip-toe, he hastened back.

On the following day the school broke up, and he went home. But, though thus separated from Els before he had in any way benefited by the reconciliation he had been so anxious to bring about, he was not altogether sorry to have three quiet weeks to himself, in which to reflect on all the errors of his conduct and to form resolutions for a more prudent behaviour in the future. Besides, the holidays would form a sort of break to divide his old life which had been filled with mistakes, from that he was going to lead when he returned. Innumerable indeed, as he could now perceive, had been his errors; but they all, he thought, might be referred to the attempt to keep Els to himself, in which he had unfortunately engaged. He wondered how he could have been such a fool: he surely might have known that so outrageous a pretension could not have ended otherwise than in disaster: certainly Els, in resenting such behaviour on his part, had but acted as in like case he would have done himself. But the next time he would be wiser, and not only avoid the cardinal error he had fallen into in the past, but walk, as it were, so carefully as to render it absolutely impossible that anything he did should give offence. And having thus satisfactorily found out, as he imagined, the cause of their estrangement, and having made all sorts of resolves as to how he would behave in the future, he grew impatient for the holidays to come to an end, being anxious to see how the plans he had thus formed in peace would stand the strain of actual warfare. And then at last the long looked-for day arrived and he went back.

On the first Saturday after the school had once more met, Orr and some five or six of his friends were stopping on their way from dinner for a moment's chat in the Market-Place, when all at once there was heard a great noise of laughter and cheers, and then a little crowd of boys came pouring through the archway which leads to the dormitories; one a few paces in front was carrying, with head thrown back and stomach well stuck out, an enormous drum which he thumped incessantly with all his might, while the rest were shouting at the top of their voices:

> 'See the conquering hero comes!
> Sound the trumpets, beat the drums!'

And then Els appeared, borne aloft on Arundell's shoulders so that he nearly touched the top of the arch as they went through. He had just put on for the first time the brown leather shoes, shorts, thin jersey with red silk cross patée embroidered on the breast, and straw hat with broad diagonal ribbon of red and white which, in common with the rest of the Eight, the cox was allowed to wear; for to that dignity it was that on the preceding day he had been advanced by Orr. So, as he was carried by, bending backwards and forwards with a charming grace to the motion of his steed, Orr, from where he leant against one of the piers, gave a playful pinch to the boy's bare leg. He in return made a sudden swoop at the other's silver-tasselled velvet college-cap, the emblem of his Senior Prefect's rank, and was already waving it over his head with a triumphant air and a cry of 'Quis?' when Orr's hand shot out and he was caught by his wrist, the small bones of which were as nothing in that muscular grasp. But he, unwilling at once to surrender his prize, strained hard to get free, while Orr, looking up at him with a smile, continued, without any apparent effort, to hold him so tight that he was unable even to move, much less unclose those iron fingers.

And 'I say,' the big boy laughed, 'aren't we getting strong just?'

And, 'Yes, ain't I?' answered Els, as he at length let go: 'Just feel my muscle!' and doubling his bare arm, he held it down towards the other with a half-serious air.

'Ah,' said Split Mug. 'But it's his legs he's really proud of!' and, he poked at them delicately with his forefinger. To which remark the only reply Els made was to stretch out first one and then the other, and look at each in turn with a delightful air of satisfaction. Then in a voice of assumed command he bade his steed set him down, and, as this latter stooped in obedience and he was clambering off to seat himself on the rail beside Orr, he caught sight of his friend Rosy standing in the archway which he himself had just come through.

Jaspar always disliked being near at hand when Els was with those to whom he himself, as he knew, was only a wretched smug, and he would certainly, had it been possible, have avoided meeting him now. But it was quite unawares that he had thus run into the midst of them all, and by the time that he had recovered himself sufficiently to think of retreat it was already too late, for Young, who had been hovering on the outskirts of the group, and whenever they laughed following suit obsequiously, slipping quickly in between him and the door at his back, was now standing right in his path.

'Now, then,' he cried blusteringly, 'where are you coming to?'

Jaspar coloured up, but, hoping he might persuade Young to let him escape before the general attention should have been drawn their way, still kept his temper and even affected to laugh.

'I say, let us go, there's a good chap!' he said, in a low voice. But he felt he would have given much to have been able with one straight blow between the eyes to have knocked down the ugly devil he was thus humbly addressing; who for a moment seemed to hesitate and then, while he stood waiting, still with that submissive smile and air which all the time he despised himself for assuming, gave him a sudden and violent shove and drove him cannoning up against Split Mug, who in his turn viciously pushed him away – and even in the hurry of the moment he yet had time to feel and resent the sort of disgust with which the other struck out with both his hands, and the offended air with which he began to rearrange his disordered tie. But, meanwhile, he was being bandied about from side to side so fast as altogether to prevent his regaining his balance, while his ears were filled with a confused sound of contemptuous laughter, in which he presently heard Els join; whereon, stung into sudden fury, he rushed at Young in such a blaze of passion that this latter, in a funk, stepped aside and let him escape. There was a pause, then Orr, clapping his hand to his pocket, cried:

'What a beastly nuisance! I've gone and left the key of my lock-up in my cubicle!'

Els, who had been sitting on the rail, swinging his bare legs, jumped widely off, and, springing to attention, saluted.

'Shall I go and fetch it, sir?' he said.

'Will you?' said Orr.

'I'm gone!' he cried. 'Look!' and in a moment was out of sight.

Jaspar was fond, no doubt, of humbling himself before Els, but it must be voluntarily and after his own fashion; above all it was necessary that it should not be in such a way as to make him ridiculous. And while it would have been bad enough to be turned into a laughing-stock, it became absolutely intolerable when this was done by those who were Elsie's greatest friends, and who might therefore be supposed to be acting, if not at his instigation, at least with the assurance he did not disapprove; and a feeling of almost uncontrollable fury against the boy took possession of his soul, immediately succeeded by one of depression, as he recollected how powerless he was. But at least, if ever Els should try to speak to him, he could cut him dead.

That same evening he went up to Mr. Clarke's rooms in the house to have some Latin verses corrected. He knocked at the door; but the only answer he received was a sound of laughter from within, and again he knocked, and louder still again, till suddenly the noise stopped and a voice called out, 'Come in!' The don was at his writing-table, with Els by his side, who smiled at him as if nothing had happened. But he only replied with a cold stare of haughty surprise, and he was pleased to find himself still able to maintain this look, even when the dancing eyes he knew so well were plunging into his own. He had hardly dared to hope so soon to have a chance of carrying out his intentions. He could have wished indeed that they had met when a lot of others had been by so that the affront might have been public, but, wherever it was, the shock to Elsie's vanity would be still the same. Meanwhile, Mr. Clarke had perceived that his pupil's attention was wandering.

'You young rascal!' he exclaimed, and pinched the boy's ear.

'O-o-h!' cried Els, and laughed and put up his hand.

As for Jaspar, he had stopped a few paces off, and now stood bolt upright, by his serious and worthy air expressing that protest against such behaviour on the part of a master which their relative positions forbade him to put into words.

'Well, what is it you want?' asked the don at length, as he wheeled sharply round. What a difference there was between the tones in which he and Els respectively had been addressed! And he explained why he had come.

'Oh, yes, of course!' cried the don; then added in a chill voice: 'Your verses are disgraceful!' and so, swinging round again on his chair, began once more to look over Elsie's theme. Then again there was a knock at the door. Mr. Clarke dropped his pen upon the table, leant back, and looking over his shoulder with a resigned air: 'Oh, come in!' he said, and Orr walked into the room; he and the don, as Jaspar thought, greeted each other rather as man and man than master and boy.

'I hope, sir, you're very strict with this young scamp!' said Orr, and laid his hand on Elsie's shoulder, who looked up at him with a gay laughing glance of what to Jaspar seemed the most perfect friendship. Then, as the correcting still went on, Orr began to give him little sly pinches behind. Els did what he could to protect himself by putting out his open hand, but without much effect, for then Orr took to making rapid dabs at his palm with one finger, which the boy tried vainly to close all his upon. In the middle of which he laughed, and was taken up rather sharply by the don.

'Yes, sir!' said he, and began to pretend to pay great attention, but a moment afterwards looked back over his shoulder at Orr, and made a little grimace as who should say, 'There! I knew how it would be! It's all your fault!' Suddenly Mr. Clarke, as if remembering that Jaspar was still there, cried angrily:

'It's no use your waiting now, Tristram; don't you see I'm busy?' And Jaspar turned on his heel without a word and left the room.

But this was only the beginning of a period during which he was obliged to be a spectator of Orr's triumph, the rival to whom, at first despised, then hated as he saw him beginning to gain ground, he had now at last been compelled to leave the field. Nor was it only occasionally that he met the two together; at all hours and everywhere he had to see his enemy occupying that place in Elsie's life which not so very long ago had belonged to him.

If he went down to the river they were there. Now it was Els alone who would be sculling in his whiff, made more charming than ever by the serious air with which he was obviously doing his best, being rather frightened, as it seemed, of Orr who, bare-headed and bare-legged, came racing at full speed along the towing-path, keeping his head turned towards him and, as he ran, shouting out words of command, exhortation, and abuse; and now it was the Eight that would go leaping past over the water, Orr rowing stroke and Els over against him, his every faculty absorbed in steering, the lines tight-grasped in his hands, and bending backwards and forwards with the rest of the crew as with a clockwork regularity they rose and fell. Then, as he himself continued on his lonely way, once more there descended upon everything the silence that had for a moment given place to this rush of life, but now was only broken by the soft whisper of the stream among the reeds. Sometimes, as he went up by the field-path through the standing corn, he would stop for a moment and look back: to the left the river flowed away towards the Lydiat woods, and, just below, the mill, bestriding the rushing water with its two dark arches, shot its tall tapering, chimney-shaft, all black at the top, into the air. Then, as he waited, Orr and Els, one after the other, came climbing over the stile; round the latter's neck was wrapped a soft white woollen scarf, the loose ends of which were flung picturesquely over his shoulders; his jacket was open, and his almost transparent jersey, pulled down outside his shorts, lent to his figure something of that indescribable charm possessed by those pictures of mediæval pages whose jewelled belts you always saw worn low over their hips. And once again, in Upper Dormitory, as he passed along the broad central aisle to his own cubicle, he would find them still together: Orr's head was round the corner of Elsie's curtain; the boy's delightful laugh mingled with the splashing of water. Just above, there hung forward a large picture of the Crucifixion, in which everything but the bowed head of Our Lord and His outstretched arms was lost in deep brown shade.

But it was on Sundays that he suffered most. As soon as dinner was over, he would take a book and go off to the bowling-green, where, stretching himself out full length upon the grass, he would prop his chin in the hollow of his hands and begin to read. High overhead the tall limes met and, shutting out with interarching boughs the garish rays of the hot sun, only let through a subdued and mysterious light that well accorded with the drowsy murmurous hum of bees and the ceaseless rustling of leaves which filled his ears, and presently sent him into a waking dream. Then, looking up, there were Orr and Els and half a dozen of their friends coming in his direction. The boy was bareheaded, and behind his ear was stuck a rose – after the fashion, was it not, of the gallants of Elizabeth's court? His tie was of that pale-blue silk the school affected, the delicate tint and material of which for the most part made the wearer's complexion dark and coarse, but his only more soft and fair; his turn-down collar worn outside his Eton jacket was wide and spotlessly white, and the lines down the middle of his trousers had somehow the same effect as those on the steel legpieces of the young St. George of whom an engraving hung over the mantelpiece in the Butcher's study. But as down at the bathing-place he appeared so perfectly formed as no more to want a covering than does a statue; now you scarcely stopped to consider the clothes for the body which, as it were, shone through them. So, his old untidy gown swaying as he came with a rhythmic grace, with a delightful boyish swagger he advanced over the sun-flecked turf, the youngest and smallest of them all, yet certainly the one whom first a stranger would have noticed. For while he walked a little in front of the rest, as though not so much an equal as a prince at the head of his court, the resemblance was continued by the way in which each there was evidently trying emulously to find favour in his sight above the others. And though for one brief moment Jaspar made an effort to persuade himself it was contempt he ought to feel for him, and felt; the next, as the group passed by so close that the gown of the nearest almost touched his head as he lay on the grass, he caught a word, from which he knew that Els was telling one of his stories, and his thoughts were once more in a tumult and beyond his control. He himself had only heard a few, but those, now for ever forcing themselves upon him, coloured all his notions of life, so great had been the effect produced by the union of matter, already strange and troubling by itself, with a manner in which an air of cherub innocence and a voice of extraordinary sweetness combined to force you to think twice before you could understand what had been really meant. And then, laughing loudly, they all disappeared up the steps at the farther end.

Of course he knew that, in spite of all he said to the contrary, he could easily have avoided these rencounters; but so far from attempting anything of the kind, rather he took every opportunity of throwing himself in the boy's way. And often, just as he was setting out for a walk, the mere sight of something belonging to Els – a cap – a book – would be enough to bring him up with a sudden shock, and to keep him hanging about for hours, in the hope of one of these same meetings which, over in a second, never failed to leave him more restless and unhappy than before. But indeed the boy was hardly ever out of his thoughts, which had always the same refrain: 'Et tu, Brute! Et tu, Brute!' Anything else he could have borne, but not this having been forsaken by his own familiar friend. He must then after all be no more than human, this boy-god, whom he had adored for so long and with such noble constancy! But even to himself it was only, as it were, under his breath that he made this acknowledgment; as far as others were concerned, he still was careful not to let slip a single word that might lead them to suspect his faith was shaken; on the contrary, he rather enjoyed being laughed at for the way in which he persisted in speaking of one who had treated him so very ill. He affected too a kind of generous anger in denying the truth of the things that now were said about the boy. Not that for a moment he really thought his soul was as immaculate as the white and red of his cheeks; but somehow it pleased him to believe that to be false, which all the time his reason told him was true.

One wet Sunday afternoon Els was with Orr in his study in Upper

Octagon. He had cleared the trestle-table of its books and thin cheq-
uer cloth, and having spread all his fishing-tackle round him on its
ink-stained deal top, had become absorbed in the composition of a
certain kind of fly of which he intended to make proof on the trout
in Bartley Water so soon as he should be back home. Orr had been
lying reading on the old broken-springed green-rep-covered sofa, but
now, having let his book drop upon his lap, was considering his small
companion's earnest face as it was bent over his work. Then reaching out his hand, he passed it caressingly over Elsie's thick-clustering
curls, who, clasping his fingers behind his head and stretching himself
and tilting back his chair, looked round with a smile.

'I've sent for our friend Rosy,' said Orr, 'for a talk! If he *will* go on
getting caught out of bounds we shall have to give him a Prefects'
licking!'

'Oh, well, I think I'll be off then!' said Els, and let down his chair.

'What rot!' cried Orr, 'what ever do you want to go for?'

And as a knock was heard: 'Ah, here he is!' he added, 'Come in!'

And the handle turned and Jaspar appeared.

It was already quite bad enough that he should thus have to obey
Orr's summons at all, and humbly come to receive such punishment
as he might choose to inflict on him for his offence; but it was really
too much that he should besides be forced to see such evidence of
the terms on which his enemy now lived with his sometime friend.
And though he could not help flushing up, for one moment he looked
Orr full in the face, and thought that in that glance he met him, not
as a small boy a big, but as foe meets foe. And then he dropped his
eyes, and so stood stock-still in the middle of the floor and listened; or
rather seemed to do so, for indeed, so far from trying to attend, he did
his best to think of other things, and though not altogether successful – for every now and again he could not choose but hear what was
being said – for the most part Orr's words fell meaningless upon his
ears, and even seemed to help his thoughts to wander. And all the time
he somehow felt as if Els was quite aware of what was passing in his
mind, and knew that, while he did not in the least find fault with Orr,
who, always an enemy, was in his right to triumph in whatever way he
chose, he could never forgive one who had been a friend, for having
got him spoken to like this by the very rival he had been left for. Badly
enough in all conscience had Els behaved when in the Market-Place
he had seen him put to open shame, and not only not flown to his

help, but even joined in the laugh; but far worse was his conduct now in having had him summoned by Orr that he might enjoy the spectacle of his humiliation. And enjoy it the boy did no doubt, though he never once turned round, and all that Jaspar saw of him was the back of his crisp head and the tendrils of hair which curled at the nape of his neck, and his wide collar and, through the back of the kitchenchair he was sitting on, those light grey trousers he always wore on Sunday, and his Eton jacket of black ribbed cloth, the point of which, as he leant over the table, stuck a little out. Nor was it only Els he thus closely observed; he also, though apparently never raising his eyes, contrived to see what sort of place he was in. This then was where, secured from all danger of intrusion by his dignity and even more by the fear he was held in, Orr, his successful rival, passed so many happy hours with his faithless friend; and how much this latter was at home he could judge by his keeping there, on a Swiss bracket in the corner by itself, the cup he had won for the Junior Hurdles in the Athletics last half. Of the same curious wedge-shape as that other study in Lower Octagon, in which, not long after they had come, he had found Els, the walls, like those, were merely partitions of dark-stained deal; here, they were hung with photographs of school groups, Eights and Fifteens which, on one side, were surmounted by a red-bladed oar. Fixed over the table was a bookcase, the shelves of which, edged with gilt nails and a fringe of green, were filled, partly with yellow-back novels and in part with school-books; a number of silver and pewter mugs, won at various times by Orr, were ranged in a row at the top. Curtains of faded green depended from a wooden pole on either side the two small trefoil-headed windows through which, as now and again for an instant the rain lifted, he caught glimpses of the long range of the dormitories upon the right, the garden and, beyond, just a corner of the Field. And he thought how much better *he* would furnish his study when he had one, as now at any moment might be the case. Then suddenly it stopped, this voice, that had been going on so long, and he woke up.

'All right! you can go now!' he heard Orr continue after a moment's pause: 'and I advise you to remember what I've been saying!'

So, without a word, he left the room, yet not so quickly but that he was able to see Orr's expression change once more and Els turn round: they were evidently both delighted to be again alone: and as he crossed the landing outside he heard them laugh – at him of course.

'And after all I've done for him too!' he said, as slowly he passed out between the fluted oak pillars of Upper Octagon door and began to descend the stairs.

It was altogether beneath his dignity to stoop to reproach the boy for his ingratitude; but he saw no reason for not doing his best to make it known how worthless he really was. He would at the same time no doubt have to let it be seen how foolishly he himself had behaved; but at least he would have the satisfaction of preventing Els from betraying others. And as he went about explaining all this to any one he could get to listen, he found means of making capital of the very folly of which, even according to his own account, he had been guilty, by somehow giving you to understand that it was the noble confidence he had displayed, which had made it easy for one so lost to every good feeling as was Els to take him in. The moment of course he had found out the boy's real character, he had given him up. But though he affected to be greatly distressed at the sacrifice thus imposed on him by his own self-respect, he yet was almost as happy as he had ever been. He would, he thought, have much preferred to have sung the boy's praise; but, since this was become impossible, it was something still to be able to talk of him at all, if only in the way of abuse; indeed, he was by no means sure that this latter did not, on the whole, give him the more pleasure; for, as he applied to him the very coarsest and ugliest terms he knew, he would experience such a thrill as he could not remember having ever felt before. And while he enjoyed the effect that, on himself at least, they produced – for in word he was as modest as when first he had gone to Rose Hill – he had at once the amusement of standing forth as a champion of a goodness he thought silly in others and certainly did not practise himself, and of knowing that he had broken with Els on quite other grounds than those which he thus pretended.

# CHAPTER XII

And now Gaudy Day was come, the Feast of St. Peter, the School's Patron Saint, which was always kept with every circumstance of ceremonial rejoicing. In the morning there had been Chapel, and then speeches in the Big Schoolroom, and a great lunch in Gymnasium; and in the afternoon the visitors – for the most part the fellows' mothers and sisters – had strolled up and down the Bowling Green, while, from a temporary stand put up just where Jaspar always lay on Sunday afternoons, the Choir had sung glees to the beating of the Precentor's ebony staff. Els had gone about with a tall stately-looking lady – his mother no doubt – and a little, dark-haired short-skirted child, the sister, he supposed, whom he had occasionally heard him speak of. Once or twice he had thrown himself on purpose in their way, but none of them had seemed to notice him, and all the pains he had been at with his bearing were entirely lost. So, drawing a little back, he had contented himself, with watching them, as, with the rest of the gaily-dressed crowd, they slowly passed and repassed before him; and while he could not but acknowledge that they were by far the most aristocratic-looking trio there, he reflected with great bitterness on how by rights he ought to have been at their side. But he was all alone: not only had no one come down to see him, but in the whole wide world there was nobody except the Binneys he could have expected to do so; and for them, he was only too glad that they had stopped away. Nor had he any longer a special friend, with whom, like so many he saw, to have gone about arm in arm; he was not even able to join one of the noisy groups who passed, laughing and talking, backwards and forwards over the grass.

So when evening arrived and it was time for the Play to begin, he felt too down at heart to care to go; yet, as he liked still less the prospect of being left alone in the silent and deserted schoolroom, he resolved to follow the others. The night was sultry and starless, but from the open door of Gymnasium streamed a long shaft of light, for which he made across the wide open gravel-space the end of School abuts upon. Outside this sort of path, all was thick blackness through which could just be seen looming, vast and mysterious, the building itself, and the tall dark motionless trees on either side. But resolved still to keep to himself as much as possible, he took his place at the back, and so, in shadow and with no one near, was free to give way to those thoughts of melancholy and desire and nightmare-apprehension, which were oppressing him. And as he sat, he felt himself turning to stone, while even his eyes, life's last retreat, could only look straight out in front with a fixed and unblinking stare. Figures he could see were moving to and fro on the stage, gesticulating and talking, but he gave them little heed, every faculty being absorbed in the gaze he had fastened on the set-piece at the back. And momentar-

ily this grew in brightness and size, the while the rest of the building
appeared with equal pace to fade away into darkness and insignificance. It evidently represented some town upon the coast of Italy or
Greece: to the left, a mass of yellow houses with green jalousies and
ribbed red tiles descended in terraces to the harbour's edge where
floated a crowd of gaily-painted boats; they and their sails alike were
of a shape and colour quite different from those of the dull lettered
and numbered fishing-smacks he had so often seen drawn up on the
narrow steep beach at Rottingdean, or, from the cliffs, caught sight of,
as they moved slowly over the leaden waters of the Channel; to the
right, a deep-blue sea stretched, far as the eye could reach, until it met
the cloudless sky: and on all was a light that, neither of sun nor lamp,
seemed more appropriate than either to a land which was surely that
of the fulfilment of hope. And his heart ached with longing after a
place where, under new and fairer skies, happiness would at once be
his, and he would live in that perfect union he had always aimed at
with an Els who would be different from the boy he knew and yet
the same.

Then suddenly there appeared upon the stage a figure which
was the very embodiment of his dream. Never had Els appeared so
handsome; while his everyday clothes – and even they had seemed
better than those of others – had been exchanged for a costume as
much more delightful to look upon as he than his ordinary self. It
was a page's suit of blue and white satin, all a-flutter with ribbons
and bows; over the Vandyke collar fell, in great loosely-curling rings,
long love-locks of soft gold hair; his slim and shapely legs were cased
in delicate white silk stockings, and he wore high-heeled satin shoes
with huge rosettes; one hand carried a plumed hat, the other pressed
down the hilt of his sword; and here and there he moved with a gal-
lant grace and spoke his words, the while his short cloak swung this
way and that from his shoulders. All at once, darting to the front of
the stage, from its scabbard of silver and blue velvet he whipped his
rapier, and shaking it with a gesture of defiance above his head till it
flashed again in the light, burst full-throated into his song. It was that
of the School, and scarce had he finished the first line than they one
and all, as if swept out of themselves, sprang to their feet and with
an absolute roar chimed in. But Jaspar still kept his seat; not that he
was not moved, but he wished to prove to himself he was above the
vulgar passions that swayed others. Then, as he sat in his corner at the

back, his eyes wide open, yet seeing nothing but one great blaze of light and, in its midst, that beautiful and dazzling figure; and his ears filled with the thunder of those hundreds of voices, slowly, as if under the compulsion of some outside force, he began to rise, and leaning forward, clutched at the rail of the chair in front, the while it seemed to him as if his soul, straining towards the heaven that had opened before it, was trying to drag his body after.

Suddenly the curtain fell; and as he made his way back, jostled in the semi-darkness among the noisy crowd of fellows who were streaming out, his former notions of pride and honour fell away, and, abandoning all thought, not only of reigning alone in Elsie's heart, but even of doing so on equal terms with Orr, he told himself he would be more than content if still he might keep a part, however small, in the vision which yet dazzled his eyes.

It would be impossible, he knew, to get a word with the boy that night, or even to send him a note, but he thought it would ease his mind if, before he went to bed, he composed one to despatch next day; and so, no sooner was he back in his cubicle than, taking a piece of paper, he placed it up against the partition, so as to get the benefit of the light which from the gas in the middle fell over the curtain-pole, and wrote:

'My dearest Els, – I am ridiculously foolish I know, but still I do not want to quarrel with you altogether; and so I beg you to forgive me. But before you forgive me, I must inform you of a few facts, which I can only do by word of mouth. If you forgive me, therefore, tell me as soon as possible. If I am not told I am forgiven before tea, I shall know I am not. – Till then, believe me, yours penitently,                    J. T.'

So, content now he had done all that was for the moment possible, he fell asleep.

The next morning at breakfast he gave the precious folded paper to one of the servitors to take: he would have liked, had he only dared, to have warned the man to be very careful not to lose it, nor to let it fall into any other hands than those for which it was intended; but he let it go with a careless air, as if it had been of no more account than the dozens of others which were daily sent about at meals. And then in school he began to talk of Els to his next-door neighbour on the form. It was not the first time by many that he had done so, and the other had on each occasion warned him how much better it would be to give up thinking of one who so little deserved regard, and he had listened with pleasure, feeling comfortably superior the while in being able to have relations at all with one who occupied such a distinguished position; nor did he ever fail to let it be understood they were much closer than was really the case. Now, as he talked of his desire to be reconciled, and heard the other point out how well he was rid of the boy, and how very silly it would be of him to allow himself again to be entangled, it pleased him to think that he had already written and despatched a note which must presently bring about the very state of things thus earnestly deprecated. Meanwhile he answered, yes, he knew all that, but he could not help it; and on this theme he proceeded to expatiate with the greatest warmth, wishing to astonish his friend, and feeling there was something fine in such a weakness, and spurred on by the sound of his own voice. Besides the fact that, morally speaking, Els was unworthy his love, far from diminishing, only increased it; and whatever he might have done had the boy been all he should, he found it as it was quite impossible to give him up.

Then, once alone, his thoughts flew back to the note. Had he said too much? Or not enough? And from these reflections he was always being roused by fancying that some servitor whom he saw in the distance, was surely bringing him the reply. So, as the day wore on and still no answer came, he began to set his wits to work to prepare some loophole through which, should none arrive before the hour he had fixed, he might still escape and take refuge in hope. Was it not tea-time on the following day that he had settled as the term beyond which he would not wait? Perhaps the note had never reached Els after all? Or was it the answer that had gone astray?

And then at last the bell began to ring for tea, and he went off to Upper Hall. This was a meal of which he had come to be very fond. The great high room was always cool, kept so by its thick walls and by the outside blinds which were let down the moment the afternoon sun began to fall on that side of the house. And while it thus afforded a pleasant contrast to the heat out of doors, the soft dim light that filled it was grateful after the glare. Just opposite where he sat, one of the tall windows, wide open, showed under the semicircle of its blind, a small piece of the bright green turf of the lawn; round the edges trailed two or three loose branches of a climbing rose that now and again would gently wave as they were stirred for a moment by some puff of wind; and this, with the hair of the boys about him still wet and their faces freshly dipped from bathing, filled him with a delightful sense of summer life; not as he had known it at Telscombe, baking and breathless, at the bottom of a valley close shut in, and in a tiny stuffy room, but as a thing of cool shining rivers, wide smooth lawns, shady avenues and rustling trees. From the lofty walls, panelled to the ceiling with squares of dark lustrous oak, here and there looked down, from out their frames of tarnished gold and the impenetrable blackness of their backgrounds, half a dozen or so heads of those benefactors for whom in their Grace they daily prayed. Over the stately mantelpiece of marble, pillared and carved, was affixed a trophy of the College Arms, a dove striking down a serpent with its claws, and the legend 'Sicut Columbæ' round about. Opposite him sat Young; and now, when they were half-way through their meal:

'Rosy,' he said.

But he gave no sign that he had heard.

'Rosy!' the other cried again, and letting himself slip a little under the table, but clinging still with his hands to the bare massive edge of oak, he kicked at him underneath. But still he said nothing, only tucking his legs out of danger under the form.

'Rosy!' once again cried Young.

'Well, what is it?' Jaspar asked, but did not take his eyes off his book.

'I've got something for you from Els!' he said.

'Have you?' he returned, in what he hoped was an indifferent and unmoved voice, though he could not but fear that his excitement must be generally obvious.

'Will you have it now,' continued Young, 'or wait till you get it?' and with that he stretched out his hand across the table, showing from out his tightly-doubled fist a corner of what looked like an envelope. For a moment Jaspar sat quite still, affecting not to care, until at last, Young's hand being now quite near, he made a sudden grab. But the other was too quick for him:

'Oh no, you don't!' he cried, and drew back. And then, as through the doorway into Middle Hall he saw that behind the Warden's great chair of state the servitor was standing with his trencher-cap ready to hand him so soon as he should rise for Grace; and by that sign knew that the end of the meal was near:

'Well, here you are then!' he said with a generous air, and gave the

envelope which Jaspar received with an elaborate affectation of indifference, so that if after all it should turn out to be a sell, he might be
able to pretend that he had never been taken in. Recognising, however, Elsie's hand outside, he opened it, and was preparing to draw
out its content, when he perceived that there was nothing inside but
the scraps of his own note. Surprised, he raised his head to look at
Young, and, as he did so, met his eyes fixed on him with an air of
the most malicious mockery and triumph; and just as the words, *Per
Jesum Christum Dominum Nostrum!* came booming in in the Butcher's
mellow voice, he seized his tea-cup, and in a gust of disappointment
and rage, hurled it straight at the other's head. But Young had time
to step a little aside, and it went crash against the wall behind. The
noise was partly lost in the slight confusion that always attended the
passage of the dons through Upper Hall on their way out; but the
Prefect, whose table it was, had seen him.

'Five hundred lines, Tristram!' he called out.

But Jaspar scarcely heard, as he stood there trembling with passion,
and feeling as if in another moment he would have flown at Young
with one of the knives that lay there on the table so ready to hand.
Indeed this latter was so alarmed at his air that he did nothing more
to revenge the insult than bluster, declaring with much affectation
of magnanimity that since the young squit had got his lines he was
content, and would not himself punish him any more for an attempt
which after all had failed. But Jaspar, though he heard him speaking,
understood not a word, and only walked slowly out of the room.


## CHAPTER XIII

Of course Jaspar's wiser judgment told him that all possibility of reconciliation was now at an end, but still for a little he clung to the hope
that some change for the better in his relations with Els might even
yet be brought about, were he to take the one step his dignity allowed
of, and return the old silver pencil-case which, though he knew he
had really bought it of the boy, he had always tried to make believe
was a sort of Essex's ring. And if he sent back Elsie's presents, surely
Els must send back his; and there were any amount of things he had
given him that he would be very glad to have himself.

But before he could arrive at any decision on the point, he found that he had sunk into such a state of torpor he could hardly force himself to get up and dress in the morning or, when once he had sat down, to move. And so far now was he from ever knowing his lessons that he did not even try to learn them, doing nothing in Preparation, but, with a fixed, vacant stare, gaze at the book open before him till the whole page was blurred; while when impot followed impot in such quick succession that before one was finished he had always another to do, he was rather glad to be able so to get through his time as to give his recollections no chance of rushing in, which only waited for an instant's emptiness to flood his mind. He even began to look forward with a silly curiosity to the moment, now surely near at hand, when he would be sent up to the Butcher to be swished. Perhaps, too, they would take away his scholarship – he had heard of such things being done – but it appeared no more than right that, as that which had enabled him to gain it had been lost, so the prize itself should pass also out of his possession. And the worse he could make his case, the better he was pleased; it seemed as if, in so doing, he were somehow revenging himself on Els.

'I can't make out what's come to you of late!' said Toady Maude one day. 'Aren't you well?' But answering not a word, with a half-stubborn, half-sleepy face, he kept his eyes still fixed on his book.

'Oh, well,' observed the don with a resigned air, 'I suppose you'd better write out the lesson as usual!'

And without even an attempt at protest he sat down, and leaning back against the wall closed his eyes, and with much ostentation affected to go to sleep.

'Tristram!' cried the don. And as he looked up with a pretended start: 'Why don't you attend, you silly fellow?' he said. Yet far from being grateful that his cheek should be thus forgiven, Jaspar was only angry his heroics should so have missed of their effect.

'I can easily get a crib!' he muttered. Toady however, with a kindness which only irritated him the more, pretended not to have heard, and the lesson went on. But when it was over, and most of the form were indeed already out of the room, he called him back, as, slowly, the last, he followed, and essayed once more to find out to what was due the change that had of late come over him.

'What's the matter?' he asked. 'Is it anything in which I can help you?'

And standing there before the desk with sullen face and hanging head, Jaspar thought how glad he would have been to have opened himself to such unexpected sympathy; but something in him, which was quite beyond his control, compelled him still to answer with a 'Nothing, sir! why?' which, even as he spoke, he knew was tantamount to a definite rejection of the assistance the don proffered; who indeed appeared to consider it as such, for he said nothing more, but presently looking up from the mark-book he was busy over: 'I don't want anything!' he said in the coldest of tones. 'You can go!' And Jaspar turned and went slowly off. Now that all chance of doing so was over, he would have given much to have accepted this offer of help: and vexed with himself on this account, he was no less ashamed. Not only had he wantonly rejected the sympathy that he needed so much, but, by his behaviour up in form, had traded most unworthily on Toady's forbearance; for, of course he never would have dared to show his temper like that to any one, whether master or boy, who he was not sure would put up with it.

Meanwhile, ever since he had turned on him in Hall, Young, apparently giving up all thought of actual attack, had confined himself to setting as many of the fellows against him as possible; nor without result; for presently, apathetic as he was and dull, he could not help noticing a change in their behaviour towards him. He had only to sit down, to see those on either side with affectation slide away along the form as from something unclean, and however loudly three or four might be laughing and talking together, as he came up they would fall silent, and so remain, ostentatiously waiting till he should be once more out of hearing. But really he was not surprised at Young's success, for while all the smaller fellows, and even many of the bigger, were only too glad to do anything to pleasure one who could, if he chose, be so disagreeable; he, on his side, could not expect that any one should care for him who not only had made no attempt to acquire friends, but had plainly shown that, so long as he could have Els, he wanted no one beside. But by and by – no doubt he thought he would put up with anything – Young grew bolder, and from words proceeded to deeds. One night as he was going down the broad central aisle of Upper Dormitory on his way to bed, he became aware of a number of heads peeping in great excitement round the curtains upon either hand, and wondering vaguely what they were waiting for; and then, reaching his own cubicle, he saw that it had been made hay of, and at the same moment heard them all laugh. He had still, however, enough command over himself to let no sign of what he felt appear, but, as though he had perceived nothing amiss, without looking round or even hesitating, went in and pulled-to his curtain. The next morning, when the last bell rang, and it became necessary to go out again among them, he stopped for a moment to arrange, as he told himself, the mask he hoped would hide his real feelings from the many pairs of eyes presently, no doubt, to be looking at him with a cruel amusement; for he was fully purposed that at least his enemies should not have the satisfaction of seeing how much they had been able to move him. And indeed he had been greatly disturbed by an act which had showed him that not even in his last refuge could he count himself safe; and besides was proof of the existence of that general conspiracy against him, as to which, up to then, he had only had vague fears. His heart sank lower and lower, as every moment he more clearly perceived how powerless he was to offer any defence. Against two or three, perhaps he could have made head; but how fight half the school? He only wished they would send him to Coventry. It was Young, of course, whom he must thank for standing in the way of a sentence that, while condemning him, no doubt, to solitude, would at the same time have given him peace.

But still for a few days nothing happened, and he had almost forgotten his fears, when one morning as he was going down Covered Passage, he noticed two or three fellows who were talking together turn and look at him in a curious way, as he went by, the while they said something about 'After Roll!' and 'Yes, he won't like that!' and these vague allusions filled him with all sorts of fantastic terrors. It was not that he dreaded any actual bodily pain, so much as he was fearful of its being intended to put on him some strange indignity that would prevent his ever again feeling at ease before any one who had been by, or even so much as heard the tale. So when that same afternoon four o'clock chimed from the tower, and at once the bell began rapidly to clang for Roll, he was struck motionless by the thought that now indeed his time was come, and spell-bound in his chair – it was in the Library he was sitting – gazed in a sort of trance at the books and forms and tables; they seemed sentient things; and he envied them that happy freedom from troubles which, from their air of perfect unconcern, it was clear they enjoyed. Then, with a violent effort, he broke the charm, started from his seat, and went out. But scarce had he shut the door when it occurred to him that after all he could at once disappoint his enemies and save himself by the simple plan of stopping away; he would, of course, be given a few hundred lines, but there the matter would end; and still his feet continued to bear him on in the direction of school, as if obeying some mysterious outside force against which he himself had no power of resistance; and as, one after another, different fellows passed him by, it struck him vaguely how great could be the moral distance between those who physically were yet so close. But might it not be possible by some desperate and con-centrated effort of will to become one of them instead of himself? Then down the broad slippery balustrade of the staircase that leads to Upper Dormitory, Baring came swiftly shooting and, landing almost at his feet, cried out:

'Oh, it's you, Rosy, is it? You're going to catch it, I can tell you!'

'Really!' he said in a tone of the utmost disdain; but even as he spoke he felt he must be changing colour, so low did his heart sink at thus having its worst fears confirmed.

Then, come to the Market-Place, he stopped, for, now within a few yards of School, he wanted to take advantage of the last moments he would have to himself to prepare for whatever he might be going to suffer at the hands of those into whose midst he was about to plunge, and dim echoes of whose uproar he could already hear. Yet, though there was no one in sight, he could not consider himself by any means safe from view, and so had resolutely to suppress any out-ward sign of what he really felt; but all the while, though it was not so, yet it seemed to him as if his lips were tightly compressed and his fingers clenched. He was gathering together his soul to gaze up into the cloudless sky with such intensity of effort as might perhaps suc-ceed in piercing its blue depths and finding something beyond which should give him assurance that in spirit at any rate he was not alone. And he prayed to be spared the trial which, unless it should please God to grant his request, must now in a few minutes begin; or, if that could not be, that at least strength to endure it might be given; and even as he did so, the thought crossed his mind, how absurd it was to trouble the Almighty for such small matter. Then the tension relaxed, and, coming back to earth, he looked about, almost surprised to find himself where he was. Just in front was the little sunk-garden with its carpet flower-beds of geraniums and lobelias and calceolarias; beyond, two yews, the sombre and motionless foliage of whose intermingled boughs made everything else appear more bright; and then the lawn;

and then, rising massive and square between the trees on either hand, the House, a ponderous mass of dark red brick, surmounted by a heavy overhanging cornice of white stone, with which same material the corners also were clamped and the windows framed; and suddenly, from behind the Octagon appeared a waggonette coming rapidly round along the drive; the harness of the horses flashed in the sun; and again, as in the Library, he was struck with the peculiar air of absolute disregard of himself and all his concerns which was worn by these inanimate things.

And now, a sign it was about to stop, the bell began to ring faster and faster, and he turned away and went on into School. For a moment he was almost stunned by the noise, for not only was every one shouting, laughing, talking, bear-fighting all at once, but there was besides an incessant scraping of forms and banging of desk-lids and trampling of feet, while still above all else you heard the precipitate clanging of the bell. But nobody interfered with him, nor even spoke, and, threading his way through the crowd to the farther end, he took his usual place. Then suddenly there was silence, for the Butcher had appeared, and followed by Orr whose call-over it was, now came walking slowly up towards the daïs. Behind them the arched door was just being shut, when, happening to look that way, he saw that some one was pushing against it from outside, and round the corner appeared Elsie's laughing face. For an instant Oliver the Senior Inferior hesitated, then let the boy squeeze through; he was in flannels, and was still hitching his gown over his shoulders, as not stopping to consider which was the best of the many invitations to a place that were being made him by vigorous signs of heads and hands, he slipped into the nearest seat, the occupants of which, evidently only too pleased to have him there, laughingly crowded up to make him room. But already Roll had begun; and as from the pulpit at the corner of Recess, Orr, in a swift monotonous voice went on reading out name after name, and in endless variety of tones one after another the different fellows answered: 'Adsum! 'dsum! 'sum!' Jaspar thought that, from the advantage of that height, his enemy seemed more than ever to dominate them all. So at last the list was done, and Orr came down and followed the Butcher out; the rest of the school went thronging after, jostling each other in the narrow gangway, but careful not to press upon their Senior Prefect's heels. For a moment he had thoughts of pushing to the front, and so getting clear away under protection of the respect with which

Orr's person was regarded; but he could not away with the notion of owing escape to such a source; besides, even so, there might be a scuffle, and if he really must choose, he much preferred an open fight, even though it should end in a licking, to a safety that could only be bought at the price of a vulgar brawl. So, resolved to show no signs of fear, he was following among the very last, when he heard a hiss and then another and another and another till the air seemed sibilant, and though he was far too proud to turn round, and still moved on with the same slow deliberate step, he began anxiously to wonder whether he should get to the door – now but a few paces off – without being hit from behind; and of this he doubted the more as he could feel that those who had hitherto been between him and his enemies, had now drawn aside, as if on purpose to leave him open to attack. Then suddenly there was a sound as of something rushing and fluttering, and a book – a dictionary he judged from the crash with which it banged against the wainscot – came whizzing within an inch of his head; and then he had turned the corner and was safe.

A few days after he was in his study in Lower Octagon – he had had it given him but the week before – busy arranging his books, when he heard the door at the farther end of the passage open and with all its usual noise of ropes and weights swing-to again, and looking up saw Young. He was caught, and without a hope of escape; to get out of the window was impossible; it only opened at the top and the framework of its lozenge-panes, for all it looked so innocent, was of iron; nor would it be any use to barricade himself, for even if he managed to shut the door before Young could interpose his foot, a single charge would be enough to burst the lock; and so he merely went on with what he was doing. Then Young came in, and without a word, shoved in between him and the shelf. But he only turned away, and moving to the window, pretended to be occupied about the plants that stood in a row on the inner sill; yet all the time he was conscious that this affectation of indifference was useless, since of course Young knew how much he disliked his being there. And now, hitching himself with a careless insolence on to the table and swinging his legs:

'I should like to be friends again, Rosy,' he said jeeringly. 'Couldn't I do for you now instead of Els? Turn round and let's see your pretty face! Don't you know it's very rude to stand with your back to a gentleman when he's speaking to you? Turn round, will you, you obstinate young devil!' he added, suddenly changing his tone.

Still he was silent, wondering what he had better do. The hate which, at that moment, he felt towards the bigger boy was so intense that once more, as on the occasion of their scuffle in the Market-Place, he would have given much to have sent his fist straight from the shoulder into the detested face that now was grinning so close to his; only he could not decide whether to hit out at once, or to wait yet a little in the hope his enemy would presently get tired and go off of his own accord. So he continued to balance and consider till he sank into a sort of dream, lulled by the question: 'Shall I? Shall I not?' which was mechanically going on in his head, when, with the coarse laugh he knew so well, Young pushed up against him; and snatching up the large clasp-knife that still lay open on the ledge – he had been using it to trim his flowers – he made a furious backward lunge. With a cry of 'Damn you!' the other sprang back:

'You young blackguard!' he exclaimed, 'I——'

'If you ever dare touch me again,' he cried, 'I'll stick it into you! And now get out of my study or I'll make you!'

For a moment he saw Young gazing at him, open-eyed and open-mouthed. Then:

'Just you drop that knife!' he cried.

But he for all answer made a step forward, and backing hastily out of the door, Young only spoke again from the safer ground of the lobby; and:

'Will you put that down or not?' he asked.

'No!' he cried defiantly, and still stood on his guard.

'Oh, very well then!' exclaimed the other; 'but you'll be sorry presently, I can tell you!' and so went off.

He was glad to see him go; already he felt that he was *acting* a passion which, in its beginning, had been real, and he was only too conscious that, had he been attacked, he would not after all have dared to use the weapon his momentary rage had put in his hand. Indeed, when he thought of the threats his enemy had made, he was almost sorry for what he had done, and for a while went about expecting at every turn to have fall on him, irresistible and sudden, the revenge which was only, he was certain, delayed in order that when at last it came, it should come complete. But as time passed, and still nothing happened, he began to take heart, and even to congratulate himself on having been so bold; for all personal annoyance now entirely ceased, and he had only to put up with seeing Young affect exaggerated airs of disgust when he came near, or make in his hearing such remarks as, 'That young smug! I wouldn't touch him with the end of a barge-pole!'

But so long as he was left alone, he was not only quite content to have him behave as he did, but would actually have been sorry he should have done otherwise, enjoying the contrast thus offered between what their relations really were and what such means caused them to appear to the rest of the school.

But very soon even this form of molestation ceased, and he was left altogether to himself. And so solitary did his life become that now and again he could not help thinking he would rather have put up with anything than see everybody in the place behave as if unconscious such a person as himself existed at all. Yes: certainly he was more miserable than he had ever been before, even in his darkest Scarisbrick days. Then he had been ignorant of what was meant by happiness; now he knew, and could compare his present with a former and far different state: besides, he had now to bear a pain of which he had had no previous notion, the consciousness that what he suffered came from his own familiar friend in whom he had trusted. Nor had he then been troubled with either of the feelings that now added not a little to his wretchedness: an angry sense of labouring under an injustice – for why should he be always singled out to suffer? – and a melancholy induced by the fear that he must surely be predestined to failure, since, sooner or later, everything he attempted was certain to 'break under his hand': and with this last phrase he was so much pleased that he was for ever bringing it in, and often quite alone, as he talked to himself. Yet perhaps after all his ill-success was due to his own mistakes. Would it not be well to try and draw such lessons from the past as might keep him from falling into the like again? Just then of course the best thing he could do was to 'stop still' – again a favourite phrase – so as by and by to be able to make an entirely fresh start. Meanwhile, not only did this plan seem more agreeable to his pride than any other, but even offered, as he thought, some hope of revenge, for surely it would be a kind of revenge to appear content, and so, by showing his enemies he was not to be moved by anything which they could do, disappoint them of the pleasure they were doubtless looking to get from the spectacle of his misery. Moreover, in the event of any of the dons noticing how he was left alone, he would by this device be able to make them think it to be rather he who avoided the others than they him.

So when, at the instance as he at once concluded of Young, he was turned out of Upper Hall, not only did he not protest, but he even tried to pretend he did not mind. And this too in spite of the alteration having been announced in the most humiliating manner possible. For when one day he would have taken his accustomed place he found it already occupied by England minor, and was curtly informed by Ashley, the Prefect, that for the future he was to sit in Lower Hall. So, flushing up as they all began to laugh and jeer, he left the room, which, even on the hottest of those burning summer-days, had still been cool and shady; where, looking out through wide-open windows into the garden, he had always been able with his eyes at least to escape his surroundings; and went instead to one in which, in a hard dazzling glare, he had nothing better to consider – for he was set with his back to the light – than the faces of those opposite and beyond a bare white wall. Moreover, while the table whence thus contumeliously he had been driven had had at its head a Prefect who could keep order whom all liked, and, for company, fellows of some age and standing; that to which he had been sent was under Smith, only a Senior Inferior, and so despised, even by the very smugs who sat at it, that he had to let them fight as they would over their food and rest content with getting the first help himself. Then in Upper Hall he had had, what he liked, plenty of elbow-room; but here, so tightly were they packed on the form, it was all he could do to raise his hands to his mouth. And not only were they the dirtiest and ugliest little smugs in the place, his new companions, but, which vastly increased his shame, nearly all were younger than he; while far from treating him on that score with respect they seemed rather inclined to try and make him pay for its being considered a punishment to be sent to be with them. No doubt, not only did he never try to make friends, but he did not even attempt to hide what his feelings for them really were. For, though deprived of all distraction by no longer having any window to look out of, and by further being forbidden to read – of course another effect of Young's pursuing malignity – he was resolute not to do anything that could be wrested into an admission on his part that he was no better than they. At the lowest table of all, he would still maintain that his proper place was with Els at Orr's in Middle Hall, and the only result of his being brought into this close physical contact with them, and of being deprived of all means of diverting his thoughts, was to cause him to retire further than ever into himself in a desperate effort to escape contamination.

And as he refused to take advantage of any of the opportunities thus given by Hall of escaping from his isolation: so did he likewise by the many others that the hourly necessities of the school-routine afforded: as, when his form had to wait outside their room until the don appeared who was to take them, leaving the rest to gather about the door and talk, he would go and lean over the parapet of one of the fives-courts close at hand, and try to forget himself and where he was, in gazing up at the sky; and the vane of the Clock Tower, gold-glittering against the blue, would catch his attention, and downwards his eyes would travel slowly over the gable of the roof and the stepped buttresses drawn out at each angle to form side-walls for the courts about its base till they rested at length upon the flags below; up in one corner lay a broken bat. But all the time he had been half listening to what the others had been saying. How much better than most of them he could, had he only been allowed, have played a part in the conversation! As it was, they must imagine he was taking a last look at his lesson, and set him down as a wretched swot, and a swot too who did not succeed.

Then out of school he was alone not in spirit only but in body too. No doubt when the first sounds were heard of the quadruple chimes that preceded the striking of the hour, and everybody jumped up, and, laughing and talking, making plans for the afternoon and calling one to another, went hurrying past him, now on this side, now on that, he also, though at a much more leisurely pace, went off to Upper Dormitory: but by the time that he had changed into his flannels the whole place was silent and deserted; and as, to the sound of his own footfalls on the bare boards of the floor, slowly he walked down the long central aisle, the curtains on either hand pulled back, let him look into each successive cubicle as he went along. Scattered over the beds, or left lying untidily on the floor, were the jackets and waistcoats and trousers, socks, shirts, ties, boots, which their owners had been in such a hurry to pull off. Once he stopped in front of Elsie's cubicle; against the end of the partition was pasted a slip of paper inscribed in large round text with that title he could hardly ever see without repeating it to himself, and wondering, as he weighed the syllables, what they represented to him. On the left, hanging from their black shiny hooks against the long panels of dull buff-coloured wood, were the boy's surplice, tattered gown, and old limp broken-cornered college-cap; on the other, all more or less awry, some half-dozen pictures of a kind that clearly showed, he thought, how poor was his taste, a few hunting-prints in those cheap gilt frames, and a crudely coloured photograph – it was one very popular for the moment in the school – of a woman in a loose trailing purple robe, who, with one hand holding on to a great cross of rough-hewn rock, was reaching down the other to help a companion in blue scramble up out of a dark-green sea, above whose storm-tossed surface just emerged one desperate clawed brown hand. Below, with its single bolster, was the boy's narrow bed, its hard outlines covered with a gaudy railway-rug, and in the hollow, just as they had been thrown down, a little fallen pile of school-books. Then, cautiously glancing round to see if anybody was about, he ventured in. The deep-splayed sill of the lancet-window was littered with all sorts of odds and ends, conspicuous amongst which, in a frame without a glass, and half-hidden under a torn and crumpled letter, beginning: 'My darling Lance,' was a photograph of the little girl whom he had seen with Lady Adelaide and Els on Gaudy Day. He was just stooping to examine it, when his eye was caught by another, the mere sight of which revived, only for a moment indeed but with extraordinary violence, those feelings about Els and Orr that now for some time past had left him alone. It represented the two together, Orr sitting down and Els leaning familiarly upon the back of the chair and looking straight out at you over his big friend's shoulder with that tantalising expression he had so often seen: lips dimpling, as if about to break into a smile, and those wonderful eyes, brilliant and dancing with amusement at you knew not what. He had still the thing in his hand, finding an extraordinary pleasure in increasing his pain, when he thought he heard a noise at the farther end of the room, and slipping quickly out, began to walk away.

So on through the deserted brick-arcade of the Market-Place he went, and down Covered Passage whose tunnel seemed longer than ever now that he could look right to Chapel door at the farther end and not see a soul. And presently the oppressive silence, and a fancy he was the only living thing in the whole of that maze of studies, dormitories, class-rooms, passages and halls, produced on him such an effect that, as he passed, first, on the left, the half-open door of the Prefects' Study, and then, upon the right, the turning which leads up by a slight incline to the House, he was really half-afraid lest from one or the other some awful form should start: nor was it till he was out in the sunlight and the open air that he ceased nervously glancing back, and felt as if, without danger of the devil answering him, he could once more talk out loud to himself. Then passing along the terrace that runs under Hall windows, he crossed the Bowling-Green and the disused archery ground, where the grass always grows so long and rank, and at last coming out into the park, began to descend the slope to where the stagnant waters of the pond, half-hidden now in their summer-growth of rush and arrowhead and lily, lay shining with a curious metallic lustre in the hot afternoon sun. Then, turning to the left, he would slowly walk along the farther side of the water. Sometimes he would find amusement as in days of old by imagining that in this little indentation of the bank he would have a harbour for his fleet, and on that miniature peninsula the fort which should defend it, while behind that point the blockading squadron should lie in wait, and from – and then he would stop: he was really now too old for such childish dreams.

## CHAPTER XIV

Nor in the holidays did he make the least attempt to indemnify himself for this enforced solitude at school by trying to be better friends with the Rectory family. Indeed he rather seemed to be more anxious than ever to keep out of their way. For when by himself he could at least forget, whereas, so long as one of them was near, the very fact of their presence reminded him of Bridwell by making him think how different was the life he led there from what they on their part no doubt conceived it. And besides, after having talked so much of Els, now not even to mention his name would have led to all sorts of questions as to the cause of so sudden a change, and of consequence either to his having more and more to draw on his invention for the incidents of a friendship that had no longer any existence in fact, or to his being reduced to confess how matters really stood – an alternative his pride would not for a moment let him even consider. Last of all, he was ashamed to take at home a position refused him at school.

And while on the one hand there were thus several reasons for his wishing to keep to himself, he could not, on the other, see anything in the amusements of the place to make it worth his while to put up with a society so little to his taste. For all that he ever had a chance of doing was to drive in the pony-carriage with the girls. It was not even as if they ever went on any of those excursions, that yet would have been so easy, to Brighton, Newhaven, or Lewes, no one of which places was more than a few miles off across the Downs. All they did was just to go over to Rottingdean to buy various stupid things for the house – purchases in which surely even *they* could hardly expect him to take much interest. And so great was his dislike to having to accompany them on these occasions that he was even glad when they came to a certain long steep hill, and, under pretence of lightening the carriage, he could get out, and for a few moments at any rate be once more alone. And while, behind, the old white pony, with much creaking of his harness and puffing and blowing, slowly zig-zagged up the road, he went on ahead as hard as he could, trying to find in violent physical exertion some outlet for the rage that was consuming him: a rage which went out against everything in sight, from the sun, beating fiercely down out of the cloudless and dazzling blue sky to the steep chalk slopes of the cutting upon either hand that reverberated the glare and heat on to the small black figure climbing up between them at such a furious pace. At the top he would stand and wait, looking darkly down the while upon the village at his feet, a confused line of trees and grey and red roofs stretched out at length along the bottom of the valley at right angles to the sea; above it hung in the moveless air a thin veil of smoke; on the farther side swelled up another grassy hill, smaller, but otherwise like that he stood on, over which went curving the white Brighton road, while on its crest a squat black mill spread out four thin arms against the sky. Presently he heard the carriage coming up behind, but still, as if absorbed in reverie, gave no sign he knew them to be there, and it was not till they had called him several times that at last, with a start, he affected to awake and, going towards them, once more clambered up into his seat at the back. Then whichever of the girls was driving gave the pony a cut with her whip and they began to rattle down hill until at last, passing on the left a hedge of ragged tamarisk, they turned the corner into the one long street that composed the village. They, for their part, went about to their different shops, but he was left to follow slowly, now to this one, now to that, with the pony and trap; and though, already sick of the pebble-built cottages and brick side-walks, the time seemed very long as he sat outside and waited, yet was he glad at least to be spared going in. So at length they would start upon their journey home, his feet entangled in the heaps of parcels the bottom of his perch was now encumbered with.

Of course he always did his best to avoid accompanying them upon these drives, but it was seldom he succeeded; for when he would have refused their invitation, the girls would hurry off to their father to return almost instantly with a 'Papa says you are to go!' that admitted of no dispute. At last, finding he was never safe so long as he remained anywhere about either garden or house, he took to spending every moment he could upon the Downs. And, with many a fearful glance backward, he would steal a-tiptoe down the path, pass out under the chestnut that grows aslant the gate, and, shutting the low wicket softly after him so that the sound of its swinging-to might not betray his flight, begin to run as hard as he could: past the pent-house that shelters the windlass of the Rectory-well – the rusty chain was hanging loose and the tall barrel-shaped bucket was standing on the closed flap-doors – past some small cottages whose tiny windows were blocked up inside with geraniums and suchlike plants; past the yard of Walrond's Farm with its open sheds and round green pond; under the terrace mound from which the toy tower of the church overhangs the road as it goes up, and under the row of cottages beyond upon the left, until at last, when now he was half-way up the hill, he would stop to take breath, and for the first time look back to see if any one was coming after him. But there were never any signs of pursuit, and so, turning again, he continued on his way at a more leisurely pace till, reaching the top, he would climb the long barrow that marks the highest point of the hill, and there for a moment stand, now looking down at the village in the hollow beneath – it seemed to have clustered round the church-tower – and now over the open Downs beyond which again there stretched, far as the eye could reach, the wide arc of the sea.

Then, drawing a deep breath as if at last relieved of some heavy weight, he turned his back upon the village and struck out south for the coast. For yet a little way the numerous cart-tracks with which the turf was deeply scored did not allow him to forget that Telscombe was still close behind, but soon their wavy lines began to spread wider and wider, and at length were merged altogether in the open – like the maps of the delta of the Nile – and there was nothing left to recall the place he hated with such intensity. The rounded back of the hill was still indeed too broad to let him look into the valley upon either hand, but it interfered in no wise with his view of the Downs as, softly rising and falling in every imaginable variety of curve, they stretched away out of sight, here towards Brighton, there to Newhaven and the Ouse; in front there spread wide the great semi-circle of the horizon where blue sky went melting down into haze to meet blue sea. Sometimes, as, with his head a little forward, he pressed on, he would fancy he could cross afoot those miles and miles of twinkling waters, and reach that misty line he had fixed his eyes on with that far-away gaze he always liked to feel they wore. But all conspired to send him into a kind of trance: for there was nothing to hinder his wandering where he would or to remind him of the fact that these hills, solitary and boundless as they appeared and free, had yet inhabitants and owners; and, as by music, he was lulled by the soft tinkle-tink of the sheep-bells, the carolling of the sightless larks above his head and the whispering of the breeze as it passed, which was yet so light that if he stopped for a moment it stopped too. Then as that great sweep of turf broadened out and began to slope downward before him, there came into sight the scalloped line of the cliffs and ended abruptly the interflowing hills; and the singing of the larks and the tinkle of the sheep-bells ceased, and nothing could be heard but the sea. He had heard it indeed almost from the moment he had reached the brow of Telscombe Tye; but then it had been faint and scarce to be distinguished among other sounds; now with every step he took it grew louder and louder. So coming to where the Portobello flagstaff with all its stays and halliards stood out white against the blue of the sky, he would cross the road and turn westward along the wide strip of turf that runs between it and the edge of the chalk cliffs, always taking care to keep within the line of circular white patches that serve to guide the coastguardsmen upon their rounds at night. On the one hand, above him were the Downs; on the other, beneath, the sea with its various coloured streams, the only sign of life on its wide expanse a motionless dark-sailed fishing-boat, and perhaps, right away on the horizon, from some steamer out of sight, a faint trail of smoke; and he could hear the waves breaking on the beach below, and the rattle of the shingle as the undertow went back.

Often, however, instead of going down to the sea-shore, he would start by the track that skirts the north wall of the churchyard. Nor, as he breasted the slope beyond, did he ever fail to stop and turn and for a moment consider the little village as, half-hidden among its trees, it lay in the bowl of the hills; and then he would make at once for the line of downs which form that side of the Ouse valley. And as he walked along their crest, he would draw himself up, assume a certain proud pose in the carriage of his head and, with what he considered a glance of mastery, look round. Plain to the eye in the midst of all that green gleamed white, far away on the left, the two great semi-circular chalk-pits just outside Lewes; to the right, at the other end of the chain, the grey roofs of Newhaven spread out, above which shot up the huge triangle of a pair of giant shears; in the middle were the masts and yards of the ships at anchor in the river; and a background of blue sea and sky relieved the whole. At his feet the round tower of Piddinghoe Church stood forward on its little bluff, and beyond there flowed the Ouse; only, sunk deep between its banks, there was nothing but an occasional sparkle to show you where it went curving. The wide alluvial plain through which it wound its way was surely very like the Pontine Marshes; and the resemblance was increased by the herds of shaggy black oxen with wide-branching horns that, knee-deep in the deep grass, were always grazing there. Then, as his eyes rested on the long line of hills on the opposite side, the sense of domination he had got at first from looking down from such a height gave way to a feeling that they were as a wall shutting him in from the great unknown world that surrounded the little corner of the earth he lived in: he almost believed that, could he have crossed them, he would have found the country beyond quite different from any that he yet had seen, and presently they even appeared to him to have put on a certain sphinx-like air as if conscious of the mysteries that they were hiding.

At other times, as soon as he was out of the gate, he would turn to the left and, passing up under the trees that here overhang the road, would make his way across the hills to Basdean Farm. And though nothing would have induced him to enter the house, or even to venture within the broken fence, he was very fond of stopping and gazing at it from some spot far enough off, he hoped, to be beyond the reach of the influences that surely reigned inside its walls. For something about it there was that to his mind was very uncanny, as, solitary and deserted, it stood there in that lonely nook of the Downs. Never yet had he seen any one about the place, and indeed the door in the middle with its faded paint looked as if it had not been opened for years, and the moss-grown steps as if they were never trodden, or, at least, not by mortal foot; while the whole front, darkened by the gloomy shadow of a huge ash, wore a sinister mysterious air. He

wondered what had been the crime that thus had made accursed not
alone the place itself, but the whole of the long winding valley at the
head of which it stood; for he could not but think that this latter too
was shunned both by man and beast, since never there, as everywhere
else upon the Downs, did he see either a ploughman with his team
of oxen, or a shepherd and his flock, whether along the crest of the
hills on either hand, or on their grassy slopes over the rounded hol-
lows of which moved, one after another, swiftly and noiselessly, the
shadows of the great fleecy clouds that were floating lazily across the
deep blue sky. Even the sounds he heard were few, and rather of a
kind to accentuate than to disturb the profound silence that, as in a
nightmare, kept him spell-bound: the melancholy cry of a gull, the
cawing of a rook, or the trill of a lark as, suddenly coming into sight
above his head, with wings now rapidly fluttering, now outstretched
and motionless, it would sink lower and lower until at last it dropped
like a stone out of sight into the grass and all was still except for the
dull swishing noise his feet made as they brushed against the thyme,
the bedstraw and the vetch with which the springy turf was powdered
gold and purple. He had not forgotten the botany that he had learnt
at Bridwell, and was always pleased when he could give a name to
the flowers he met with in his walks. And as he went on, more and
more conscious of being absolutely alone among the hills, and fancying at every step he took he was adventuring himself farther and farther into a region over which there had been cast some fearful spell,
he never turned a corner without half expecting to come suddenly
upon something he knew not what, the mere sight of which would
be enough to strike him helpless with terror.

But now, as he began to mount, first one and then another hill
opened down before him till at length he came up on to a crest
whence you saw them all at once melting one into another after such
a fashion as left not a single inch of flat ground visible; they resembled on a vaster scale their neighbour sea, as often from the edge of
the cliffs he had looked out upon it heaving after some great storm.
And here at last he could feel safe from those evil spirits, his terror
of whom had up till now prevented him from looking round; for no
doubt but that at the limits of the valley their power ceased. Besides,
he was reassured by once more seeing evidences of man's presence in
the shape of a great white square of land newly ploughed, a brilliant
patch of yellow colza, or a field of corn over which the wind, with

an infinite and ceaseless rustling, went passing in successive waves. And at the end of the softly interflowing curves of the hills he caught a glimpse of the straight broad shining line of the sea, the glitter of which seemed to make more apparent than before the want of shade in a landscape solely composed of blue sky, green grass, and dazzling chalk. Sometimes even he would see the figure of a shepherd standing out dark and solitary on the ridge of the opposite hill, along the slope of which his flock would be dotted white; or perhaps would meet one as, long crook in hand and mongrel at heel, he followed his sheep that, browsing as they came, were advancing in a straggling line over the turf. Then as he went back he would amuse himself by fancying he was the general of some great army, and, with what he liked to think an eagle gaze and a Napoleonic air of command, would look round as on a battlefield. Behind that hill he would conceal his reserves; up that one over there he would send his Old Guard storming in a last desperate charge with orders to carry the position or perish to a man in the attempt. What gaps were opened in their undulating lines as they rushed on! But, closing up their ranks, they still advanced, leaving the hill-side behind them thickly strewn with dead and dying. He could hear and see the musketry as in flame and smoke it flashed from the furze bushes along the top, the while, above everything, could be heard the roar of the artillery from a battery away upon the right.

Now and again however after walking miles in perfect content, suddenly all his energies seemed to leave him, and, feeling as if he scarce had strength to drag one foot after the other, he would begin to wonder how ever he was to get over the dreary distance that still separated him from home, where at least he would have something to read and so be able to avoid suffering from that absolute incapacity to think which he always so greatly disliked.

Yet wherever he went he still felt that after all he was only a prisoner out for a while upon parole, who must very soon be going back to gaol. And as on his return he walked slowly up the garden-path he would scowl at the low double-gabled front of the house: it surely knew that once more the hour was come when, under the compulsion of some mysterious power against which it was impossible to fight, he had again to constitute himself a captive within its hated walls. And: 'Late as usual!' would his Guardian observe in freezing tones as he entered the dining-room to find them already more than half-way through high-tea.

'I——' he would begin.

'Not a word!' the Rev^d. Orlando interposed, 'Not a word! You know I don't like excuses!'

'How do you ever expect to get on if you're so unpunctual?' Mrs. Binney chimed in, from where she sat at the opposite end of the table, half-hidden behind the urn.

Then, as he was engaged in accepting the tea, the butter, the bread and the cold meat that Rose and Violet were handing him as if under protest:

'Where have you been?' the Rev^d. Orlando inquired.

And well did he know the tone in which the question was put; it always seemed to him as if he could hear his Guardian saying as plain as though he actually had uttered the words: 'The boy has been doing wrong, but I have told him of his fault, and I must now show him that I did so from no prejudice against him on my part, and that I am quite ready to take an interest in what he does.' And however much before he might have felt disposed to open himself, yet at this question it appeared to him as if he had suddenly been rendered, not so much unwilling, as unable to speak, and all he could say in reply was: 'Oh, I don't know! Nowhere particular!' There was a moment's silence, and then the Rev^d. Orlando addressed himself to Mrs. Binney with an air Jaspar interpreted to mean: 'This young cub is not fit to be spoken to! Let us leave him alone!' Nor during the rest of the meal did any of them pay him the slightest attention.

But it was not only in the Midsummer holidays that he loved to roam over the hills: he was equally fond of doing so at Christmas. Sometimes the sun would shine coldly down out of a pale blue sky on to a landscape all covered with snow. The russet copses and even the haystacks would look by contrast nearly black, and the hedges, to leeward of which lay great white soft wreaths and swathes; and he would stop as he went along, not only the sole living thing, but the one sign of life in the vast dazzling hollow, and, in the absolute silence, listen for the distant breathing of the sea that, dim and misty, lay straight across the concave valley-end. But generally, while in the deans something of summer sounds and colour still lingered in the singing of the birds and the vivid red and orange of the roofs, all else was of a neutral tint, and under a sky of unchanging grey the bare rolling hills lay spread out whitey-brown, except where patches of furze made dark blotches against their sides. And, as he walked, his ear would be caught by the thumping of a flail in some lonely barn, and he would stop for a moment, and through the wide-open doors watch it, as now it descended with a thud, now was flourished above the wielder's head whose shirt stood out dimly white against the dark background; or he would see upon a distant hill-side what at first appeared to be a few tiny motionless black dots till, looking again, he perceived that they were moving, and were indeed a team of oxen at the plough; in the still keen air you just could hear the creaking that they made as they slowly advanced, while, as they reached the top, the driver's goad would show for an instant lance-like against the sky.

But what he liked best was to follow the cliffs, where always the wind blew with such force that he could nearly lean against it as he went, and where sometimes a more than usually furious gust would bring him for a moment quite to a stop. And going as close as he dared to the edge, he would straddle his legs and cram his hat down upon his head, and while everything that he had loose, his handkerchief or the tail of his coat, would flap as if about actually to be torn away, he would stand and look out to sea. Sometimes, blowing off shore, the gale would catch the monstrous tops of the waves as in long lines they came rushing on, and send the foam streaming behind on the air; like smoke, he thought, or the white floating plumes of a squadron in its charge: at others there would only be a wide expanse of troubled leaden-coloured waters over which he would gaze out towards the horizon, inexpressibly desolate, veiled in mist. The mere scene itself was already enough to make him forget his own personality, but his abstraction was rendered still deeper by the sounds that filled his ears: the melancholy music of the telegraph wires just behind, the plaintive cries of the gulls, the blowing of the wind and, above all else, the noise of the sea, whether it was the ceaseless roar of the incoming tide, or the long-drawn rattle of the shingle as, with a shaling noise, the undertow went back, to be followed the next moment by the thunderous crash of the breaking wave. So at last he would awake, and, from having been almost a part of these sights and sounds, would feel as if once more contracted into himself. And as he went back the sky would lour, and there would come creeping up from the Channel a mist that, thin at first and transparent, would gradually thicken till, having completely hid the dark sullen tops of the hills along which at first it had lain, in soft huge waves, slowly but without a moment's stop, down it would come rolling over their sides. And lonely as the uplands always seemed, there was at such times a something mysterious about them that struck him, not as in summer did Basdean Bottom merely with alarm, but rather with a sense of awe, as if from out those impenetrable mists, as of old from the clouds with which once the top of Sinai was veiled, God might presently be expected in lightnings and thunder to declare His will.

So was it always with a feeling of great relief that he got back and found himself protected once more by the presence of human beings and safe in a warm well-lighted room. Yet presently his attention would be drawn by the manner in which the wind was moaning round the house and rumbling down the chimney: on stormy nights, while, at one moment, tired out, it would drop so completely that he could distinctly hear the steady pattering of the rain on the tiled path outside, at the next it would hurl itself with a dull thud against the window-panes as though it would have beat them in, and often indeed would make him with a start look up from his book, half expecting to see their whole framework blown inwards, and the Devil, as no longer content with the Downs already by general consent given up to him at night, burst in, as the Flying Dutchman is represented doing in Marryat's story of the *Phantom Ship*. Perhaps too from some remote part of the house would come a dull and distant crash, as if the evil spirits by whom they were being beleaguered had at last effected an entrance. But what he most disliked was his Guardian's fancy never to allow a blind to be pulled down or a curtain drawn, and he was thus always in a state of alarm lest, were he to glance that way, he should see, pressed up against the panes, the white ghastly faces of the dead staring in at him with eyes like those the illustration gave to Nightgall as he gazed at Mary and Simon Reynard through the little window in the Bloody Tower. The warmth and light of the room must surely attract them from where, under their mounds of ragged grass, they lay in the churchyard just up the road all in the cold and dark and wet. Nor did his superstitious fears grow any the less when he went upstairs; and he would try to get to sleep as soon as he could, lest he might be left the only one awake of the household, and so more especially be exposed to visits from ghosts and devils whose power, once the lights were extinguished and every one fallen asleep, became, he conceived, as great indoors as out: just as, as the fire died down, the exterior cold came into the house. Yet often he would be woke with a start by the sense of there being some one in the room, when, reluctant to disturb his Guardian except in the last extremity, he would light his candles and sit up in bed and so for hours remain, not daring, however tired he grew, to turn on his right side or his left lest the Thing whose appearance he dreaded should be able to steal on him at unawares; and keeping his eyes fixed on the door and his ears on the stretch for the slightest sound. At such times he dared not even seek a defence against his fears by endeavouring to persuade himself that there were no such things as ghosts lest, by such scepticism, they might be provoked to give him some appalling proof of their existence; and could only try to quiet himself, now by repeating the Lord's Prayer or *Domine, in manus tuas*, now by recalling every story of a certain kind that he had heard and everything of the same sort that he had seen. So one o'clock would strike from the church-tower, and two, and three, and four, and five, and even six, until at last through the little window at the foot of his bed he would see the first faint saffron glow of dawn rising from behind the crest of the opposite hill, and with a sigh of relief would sink back upon his pillow and shut his eyes, and fall on the instant asleep.

# CHAPTER XV

And all this time at school he had been little by little venturing out of that fastness within himself in which at first he had taken refuge. He had begun, not indeed by ever volunteering a remark, but by answering such as others addressed to him with something more than the curt repellent 'Yes' or 'No' which had for a while been all in the way of a reply that any one had been able to obtain. But he had still for some time remained very cautious, and had always held himself ready on the slightest sign of danger once more, as it were, to retreat. And this had been specially the case when he had had to do with new fellows, his manner towards whom was always very constrained, for he knew that, were he to yield to the temptation of taking advantage of their ignorance of what his position really was, he would only be exposing himself to the mortification of seeing their behaviour towards him change so soon as they found out how matters stood. Yet sometimes, for all his care, he had met with what he considered a rebuff, when, too proud to make any attempt whether at defence or recrimination, he had confined himself to assuming towards the offender an air of

killing disdain, though all the time he would be nearly crying for vexa-
tion to think how powerless he was to revenge himself as he would
like; and for the hundredth time he would resolve to remain for the
future absolutely shut up within himself. As for the few who had
always been friendly, them he privately held very cheap; they could
not possibly be worth much if they could find no one better than
him; *he* would have chosen very differently had *he* been in *their* place;
and he would compare them in his mind with Els. He was still indeed
in bondage to the boy's face, and now and again the old pet name
of 'Raven,' pronounced in those tones that even in memory were so
strangely moving, would come sighing softly in his ears, and he would
have no little ado to prevent himself rushing off then and there, and,
in such an overmastering transport of emotion as must surely, he
would think, break down all barriers, insisting on being once more
friends.

It was only natural, however, that a leader should despise those
whom he led, and a leader after a certain fashion he was now become.
It certainly was not, he saw, to any success in work that this ascendency of his was due, for though his place in school was above the aver-
age, and might, according to the dons, have been still higher had he
done his best, he much preferred remaining where he was and being
held capable of more, to trying openly, and so acquiring perhaps a
name for hard work, but only too probably losing what he valued far
more, the reputation of being cleverer than others. And still less did
he owe his influence to skill in games. He had indeed played at nothing since he had left Rose Hill. When first he had come to Bridwell his
relations with Els had so engrossed his attention that he had never had
a moment left for other things, and then for a while his only thought
had been to keep as much as possible to himself, and now he was far
too anxious to avoid placing himself at a disadvantage with regard to
others to allow of his attempting anything he could not do as well at
least as they. He would much indeed have liked to have been able to
descend into the arena, and there have shown himself as all at once
immeasurably the superior of the rest; but, since this might not be,
he would hold altogether aloof. He even tried to persuade himself
such things were unworthy his regard; yet he never really ceased to
regret the inactivity to which, as he thought, he was condemned, and
when there was any talk of how well so and so could run, or play
cricket, or what not, would listen with an envy made none the less

by the necessity of refraining from the disparaging remarks his feelings would naturally have found vent in. It was rather to his powers of talk he owed such influence as he had: although of course it was not this that first had made his study a sort of general meeting-place for the set he lived with, but rather its convenience of access, and his own readiness to let it be used as a place to play cards in. He was, indeed, at first only too delighted to have at length a chance of seeing what this same gambling was, of which he had heard so much. But presently, not finding in it the pleasure he had thought for, and seeing beside that, while it wasted his money, it made him, the host, of no more account than anybody else, he persuaded the others it would be ever so much more amusing just to talk. Generally it was he who took the leading part in the conversation, but now and again he would retire into the background and confine himself merely to looking on. He liked to see the effect produced by these momentary withdrawals and to have his silence remarked; besides so he could better enjoy the feeling of pride with which his heart would swell as he reflected it was not he who went to others, but others who sought him. Nor was his complacency the least disturbed by the knowledge that they were drawn thither quite as much by the prospect of the biscuits and cocoa his hospitality dispensed as by any charm in him, for were not these, too, after a fashion a part of himself?

But in the summer-half he found his friends had many more amusing things to do than to listen to him, and in play-hours at any rate he was still almost as much alone as when after his final quarrel with Els he had become a pariah. And now, as then, his chief mode of beguiling the time was to take long walks by himself. Often, however, he would go no farther than a little copse which lay just outside the Park in the low ground at the farther end of the Pond. And on his way he would for a moment stop and look up at what was known as the Bridwell Oak. Those wide-spreading branches, now only kept by props from sinking altogether to the ground, had first, so the school-story ran, bent under a load of Roundheads taken prisoners close at hand by a troop of Prince Rupert's Cavaliers. But it was not so much of this he thought, its one appearance in the twilight at least of history, as of the many assignations and fights which, favourite rendezvous that it was for both, it must have seen. Presently, mounting a bank, he would step over some brown dead briars with which an attempt had been made to bar the way, and so plunge down into the underwood and out of sight. For a while the necessities of forcing his passage through the bushes took up all his attention, but by and by he reached the particular nook he always made for, and felt that at last he was alone, and free in security to give a loose to his imagination. Then, when later he would meet the others again at tea, he felt as if somehow between him and them there had a gulf been fixed by all the fatiguing emotions he had gone through, and the thoughts he had had in the wood. Now and again he would even wonder whether the various occupations in which *they* had passed *their* afternoon were not more *manly* than that in which his had been spent, nor could he get rid of these disturbing doubts until he thought of asking himself by what right that adjective was to be applied rather to what *they* than to what *he* had done. 'Twas a question he conceived it would be hard indeed to answer satisfactorily, but he was ready to abandon all the advantages it secured, having yet another to put to which he was convinced there could be no possible reply. Why should one wish to be *manly* rather than the reverse?

On Sunday mornings he had of course to go to Chapel with the rest, but, though thus constrained to be present in the body, it was always possible to be absent in mind, and he derived no little satisfaction from the thought that, in so doing, he was rendering the intentions of the authorities of no effect. Indeed he had long ago freed himself from those trammels of belief in which the others, dons and boys alike, seemed bound, and was, if anything, all the prouder of the achievement as it appeared the result rather of a superior natural instinct than of any laborious process of thought. At least it was not due to any desire to do as he liked without fear of being reproached by his conscience, for he had never been so yet, and, though well acquainted with the meaning of the word 'regret,' of that of 'repentance' he was still quite ignorant. So he would listen to the gabble of that General Confession he knew so well without ever for a moment wishing to join in it, though when, in a slow and solemn voice, the Warden, erect in his canopied stall and from that height dominating all the bowed heads and kneeling forms, began to pronounce the Absolution, he would bend lower and lower over the desk and listen as to some magician's abracadabra possessing magical powers of he knew not what effect. But for the most part the whole thing, prayers and lessons and anthems and psalms, the squalling of God's glories by godless boys as he called it from a line he had somewhere seen, seemed merely but another of the bores incident to school-life which, once he had left, he would no longer have to put up with, and he made a calculation that, even taking it as necessary to go to church once a week, he had attended enough services at Bridwell to free him for the next five years at the very least.

And then at last that hour came which in the whole week he liked the most – the interval between Roll at four and Evening Chapel at six; for then, there being nothing else particular to do, those who were in his set were quite willing to listen to him talk. He would take them off to the Bowling Green, and there, pacing slowly up and down, hold forth; he could never be persuaded to sit, declaring that he found it impossible to think when he was still, and that his body must be in motion if his mind were to be moved; but besides, he was very proud of this power of his to saunter; it was one he maintained that no one there but himself possessed. And as he always found he could best think his sensuous thoughts when with but little on, so now the sense of stiffness he used to fancy there was in his Sunday clothes, and of state in the gown he was so fond of picturesquely clutching with one hand and making swing out as he turned round, caused him somehow to feel as if his air and words should have a correspondent dignity. Besides, it seemed to him as if a certain amount of parade were necessary on the part of actors who had to perform upon a stage where everything combined to produce an effect at once of peace and state: the wide lawn so soft to the feet, to the eye so trim, the tall lime avenues that on three sides shut you in, the massive block of the House on its terrace of sloping grass, and the view of the Park as it descended gradually to where in the hollow lay the Pond. Then presently as the afternoon wore on, and the sun, declining towards the rising ground on the farther side of the water, now began to shoot its long level rays between the trunks of the trees and bar the velvet turf with broad stripes of shade and mellow light and flush with a ruddy glow the old red-brick walls of the House, from the Clock Tower far away out of sight the bells would sound. So soft were their notes at first they could scarce be heard, but soon they made the whole air seem full of their chimes, and here and there over by the Market-Place figures in white would be seen flitting to and fro. By and by some obsequious friend would be sure to bring him out his surplice; he was always fond of wearing that voluminous and rustling garment, but never more so than when, as at such times, he could endue it as though indeed it had been some robe of office proper to him alone, and when besides he could imagine his soul was acquiring something of the spotlessness of its pure white folds and was by so much the more in accord with those longings for perfect love and content and rest with which he was always filled by the solemn calm of the evening hour, long shadows over grass, motionless trees, the sound of bells, and a setting sun.

Chief among the subjects he discoursed upon was Love. He liked to think he talked of it very much after the same fashion as might have done one of the guests at Plato's Banquet – though indeed this was a piece of which, except by hearsay, he knew nothing. And he would listen to himself almost, except that it was with far greater pleasure and attention, as if it had been some one else speaking, and would flatter himself he was the founder of a new school of philosophy, that his companions were his disciples, and the garden where he walked a second Grove of Academe. And while to have talked of Love at all would have been a source of no small enjoyment, the subject being one that pleased him in his most passionate and fantastic part – how much did not that one word mean? – to do so in this laughing way, to mock at the very notion and to turn it into such ridicule as he had at his command, gave him the same sort of pleasure as he had formerly derived from speaking ill of Els while still he knew that in reality he was as fond of him as ever. In truth it almost seemed as if the passion he thus attacked was as much a living thing to him as in his day had been the boy, and as if he thought that, with better luck than in that case had ever been his, he could, by thus abusing it, make it feel something of the suffering it had inflicted on him. Moreover by thus laughing himself he forestalled any possibility there might be of others laughing at him, and put on, as it were, a panoply of sarcasm that ought, he conceived, not only to defend him from all attacks from outside, but to save him too from himself by making it impossible for him for very shame ever again to indulge in a sentiment for which he had expressed such contempt. He was always careful not to mention names, but everybody knew, he felt, to whom and to what he referred when he confessed that he had been very silly, and could not now conceive how ever he could have made such a fool of himself. To have been popular with all would doubtless, in part at any rate, have made up for his failure to obtain the affections of any single one, since, while satisfying in some sort his need of love, it would have pleased his vanity; but here too he met with ill success. Not that, as he told himself, he was so foolishly modest as to affect to be ignorant that he enjoyed a certain influence in the school, and that there were any number of fellows who professed to like nothing better than to be with him; only among them all there was not one, he thought, on whom he could count as a friend. And while this failure of his to achieve popularity filled him with as much surprise as did the abortiveness of his efforts to win love, it caused him to be for ever anxiously watching for any signs of that general conspiracy against him, which he was always expecting to break out, by reminding him on how very slender a foundation the structure of his influence was raised. Yet even so he was still incapable of devising any means to preserve the edifice itself intact, and seemed to think that if, in the event of the whole thing coming down with a run about his ears, he still could keep his pride unwounded, he ought to expect no more. And, with this end in view, he would make believe he did not the least care for any of the advantages his position brought him, but that he was all-sufficient to himself, and liked nothing so much as to be alone.

His other favourite subject of discourse was Authority: to which, both in its symbols and its exercise, he bore a huge dislike; and had done so ever since the time when he had seen it, leaving the rest at liberty to make his life as wretched as they pleased, in a hundred different ways interfere with his enjoyment of such slender means as remained to him of lightening his troubles. And the feeling was now confirmed when, arrived at a position in the school such as entitled him, he considered, to aspire to any dignities it could afford, he saw them always bestowed on others and himself left out in the cold. Nor could he understand in the least why this should be. Of course had the dons but known him as he knew himself, such conduct on their part would have been intelligible; but, as it was, he feared he could not choose but see in it still another result of that hostile fate which prevented his ever keeping or even winning a friend, and made his efforts at popularity of no effect. There were, it was true, a dozen good reasons why he should not mind being thus neglected: had he not assured himself a hundred times he was above being moved by anything that either dons or boys could think or say or do? Besides, he ought, he felt, to be ashamed to put himself out about these petty school-distinctions; in the world, the real great world, it would be very different. *There* his talents would speedily obtain that recognition which was at once their due, and necessary to their proper display; and last of all he told himself that, like the old Roman with his statue, he had far rather it should be a matter of surprise he was not a Prefect than that he was. But yet he was still far from being consoled, and Moreover could not help thinking as he talked that all the time his hearers were reflecting within themselves it was a case of sour grapes.

At first indeed he had been cautious as to what he said about the dons lest his remarks, coming to their ears, should hinder his obtaining what they alone could give him; or lest he should one day be in a position that might render it possible for those who had heard him talk to come and taunt him with not carrying into practice the theories he had advanced in less responsible times. For still at every fresh disappointment he made sure that on the next occasion at any rate his turn would come. Yet he had already begun to fear he would never please those in authority over him, when one day at the commencement of a half as they were come together in the Big Schoolroom to see the new Prefects made, he heard Elsie's name called out, and the boy left his place and went up to the daïs, where the Warden, standing over him, pronounced the sacramental words: '*Præficio te alumnis Petriensibus!*' and so put on his head the white-tasselled cap that was the badge of his new place. Several fellows turned round to see how he was taking this promotion over his head of his former friend, and, knowing this, he did his best to assume a look of the most perfect indifference: his pride forbade him to let any one perceive what he was feeling. Yet indeed he was deeply moved. In the case of every previous appointment he had been able to derive some little consolation from the thought that the chosen boy was older or higher in the school or had been longer there than himself; but now one who came after him was preferred before him; and even if he had been selected to fill the very next vacancy that occurred it would still, he felt, have been impossible to have stomached being junior to one to whom indeed he was ready to allow the possession of every charm and grace, but who after all was younger than he, and below him in school; nor had by any means a character so good – though no doubt it had improved of late – as to outweigh these disadvantages.

# CHAPTER XVI

So from that very moment he gave up all notion of any further attempt to stand well with the dons. He would have been glad enough to have done so, he thought, had not the gross injustice with which they had chosen to behave rendered it absolutely impossible. For the future it should be a case of war between them to the knife. No doubt circumstances would prevent its being an open one; and yet he was not altogether sure but that the pleasure of knowing how little they were aware of his state of mind did not more than compensate for that he would have felt, had they realised how ridiculous he was making them and all their doings in the eyes of the rest of the school. It was also true his power must continue to lack that outward show the sanction of authority alone could give; but then it was entirely the work of his own hands, and so a source of far greater pride than could possibly have been any dignity he had owed to others: and besides, its only bounds were such as were imposed by his ability to get it recognised and obeyed. Moreover, he was at last relieved from that obligation to keep the door of his lips, his constant infractions of which had made him so discontented with himself as showing him how incapable he was of doing even so simple a thing as hold his tongue: and the liberty of railing, in which he was now able to indulge unchecked, not only afforded him that pleasure he always found in the fact of his speech belying his thoughts: – since, even as he spoke, he knew there was nothing he desired more than that he so violently decried – but enabled him besides to feel, as he glanced up at the windows of the Butcher's Study, the same sort of delicious thrill as must, he fancied, have had a knight of old when he stood in front of the dragon's cave and dared the beast to come out and fight: for behind those panes resided the supreme authority of the school. And still he wondered within himself, as years ago he had done at Scarisbrick, what it was that kept each one in his place. Might it not be possible to break the spell, and in one instant dissolve the whole fabric of their society simply by getting everybody to refuse to do as they were told? In the meantime he seized every opportunity not only to disobey rules himself, but to encourage others to do the like. And while he looked on his successes in this way

– so long as nothing was discovered – as so many victories, he found he was always able to turn them to good account for the purpose of raising still another laugh against his enemies, the dons, and the profound ignorance in which they lived of what really went on in the school. Why he could have told them things – and about himself too – that would have made them stare again!

Nor was it only at his rulers that he loved to scoff: he was equally contemptuous of the various customs that obtained in the place. What, for instance, could be more ridiculous than for such a mushroom place to fig itself out in all the mediæval trumpery of Latin graces, surplices, prefects, and gowns? And surely the very height of absurdity was reached when it came to their having a Gaudy Day! Let Eton, if she liked, have her Fourth of June: but for them to indulge in anything of the kind was only to provoke comparisons where they could least be stood. No doubt there was a pretence that the celebration was in honour of St. Peter, on whose festival it was always held, but it was obvious it was equally designed as an advertisement. Just so he had heard in London, on the Queen's Birthday, artful tradespeople set out transparencies with 'God bless the Queen!' at top, and underneath, 'Try our phenomenal sugar and our noble tea!' While even supposing this were not the case, then, in his view, matters were only by so much the worse, since none but the veriest fool could surely in the present day invoke a saint and hold a feast in his honour. Even the buildings themselves did not escape the ridicule with which everything was now assailed. He would have given much to have been able to throw Bridwell society into confusion; but would have been still more pleased if, at the same time, he could have laid its habitation in the dust. It was lack of power, he thought, not will, which was all that in both cases stood between him and the accomplishment of his desires. Yet he could find nothing more forcible to say than that it was a pity such a fine old country-house should be inhabited by a pack of boys, and that its lovely gardens should be spoilt by the sham Gothic galleries, jerry-built chapels, tin passages, and all the other nondescript erections that had been put up. And now and again he would wonder how it came about that, while his indignation was so hot within him, the only words he could find to give it expression were so poor and cold.

But though there was thus nothing all reverence for which he not only repudiated for himself, but tried to destroy in others, he would still maintain that, could he only have found something worthy such patriotism, such religion, or such love as his, no one would have been readier than he to sacrifice himself. And by these means, not only did he set himself on a pinnacle as one for the satisfaction of whose finer nature more was required than was enough for the common herd, but he himself for the moment could not possibly have told whether or no he really meant what he said, so eloquent was his tongue, so moving the peculiar tone he at such times affected, for the appearance of which he would wait as though for something independent of his will. Yet, even as he spoke, he was dimly aware that, when he thus expatiated on the devotion a follower owed his chief, it was always in the position of the latter that he put himself. Then all at once, fancying he observed in his hearers a disposition to laugh, he would endeavour to recover the ascendency he thought he had for a moment lost, either by becoming more paradoxical and more severe than ever, or by stopping short, and changing his tone and making fun of what he had just been asserting was the dearest wish of his heart. And as he appeared never to care for what he had, so likewise did he always disagree with what he heard; and did anybody ever seem disposed to be of his opinion, on the instant he would veer round, and with might and main defend the very view which but a moment before he had been attacking. Thus a Nihilist among Tories, among Radicals a stickler for the divine right of kings, a believer among those who doubted, a sceptic among such as believed, he seemed to be without any opinions that could properly be called his own; indeed he was often accused of inconsistency and asked what he really meant. But he was always ready with his reply. Never, he said, did he do anything so commonplace, so dull as 'mean'! How was any one to talk at all if one might only say what one really 'meant'? He for his part altogether failed to understand why such importance was attached to what one said; at any rate he was not going to wear his heart upon his sleeve, and was quite resolved that none should ever know – and here he assumed his moving tones – what he really thought. Thus, under pretence that his opinions were too sacred to be divulged, did he try to hide no less from himself than from others that he had none at all, while still, if anybody took him at his word, he was always vastly put out.

Even in his worst troubles he had never been able altogether to give up those various little affectations that had had for their object to make him remarked; and now that he was in a position where he could hope they would have an even better effect, it was only to be expected, both that their number should increase, and that his views as to the purpose he desired them to serve should be enlarged. For now his object became to persuade his companions that there was something about him of the divinity which hedges a king; and he made it his study never, even in the smallest things, to be seen to try for anything he was not sure to get. Others might hurry if they would, but he must seem always calm; if he must be late, he must, but at least no one should ever say that he had run, and then at last, quite out of breath, had the door slammed-to in his face. It was too in his opinion only right he should now be always well-dressed, and he devoted much time to considering the question what to wear. Not that of course he ever let it be perceived what pains he was at in the matter; on the contrary he would declare he had far too much to do to be able to give the subject more than a passing thought; while did any one by chance inquire how much some certain thing had cost, with what he considered the magnificent carelessness of a grand seigneur of old, he would reply he had never asked. When he wanted a thing, he said, it was necessary that it should be his, and he never allowed any sordid question of price to stand in his way. Indeed his love of posing was so great that even in the most ordinary conversation, quite neglecting to consider what he really thought, his one desire was to say something which should produce a great effect. And often, the better to attain this end, he would affect to be absorbed in his own reflections so that when at last he spoke it might appear as if he in a moment could definitely pronounce on subjects as to which, after all their long discussions, others were still disagreed; and, in a brief decided tone, he would give utterance to some oracular remark designed, if not to settle the question at issue once and for all, then, at least, to show it in some new and hitherto unsuspected light. Nor was it only his views that he thus strove to impose upon his companions: he desired too to oblige them to follow his moods: at one moment full of that joyous confidence in himself which he had of late regained, and with his heart swelling at the consciousness of his power, he would endeavour to inspire them with those spirits which were so exuberant that it was all he could do to keep from shouting aloud for very joy; and at the next, assuming an air of melancholy and abstraction, he would presently make them as dull as he seemed himself.

But still he was very far from being content with his position. True, it was one in the gaining of which he had been helped neither by the possession of such athletic powers as those of his old enemy Orr, nor by having lots of money and being good-looking like Els. And yet, while thus depreciating the popularity of others as being the result rather of natural causes than, as with him, of merit, he seemed to look upon these wits of his, to which alone it was that he owed his success, as not so much any necessary part of himself as something that belonged to him in no more intimate sense than the furniture of his study or his clothes or books. But, this apart, what had he to be proud of? He was one of those, no doubt, who ruled the school; of one section, indeed, and that by no means the least important, he could boast himself the undisputed leader; yet, even allowing for the fact that he was without the official recognition which in their time they had enjoyed, he could not believe that he, or indeed any of his fellow-rulers, occupied relatively to the rest the same position their predecessors had held towards him when *he* had been a smug. And this consideration reminded him of Orr who even now seemed still in his way; for when he himself could not choose but think that his having risen was due less to any deserts of his own than to the fact that his enemy had left, it was only natural to suppose that a like reflection had occurred to others too, and that every time they saw him swaggering about they thought how very different would have been his behaviour had Orr still been there. And if he was thus unable to look on his position even in the School as great, what must he think of it in respect of the outer world? Why, long before he had reached his age, Ivan the Terrible had cut off his boyards' heads and seized in his grasp the reins of power. Thus was it that through the very great-ness of his ambitions he ceased to have any at all, and that his dreams of what might, in other circumstances, have been his, put him quite out of conceit with what he had.

But there were other reasons for his not taking that part in the government of the School which he might well have done. In the first place, he was fearful of putting his power to the touch, lest, after all, he might find it not nearly so great as he had thought; and in the next, while keeping in the background saved him from the pangs of that shyness he never failed to suffer from whenever he had to stand out alone and do anything before others, it at the same time accentu-ated, he fancied, the contrast already in his eyes so pleasant, between the unimportance of his ostensible position and the greatness of that influence, which, when he so chose, he could exert. Nor was this the only way in which he strove to avoid all danger of a shock to his self-esteem. He was scrupulously exact in his obedience to rules. To have been punished, even by a don, must, he felt, have lessened that respect with which, as something apart and separate, it was his aim to be regarded by others; while to have had a Prefect give him lines would have been an indignity the mere thought of which was more than he could bear. It was however only when there seemed to be a chance of his being found out that he was thus careful as to what he did or left undone; where there was no such risk he made his own good pleasure his sole rule of conduct. And he even contrived to turn his disobedience into a means of still further exalting himself in others' eyes by declaring that, while in matters of indifference he had no objection to conforming to rules, he would never allow them to stand in the way of his gratifying a desire. Yet while such was the view he affected to take of by far the greater number of such breaches of discipline as he committed, there were some he was at great pains to conceal; not because he considered them to be *mala in se* – nothing that he chose to do could ever in his eyes be wrong, his honour and good taste being, in his opinion, quite enough to guard him from all disgrace – but because to have been known to have committed them would have argued, he thought, a share in weaknesses from which, properly to play his part, he ought to seem free.

As to the Prefects, towards them he maintained an attitude of what he took for the most graceful dignity as of one who recognised the higher rank that was theirs by law, but at the same time knew, and knew it was a fact acknowledged by all, that the intellectual superiority was his. Just so, he conceived, might a great commoner have yielded the *pas* to some obscure marquis or duke. Indeed his manner to them grew more deferential every day, as every day he became more and more convinced that it was only opportunity he lacked to show himself as much greater in deed, as clearly he was already in thought, not only than those whose prowess in games it was that had been chiefly instrumental in putting them where they were, but than those who owed their position to their place in school. And at every turn he found additional proof of their inferiority to himself in the smallness of their powers of talk as compared with his – and he had come to think that who could not talk could do nothing – in the way they accepted and respected the institutions of the place, and lastly, in the

simplicity with which they let themselves be taken in by all his affectations of respect. And he began to long for the day to come when at
last he should go out into the world – the real great world which was
so different from that wherein till then he had been cribbed and confined. At least it would give him scope for that desire for action with
which he was consuming. And from time to time he would almost
think he could catch vague echoes of the great battle that it seemed
to him was for ever rolling and surging round him upon every side,
though the impalpable walls that shut in Bridwell not only prevented
him from then and there sallying forth to take his part in the fray, but
even from having anything but the vaguest notion of what sort of
fight it was that was going on. Now and again, indeed, his impatience
to be up and doing would become so great that he would long to leave
words if only for such things as school could give, and would imagine
himself the general of another army of giants, leading a desperate
assault, of what kind he did not know, against the vague Olympus
the dons appeared to him to dwell upon. And yet so far was he from
making any effort to satisfy, in however small a degree, these desires,
that, on the contrary, he did what he could to get his life arranged in
such a manner as to diminish still more the already small amount of
thought he bestowed upon its circumstances. He had perceived that
in proportion as he was the more rarely called on to exercise his will,
so did he become more free to indulge in what were now the two
great pleasures of his life, sensation and thought; and with this end in
view, while he tried throughout all changes to keep the same cubicle,
the same study, and even the same places in Chapel and Hall, for such
consideration of matters of daily life as he found it absolutely impossible to avoid he would set apart a certain portion of every day, so that
at any rate during the rest of it he might remain undisturbed, and
taking one after another in order, he would at the end draw up a sort
of mental table, his *état d'affaires* as he called it, wherein he elaborately
set out how No. 1 was in this state, No. 2 in that. It was true, no doubt,
that such a mode of life rather increased than relieved that necessity
to creep under which he laboured, but with his eyes now fixed on
the outside world into which he was presently to go out, he made
but little account of what his position might be in that of school; and
then besides, there surely ought to be ample compensation for any
restraints that hampered his person in the absolute freedom to soar
that his thoughts enjoyed.

For some time past he had had a great desire to be friends once more with Els: they never of course could be so again in the old way – they were both of them too old for that – but he would have been very glad to have been able to think they were again at one. Moreover a reconciliation would mean that he would be admitted into the Set with whom his relations had hitherto been a little difficult owing to the fact that so long as he was there the subject of Els had to be tabooed. And though he could hardly hope ever to reign over them after the same fashion he did over his own followers, yet, after Els, he would, he made no doubt, become the principal personage, and thus the most important of the school, since he would be equally a leader among such as were clever and worked, and such as were handsome and idle and well-dressed and rich and good at games: a position it was only proper should be his since in his own person he united the best qualities of the two classes. He was therefore proportionably pleased when one day he learned through a common friend that Els too was anxious that their longstanding quarrel should be at last made up and proposed himself to take the first steps towards a reconciliation by coming to pay him a visit in his study. So on the following Sunday, as he sat talking to two or three of his more particular friends, there was a knock at the door, and with a 'May I come in?' in the voice which he knew so well but which, often as he had heard it, had not for long been addressed to him, his former friend appeared. He for his part got up, and, thinking to himself the while that their meeting was quite an historic event – the reconciliation indeed of two potentates, each in his own way of equal might, who had long been at enmity together – held out his hand with an air of theatric grace: he wished it to be understood that it was the other who had been in the wrong but that he was too generous to stand upon his dignity. So Els, perching with easy grace upon the edge of the table, sat and talked, while he, remaining in the background merely looking on, did his best the while to turn to good account this opportunity of considering his former friend close at hand. He was still as handsome as ever and his figure as graceful, but there was something about him that irritated while it pleased. Nor was he without a certain feeling of jealousy as he saw how much he was charming the three others he was talking to. Then presently as the bell began to ring Els, whose turn it was that afternoon to read Roll, linked his arm affectionately in his and so, talking gaily all the while, walked off with him into School.

And as they went along everybody on their path gave way, interchanging with Els as they did so, a smile or word: he was glad it should thus be published to every one that they were reconciled, and all the more so because, from the fact of its being Els who had taken his arm and not he Elsie's, he hoped they would draw the conclusion that it was Els who had made overtures and not he.

But their friendship thus renewed was of short continuance, for three weeks afterwards the school broke up for the holidays and the last half they were either of them to spend at Bridwell came to an end. Els however made him promise to pay him a visit at Tremlett before he went abroad to learn German as it had been settled he was to do some time that autumn.

## CHAPTER XVII

Jaspar had expected to leave for Germany at once and was much disappointed to find he was not to start for another three or four months; and the regret with which he learnt this news was much increased by the consciousness that there was not one of the Rectory family but was as sorry as himself that he would have to stay with them so long. And, as before, he spent every moment he could upon the Downs. Indeed he was even more anxious than of old to avoid driving out with the girls since, to all the reasons he had formerly had for so doing, now was joined a dislike of being seen in such a conveyance as the old pony-carriage. Its leather was dull, and cracked in lines and circles; here and there from the faded cloth of the cushions the horse-hair was gaping out; the original colour of the paint had long disappeared, and the very framework itself was only held together by a number of rough pieces of iron that had been nailed on from time to time by the odd man; while as for the perch behind on which he had to sit, it was only kept from altogether parting company with the body of the carriage by a network of rope. And the animal that drew this shandrydan was worthy of his place between the shafts; it was the same old white pony that had been there ever since he could recollect and now, in the extreme of age, flog as they would with the lashless whip, or even prod, standing up, with their parasols, neither Rose nor Violet could ever get it, even for a moment, to move out of the jog-trot at which, its head between its knees and half asleep, it lolloped along. Not that by any means there was nothing but this at the Rectory which he was ashamed of: only with regard to the rest he had no choice but to put up with it as well as he could; and indeed so used was he to doing so, he would have been content could he have felt that those who knew him, knew how great was his scorn and dislike for all persons and things in any way connected with what, for want of a better, he was obliged to call his home. But he had no desire to have the fact of his being a member of such a family more widely advertised than he could help, and was afraid lest, were he to drive out, strangers who met them might suppose that he belonged to that shabby old turn-out and those common-looking ill-dressed girls. He wished to goodness he had no people at all, and stood alone, responsible for nobody and nothing but himself and what was his.

And while to go out with them was thus a thing he always did his best to avoid, if he stopped indoors he was obliged to listen to what Mrs. Binney had to say as to her dislike of seeing people 'hanging about.'

'I'm sure,' she would cry, 'you never see James idling! Why can't you go and do something too?'

As if he would not have been only too glad could he have found anything worth being done! But he was not going to put himself about for the mere sake of 'doing something' in the sense in which she used that phrase; and once or twice he ventured to hint as much.

'I don't know, I'm sure,' she retorted, 'what you mean! If you think we're not good enough for you, you ought to get your swell friends, the Southwoods, to ask you to go and stay with them! But if I were you, I should wait to see if I could get the bread and jam I wanted before I quarrelled with the bread and butter I had!'

So, as he wandered over the hills, he was for ever complaining to himself with an: 'I think Els ought to ask me as he said he would! And though I don't particularly want to go to Tremlett, I do want to get away from here!'

Often at such times there would come over him a feeling of furious impatience at the fate by which he was being kept in such a beastly hole. If he could but have got out into the world and so at last begun really to live! And he would compare himself to the yellow-beaked white-plumaged gull that, with one wing clipped, fluttered and hopped about the garden, uttering from time to time, with wide-open beak and head thrown back, the melancholy note he so often heard along the cliffs. His fancy thought it was lamenting the days when, instead of having to hobble pitifully about a wretched little piece of ground, shut in on every side by hedge or wall, it had the boundless sea and the whole extent of the Downs over which to sweep at will.

At other times he would liken himself to the tiger in the circus at Newhaven that he had gone to see last holidays. With what restlessness it had paced up and down behind the bars of its short narrow cage! With what a savage growl at every turn in impotent fury it had reared its huge supple-limbed bulk up against the corner of its pen and so resumed its tireless walk with as little interruption in its movement as there was in that of the waves as they sank back into the sea after heaving swiftly along the smooth brickwork curve of the Black Rock groyne. But as for him he had not even the bars of a cage that might have served as something tangible whereon to wreak his spite, but must be content with trying what bodily fatigue would do to cure the restlessness he suffered from. Yet fast as he walked – and he seemed to storm up the hills – he could never succeed in getting over the ground at anything like the pace he wished; while, though he would often do as much as fifteen or twenty miles at a stretch, he never thought he had been far enough, but always came back with the resolve to go twice the distance on the following day. He would choose some distant point as his goal, and, hardly looking again away, even to see where he was setting his feet, would make for it straight, over grass and plough, through gorse, through briar, up hill and down dale; there was a certain pleasure in this kind of triumph of his will that thus carried him on to his journey's end regardless of what lay between. He liked to imagine that the far-off hill for which his face was set was in truth the ambition of his life and that he was pressing towards it with the absolute indifference for anything he might trample down or push aside, which he had already made up his mind he would feel. He would have been glad now and then by way of a change to have gone to some place or other farther off than any he could reach afoot; but here his want of money was in the way. And he resolved that happen what might in after-life this want at least should not be one from which he would suffer. Not that he doubted for a moment he would be successful in other respects, feeling sure that with men and women he would get on much better than he had done with boys. For he readily acknowledged to himself that his life at school was hardly to be called a success; and had often declared that in all the years which had elapsed between his first going to Scarisbrick and his leaving Bridwell the only things he had learnt were a few dog-gerel rhymes out of that old green-covered Latin Grammar and the habit of having a bath every morning.

But what now made his life so hard to be borne was the fact of its being just such as he would have wished to live with that ideal friend whom still, in spite of every disappointment, he was always hoping to meet. The lovely summer-days that were now so long would then have passed all too quickly. How jolly it would have been to take him his favourite walks and bathe with him from the little beach! And the way in which he always walked so fast that his shins would ache again, was due in no small measure to the fancy that behind that haystack or that barn or on the other side of that hill he would find at last what for so long he had been vainly seeking. And many and many a time, catching sight of some small solitary figure in the distance, would he hurry towards it, forgetting all his imaginings in the hope that now at length reality was about to take their place. But it was only some old shepherd whose soil-encrusted clothes and wrinkled weather-beaten face, so far from giving him assurance that here was one would serve his turn, made him rather conceive that such a creature must surely be of different flesh and blood from himself. So, slackening speed, he would pass by without a word, smiling to himself at the way he had been taken in and at the thought how little the man knew his mind.

And then one afternoon towards the end of May he received a note from Lady Adelaide, but had only time to make out that it contained an invitation to come and stay at Tremlett, when Mrs. Binney, her curiosity excited by so unusual an event as his receiving a letter, could restrain her impatience no longer and inquired what it was. Without a word he handed it over and, turning away, began to look at one of the books on the table; he hoped thus to make her understand how greatly he disliked this inquisitiveness as to his most private affairs.

'That *will* be nice for you!' she said and gave him the letter back. 'You had better write and say you'll come on Thursday. The cart must go over to Rottingdean that morning, and it could take your things at the same time.'

But he, irritated at finding it thus assumed he would accept, replied he did not think he should go.

'Not go!' she cried in astonishment, 'and why not, I should like to know?'

But here, in the passage outside, the maid began to ring the bell for high-tea.

'We shall see,' she cried, 'what your Guardian will say!' and so went out.

They had not been long at table when Rose turned to him:

'You seem very silent, Jaspar!' she said; 'is anything the matter?'

'How can you ask him such a question?' interposed Violet. 'You know he never thinks we're worth talking to!'

'My dear,' said her mother from behind the dull worn plated urn where she was pouring out the tea, 'how can you be so absurd? The idea! By the by, papa,' she added, looking down the table to where at the other end the Rev^d. Orlando stood and carved the great brown flap of tough beefsteak that filled the dish before him, 'by the by, I haven't told you yet that Jaspar's received a most delightful invitation from Lady Adelaide Southwood to go and stay with her at Tremlett. She writes a charming letter – places no limit to the visit – altogether most kind!'

'Well, I'm sure,' commented Violet, 'you ought to be very grateful, I should think! Such nice people too, to know? I wish you could have managed to have introduced us!'

'Yes,' cried her mother, 'and then she would have asked you two girls instead. Living all alone like that in a big house she must want a companion dreadfully. And I've no doubt one of you wouldn't have minded going for a month or so if papa and I could have made up our minds to spare you.'

'And I could have painted her picture!' added Rose.

'Besides,' put in Mr. Binney, 'who can tell? One of them might have had the luck to pick up a husband!'

'Luck indeed!' ejaculated his wife; 'I think the luck would have been on the other side! Our girls are much too happy to——'

'Would you give me my tea, please?' struck in James.

Mrs. Binney handed him his cup and then went on: 'But what I was going to tell you was that he says he won't go.'

'Eh? what?' cried Mr. Binney in loud surprise. 'Won't go?' and then turning, 'don't attempt to talk that sort of nonsense to me!'

'There! what did I tell you?' Mrs. Binney observed.

'I didn't say I wouldn't go!' he answered, 'I said I didn't *want* to go!'

'And why not, sir, pray?' Mr. Binney asked. 'Here's a lady in the high position of Lady Adelaide Southwood paying you the honour and compliment of inviting you to her house, and all you say is you don't *want* to go! And why don't you *want* to go, if you please?'

'I don't know!' he said, 'I don't want to!'

'What do you mean, sir?' roared Mr. Binney, 'by speaking to me like that?'

Jaspar cast a side glance along the table; his Guardian's great hairy hands were quivering and their swollen veins stood out.

'As long as you're under my roof, you will have the goodness to understand that I'm the master, and, by God, I insist,' and here he brought his fist down on the table with a bang that made the cups and saucers rattle, 'I insist on your treating me as such with proper respect! You've a nasty sulky way about you I don't like at all! I daresay you think you're too old to be flogged, but I advise you not to make too sure, or you'll find you're mistaken!'

'I don't see——' began Jaspar, but still without looking up.

'Don't talk to me, sir!' thundered Mr. Binney again, 'I won't have it! Do you hear? I won't have it! God bless my soul! As long as you are here I insist upon your obeying any orders I choose to give!'

'Oh, I daresay,' Mrs. Binney put in, 'he didn't mean what he said after all!'

'My dear,' said her husband, 'I wasn't speaking to you!'

There was a moment's silence, then Jaspar began again: 'But——'

'Don't attempt to argue!' roared Mr. Binney. 'My orders are absolute! You will write and tell her ladyship that you will be delighted to accept her kind invitation!'

Jaspar said not another word, and even the others during the remainder of the meal only conversed in the lowest of tones.

The following morning after breakfast he abruptly addressed Mrs. Binney with:

'Will you let me have some money, please?'

'Money?' she repeated in surprise. 'Why, what ever do you want money for, I should like to know?'

'I'm going in to Brighton,' he explained, 'to order some clothes. If I am to go to Tremlett, you'll have to give me some clothes to go in.'

'I don't know what you mean, I'm sure,' she said; 'you've got that brown suit, haven't you, you had last term?'

'It isn't fit to be seen now,' he answered. And then added: 'Besides, I want a hat and a whole lot of other things!'

'A new hat!' she cried; 'why, you had one only the last time you went back to school!'

'Well, it's worn out now anyhow!' he said.

'Really, Jaspar,' she observed, 'I can't imagine what on earth you do with your new things! Now there's James———'

'I'm not going to go about like him!' he cried, 'with a hat green with age, and boots that look like knobbly plum-tarts!'

'Well, I'm sure,' she retorted, 'he always seems to me to look very nice! And anyhow, he managed to go all through school taking scholarships and prizes and not costing his parents a penny for all his green hat and knobbly boots. Handsome is that handsome does, Jaspar!'

But this was only the beginning of a series of battles between them over the various articles of his outfit, the campaign lasting the whole week that elapsed before he started. It was only brought to an end the very day before he went by his securing a desk for ten and sixpence, while she was eager he should take one which, after much bargaining, she had persuaded the shopman to let her have for eight.

'You've got the ideas of a prince!' she said, as they went out.

The next day he left, and as he walked over to Rottingdean across the hills on his way to meet the omnibus, he found himself, much to his surprise, regretting the departure which only twenty-four hours ago he had been looking forward to as a happy release.

## CHAPTER XVIII

He had, of course, long vaguely known that Els was immensely rich, but not until he actually arrived at Tremlett Chase had he understood what a vast difference this fact implied in their respective modes of life. As the dog-cart that had been sent for him drove up to the entrance, from one of the heavy-looking stone lodges which stood at the opposite ends of a great semi-circular grille, an old woman came out, and, evidently with no small effort, pulled back first one and then the other of the tall gates of hammered iron, the delicate arabesques of which were ensigned by a gilded coronet. And as he looked up and saw this emblem of dignity shining bright against the deep blue sky, he thought it somehow gave ironwork, and stonework, grass and trees, an air different from that they would have worn had they belonged to an owner of less high rank. So, to the deadened sound of the wheels as now they rolled smoothly over gravel, he went on up a broad avenue of stately elms. He fancied he had left his past on the other side of those splendid entrance-gates; all he could see was his; and at length, in the inheritance of everything the wealth and power of a score of generations had accumulated for his enjoyment, he was about to lead a life which would be free of all that scuffling and promiscuity he so disliked. And the Chase itself, from the glimpses he caught of it under the boughs of the double row of trees on either hand, seemed just such a place as he loved to wander in, having in its delightful little knolls and dells all scattered up and down with hawthorn and oak and standing deep in bracken, that air of being a whole country in miniature, which had made him so fond of Scarisbrick in the days of his band.

Presently the house itself came into sight, and as they approached and he perceived how great was its extent of front, large as had been his notions of the sort of building he would get to at last, he saw that they had fallen short of the reality; it was rather a royal palace than the country-place of a subject, however rich and noble. Once, however, indoors, the bustle of arrival prevented anything more than a general impression that the interior fully kept the promise of the outside, and it was not till a few minutes before dinner that, finding himself alone in the Silver Drawing-Room, he again had time not only to see, but, as he saw, to think. He was greatly struck as well by its stately proportions as the fashion of the decorations and furniture. The lofty walls were covered with some stuff which, on a silver ground, displayed in velvet on velvet baskets of red and green conventional flowers; from the coved ceiling depended motionless at the end of a long red silk tasselled cord a great crystal and silver chandelier, and over the dark lustrous mahogany doors chubby amorini, leaning towards each other and stretching out their hands, held up a coronet like that over the Park-gates; under a white marble mantelpiece so high his head scarce came up to the level of the opening, was a bank of hot-house flowers among which gleamed two tall elaborate silver fire-dogs; and here and there in the darkening room the light shone upon the polished floor which was unencumbered by any furniture, what little there was, set away against the walls, for the most part consisting of large heavy gilded sofas and chairs: many of them, having the coronet and cypher carved into their substance, really seemed as much constructed especially for the family as the house itself. Every-

thing seemed to have an air at once of pride and expectancy, as if waiting for the entrance of a sovereign who, with all the ceremonial of a
court, would presently come in, attended by White Staves and Gold
Sticks, Pages of the Presence and Gentlemen of the Great Chamber.

And as this reflection crossed his mind, the door opened, and there
appeared the same tall beautiful stately lady he had seen with Els on
the Bowling Green at Bridwell on that Gaudy Day long ago. Advancing with a smile, she held out her hand and made some remark about
being very glad at last to meet one she had heard so much of. He
was just murmuring some confused response, the while, with a vague
feeling of uneasiness, he wondered what it was she had been told,
when Lord Augustus, her brother, came in, and almost at the same
moment there was the distant clang of a bell, the door opened once
more, and the butler having announced dinner, his lordship, who was
indeed the only other person stopping in the house, without waiting
for Els, gave his arm to his sister and went out.

'So sorry,' he said, looking back over his shoulder at him, who,
doing his best not to tread on his hostess' train, was following: 'So
sorry we haven't got a lady for you! I'm afraid you'll have to take
yourself in!' And he gave a hearty laugh.

'Was Lance always late at school?' Lady Adelaide asked. 'He always
is here!'

During dinner he scarcely spoke, in part from shyness and in part
because his attention was much taken up by Lord Augustus. For the
first time in his life he now saw one who not only lived in that Great
World of Secretaries of State and Peers of the Realm, Blue Ribbons
and Princes of the Blood, of which he had dreamt so often, wherein
he too one day, he thought, was destined to play a part, but was, as he
knew, himself an Excellency and a Right Honourable, an Ambassador
Extraordinary and Minister Plenipotentiary, a Privy Councillor and
Grand Cross of the Bath. And as these pompous titles sounded in his
ears with equal pleasure and no more meaning than, when reading the
*Decline and Fall*, he had found in the repetition of those of the Sebas-
tocrator and the Cæsar, the Panhypersebastes and the Protosebastes,
the Protovestiare and Great Logothete, from the opposite side of the
table he considered him as one newly returned from some wonderful
and distant land whither he himself was at that very moment setting
out. It was true that neither in appearance nor ways did his lordship
give the least support to any of his notions as to what the great ones

of the earth were like, since not only did he fail to discover any trace of that air of distinction which he had understood enabled you in all circumstances to recognise the high-born great, but he even ate after such a fashion, with such champings and chumpings and gollopings and such a messing of his moustache with soup and sauce as must, he conceived, have led any one ignorant of who it was to set him down as not more than a gentleman, but less. Yet, though for a moment discomposed at this upsetting of his theories, presently he came to see in what at first he had taken for an argument against them, only another proof of their correctness. It was clear that the highest equally with the lowest ranks were careless as to their manners because both knew, these as below, those as superior to such considerations, that their position in society was quite independent of how they behaved. But before dinner was over, what with the fatigue of so long a journey and the unaccustomed excellence and variety of the food and wine, he had grown too sleepy to trouble his head with these or any other thoughts, and he was very glad when, soon after they left the dining-room, Lady Adelaide observed he must be tired and suggested his going to bed. Half-an-hour later he had fallen asleep, having scarce had time to think how deliciously soft the mattress was and how curiously perfumed and delicate the sheets.

The next morning after breakfast Els proposed a game of lawn-tennis, and: 'You play, don't you?' he added in a tone that made it impossible to answer otherwise than in the affirmative. He hoped he would at least be able to get out of playing then, but, one after another, his objections were overborne, and in a few minutes more, a racquet in his unwilling hand, he was on his way to the ground. He would have gone to a duel with less heavy a heart, since even death would have been preferable to the disgrace he could for the moment see no means of avoiding. And as he went along he put up a silent, but intensely earnest, prayer that even now at the eleventh hour something might happen to save him. But there was no response, and presently he found himself facing Els across the net, and obliged, if he wished to escape the double shame of having both his incapacity and his lie made manifest, to adopt the only means of escape that yet remained, and pretend not to try. At first Els only called him a lazy chap, and said he was sure he could play well enough if he liked, but when he continued to pursue his plan, and made no other reply but a faint smile – whereby he intended to express, but for himself alone, a sort of contemptuous pity for his friend's ignorance of his state of mind – the other, who could never bear to see any one not in earnest over a game, grew cross:

'Oh, it's no use going on,' he cried, 'if you won't try!'

And as he, of two evils choosing the less, preferred it should be thought that he would not, rather than that he could not, play, Els, after a few more strokes, stopped suddenly.

'I think, after all,' he said, 'I'd perhaps better go and see the game-keeper as I intended. Will you take in the racquets?'

So Jaspar, turning, went slowly back towards the house, and, 'Aha!' he said presently out loud with a glance over his shoulder and a know-ing wink, 'Aha, I thought I'd choke him off!'

But for all this he was much put out that he, whose constant desire was to please, should be compelled to appear thus disagreeable. He could not understand how it was that he should be unable to do at all what dozens of others, whom he rightly looked down upon, did well; but he tried to think his incapacity in this respect should be rather a source of pride; he could not fiddle, but he could make a small town a great city. Yet this, though an excuse sufficient for him, was hardly one he could expect should be enough for others, and he felt he would be very glad when he had done something, as one day he would, that in the eyes of the world as well as in his own should set him above that obligation to be like others which he was always finding so dangerous to his pride. For the moment, as he reflected on the many shifts he foresaw he would be put to if he was to avoid on the one hand being considered disagreeable, on the other being held a muff, he wished he had been a woman, and so able unquestioned to do as he liked. He quite envied Lady Adelaide the peace of mind with which she could listen, whatever were the plans for the day that were being made.

Yet, though much relieved when he found he was never asked to accompany Els and his sister in their morning rides, he was none the less vexed at heart to have it thus taken for granted that he was one who must always be left out of account whenever there was any-thing to be done. But, although divided between these two opposite feelings his manner was constrained and awkward, he still persisted in being present at the start, and, as the hour came round, would issue from the great carved oak doors of the hall, with much gravity acknowledge the groom's salute, and so, advancing to the edge of the steps, stand and look down at Nita's rough Mexican pony and Elsie's glossy-coated chestnut. He would have given much to have been able to leap on his back and have been found when they appeared turning and winding him in such a way as to fill them with surprise and admiration. If only he could have had the courage honestly to confess he could not ride but would like to learn! For he longed to know what it was in the fresh morning air to go galloping at full speed over the turf while consciousness itself was lost in the pleasure of motion. But his pride could never away with the thought of an acknowledgment that must reflect not only on himself but on his birth: – for surely ignorance of the horseman's art was a strong presumption against one's being gently born; and, careless what secret pains a thing might cost to learn, in public it was rather by witchcraft than wit that he always desired to appear to work.

Presently Els would come out slowly buttoning his glove, descend the steps and mount the horse that was an appanage of his rank at once and a sign of his wealth. And when Jaspar considered him sitting there in his saddle and bending with easy grace to every motion of the animal, at sight of all the charms united in his person as well those of beauty and youth and health and strength that could be seen as those visible to the mind's eye alone, he felt at once repelled and attracted; to which effect there was not a detail in the boy's appearance but contributed, down to the small shapely, polished boot with its spur, the toe of which rested in the stirrup so firmly yet so lightly and with such a royal air of mastery. And at one moment he would think his friend's barbarism far more aristocratic than all the super-subtle refinement upon which he prided himself so much as in reality setting him above those who at first might seem his superiors in money, rank, good-looks, and powers of mind and body; and the next, by way of asserting his own merits in the tacit comparison he was drawing, he would do his best to believe that after all the sports the boy was such a master of were only fit for bumpkins and boobies; while as for the race of country-gentlemen he was sprung from, their baseness exceeded that of any other men who had ever lived in the world.

But now Els began to get impatient, and: 'Nita, Ni-ta!' he would shout; a faint small cry would be heard in answer from an open window in the opposite wing, and in a few minutes more the child herself would appear. One hand gathered up her curiously-cut skirt, the other was filled with sugar for her pony and bread for the pigeons that, scarce waiting her call, came shooting down, fluttered for a moment when now but a little way above the ground, and so at last alit and began to feed; as for the pony, he would be nuzzling and lipping at the sugar she held up to him on her outstretched palm. But now her brother would cry, 'Oh, come along, Nita, do!' and she, giving Jumbo's neck a last hasty pat would let the groom swing her lightly up into her saddle, would bend for an instant to arrange with him her skirt, and so go off. And as under the flickering shade her pony went cantering away by the side of his bigger companion, who, with much tossing up and down of his head was going prancing along all on one side, her skirt fluttered and her hair danced upon her shoulders, and she would put up her hand to secure her hat more firmly on her head. The groom would walk slowly away in the direction of the stables, but Jaspar would stop to watch them till they disappeared out of sight down the Long Walk, when, turning his back on the courtyard, now once more silent except for the summer-sleepy cooing of the pigeons, he would go in-doors. And so he passed through the hall that struck as cool as on former hot summer-days had done Bridwell Chapel of which indeed it reminded him in its size and shape and gabled roof. But the resemblance was one he only noted vaguely, as he did the antlers that hung here and there on the walls, the huge yawning fireplace with its great iron dogs and the stone-flagged floor half-covered with Turkey rugs, for he was thinking how sorry he was that he had ever come. But for his fear of what the Binneys would say he would have gone back at once.

It was always to the Library he went. The soft vellum pages of the missals that gleamed with burnished gold, and had the colours of their illuminations still as fresh as when monkish hands had laid them on; the musty smell that exhaled from the pages of the tall old folios, the wormholes so many were drilled with, their quaint bindings and curious type, deepened that sense of remoteness from the world with which the absolute quiet had already impressed him; for the only sounds you ever heard were the swinging tick-tack, tick-tack of a big clock, through the wide-opened casements the faint stirring of the wind among the limes and the occasional note of some unknown bird: otherwise there was the silence and retirement of a desert with the severe and grandiose sense of a palace interior. And here he would often spend the whole morning ensconced with a book in the corner of the cushioned seat of the great bay-window that went up many-storeyed the whole height of the lofty room. But fond as he was of reading for its own sake, he still did not care to lose what credit could be gained from being thought to read for pleasure such books as none others of his age ever looked at unless obliged, and when therefore, as he sat one morning in his accustomed nook, he heard the door open, he dropped Maxwell's *History of the Irish Rebellion* – he was just enjoying Cruickshank's plate of the burning of the barn at Scullabogue – and snatching up the *Faust* he had been careful to lay ready open at his side, pretended to be too much absorbed to know that Lady Adelaide was there. At last she spoke:

'You seem to be interested in your book, Mr. Tristram!' she said and smiled.

With an affected start he looked up.

'And where,' she went on, 'and where are Nita and Lance?'

'Oh,' he said with an indifferent air, 'they're gone for their ride!'

He wanted if he could to get Els into a row for neglecting him and at the same time not to let Lady Adelaide imagine it was otherwise than of his own choice that he was there. She asked whether he would care to walk with her down to the village whither she was then on her way; and the words were scarce out of her mouth before he had made up his mind he would accept the invitation, but fearful lest she should for a moment think he wished to be elsewhere than where he was, it was still some time before he let himself be persuaded to come.

'I wish Lance were more like you!' she said as they went out; 'more fond of books! He seems to care for nothing but hunting and shooting.'

But this was only the first of many expeditions of the same kind that he and Lady Adelaide made together. And he was always glad to go; for he found something as pleasant as new in the signs of respect with which they met as they went about. It was true of course that they none of them were meant for him, but still he felt a swelling sense of pride when he saw the children going bob and bob, and the occupants of the cottages all rise in confusion when they appeared in the doorway. The woman of the house with a corner of her check apron would hastily wipe one of the wooden chairs, and, pushing it forward and begging her ladyship to sit down, herself step back a pace or two and so remain respectfully standing; as did he likewise, hat in hand, considering that he thus displayed towards the cottager the lofty courtesy of a grand seigneur, and towards Lady Adelaide that graceful deference it was only becoming he should pay to one he had begun to look on as a sort of queen. As for all the suffering and misery which as often as not she came to relieve, it was so far from moving him to any feeling of compassion that rather he was glad of the additional opportunity of being graceful that it afforded his dear lady. Such was the term under which he now liked best to think of her. It was that he preferred of all those he had so far discovered in his reading, during the course of which he was always on the look-out for any descriptions that might fit her, or people she might be compared to. For the moment he thought she was like no one so much as her he always spoke of, *ore rotundo*, as Marie-Antoinette-Josephe-Jeanne de Lorraine d'Autriche. Both had the same proud smile hovering about the corners of the mouth, the same thin nose with its imperial curve, high-arched eyebrows, well-opened eyes and high forehead from which the hair was swept back in a roll; Lady Adelaide's was of a soft silvery grey that had much the same effect as must have been produced by the powder worn by the Queen of France. Then too, like her type, she had a certain beautiful haughtiness in the pose of her head, a carriage that made her look taller than she really was, and in her every movement a gracefully-assured dignity such as could only belong to those great ones of the earth, who from childhood up have been used to see all in their path open out in backing lanes as they draw near. Even her hands, delicate but firmly modelled, seemed fitted rather 'to sway the sceptre and to grasp the orb' than for any of the meaner purposes of life. Surely no vulgar worries could ever approach one so placid-beautiful, so royal-high; when troubles came – as who can control his fate? – they would be of a tragic and ennobling, not of a mean and petty sort. And them she would meet with the lofty and unwavering courage which surely belonged to the proud soul that looked out from those clear grey eyes. Like Marie Antoinette she might be compelled to bow her head before men, but her undaunted spirit would surely never deign to stoop before any but God.

One reflection however there was which now and again made him feel uncomfortable: what was the exact rank in society which this same mistress of his considered he occupied. For while at one moment her manner, always gracious and kind, would completely dissipate his alarms, at another he would be so far from considering this a favourable sign as only to see in it a proof of her regarding him as an *espèce*, and so of course as one to whom it would be in the highest degree unbecoming on her part to show any variance of mood.

And though he would never have consented to acknowledge, even to himself, that he was not her equal; and now he would base his pretensions on the fact that after all his birth, if not as illustrious as hers, was still gentle, and therefore in all essential points as good; and now would affect to hold——such accidental distinctions as absurd; yet having in his heart of hearts an uneasy consciousness he was nothing of the kind, he was ever on the look-out to detect and resist the slightest attempt on her part to assert a superiority he resented the more, as he felt himself the less able to deny its existence. Indeed so tender was he on this point, that more than once it happened that some remark which he had at first taken for a compliment had presently become an effort to console him for what to her no doubt was an inferiority so evident she could afford to be magnanimous; and if there was one thing more repugnant than another to his pride, it was the notion of being pitied. But this was a view he never held long, choosing rather to see in her selection of him as a companion a proof of his belief that his powers of mind were of a calibre which fitted him far better for the society of his elders than for that of those of his own age.

And in this notion he was presently still further confirmed by the conduct of Lord Augustus. Up to then, except at meals, he scarce had ever seen his lordship, who appeared to spend most of his time in the Justice-Room which was specially affected to his use, and where, as Jaspar understood, he was engaged in all the voluminous and important correspondence entailed by the seat in the House which, now retired from the diplomatic service, he occupied. On the rare occasions that they met he had been treated with a lofty assumption of his being not only a child, but one of a rank altogether below notice, and whenever he had ventured to join in the conversation, had been looked at in a manner that had caused his voice to die away in his throat, while Lord Augustus, not even making a pretence of answering him, had treated his remarks merely as if they had been some momentarily disturbing noise and gone on with what he had been saying as if nothing had happened. Once or twice he had even ventured on a little joke, but his lordship had always declined to laugh, apparently being of opinion that in so doing he was taking advantage of a chance of putting down one whom hitherto he had merely considered as of no consequence, but who now was developing into an objectionably pushing young man. Such treatment would by itself have been galling enough, but it was made still worse by its contrast with that accorded to Els and by the fact that any retaliation seemed out of the question. All he could do in way of revenge was to laugh in his sleeve at the old gentleman's manners and appearance and mental powers. He would have doubtless preferred to be able to tell him to his face what he thought, yet he was almost consoled when he reflected on the vast difference there was between his real opinion of his lordship and what this latter in his conceit and pomposity no doubt believed it to be. And while in his personal appearance he was ugly, ungainly, slovenly; his intellectual gifts were very far from making up for the deficiency; at least if one might judge from his conversation. But indeed he could never get over his surprise that here in this palace the general talk was not a whit better than that which went on in the stuffy little rooms and tiny garden of the Rectory. What on earth did one so stupid and dull ever come into society for at all? Certainly he, with his exquisite inborn sense of art and all his brilliant philosophy, was immeasurably the superior of this dirty old gentleman with his stale jokes and stupid remarks about the weather. And if this Lord Augustus, being thus by nature, could yet become what he was, to what high dignities might he, Jaspar, not reasonably hope to attain with talents such as his?

Sometimes his lordship would take him out for a walk. He enjoyed being seen in the society of so great a man; and was only disappointed when it was strangers they met who, not knowing his companion, instead of gazing at him with becoming awe, would stare in surprise at the big fat untidily-dressed man who was tramping along and talking so loud: he would much have liked to stop and explain who it was and point out that he was too great a personage to be under the necessity of thinking about his clothes. And Lord Augustus would hold forth, flattering him immensely by employing such phrases as 'People like you and me!' after which his step would be sensibly lighter; and by turning to him every now and again with a 'What do *you* think?' And he would give not what really were his views, but such as would, he thought, be most acceptable to his hearer. Only he never felt quite sure what these might be; and more than once indeed discovered he had shot altogether wide of the mark. And he had other disappointments too, as when Lord Augustus failed to express the least surprise at the intelligence and information of which he considered he had given proofs, or remarked of some opinion: 'So I thought at your age!' And it always annoyed him immensely when his lordship spoke of his ending perhaps as an Assistant-Under-Secretary, or even an Under-Secretary. An Assistant-Under-Secretary! or even an Under-Secretary! He!

# CHAPTER XIX

And yet, though fond of these walks, he was as much so of being alone, since only then could he indulge undisturbed in those dreams of ambition to which indeed he was always given but which this sort of conversation especially served to provoke. Not that he had in any wise made up his mind as to the exact way in which he intended to be great: he only knew he was indifferent whether it was love or hate that he inspired so long as he was not left without influence at all. Of this however there was, he felt sure, so little danger that even when his fancy discovered in his own face the same signs of predestination to an unhappy fate as he tried to believe he saw in the picture of Charles I. in the Grand Saloon; while he considered it quite possible he might, like him, have a tragic fall, it did not for a moment enter his head that he would never climb. And were there not a dozen excellent reasons for this assurance? Others had succeeded. Why not he? Surely the mere fact of his having ambitions implied possession of means to gratify them, if you only considered that no one else had any at all. As for the way he had failed at school, in that he saw an earnest of victory, not a type of future defeat: very few who had made themselves names in after-life had ever been distinguished as boys. And so confident did he feel of success, his only fear was lest some one or other of his Bridwell contemporaries should outstrip him in the race and thus inflict such a humiliation as, short though the time might be before he wiped it out, would even so be terrible to bear. But this was a danger it could scarcely be hard to avoid. He would give himself till thirty – and that was already four years beyond Napoleon's age when he made his Italian campaign – and if then not great, would go away and hide. How could anybody pass such years and, seeing themselves still obscure, not shrink away, overwhelmed with shame, from every eye? Once or twice, transported by these swelling thoughts, with a victorious air he stamped on the ground, feeling as if he could command the entire world, not only mankind, but earth and sky: there was nothing, he conceived, he could not do. And as, thus dreaming, he walked slowly up and down the terrace, from time to time he

would stop, and, with one foot put lightly forward, all his weight resting on the other, and his hands à la Napoleon, behind his back, would
stand, his gaze fixed upon the ground as lost in thought. 'Er – er,' he
would murmur, 'what was I saying?' Then, drawing himself up, he
would consider the scene; and into his eyes he felt come an expression that seemed to him to unite at once the dreamy wistfulness with
which at home from the edge of the cliff he had looked out across the
moving sea towards the distant horizon, as if it had hid, not France,
but the land of his desires; and the commanding haughtiness wherewith from the crest of the Front Hills he had contemplated, spread
out below, the hedgeless chess-board fields, the white windmills and
the spire-marked villages of the Sussex Weald. It was only from this
one spot indeed he could obtain a view of anything like the extent he
had used to get on the Downs, since, as for the country round, what
with copses and tall hedges and hedgerow elms, cottages and barns,
palings and gates and walls, you could hardly see a yard ahead. But
from here his gaze, travelling over the Chase as it sloped away at his
feet, and over the shining lilied surface of the lake, was only stopped
by the hanging-woods on the opposite side that mounted from the
water's edge and shut in all.

And while the distant prospect thus filled him with notions as
grand as vague, the evidences of wealth and state that he perceived at
hand gave a more definite form to his wishes and made him impatient
for the day when he would have for his own just another such garden,
with like banks of turf and lawns so trim as rather to seem laid with
velvet than grass, like orange-trees ranged at equal distances in square
big-handled green tubs, like tall white marble vases over whose out-
ward-curving lips fell the most brilliant-hued flowers and like smooth
gravel paths, so broad that Le Roi Soleil, accompanied by his whole
court in their hoops and whaleboned skirts, might have moved along
them as much at ease as on those of Marly or Versailles. Now and
again, indeed, he would fancy that all he saw was really his, and that,
like Fouquet at Vaux, he was actually on his way to receive his sovereign who had come to visit him in this his palace whose splendours
far outshone the most magnificent of those belonging to the Crown.
And so strong would the hallucination on occasion become that he
would take a few steps forward and stretch out his hand as if in truth
about to greet a royal guest. And whenever, as he went about, he
encountered a groom or gardener, he thrilled with delight as the man

respectfully touched his hat; at such times he felt, he thought, as must an Englishman when in presence of a member of some one or other of their innumerable subject races. Yes, he was certainly one of the lords of human kind, and there was a something about him that compelled his inferiors to recognise the fact at a glance.

Sometimes he would climb the dark turret-stair that led round and round to the top of the Gate Tower; each step was a rough-hewn slab of solid oak and the newel itself an entire tree: and, coming out at a sort of little hutch, cross the ridged lead roof, all cut and scored with names, and go and lean against the lichen-stained battlements. For a while his gaze would not travel beyond the house itself, which, with all its roofs and chimneys and courts, appeared from here more like a town than any single dwelling-place; indeed, he still scarce knew his way about the maze below of passages and rooms and halls; and then it would stray to the surrounding lands that, far as the eye could reach, had for centuries belonged to the Great House. He liked to think of all the crimes he felt sure had been committed whether to win or keep what he was looking on.

But most of his time he spent indoors, wandering from the State Bedroom to the Grand Saloon, from the Grand Saloon to the Tapestry Chamber, from the Tapestry Chamber to the Matted Gallery, and with chin tight-stretched staring up at pictures whose dark unintelligibility and remoteness from anything in nature that he had ever seen impressed him with a high sense of their value; and now stopping at the foot of the State Bed, and thinking of all the stories of births and deaths and bridal nights which it might have told, that lofty plume-topped structure within whose curtains of faded crimson velvet and tarnished gold-lace each successive lord of Tremlett had in turn for generations past been born and bedded, had died and lain in state; and now looking up at the famous tapestries that, as the story ran, a queen had given and an empress vainly coveted, and considering their representations of the various palaces of the French king with huntings and figures and curious gay-plumaged exotic fowls. Sometimes he would come across parties of tourists whom the housekeeper was showing round, and with much ostentation would pass on before them into places where he knew they were not allowed to go: he liked to see them try to follow him, and to hear Mrs. Harris calling them back while she explained that 'that gentleman' was staying in the house. It gave him a delicious thrill of pride to think that he was enjoying as equal, friend and guest what these base and minor sort of people could only catch a passing glimpse of, although once, as he stood before a picture pretending to be lost in contemplation, he was much annoyed to overhear one of them remark as they went by, 'He thinks we're admiring him!'

But it was in the Matted Gallery that he liked best to spend his time, and it was never without a feeling of being now at last on his way to a spot where not only was he happier than elsewhere, but also in some sort at home, that he would open the carved dog-gates at the foot of the staircase, mount the slippery and echoing oak steps, and, through the double arch at the top, see the room stretching before him in its unbroken length of two hundred and twenty feet. One side, the left, was almost entirely taken up by a range of mullioned windows looking out into the courtyard; through their diamond quarries the sun cast trellised shadows on the floor. Between each, affixed against the wainscot, were trophies of bows and bills, helmets and breastplates, swords and guns; in any ordinary house they would have been there, he thought, merely as appropriate decorations; here they were rather arms that had simply been allowed to remain where hung by the hands of those by whom last they had actually been used. On the opposite wall in one long row were portraits of the various lords to whom all he had seen since he had come, or could at that moment see, had in turn belonged; who, equipped with those very arms, at the head of their dependants whom the same stores had also furnished forth, had in the succeeding centuries gone caracoling out from the courtyard below, as every morning now did Els, on their way to fight with Alva or Cromwell, Monmouth, the Pretender, or Napoleon. And as he walked slowly down the almost endless-seeming line, the consciousness that he was on terms of the most intimate friendship with the descendants and successors of all these lords and ladies appeared in some sort to answer the question that as a boy he had so often propounded to himself, of what would have been his station had he chanced to live in other days. Besides, under the silent gaze of those who had helped to make history, he felt as though he too were playing a part on the historic stage, and in his turn were performing before an audience, not a member of which but had also in his time been an actor, though now by death reduced to being a spectator from another world of what went on in that he had had to leave.

Pictures of the earlier owners were naturally wanting, and he could only imagine what that 'Lord Trimlette' had been like, of whom the Froissart in the Library told. But there was a full-length portrait of that descendant of his, fourteen of whose immediate relatives had lost their heads on Tower Hill, two died prisoners within the Tower walls, and four been attainted, who for his own part had taken 'in lawfulle warres Lewis de Orleans, Duke of Longeuile and Marquis of Rotueline prisoner at the iurney of Bomy by Teruane the sixteenth day of August, Anno Henr. 8. 5,' and had so succeeded in having his paternal coat of 'argent, on a bend gules, between three pellets, as many Swans proper,' 'rewarded,' as Gwillim had it, 'with a Canton Sinister, Azure, thereupon a Demy ramme mounting Argent, corned Or, between two flowers de lis of the last, ower all a Batune dexter-waies, as the second in the Canton.' Round his neck there hung the 'cheyne of fyne gold' that was set down as an item in the inventory of the things in the house which had been taken at his death; and behind his white trunk hose the floor went up like a wall. And thence onward there was scarce one of the long line whose portrait was not there, done by whoever had happened to be the fashionable painter of the time – Zucchero, Vandyck, Lely, Kneller, Reynolds, Gainsborough, or Lawrence. But it was only for a certain few he cared, and among the rest for one by Sir Peter of the Anita Southwood, who for a few short summer months had reigned a beauty at Whitehall, been betrothed to a great peer, and then, returning to Tremlett to make ready for her wedding, had fallen sick of the plague, and within three days lain dead in the Blue Room next to his. The fact of her not only bearing the same Christian name as her descendant, but even being like her in face, would at times so confuse him that he scarcely knew which of the two was alive. Indeed, the painted population so outlasted and outnumbered the living, he was half-inclined to think that it was they who were the real possessors of the place, and those who fancied themselves such but quickly-passing unsubstantial ghosts. At any rate the principal business of these latter seemed merely to add their like-nesses to the collection, which once done, it was a matter of indiffer-ence how soon they died, though perhaps it was as well if they lived long enough by some great crime or success or misfortune of which Tremlett ought if possible to be the theatre, to add also to that other collection of stories which was now so large there was scarce a corner whether in Chase or garden or house that was not haunted with the memory of what had happened there years ago. Two other portraits there were a little farther down, those of the viscounts, father and son, who had lived under Queen Anne and George i., of which also he was specially fond as having in a supreme degree that superb and lofty air as of creatures of another clay which now for some time past he had been trying with the help of a glass to cultivate in himself; the sole difference between the pair appeared to be that that of the father whose personality was altogether lost in a complicated mass of magnificent clothes, seemed begot of mere rank and wealth, while in the son it was more like that he himself was anxious to acquire, partaking of intellectual disdain; both alike had stuck their plump hands upon their hips as if the better to display their taper fingers and filbert nails.

And so at last he came to him who had immediately preceded Els. This then was the 'grandpapa' of whom he had so often in the far-off Scarisbrick days heard speak. But surely the old man's signs of age must have been exaggerated. No living person could ever have had such a rough yellow wrinkled skin, eyebrows so bristly or eyes so sunken or so lifeless, and certainly not that curious green tinge. Death, tired of waiting for one who was so long a-coming, must evidently have resolved at last to show his power, and tricked him, yet alive, in the hideous tints of a week-old corpse. It was horrible to have to think the day would come when he too would be like that. Would it not be better, while still his skin was soft and smooth and his eyes undimmed, instead of giving day and night, as he purposed, to ambition, rather, like Anacreon, to fill – as ran a translation of some Greek verses which once he had made at school – to fill every moment of his life with love? So when at last the time arrived that he would no longer be an equal partner in the game, but, old and ugly, have to resign himself to the fact that no one would ever again be as pleased with his caresses as he with theirs, he would not have to regret having thrown away any of those opportunities of pleasure which youth alone can hope for. Meanwhile in the present instance all the repulsiveness of extreme old age only made a better foil for what was already well set off by the dark panelling of the wall, the dazzling complexion and liquid sparkling eyes and curling golden hair of him who was the handsomest of the whole handsome line, the minion of the race, of Els. It was here he always stopped the longest, going up so close that his own face and that of the picture almost touched. Nor did those painted features, eyebrows and nose and cheeks and lips, only now recall what once he had known so well but seemed a part of the boy's historical inheritance, and in the eyes into which he stared so hard, he found not alone, as in days of old, a provoking smile, but centuries of domination. It amused him too to remember that this handsome laughing small boy in flannels, who was so exactly the Els he had known, and, ridiculous to think of, loved, had even then been Lancelot Charles Southwood, the Most Noble, Potent, and Honourable, fourteenth Viscount Tremlett, eighteenth Baron Southwood of Tremlett, Hereditary High Steward of Bradfield, and twenty-third lord of that Honour of Tremlett St. Mary, which, 'with all its appurtenances, and all the knight's fees thereto belonging, with Court Leet and View of Frankpledge,' had by letters-patent from 'Henry, by the grace of God King of England, Lord of Ireland, and Duke of Aquitaine,' been granted to hold to his ancestor, 'his heirs and assigns for ever by tenure by cornage from the Feast of St. Michael last past.'

And then how rich he was! If at least one might judge from the magnificence of all one saw. *His* means could not have afforded *him* a single one of those things of which here there were such numbers, and which even so formed but an inappreciable part of the boy's possessions. Why, even this very picture was by the greatest painter of the day, whose portraits he knew cost a thousand guineas apiece. He liked besides to think that Nature had joined Society in heaping gifts upon their common favourite, and that while Elsie's money and rank put one-half the world at his feet, the other was brought there by those bright eyes and the rest of those physical beauties, to name all which would have merely been to give a catalogue of the different parts of his body; while in case there might still be some to resist this double charm, there was a something in his manner it was surely impossible any one could successfully withstand. And presently as he gazed and gazed unblinking, straight into those painted eyes, he fell into a dream that had for its subject the prodigious power over men and things which was latent in the original. He compared him fancifully to a sovereign or bank note. And how completely wasted it all was on one who would never, as would he in his place have done, employ it with that cool impassiveness which would alone permit of its being utilised to its full extent! He wondered how it came about that Els was such a king of concupiscence whilst he, who was yet so near, had nothing that could make anybody anxious to win his good graces. Why should another already be in the enjoyment of what, if he achieved by the end of his life – though he was going to achieve much more – he would be luckier than most?

But though of course he would have been glad had it been he, and not Els who of the two had had the good looks, and by inheritance obtained the more excellent name; and though he could not but feel angry with *his* ancestors who had left *him* little beyond a certain number of tastes and very likely the seeds of some terrible disease, he still would not allow he was in any sense jealous. Had he not within him such a consciousness of worth as prevented his feeling otherwise than the equal, not only of the living great, of Lord Augustus and this boy, but of the dead as well, whose portraits were all around? And was not the possession of talents like his a more legitimate source of pride than that of beauty and wealth and place, since all these were bestowed on one ready-made, while the powers of one's mind were as much one's own creation as the crops the field will not produce unless first sown. He even tried to think it was only fair that Heaven should have thus provided for one who, however charming, could never certainly have done so for himself. Besides, after all, the boy's position was such as he for his part would hardly have cared to occupy. He could never have borne being known merely as the possessor of a beautiful place; to have felt that people came to see, not him, but a house in which he was only an accident that could easily at any moment be dispensed with. Had he been in Elsie's shoes he would, he was sure, have found everything spoilt by the comparison he would have always had in his mind between his power and that which his ancestors had once enjoyed, and he would certainly never have rested till he had made himself, the owner, as worthy the house as the altered circumstances of the time would allow, and brought it about that it was still he whom people thought of even amid these stately galleries and gardens and woods as they surely must of My Lord of Salisbury at Hatfield. And, indeed, with him such must of necessity be the case, since, however magnificent the seat he was one day to have – and he had already drawn the plans – it must still remain subordinate in interest to himself, its creator.

Nor was this the only respect in which he flattered himself he would have worn the golden circlet of a peer of the realm with a better grace than Els who indeed appeared rather to avoid than seek opportunities for the display of that pomp and circumstance which were only what was suited to his rank, and certainly never dreamt of having his ancestors' days kept solemnly and their memories preserved in never-dying honours. And not only was the boy thus careless and ignorant of the history of the place itself and of that of his forefathers who had lived there now for so many hundred years, but he altogether declined to listen when Jaspar would have imparted some of that knowledge on the subject of which just then he was full. He was surprised at such indifference with regard to questions which, interesting even to a comparative stranger, should surely have been still more so to the representative and heir of the House; but he had never any personal feeling in the matter till one day, having found out that an ancestor of his had married a Southwood, and reporting the discovery, and beginning to call Els coz, he fancied he detected in him signs of not being best pleased at a relationship with which he for his part had been so delighted. He said nothing, only he grew more impatient than ever for the day to come when the desire to make much of the connection would be on their side, not on his. And who, after all, were they, he should like to know, to give themselves such airs? Had any of their race ever changed the course of English history? Or made the name of Southwood a synonym for genius, courage, or devotion? Why, future times would reckon them among such families as the Lucys and the Blounts, who, however ancient and all that, owed everything but the merest local fame to a chance connection with an Immortal. What made it, too, the more absurd was the fact of his being of their blood, and so in case to succeed to the very honours from the height of which they now looked down on him with such contempt. How would it be if he gathered together all those who stood between the title and him, and sent them out to sea on a ship which he then would scuttle or blow up or somehow sink with all on board? Certainly had he been Elsie's younger brother and so with only one life between him and fortune, without a moment's hesitation he would have put him out of the way; and he would amuse himself with thinking how the deed might have best been done, the while, out of the corner of his eye, he would steal a sly look at the unconscious object of all these reflections, and laugh to himself as he thought how little the boy knew of what was then passing through his mind.

# CHAPTER XX

And while his mornings were thus occupied in wandering about the house and gardens, his afternoons were for the most part taken up in going out on the river with Nita and Els. The latter for his part generally went on ahead, and left the child and him to follow after with the sandwiches which, to make sure they had lots of jam, she liked to fetch herself from Mrs. Harris. And as he went turning with her in the maze of vaulted and stone-flagged passages that formed the means of communication between the different offices, and now on this side, now on that, through spandrelled doorways, caught a glimpse of the various servants at their work, it pleased him to see how many had to toil in menial obscurity in order that he might enjoy that ease and state and that freedom from all need to trouble about the sordid details of life, to which he was entitled at once by the right of intellectual superiority and that of birth. It was, he thought, as if he had been in some great palm-house in the midst of flowers and heat while all outside was ice and snow.

So presently, he with the basket over his shoulder on a stick, the two set off, and, taking the little footpath that slants across the flat and open piece of park where Elsie's cricket-matches were always played, went on till they came to the stile over which you get into the wood that from thence slopes down to the river. And here for a moment he would stop and look back at the house. It was the view of it that he liked best, as from its velvet lawn, the green of which looked more vivid by contrast with the darker colour of the straight and slim dwarf-cypresses, facing the western sun, it rose, a long low irregular pile to whose red criss-crossed bricks the lapse of years had given such a ruddy mellow tint as now to make it seem, not so much the handiwork of man, as equally a part of nature with the contemporary trees and grass in the midst of which it stood; and this impression was somehow strengthened by the air of serenity with which he chose to imagine that its crown of gables and twisted chimneys and high-pitched roofs stood out against the blue of the summer sky. There was surely a something human in its aspect, as in the portraits in the gallery that it contained, a something of inanimate nature. Nita meanwhile had been amusing herself with balancing on the tip of her finger her bright-red cotton parasol, but at last, growing impatient: 'Oh, come along!' she would cry, and he would turn and go after her down the winding path on which some of last year's leaves were still lying undisturbed. He was very fond of the whole hanger, loving to hear from out its mysterious recesses the faint coo of a pigeon while overhead the rustling leaves as they stirred let through a flitter of blue sky and dappled with trembling light and shade the moss-grown walk they followed. And then as they still descended, all at once you saw the river shining between the trees. So they came out again into the sunlight on to the little lawn, against the bank of which the boat-house, painted white and thatched, floated solidly on its grim-looking iron caissons. Els was waiting for them, sitting on the rustic bench that is built round the trunk of the big willow, and, as the boat was ready, it was not long before they were started, Els rowing bow, he stroke, and Nita steering.

And all at once it struck him, as she sat there just in front, that she was quite as much boy as girl. And as one of Elsie's greatest charms had been that he had something in his dress and manner and looks and limbs of the delicacy and grace of a girl; so now he took delight in finding in her a delicious flavour of the roughness of a boy. Even of the dress she wore there was really nothing but what might have equally well done for one of the other sex. Her old straw hat – she had got her brother to bring it her from Bridwell – was pushed to the back of her head, and so formed a nimbus to the dark and heavy curls that, cut-square across her forehead and falling in great loose rings upon her shoulders, framed in their turn her face; her tie was one of those of scarlet corded silk that had been so fashionable at school that last Easter half, and her jacket of blue serge was as much worn and stained as though indeed it had belonged to a boy. Its gilt buttons and gold-embroidered anchors made him think of those young middies of Marryat's, who, ever since he himself had ceased to be of their age, had exercised such a fascination over him – he had never met one in real life – as possessors of what now he had found in her, a double charm. Only of course in their case it had come from their seeming, not of two sexes, but two ages, and while in years and ways mere boys, in actions and responsibilities grown men. No doubt her short skirts proclaimed her a girl – though even they might well have been taken for a kilt – and those black cotton stockings through which he could just perceive a faint shimmer of white leg; but as his eye still travelled downwards, the boyishness of her canvas-shoes again threw him out: they were such as her brother had in his recollection used to wear. And she held the rudder-lines grasped tight in her little sun-burnt fists, and her lips were set with just the same air as he remembered to have seen in him when out with the Eight, and with just the same seriousness she bent her small body backwards and forwards to their swing. And then he would catch some passing look that would remind him, no longer of her brother, but of Lely's picture in the Matted Gallery of her great-great-great-great-aunt, and they would seem but an illustration to a History of England, those same features that but a moment before had only recalled half-forgotten passages out of his own. Nor all this time had she ever once noticed how she was being observed; she had been far too much absorbed in her steering, and her glance, as it travelled past him, had, he recognised, but seen still another of those obstacles that were always getting in the way just when she wanted a clear view of their course. Presently however she said she thought she would like to scull, and so, resting her hand for an instant lightly on his shoulder as they changed places, she proceeded to alter the stretcher, roll up her sleeves and try her sculls, and then, holding them ready to drop into the water the moment he gave the word, intently watching him, she sat and waited. Nor, when at length they once more started on their way, did her rowing disappoint the expectations raised by what he had already seen of her behaviour in the boat and by the reflection that it must have been her brother who had taught her the art.

So by and by they came to the tall black gates of Trigg's Lock which, throwing a dark shadow over the dead water of the pool, made it look so gloomy and deep that he felt sure that, had they upset, they all would have certainly been drowned. And here they had to decide whether to go through, or to turn off up the backwater to the right. Generally it was the latter way they chose, and as at his warning cry the two others shipped their sculls and ducked their heads, and the boat, shooting on between the low piles of a narrow wooden foot-bridge, left the river proper behind, it seemed as if they had all at once entered a domain which, like that of the Sleeping Beauty, was under a spell. The stream, black and sluggish, scarce appeared to move; the only sound you heard was the faint cloop of the water that the boat in its passage sent washing against the hollowed banks; and overhead an arch of moveless leaves, of emerald translucence, gave to the sunlight as it passed through a faint green tinge such as no doubt it had in those coral caves at the bottom of the sea where dwelt the mermaids and mermen of story. Nor was he the only one, as it appeared, to feel the influence of the scene. Els, resting on his oars, was dreamily watching the drops that fell at intervals from their blades, of which, though each on the instant of its falling, merged in the general surface of the stream, there was yet a succession quick enough to occupy the eye; and even the restless Nita, now erect in the bows, was as motionless as a carved figure-head. Indeed with Hector the collie in an attitude of attention at her feet, she might well, he thought, have passed for the Britannia of their small vessel with her watchful lion. Only from time to time, as necessary on this side or on that to give a stroke, the scull that, like a trident, she held upright in her outstretched hand, would be noiselessly dropped into the water, and again as quickly taken out; and once, looking back over her shoulder, she spoke to Els; as she turned her head her curls went round.

Presently, as up that mysterious arcade with a motion at once imperceptible and noiseless, they glided on, the current began to run clearer and swifter, clots of foam went hurrying by, the noise of the weir that had been at first but a distant murmur, grew momentarily louder, and, turning a corner, they came out into the Lasher Pool. 'Rowling Bay,' as it was called on the old cracked yellow map of the estate which hung in the Justice-Room; one of Nita's ancestors had brought the invention out of Brabant. And here they pulled in to shore at a clump of alders that grew aslant the stream; their lower branches yet were stuck with the dried and muddy weeds that had been hung upon them by the winter's floods; and tying up the boat, they had their tea. And while high above their heads out of sight a lark was singing, and close at hand the tumbling waters of the weir came down with a ceaseless slumberous rush, he watched now the interchanging network of wavy lines of light that went flickering along the varnished side of the boat, and now through the water, which was so clear that they seemed to be supported on nothing, the shadows that moved over the brown pebbles below – repetitions on a smaller scale of those he had seen passing across the slopes of the Downs. But at length Nita, leaning back, put her arms behind her head and stretched herself and yawned, and Els, waking from his doze among the cushions, observed it must surely be time to be going home.

The painter, however, with which the boat had been secured, had become so sodden that it was impossible to get it undone and start till Nita, kneeling down, managed to loose it with her teeth: perhaps her brother's in old days had been as pretty, otherwise he had never certainly seen any half so milk-white regular and strong; while the way in which she worried the knot vaguely recalled some delightful little animal. But even then there was still the boat to be pulled up the bank and launched again above the weir. Els, for his part, much disliked the 'beastly fag' that was thus entailed, but it was what Nita seemed most to enjoy. Taking her place at the bows, sometimes, driving her heels into the ground and leaning back, she would tug at the rope with might and main; and sometimes, facing about and putting it over her shoulder, with all the weight of her small body thrown forward, she would haul. As for Jaspar, though now indeed always a little ashamed of so childish a taste, he was still as fond as ever of anything that afforded him a chance of imagining he was some character he had read of; and this carrying up of the boat from backwater to river reminded him of a Canadian portage; while, when at last they reached the top, and, after a moment's rest, began to push it through the thick tall flags, he would fancy himself a great explorer, Johnston for instance, discovering a stream on which no white man ever yet had launched.

And so at last they set out upon their journey home, Nita once more steering while Els lay on his back in the cushioned bows and let him scull alone. But the arrangement was one he was by no means inclined to grumble at, since it left him free to regulate their pace as he liked. The slower he went the better he was pleased, since only so could the regular rub-rub of the oars in the rowlocks, their rhythmical plash and tiny gurgle produce on him their usual lulling effect, and dispose him to one of those waking dreams he was so fond of, in which it was always his effort to confound people and scenery, and make both serve merely to produce one general vague impression. Nor did he ever meet with better success than when the sun, as now it sloped to the west, would flush the child's face celestial rosy-red, and lighting up the clear brown depths of her eyes – as but a little while before it had illumined those of the water – seem to make her in some sort of kin to the brimming silver river and the green meadows whose grass-fringed edges it lipped, and to the alders and flickering aspens and tall spikes of purple loose-strife whose reflections glowed wherever the current in the shadow of the withy-beds ran still and dark. There was, Moreover, in his thought yet another bond between her and them, in the fact that these same flowers and trees belonged at that moment to her race almost as much children of the soil as they, as for the last, – how many hundred years was it without a break? – those that had preceded them in their places had been their heritage who had preceded her in hers. So slower and slower his sculls rose and fell and, lingeringly sweeping back, dragged after them, trailing and swishing and fluttering, the long weeds in which they caught. But at last he stopped rowing altogether: it appeared to him as if, in thus resigning all attempt at independence, he had got rid of the only obstacle that up to then had prevented them from being at one with the scenery through which they were moving. So presently they came in sight of the tall white sentinel-posts that stood, up to their waists in water, in a line across the weir stream, and Els raised a long-drawn cry of 'Lock.' To him it always sounded like a lament for the dying day, and the melancholy it never failed to inspire was rather increased by the thought that he could not expect to enjoy for ever that state of absolute content in which every sense of soul and body had for the past few weeks been steeped than diminished by the knowledge that there were still many days before him as lovely, as happy and as long as that whose end he was then regretting. So they passed in and the lock-gates shut-to at their backs, and, while the momentarily increasing pressure behind made the old timbers creak and groan, with a noise from every side of dripping and pouring water, the boat sank gradually down. At last it stopped, and slowly, one after the other, as the old man above pushed backward against the handles, the sodden and moss-grown gates revolved and, like the doors of some giant triptych, discovered the landscape beyond and let them through.

Once out, Els again took his place in the bows, and they settled themselves to start afresh; yet still for a moment Jaspar held his sculls suspended in mid-air and indeed was only at last induced by an impatient cry from Els to drop them in and so shatter, as it were, the mirror in which the delicate pink and blue of the sky above was so tranquilly reflected. And now their sculls began to slap over the water and the boat at every stroke seemed to make a leap; the willows bent, waving white before the breeze that had sprung up and the river, of a dull lead colour, instead of twinkling, as before, and flashing in the sun, was flawed by the gusts which went sweeping over it. Nita, who had put on her brother's covert-coat, as once she caught his eye, drew in her chest, hunched up her shoulder and, laughing, rubbed her ear against the velvet collar she had turned up.

# CHAPTER XXI

Often however Els had things to do which he liked better than going out on the river with Nita and him, and then, not caring to take the boat by themselves, they two would wander off together on long rambles about the Chase. Indeed, so much accustomed to coming out with him in the afternoon did the child presently grow, that whenever after lunch he happened to remain in his bedroom longer than she considered was necessary to give him time to fetch his hat, she would run up and thump at his door.

'You can't catch me!' she would cry, jumping back as he opened it, and so flew off. And along the endless-seeming corridors they raced, their shouts and laughter and the noise of their hurrying footfalls on the bare oak boards disturbing for an instant the profound solitude in which for the most part were left the pictures of the former inhabitants that from the dark panelled walls looked down on them as they tore past. He always let her reach the bottom of the stairs without being caught, where, indeed, out of breath, she would stop of her own accord, and, pretending not to want to let him pass, stretch out her small arms, take hold of the banisters on either side, and brace herself to resist his efforts to get by.

'You are a weak Tommy!' she would cry, as he pretended to be doing his best to make her leave go, and so gave way, and, followed by him, went out into the stable-yard. Here, while she stopped to speak to Jumbo, who was poking out his nose over the half-door of the loose-box, he, behind, leant back on his stick and looked about. Up to then the only stables he had seen had been the lean-to shed in which the old white pony was kept at Telscombe; yet, though it would thus have been but natural that these should have struck him as immense, they did not seem to be a bit too big for such a place as Tremlett; and, as he looked, he grew as proud at the reflection that he was living in the midst of such magnificence as if he had been Els and had owned it all. Two sides of the vast quadrangle were taken up partly with harness-rooms and such-like offices, in part with what their great double doors announced as coach-houses; the other two were entirely stables – or so at least he judged from their semi-circular windows high up in the wall, and their doors with those awkward ringed handles he always found so hard to open. From one of these latter two grooms were at that moment leading out Lady Adelaide's favourite bays to put them to in the barouche which was already out in the yard; their traces dangled, stiff-knotted, at their sides, their hoofs clattered and trampled on the cobble-stones.

And then Nita was ready, and they started, Hector barking, plunging about them and waving his tail, but soon settling down into a happy trot; it was almost as pleasant to see his knicker-bockered legs going on in front, as to watch Nita's short skirt swing as she walked and the wind in a sort of cadence lift her hair from her shoulders and again let it fall. Generally they went first to the lake. As they came down the slope the two swans, perceiving their approach, made toward them, breasting the water aside as in a series of little rushes they pushed on their way. In a few moments, however, one or other, anxious to outstrip its companion and get first to the bank, would raise itself half out of the water, and, beating the surface rapidly with its wide white wings and uttering an angry cry, come rushing on to where he and Nita were standing waiting with the bread. Then, their pockets emptied, they would leave the birds still worrying the last crusts under water with their beaks, and so go on towards the Golden Gates by which you pass into Hail Mary Wood, and thence on into the Chase. And as they went along the wide belt of turf that, studded at intervals with great tufts of pampas-grass, stretches between the path and the stockaded bank, 'Look,' would Nita cry, and point toward the lilies here, close into shore, so thick that their glistening leaves for want of room to lie out flat were all turning up one another's edges; 'look at that yellow-hammer over there!' and as she clapped her hands the bird would rise, and, with a dipping flight, disappear over some flags.

But indeed, as they wandered together over the Chase, now under the lichen-dappled beeches of Solomon's Mound, now under red-scaled pines knee-deep in bracken, where the dry slippery ground crunched under their feet as they went up; and now again in some little open dell scattered with sombre yews and may-trees overgrown with honeysuckle and blackberry, she was for ever crying out to him to look at something or other which, but for her sharp eyes, he would have missed; at a rabbit as it skirried away, its white scut glancing up and down, or some deer as, startled, they tripped off and stopped and stood at gaze. And this keen interest on her part in things about which he thought no girl would either have known or cared, presently confirmed him in that fancy he had at first conceived on the river, that she had in her something of a boy. And once this notion had taken hold of him, there was nothing, from the way she went scrambling about to that in which she whistled to Hector, that did not seem but another proof that he was right. Even her dress, as in the boat so now, contributed to this effect, for her thick boots with their brass hooks and thongs of leather looked, especially when covered with mud, exactly like those that Els had worn when they had played football together long ago. But indeed it was always of her brother that she reminded him; not of the brother he had known in more recent times, but rather of that young Prince Charming his fond imagination had already begun to insist had been his friend in those far-off Scarisbrick days. For though not nearly so good-looking, she had yet the same broken eyebrows which in him he had been so fond of and the same laughing eyes; even the few tiny freckles which Els had had and which had exercised upon him such a curious charm, were now reproduced in her and with the same effect. He compared them fantastically to those that speckled the warm apricots upon the long south wall. It was true that it was framed in heavy curls, this face which was so troublingly like that of the boy to whom, a boy, he had been devoted; but even this was not enough to persuade him of her being really a girl, for Elsie's lovelocks in the theatricals had been as long; and it was only when he helped her over some many-barred and bramble-topped gate or some battlemented clinker-built paling of grey rattling oak, and felt how small and pliant was her waist and how meltingly soft her dress, that he knew her not to be of his own sex. But this was not a thing that often happened, for if she could she would always jump; and then, more than ever, she reminded him of her brother, snatching off, like him, her cricket-cap and crumpling it in her little clenched fist as, setting her face, she took her run. For her language, that too, like everything else about her, had in it something of both sexes, and he found an extraordinary charm in hearing her at one time talk like a small girl and at another make use of such very boyish expressions as 'beastly,' and 'jolly,' and 'stalky,' 'feign I!' and 'no fear!' Nor while thus perpetually comparing his present relations with her to those that had once existed between him and her brother, did he forget that, still now as then, he could enjoy the consciousness that his intellect was, as he phrased it, 'stooping its lofty crest' before one in every way its inferior. And ever since he could remember anything it had been a favourite notion with him, this, of strength obeying weakness and one which several times he had carried into execution. It was a matter of indifference whether, as the former, he voluntarily submitted to the caprice of one who was pretty and younger and weaker than he, or played this latter part himself, supplying by force of character and what else he could, that which he wanted in good looks.

Yet, fond as he was of his child-companion, he was scarce less so of the Chase they thus roamed about together, and every day discovered in it, as in her, some fresh delight and beauty. The fact that it was one of the oldest in the kingdom, and that since first afforested, none but a Southwood had ever been master within its bounds, called up still more of those historic memories of which the whole place seemed so provocative, and was by itself enough to lend it a charm beyond any to which its mere natural beauty, great though that was, would in his eyes have entitled it; just as the peace of its glades, though no deeper than that he had so often found on the Downs, gave him by so much a greater pleasure, as there it needed only for any one to wish to break in on it for them to be able to do so, while here it was inviolable and might be enjoyed by none but he. And not only, If old tales were true, had it in its origin been formed by the most violent means, but within its verge the forest laws had for centuries been administered with such cruelty as might have been expected of a race whose present representative was as fond of sport as Els. And the knowledge that this was so, gave him a like sense of satisfaction as that he had when he followed Nita through the offices, and, seeing all the servants at their work, realised how many had to toil to let the great ones of the earth live that life he found it so agreeable to share.

In the house itself there was hardly a corner his imagination did not make the scene of some event that, ordinary enough perhaps at first, was by lapse of time become invested with that glamour which, for him, surrounded the past: and here there was not a spot from that high green wall, the Long Walk, which, stretching away on either hand far as the eye could see, went marching up and down across the Chase and at every turn kept barring the view, to the tiniest dell or glade, whose beauty was not enhanced in his eyes by the reflection that perhaps it had witnessed a death. He was really quite indifferent whether it had been verderer or deer-stealer whose heart's-blood once had soaked that now innocent turf, or on whose glazing eyes those elms and oaks and beeches and those bracken-covered slopes had been the last objects impressed, since in either case the sacrifice had been made for the pleasure's sake of him who was lord of it all and so in the end for his. And whereas, indoors, the fact that the setting was of one special age had contrasted with the characters, here, in the open air, the trees and grass were of whatever times the scene was laid in and contemporary with figures of all periods. But one particular spot there was of which he was specially fond; it was where a few slight ridges in the turf marked what tradition asserted to be the site of the largest of the villages destroyed by the ancestor of the child then trotting at his side. No doubt the inhabitants, bending under such household-stuff as they had been able to save, had plodded off along the very path which he and she were at that moment following; and no doubt as they looked back and saw the smoke and flames from their burning cottages mounting above the trees they had shaken their fists in the direction of Tremlett and called down curses on the head of its lord and all his race. He laughed to himself as he reflected on their folly in believing it of any use to appeal from the injustice of their fellow-men to a being who only existed in their dislike to think that their wrongs would never meet with redress. For their oppressor's posterity were still flourishing in wealth and honour on the lands once theirs, and the very act of spoliation which had stripped them of everything now served to give an additional halo of romance to his place and name. It was another proof in support of his opinion that one must depend upon oneself alone. Since all mankind was divided into spoilers and spoiled, it was to the former that for his part he would seek to belong; but in any case he would never try to console himself for being last in this world by imagining he would be first in the next.

Sometimes, crossing the river, sideways, in Indian file, by the lock-gates, Nita and he would make their way to Bower's Mill: for her part she always went prying about, climbing the steep rickety stair, plunging her bared arms into the bins of soft flour, or, up in the top loft, punching the fat white sacks which, leaning one against another, were standing ready there to be slid down the loose-hanging board into the barges below: but he, resting his elbows on the sill of the little window, would lean out and dreamily watch the revolving wheel; it was so close that he could, he thought, almost have touched it with his hand. And by and by, lulled by the heavy rumble of the mill-stones grinding overhead, and the ceaseless plash of the water which showered from the huge wheel as it came up, and dizzy with trying to follow the paddles going one after another swiftly by, he lost all sense of reality and became a part of what he heard and saw. Now and again a puff of air, fresh with the damp weedy odour of the tail-water, would caress his cheek in the same curious soft way as used to do upon the Downs the summer-breeze.

And sometimes they made their goal a certain gamekeeper's lodge called Pricklet's Hatch which stood at the most distant of all the entrances into the Chase. Often indeed they would have their tea there, sitting together in the valanced ingle-nook and eating off one plate put between them on the settle; and now Nita would hang over her ear for earring two cherries on one stalk, and, with an air that suddenly recalled her brother, turn her head to let him see; and would now, a child, trace patterns on the plate with the Golden Syrup the keeper's wife had brought out to do them honour. At their feet in the midst of a little heap of grey wood-ashes almost as soft to the touch as the flour down at the mill, still glowed the remains of the fire; and if you stooped forward and looked up you saw the sky at the top of the chimney; the daylight that descended gave a curious blue tinge to the soot.

But where they liked best of all to go was Bartley Water, the tiny brawling trout-stream that winds across the Chase and falls at length into the river at Rowling Bay; and specially were they fond of that reach, if it may so be called, which begins at the north boundary of Hindleap Walk. Here, on the sloping bank, within view of the bridge, side by side they would sit and, pulling off their shoes and stockings, step down into the brook. It was always she who went the first, at every moment turning round to look at him and laugh as, with his flannel trousers pulled up as far as they would go above his knees, he came picking his way along behind. And often she would sway and nearly fall, partly through the rush of the current, and in part because of the difficulty of keeping her footing on the slippery stones; indeed, if you did not wish to hurt your feet, you had to tread only upon such as were covered with a soft growth of weed. And up and down went the bubbles on their way and the water would gurgle against her legs, that, but a moment before so white, now looked as brown as the dim round pebbles at the bottom. As for Hector, he had followed them in as far as he had dared, but at length, grown frightened of being carried off his feet, had turned, despite their cries gone plunging back towards the bank, and now was shaking himself over their stockings and shoes; his tail in especial flourished a shower of sparkling drops. So presently with tussocks of earth and grass wrenched away from the banks, and stones scrabbled up from the bed, they made a dam and the water below now was shallowing into pools. Yet still for a while they busied themselves in stopping up the holes that, now here now there, the pressure of the stream behind, every moment growing more strong, kept forcing in their embankment; but at last, when already it was being overflowed, Nita, scrambling out, held on by his hand and, leaning over, with the tip of her outstretched toe, broke away a bit at the top and so let the water rush through.

And hence, pickaback, he would carry her, still barefooted and bare-legged, himself the same, to the cascade some hundred yards above; and here, at the foot of a moss-grown beech of which one long and slender tufted branch now and again bent down towards the stream to kiss its reflection that swayed up to meet it, she, exclaiming she was 'awfully fagged,' would throw herself down upon the ground, and, cuddling Hector to her, and laying her little cheek against his cold black nose, begin to talk to him who in response would slightly wag his tail. From time to time Jaspar would make a remark, and she would turn her head in his direction, her lower lip, red and pouting, slightly dropped. But soon, not only did he cease to speak, but even, except in the vaguest way, to think, surrendering himself wholly to the dreamy delights of a sort of trance. Overhead, near and yet far, the multitudinous murmur of that sea of leaves now swelled and swelled, and now as gradually died again away; and at his feet with a continuous rushing noise the stream went over the fall, and, flickering with a crystalline tinkle over its bed, disappeared round the corner. And while thus through his ear his brain was lulled into a kind of doze, his eye contributed to the same effect, being dazed by seeing the water going always slipping, slipping, smoothly and swiftly motionless as though of glass, over the ledge of big grey stones that formed the cascade; where it cleft the stream below was a line of foam.

It would be late before they got back, and often he would scarce have time to dress for dinner; yet even then more often than not he was interrupted by hearing the child calling to him from the terrace below, and he would have to join in a game of catch with a tennis-ball which, overhand like a boy, she would throw up. It was always either shooting past him into the darkening room behind, or falling short and sticking among the roses with which the outside wall was here thick overgrown. Nor was even this the last he saw of her; for as he hurried down to dinner, he would hear a cry of 'good-night,' and, looking up, would see her leaning over the banisters of the landing above. Her hair had fallen forward on either side her face, and over the edge of the floor was just projecting the pointed tip of one little patent-leather shoe.

Now and again however he would so far awake from the sort of dream into which he had sunk as, with a vague feeling of uneasiness, to wonder what the others thought of the way in which he was thus always going about with the child. To Els, who more than once had inquired in great surprise what was the use of a girl of that age, he gave all kinds of reasons except the true: – that he liked to be with her. He was ashamed to confess to so innocent a taste. As for Lady Adelaide, she would declare that it was really most good of him so to bother himself with a little girl. And to her, though indeed uncertain whether there might not lurk something of sarcasm in her words, he would murmur some vague reply which, while avoiding the dangers of positive assertion, might yet be enough to induce her to think that what he did was done out of a desire to repay in some slight degree the many kindnesses received at her hands; for after all, he might as well, if he could, get thanked for what in truth he did for no one's pleasure but his own.

And when he could, he would pass the mornings also in Nita's company. He first had found his way to the Schoolroom through hearing, as he walked early on the Terrace, from an open window of the upper floor the sound of scales. From the deliberate and painstaking manner in which the notes were being picked out, it could, he had felt sure, be none other than Nita practising, and, returning indoors, he had followed the sound.

'I'm not interrupting you, am I?' he said as he came in.

'Oh, but I like interruptions!' she replied.

And encouraged by this assurance, he was presently always going up to her room. Stretching herself at length on the broad cushioned window-seat, her heels in the air knocking together, she would put her book down in front, plant her elbows upon either side, push her outspread fingers through her hair, and stop her ears and knit her eyebrows with a little mowe of determination that never failed to afford him great delight. And, from where he sat at the farther end of the seat, he would look, now at her, and now, through the casement pushed open on its semi-circle of iron, into the garden below, or, about the room, at the rows of Illustrateds whose gilded backs filled the bookcase opposite; and the paper with its daisies and everywhere-repeated motto: *Si douce est la marguerite*. And he would think of all the children of whom history told as having been beloved by famous men; of the Fair Geraldine whom Surrey had seen a child on the steep orchard-slopes of the Round Tower moat at Windsor; of Stella Devereux to whom Astrophel Sidney had given his devotion while still she was no more than twelve; and of Laura whom Petrarch had loved by the fountain of Vancluse as he Nita on the banks of Bartley Water. Or he would try to finish the copy of verses with which the stream had inspired him:

> 'Pure river whose pellucid wave
>   Flows rippling to the sea
> By moor and fell thou coursest on
>   How dear thy stream to me!
>
> Ah, would that winter never were!
>   That summer suns e'er shone!
> Then – then – then – '

Or, taking up her chipped lacquer box, he would begin idly turning over the odds and ends inside, only presently to be constrained to set it down by her evident anxiety as to the safety of its treasures; that she seemed to set the greatest store by was a certain little bit of cedar pencil which, in its dints and nibbles, showed how often it had been bit by her small sharp teeth. And then he would fall to undoing the little knot of ribbon that tied her hair at the top. But she, for the moment intent upon her lesson, grew impatient at being thus disturbed, and shook her head with so petulant an air as not only to make him at once desist from his attempt, but to drive him away in dudgeon to the arm-chair at the other end of the room. He had not however been there many minutes before she came after him with her book.

'I say, tell us what this word is!' she said.

'Which?' he asked, trying in vain to make it out among all the small fingers she put on the page at once.

And so he began to translate – for all the world as he had done for Els at school – while she, perching on the arm of his chair, and passing one small warm arm round his neck, peered over his shoulder. Her hair, falling forward as she bent her head, softly brushed his cheek.

# CHAPTER XXII

But of all the days in the week, still as at Scarisbrick and Bridwell, it was Sunday that he liked best. In the morning they all went to church, walking thither down the long broad path that leads from the house straight across the garden to the lych-gate; beyond again, framed by the meeting boughs of its lime-avenue, you saw the small squat-tower with its broach-spire of shingles. The bells at every step they took rang louder and louder till at last their sound became for a moment merged in one general clash, and then, as they passed in underneath, sank into a muffled din. Jaspar always enjoyed their procession up the nave: it was that of a queen and her court. Lady Adelaide went first, her hand lightly resting among the curls that fell on Nita's shoulders. The gesture was one which never failed strangely to move him, not only as in itself beautiful but as flattering his pride in the gentle birth that, while letting him despise the rabble, at the same time enabled him to consider himself, if not so lucky in such details as wealth and rank as people like the Tremletts, still, in the most essential particular, their equal; for it showed that the feelings for her children of a mother of his own Brahmin caste were as much finer than those entertained towards their brats by the common women who filled the pews on either hand as were her features and her hands, her figure and her dress than theirs. And as he walked behind, careful to keep at such a distance as should be most proper, having due regard no less to his own rank than to hers, his back straightened and his chest swelled at the notion of being thus seen by the whole village in attendance on her who to them was a sovereign-princess; and all the time he would be trying to compose his features to such an expression as, while at once significative of his superiority to those who were doubtless looking at him, and of the exact position he occupied towards Lady Adelaide, should be also suited to one who knew that he was taking part in a great ceremony of a religion in which for reasons of state he must affect belief.

And as in house and garden and Chase everything seemed to be always telling of the glory and honour and power and might of the Southwoods; so was it here too the same in a building where there ought by rights to have been nothing but what spoke of God. The vicar himself could not wear his surplice and hood without a chaplain's scarf of their livery colours of red and white, as though to show him as much their servant as the Almighty's. It carried back his mind to the days when people as proud and well-born as he had not thought scorn to fill offices about the persons of Lady Adelaide's predecessors that now were held by common servants; but his manner towards her gracefully revived the memory of those bygone times. And in the traceried windows amongst all the Christs and saints with their haloed heads and brilliant loosely-trailing robes appeared, glowing in the same colours, argent and gules, the Southwood arms; which, carved again in wood and stone, were everywhere repeated, on corbels and poppy-heads, and with the Sponge and Nails, the Scourge and Crown of Thorns on the very font.

But chiefly was it the monuments that rendered it difficult to think of anything but these Southwoods who even in the grave still were pompous and splendid. One was actually within the communion-rails: a white marble statue in his habit as he had lived of the viscount who, so the inscription upon the pedestal at length set forth, had been 'Master of the Household to her late Majesty Queen Anne of Ever Glorious Memory.' But most were in the Tremlett Aisle which was really so crowded that it seemed impossible for another, however small, to be squeezed in. Here, on its back, on a low slab, lay the effigy in Purbeck marble of a knight whose identity had indeed been long forgotten, but whom the charges of his convex shield still proclaimed one of the dominant race; nor was he, as you mostly found them, out-stretched in the repose of death, but kept in his violently contracted brows and in every limb, even in his crossed legs, that symbol of easy rest, an animation of furious resistance: he appeared indeed rather to be drawing than sheathing his sword, and the very dog at his feet in the gathering up of all his muscles for a spring displayed the same extraordinary and savage energy. And there, put away on shelves, one over another, were the painted alabaster figures of some later members of the family, the women in ruff and farthingale, the rigidity of which seemed more in the things themselves than in the stone, the men in habergeon and huge stuffed-out trunk-hose. In the roll of the pillow upon which the elbow of one was stiffly propped – just where one puts one's handkerchief when one goes to bed – was neatly tucked a little skull. Close by, facing each other across a desk, knelt a father and mother: behind her, ranged all according to their height, the daughters of the marriage: behind him, the sons. Jaspar wished that *his* forefathers had had such monuments set up to *them*. Their omission to do so was the more to be regretted since it was one which could never in any circumstances be repaired. As it was he could only try to think that in a sense these were *his* ancestors as well: at any rate there was always the chance that, like the old Roman poet – what was his name? – whom the Metelli had admitted to the honours of their tomb-house, he might one day be brought back and laid below among those in the midst of whose memorials he then was standing.

And as he never could get over his surprise at the way both Lady Adelaide and Els accepted as the most natural thing in the world a position of which to him the advantages appeared so great that not even for a moment did he forget that very small part of them which fell to his share as a guest: so here he was always wondering how they managed not to be oppressed by the thought of how brief was their time for its enjoyment. Had he been in their place he felt certain that whenever his eye had caught the square flag in the middle of the floor, he would have been reminded of that day so soon to come when it would be raised for him, and in his turn, nailed in his coffin, feet foremost he would be carried down to make one more in the silent company that filled the dark vault beneath. Nor could he have come there on Sundays without his pleasure in all he would have had being nearly spoilt – or would it rather be fearfully enhanced? – not so much by a knowledge of what lay hid below as by a vision which, riving open the pavement at his feet, would have shown him the hideous masses of corruption or little handfuls of dust that was all remaining of those who, once as full of life as he, were now what he must soon become. As for the ignoble dead they, very properly, were out of doors; you saw their graves on either side the path, marked by a simple headstone or long board, or by nothing perhaps but a mound of grass.

And as it was this exercise of their old seigneurial *droit de sepulture* – he liked to think that his reading could illustrate the present with examples drawn from another country and age – by which the dead

Southwoods were preserved from any contact with vulgar ashes; so was it the *droit de banc* that enabled them, living, to avoid association with any less noble than themselves, the Tremlett Aisle where they sat being not only separated from the main body of the church by a screen of elaborate tabernacle-work all cusps and battlements, but raised on a sort of daïs two or three feet above the level of the rest of the building. It was only proper that any petitions which they might choose to put up should mount to the Throne of Grace unhustled by those of their dependants. But indeed he delighted altogether in this pride of prayer; for if it did not quite enable one to think that, like the king of Thrace whom Montaigne tells of, one had a god of one's own, at least it seemed to give one the *entrée* with Him whom one had to share with the fool-multitude.

But for the most part, while acknowledging that, had he been born to such a goodly heritage as Els, he would have adored, like him, his father's god and property; his pride, not finding sufficient food in such superiority as he had of birth, took refuge in the reflection that in force of intellect at least he surpassed, not only the baser part of the congregation, but those from the Great House as well; and that he had had strength of mind to burst the swaddling-clothes of a belief in which every one else, he could see, still was fast bound. It was true no doubt that he had not yet been able to bring himself to give up the old fetich-prayer of *Domine, in manus tuas* which, ever since he could remember anything, he had been used to murmur before falling asleep; but this was merely of a piece with his other trick of looking under the bed before getting in: they were both precautions, the one against ghostly dangers, the other against those of flesh and blood, which he liked to keep up, not so much from any belief in their effi-cacy as because, without giving him much trouble in the present, they might one day – who could tell? – be of use. In every other respect he had long got rid of his belief, and it was really nothing but the fact of the word 'atheist' having such an ugly sound that prevented him from openly avowing his infidelity. And presently, as he gazed about, it seemed to him as if this assurance of being intellectually above the rest of the congregation gained additional strength from the fact that the estrade on which he stood raised him above them physically as well, and he felt as if he were looking down from what was in a double sense a vantage-ground at the errors and wanderings and mists and tempests in the vale below. Nor was the prospect with pity, but rather with swelling and pride, as he thought how weak, compared to his, must be their minds, which thus could hold their faith for true, despite the fact that every age and race since the world began had believed the like of theirs. Indeed, so pleased with himself did he become that he was actually on the point of thanking God he was not as others were, and did not, like them, drink from the muddy pool of conformity and tradition, when, just in time, it struck him that it would be too absurd to profess himself grateful to a Being in whose existence he declined to believe, for not believing, and, laughing to himself, stopped short. But the next moment, noticing the fervour with which Lord Augustus was joining in with the shrill voices of the village choir, he fell to doubting whether he might not after all be wrong, and whether he would not do better to believe a religion of whose truth one so much older and more distinguished than he was evidently so convinced.

Then his glance wandered to where Nita was standing beside an altar-tomb on the ledge of which she had put her books by one of the kneeling angels, who, headless though they were, still swung their censers at the feet of her ancestor's recumbent effigy. Against the wall hung a board with an inscription in quaint thin letters of faded gold on a ground of black:

'To the Pious and Beloved Memory of Anita Southwood whose Body lies interred in the Vault below, while her Soule lives in the Felicities of Heaven and her Honored Memorie in the Register——'

And, as she moved her head, he could read the last words:

'of Fame.'

It was the epitaph of her namesake and ancestress whose portrait in the Matted Gallery was one of those he in especial loved to gaze at, and the 'Register of Fame' was De Grammont's *Memoirs*. Through the wide open-work brim of the child's hat the light, he thought, struck on her face much after the same fashion as in their rambles he had so often seen it do through the trees on the turf, dappling it with the prettiest effects of light and shade. Her hair, escaping from behind, flowed on to her shoulders in waves that went up and down like those of Bartley Water where it passed over the pebbles that strewed its bed below the fall; her eyes were cast down and there was nothing to be

seen of them but their lashes, almost as long and curling as her brother's; her small chin half disappeared in the soft creamy folds of what
he called her steen-kirk; and every now and again through the open
door would come a puff of wind, gently rustling the pages of her
book and stirring those fine threads of hair which remained too light,
it appeared, to need support, loose on the surface of the others; while
the tree outside the window would sway and its leaves, transparent in
the sun as those that overarched the backwater, would come tapping
against the panes. He tried to distinguish her voice among the rest, as
in old days in Chapel at Bridwell he remembered to have listened for
her brother's. And as then he had wanted Els to take the Communion
with him, so now he liked to fancy that this going together to church
added the sanction of religion to their friendship, and knit them one
to the other after a sort which bore the same relation to the Marriage
Service as did their constant companionship to that of husband and
wife. As they went out he would glance at the dry and broken stoup
in the porch-wall, and wish they had been Papists; then he would have
offered her holy-water after the fashion of the gallants of old; the
action was one which had always appealed to him as blending religion
and love in such a way that one could hardly tell to whom the homage
was paid, to God or to one's lady.

But fond as he was of Sunday mornings, he enjoyed even more the
afternoons, which he and Nita always spent together in the garden.
And while with knees together and toes turned in she bent over her
book as she sat in her wicker-chair, he from the depths of his, his head
sunk back into the yielding cushions, lazily, with half-closed eyes, sur-
veyed the scene. Through the arch opposite he looked down a long
grass-walk to where, at the end of the vista, the Spinario, gleaming
white against a semi-circle of clipped laurel, leaned with an intent
air over his uptwisted foot; but everywhere else a high yew hedge,
sharp-angled and close and straight as a wall, encompassed them
about; against its darker green from the vivid emerald of the smooth
turf sloped up in a bank of variegated colour a wide border of old-
fashioned flowers; the quaint grace of their names appeared to him
at once to fit and double their charm; out in the middle two great
mulberry-trees, their aged limbs only kept from sinking to the ground
by crutches, sheets of tin over the wounds where some big branch at
last had given way, littered with their fruit the grass beneath and supported, hanging crescent-shaped between them, Nita's Mexican ham-

mock that was 'a pal to her pony'; on the table close at hand the silver of the tea-things gleamed, here among the trees and grass and flowers, after a fashion quite other than indoors; and everything together formed a picture that not only satisfied his eye, but enabled him to enjoy in its highest degree that peculiar form of cultured idleness on which he so prided himself as suiting one who was simultaneously artist, philosopher, and grand seigneur.

And as at Bridwell a garden, of a summer Sunday afternoon, had always disposed him to philosophise; so was it the same here too; and he would presently begin to ask himself how it was composed, this general effect, that the scene as a whole produced. Of course each item of the composition had a definite value of its own, but he inclined to fancy that all these various causes might be referred to one original: the wealth the Southwoods had for so many generations enjoyed. It was that doubtless which had let the hedge become so high and thick as now to seem to be keeping at a distance all the heat and noise and hurry and stress of the outside world; which had brought a hammock from the other side of the Atlantic to be the summer-toy of a little girl; and had allowed more money to remain locked up in china and silver than his Guardian earned in a year. Its presence could even be traced in the bread and butter and tea and cake, that not only were far more delicious than anything of the kind he had ever tasted before, but were provided in quantities which did not, as at the Rectory, announce the fact that every penny was of consequence; and time itself to which he would have conceived it impossible to submit otherwise than did everybody else, somehow seemed different here when measured, not by the loud and hurried ticking of a cheap American clock, but by the noiseless moving of the sun round the bronze plate of a carved marble dial.

Yet, while attributing to money its due share in the total result, he told himself he must not forget the intention that originally had dictated its expense. There was not a thing on which his eyes rested but what was the realisation more or less complete of the ideal of beauty and comfort and state of each successive generation of owners; and the witness too of their joys and sorrows, hopes and fears: he used to fancy that in this double capacity all he saw had a life of its own.

So the shadows stretched longer and longer across the grass; over the top of the hedge the broken outline of roofs and trees showed solemnly dark against the sky; and the sleepy monotonous plash of the

water in the fountain that hitherto had been the only sound to break
the hush, now dropped into a kind of soft accompaniment to the
cawing of a flight of rooks that, high over head, were passing across to
the Wilderness elms; to the pure liquid notes that a thrush was trilling
from some bush close by; and to the bells of the church at the other
end of the garden that now began to ring. And from his mood of the
earlier afternoon these signs of parting day carried him into a romantic melancholy; and he fell to crooning to some half-remembered tune
the 'Wenn sich lau,' out of his *Faust*, but presently stopped to listen to
the faint sound of voices singing to the organ, now the *Nunc Dimittis*
– it always seemed to him that the last words went dying away upon
the air like a kiss – and now, 'Lead, kindly light!'

And these feelings had never been so strong as on what was not
only the last Sunday, but the last day he was to spend at Tremlett;
for his vague regrets were now made bitterly real by the necessity of
having to quit a life the pleasures of which he seemed only then to
be beginning to appreciate. For the first few weeks that he had been
there he had even longed for the hour which now was come: and
though, as one had succeeded another, little by little he had found
things more to his liking, he had still felt sure that when at length he
was 'summoned,' as he put it, 'to the field,' it would be seen that, far
from having been enervated by his sojourn in a Castle of Indolence,
he had only been rendered apter and more eager for his work by what
he rather chose to call 'a recuperative period of resolution.' It was
true that a few weeks before he had asked to be allowed to stop till
after Nita's birthday on the 20th of that very month, October; but
when his request had been refused he had set down his annoyance as
entirely due to his Guardian's stupidity at thus forcing him to begin
at once a fight which probably would only cease with his life and into
which his entrance might therefore well have been still a little delayed;
and, ceasing to take any count of time, he had abandoned himself
again to the delight of the passing hour. And now suddenly he woke
as from a dream of fairyland to find, like Thomas the Rhymer, that,
while still he felt as though only just arrived, it was long in reality
since he had come, and, what was more, that, so far from being the
readier for the battle, he was as reluctant to go forth as was Rinaldo
to leave the gardens of Armida: not that he knew whence the allusion
was, or well indeed what it meant, but the names had tickled his ears.

The next morning when they called him still, as long as he could, he lay a-bed, willing to defer, if only for a little quarter of an hour, the getting up that must put him at length within the influence of the mysterious and resistless power which from that moment onward would never let him stop till he had reached, not his journey's end abroad, but the dark and shrouded term of his life's ambitions. But at last he could delay no longer, and, with a sudden resolve, jumped up and began to dress. Nor did he so without unusual care, and likened himself the while to those state-prisoners of old days who always made such elaborate toilettes for the scaffold. Over his dressing-table, out of the wide-open window, he could see, as so often before, the shadow of the house lying sharp across the lawn still covered with a heavy autumn dew, and beyond, the laurel hedge glistened, just catching the sun; a white butterfly went fluttering up and down in front, and from the other side came the sound of the mowers whetting their scythes. But these familiar presages of a lovely day, which hitherto had only filled him with pleasurable anticipations of what the long sunny hours were bringing, now weighed on his heart with such a presentiment of unhappiness as even the fact that he was going away seemed hardly sufficient to account for.

The interval between breakfast and lunch he spent in going with Nita hand in hand to say good-bye to all their various haunts. Up to then, though often enough unhappy that he could never succeed in feeling at one with the scene, whether he tried to arrive at his end by exploring house and garden and Chase till he knew every corner, every hill, and glade, and almost every tree; or, as down by Bartley Water or at the Mill, by forcing himself into a sort of trance; still he had always been able to think that, if he failed to-day, to-morrow he might have better luck. But now he knew his desire for one that he could never hope to satisfy, and the passion that this knowledge lent it was intensified by the more than ordinary beauty of everything, for never had the shade looked so inviting nor the sky so deeply blue. And nearer and nearer drew the moment when he would have to go. Luncheon, that more than once had seemed so tedious to him, all impatience to be off with Nita, now appeared to be over in a few minutes. He had tried to eat, but hearing Lady Adelaide say something about 'to-morrow' had pushed away his plate.

'I think I'll have one!' observed Lord Augustus of some *méringues*. 'It's sudden death, I know, but I'll risk it! By the by, Addy, I didn't think much of your cutlets! I never had any I liked less!'

So presently he was at the hall-door and saying good-bye and then was just setting his foot to the high dog-cart step when Nita, running forward, half raised herself a-tiptoe, half drew down his head and, very serious, kissed his cheek. Lady Adelaide could not help laughing at this innocent display of affection, and he felt obliged himself to give a little laugh as gently he disengaged the small arms that had been flung round his neck. But at heart he was greatly moved by this woman's action done by a child. Then Els, who was already in the driver's place, a cigar in the corner of his mouth, opened the rug for him as he sprang up, the groom stepped aside from the mare's head, and as they started forward and the man ran and clambered up behind, Jaspar raised his hat with a smile, Nita, through her tears, smiled too and waved her cricket-cap, and the next moment they were round the corner and out of sight.

## CHAPTER XXIII

In the last days of the September of 1877 Jaspar quitted Bonn, where, ever since Tremlett, he had been learning German, and travelled across to Tours to do the like by French. It would have been easy had he so chosen to draw out the little excitement which naturally attended the change; but rather he sought to make it brief, as in haste to arrange himself a way of life even more regular, still more monotonous than that he had led under the shadow of the low chestnut avenues of the Poppelsdorf Allée; and he was glad to find his new surroundings such as must be of help in his attempt. For with the crucifix at the bed-head and holy-water shell – but what was it for this withered sprig of box? – and its white walls and red-tiled floor and chairs rush-bottomed like those in the churches, his low small room made actual the convent-cells he had so often read about and seemed almost to oblige him to an existence as ruled as a monk's. Nor was its outlook much other than you might have found in a real monastery, being, there, on to a garden, if so you might call it which, far too long for its breadth and shut in by high walls, had rather the appearance of a vault with its covering arches removed than of a plot of ground always spread free to the sky; while here, though indeed the window opened on to a public square, it was such as might almost have been a cloister. One whole side was taken up by the lofty dead-wall of the

Archbishop's Palace, the dreary expanse of which was only broken by the pillared entrance-gate. He was proud to find his knowledge of architecture sufficient to assign it at once to its proper Jesuit style; but something enigmatic there was besides in the very columns, so peculiar an air that you could not help falling to speculations as to the dark dreadful things which must surely go on behind. And his fancy was the more excited as the great dust-begrimed doors never opened, and even when the wicket unclosed to let in a priest or to let one out, it was only wide enough to allow of the black-cassocked figure slipping through, and then, moved by an invisible hand, instantly again it shut-to. Such must have been the gates of the Inquisition; and no otherwise had the Familiars of the Holy Office flitted in and out upon their terrible occasions. But the dark power of the Romish Church shrouded itself as of course in mystery. For the remaining sides of the *Place*, they were occupied by houses with courtyards in front, above the blank walls of which you just could see a row of shuttered attic-windows. What did they do, what were they like, the absent owners of these vast deserted hotels which, no less silent, suggested so much more than the family-tombs away on the other side of the river in the cemetery above Marmoutiers?

And not only were sound and movement both almost entirely wanting to animate the scene, but such as they were, rather appeared of a kind to accentuate than relieve its sombre character; for, apart from the occasional clapping of some *bonne's* wooden shoes over the cobblestones, scarce did you hear anything but the ringing of the convent-bell just round the corner. And every time so vividly it reminded him of school, that at length turning to account his impulse instantly to set about something fresh whenever its cracked tinkle struck on his ear, he proceeded to utilise it for the regulation of his life. It amused him to wonder to what strange popish practices it was summoning the nuns close by as him to history, to Greek or Latin, to breakfast or to go to bed. And always the last thing at night there were the alternate bugles and drums of the *retraite*. Catching its first faint sounds he would give over reading and lean back in his chair and listen as gradually they grew near and nearer, passed loudly echoing under his windows, and then, as gradually, died away and left him alone in the night-silence; if a little deeper it seemed at least more natural than that which, weighing on him with a dreadful sense of some impending evil, brooded over the whole *quartier* by day. Then one morning he woke to find his room filled with a curious reflected white light, and going to the window, saw everything covered deep with snow. The hardest winter followed, every one said, that there had been since the Invasion; and the way even the few noises there had been before now reached him dim and muffled intensified the dream-effect of his machine-like life.

But by and by as winter little by little now began at last to give place to spring, he was seized by a fever of impatience to enjoy himself before it should be too late. He was already behindhand; and really it looked as if he were going to spend his whole life in preparing to live; as if he were to be like his father, who after stinting himself for years, had died on the very threshold of the old age he had given up so much to ensure the comfort of. He never even had a chance to display the knowledge he had now – for how long was it? – been so unwillingly accumulating; and where was the good of knowing if you could not show you knew? It was monstrous he should have to be always grinding away at these beastly books; and even more infuriating to hear people praise him for his steadiness. Steady! Why, how without money could you be otherwise? They little knew who envied him his studious tastes and wished their own sons like him – little they knew how he loathed having to be for ever reading, reading, reading in provision for something that never came. Then all at once, he would remember that the more he loitered by the way, so much the later must he arrive at his journey's end, and once more he would address himself to these same books in a fury of determination.

But presently raising his head his eye would be caught by the old professor with whom he lived doddering along the path just under his window. Fancy if ever he should come to be like that, without a pleasure in life but three or four times a day, with carpet-slippered feet, to shuffle round a poky little garden and from a tin drop pinches of salt upon slugs! Rather ten thousand deaths! Not that he would object to pass his latter days in peace and a retreat, but it could only be after he had fought the good fight and had received his prize; indeed he would *like* in his declining years to plant cabbages; but as Diocletian; or to withdraw into a monastery; but as Charles v. to Yuste. He laughed as he reflected how, while he would be far away in London where the great battle of life raged hottest, whose noise had now for a long time past seemed every day to grow more loud in his ears, but which he still was only marching to; and would be hewing with his own right arm his way to victory, this silly old fellow would still be shambling along that narrow path, poor and obscure as now. Yet once perhaps he also had had ambitions. When they met at dinner he must look and see if about his mouth were the lines that always, as he had heard, marked *les ambitieux rentrés*. What if one day they should mark him? But why need he fear? Was he not, as he read his history, always coming across famous men whose qualities it was obvious he shared? And though it was no doubt true that in him either they went unrecognised or even were held for faults, it was, he could not doubt it, as with those poetic licences which, at Bridwell, had, in Horace or Virgil, found nothing but praise, but in his verses had been rewarded with impositions: while as for his never having at school been taken for anything out of the common, there were numbers in like case who in after years had yet become famous; and now it was the lives of such that more particularly he affectioned. Besides he had much reduced his demands since the time when he had thought to be a great conqueror or a crowned and sceptred king. And he laughed again as he recalled these day-dreams of an ignorant boy. Now he only asked a peerage. So, wrinkling his forehead in an effort of concentration and nodding up and down his head as under his breath he repeated a line or two of what he was reading, once more he stooped over his book.

But soon, finding that he really must have some interest in life beside his work; and desirous of changing into prayer to a definite god that vague aspiration after good success in his endeavours which, in a *bene eveniat*, his superstition recorded on the fly-leaf of all his books; he bethought him of turning to the religion of which all round were so many signs. His efforts, however, met with but little success; for while from so much as trying to reach the penetralia of the temple he was withheld by fear lest, like that old king of France, he should find himself spirited away and made a monk by force; from outside, the Popish faith, as seen at Tours, was highly repugnant to what he liked to think his sound English common-sense which could by no means away with all this fasting and confession and so often going to church. It was like these queer foreigners. In England now religion was considered out of place except on Sundays, and just a few other occasions such as Christmas Day. His sensible countrymen reserved their piety, as English officers their uniforms, only for duty, whereas these Frenchies used both every day and all day long. Moreover, these crucifixes and beads and things savoured unpleasantly of the fires Bloody Mary had lighted in Smithfield, of Cranmer's burnt right hand, and of Latimer and Ridley at the stake. Then hearing that Monseigneur, whom they were always making such a fuss about, had scarce five hundred a year, to his other sentiments with regard to the Roman Catholic faith contempt was added; surely a religion could not be much worth which gave to its archbishops no more than that. And he began to affect little airs of superiority as being of a country where bishops, let alone archbishops, received more in a month than Sa Grandeur in a year. He was only surprised that, explaining all this, his hearers did not openly confess their envy of his fortune as belonging to a nation so highly favoured, and deplore their own which had assigned them to one of such obvious inferiority. So once more with redoubled ardour he fell to work.

Now and again, of course, a moment came when he grew really too tired either to read any more or write, and then he would go down into the garden, drop into the wooden seat at the bottom, and, fixing his eyes upon the ground and keeping as near as possible motionless, his hands in his lap, try to fascinate himself into a trance. But every moment the contrast grew more unbearable between the tumultuous restlessness that made his heart beat so fast and his ears burn and his head ache, and the absolute inactivity his circumstances compelled him to, which somehow appeared increased as well as symbolised by the loose-limbed weariness of his attitude. So, jumping to his feet, he would fall to pacing up and down the path with such furious large strides as reduced the garden, small already, to the dimensions of a cage. He felt as if he could with ease have done a thousand deeds of heroism and daring. Had he had but the chance he too, like young Königsmarck, his sword between his teeth, would have swum, naked, through the midst of the battle and, alone, have boarded and taken a Turkish galley. Even if he had known how to ride – why had he not learnt when he had had a chance at Tremlett? – if even he had known how to ride he could have sprung into his saddle and galloped and galloped and galloped straight ahead, loose-reined, red-spurred, till all at once his horse, worn out, fell headlong under him. Or, but that he wanted money, he could have set off travelling; and in an instant his fancy had hurried him to the great junction of St. Pierre les Corps, and he saw the long expresses come steaming in, bound now for Paris and now again for the south; he would have liked to climb into a carriage and travel for days without stopping. But so far were his means from permitting him aught of the kind that, even with the help of such small pilferings as he could effect out of the money he got from Mrs. Binney for extra-masters and books and pens and paper, he could only contrive to save enough for an occasional day at Amboise, Chenonceaux, or Blois. For a little he tried to amuse himself with the thought that he, who was destined to act so great a part on the historic stage, was now among scenes before which in times gone by many a famous drama had been played out. But suddenly every stone would begin to cry shame on him for wasting those hours in dreams of which there was not a minute but should have brought him a little nearer his goal, and he would hurry back, resolved to work fourteen, fifteen, sixteen hours a day. And even when far too weary to understand, still, bent over his table, he would oblige himself to read on until his head dropped forward on the open page and he fell asleep.

Then one afternoon as he was going home along the Rue Royale, suddenly, face to face, he met Orr. He had given him scarce a thought since leaving Bridwell; now, simultaneously, he recollected how then he had sworn the most solemn oaths that if ever in after-life he came across him he would be horribly revenged; and found all his anger burnt out. He tried at first to rekindle the flame, but soon desisted, recognising that the last spark was dead; besides, he was ashamed of attempting what was so clearly beyond his power. Yet he could not but feel angry with himself; it was surely a mark of a weak nature, this inability to keep hate alight; though he did his best to think it rather a virtue, since the proud were seldom revengeful and the great, never. Or did he rather forget his wrongs only because he could not avenge them? And his sense of irritation was yet further increased by the fancy that still, as at Rose Hill and at Bridwell, Orr regarded him with contempt; a sentiment he for his part, as then, so now, never, try as he would, could meet with anything but admiration and envy. Nor were these feelings roused only by such physical characteristics of his old enemy's as had mere general implications, his height, for example, bull-neck, broad chest, and muscular arms, but more by those which argued moral qualities; the firm-set lips that spoke of conquests over horses and women, and the virility and decision of his gestures and walk and of the tones of his voice, inferring courage and resolution and knowledge of the world.

He found it impossible to conceal even from Orr's companions, let alone from Orr himself, what, in this last respect particularly, he knew

only too well that he lacked; but now he would maintain it a possession a Christian gentleman was far better without; and now attempt
to make up for what in practice he wanted by the enunciation of par-
adoxes of an audacity, and of theories of conduct so cynical as, he
could see, to overshoot his mark and pass belief. And while he would
be vastly put out at failing to persuade them that he really meant what
he said, or equally if they displayed no eagerness to listen; he would
be as much so when they showed their appreciation by over-persuad-
ing him to stop when he would have been gone; for, though flattered
at their desire for his society, he told himself it was altogether unworthy his character thus to be led into doing what he ought not. But he
tried to think it was only in matters of indifference that thus, against
his wiser judgment, he let himself be talked over, and that in affairs of
weight he would have known how to stand firm. And whenever, willing at once and against his will, he was carried to theatre or café, he
did his best, by affecting a serious and preoccupied air, to show how
far he was above both the amusements he was taking part in and those
he shared them with. Captious persons of course might say it had
been better done to stop at home; but how then could he have demon-
strated his superiority? And while he was hugely offended when none
took notice of his looks; if any asked what was the matter, he would
answer, 'Nothing!' but in a tone he meant to imply, 'A great deal.' He
even tried to imitate – which Henry was it? – and never smile; but
when again and again he had caught himself laughing heartily, casting
about for some device by which at once to continue his affectations
and let his nature have its way, he hit on that of giving free vent to
his mirth and then all at once checking himself and compelling his
features once more into their preoccupied expression. And so successful was the plan, so puzzled he could see were those he was with at
the abrupt manner in which thus he went from grave to gay and back
again to severe: that he was even encouraged to try still to improve his
manner of effecting the transition by practising it before his looking-
glass.

    Nor was it only that Orr himself would often carry him off; he
introduced him too to some cousins of his, Mabel Brown and her
mother who lived at the Châlet in the Impasse Heurteloup, and for a
while he tried to fancy himself in love with the girl. But it was a passion against the grain, and when towards the end of June she and Mrs.
Brown left for England with Orr, though once more without a soul to

speak to, he was by no means sorry to be released from the necessity of any further efforts at making believe.

And day by day the heat grew more unbearable. For a while, all but naked on his bed, he would turn impatiently now upon this side, now on that, and try a dozen different postures in as many minutes, till at last, feeling as if he must presently suffocate in such a box, he would jump up and dress and go out; but only to change bad for worse; for with a dazzling blue sky overhead, dazzling white houses on either hand and, underfoot, hot pavement as white and dazzling, he seemed to be shut in a vast furnace; and ever before him was a mirage of cool dim lofty spacious halls and shady avenues of low-spreading chestnuts or tall limes and broad streams sparkling in the sun and willows tossing their leafy arms in invitation; while his ears were filled with the music of rustling boughs and the drowsy hum of bees and a pigeon's coo away in the depth of the wood and the sound of rushing water. Nor was his desire toward these things only as pleasant in themselves, but because, figured after the likeness of what summer had given him at Rose Hill, at Bridwell, and at Tremlett, they stirred besides vague longings for that something to occupy his heart, which, whether for pleasure or pain, had at all three places been his.

Then, what time the *volets* again were opening and the white-capped women came out to sit and take the air and gossip on the pavement in front of their shops, he would follow the Rue St. Etienne to where, broadening, it debouched on to the quay just opposite the Pont Suspendu. So, leaning on the rail, he would look down stream and, taking off his straw hat, let the evening breeze now springing up pass with the touch, he thought, of some cool soft hand over his hot forehead. A mile away the Pont Royal, striding in an endless succession of arches, now over river, now over dry sandy bed, showed dark against the sky where the sun was going down with a splendour that foretold as burning a day for the morrow as that then drawing in. But each sunset outdid the last in magnificence. No wonder Turner had come there only to see them. Below, as with a sensation of hanging in mid-air he felt the spider-thread of the bridge sway with every passing footfall at his back, swift and clear and dimpling flowed the Loire, wide still but in depth a rivulet. For here again its waters had so shrunk that great islands were showing their rounded backs like the rocks as the tide went down under the chalk cliffs at home. Faint sounds of singing came from among the tall poplars of the Pré Catelan where Orr had promised one evening to take him. At that distance they might well have been the angelic voices of one of his favourite hymns echoing in welcome to the pilgrims of the night from a shore towards which, now for ever having done with this harsh world, he was being gently wafted as over some mystic sea.

So his thoughts went back another stage, and a yearning as sudden as intense seized him, not so much after the long glorious English summers he had once enjoyed with all their dear sights and sounds as for that brief period when happiness and innocence had both at once been his; a period that in each feature was recalled by Elsie's name no otherwise than those of Elizabeth or Anne by theirs. And he repeated a line he had come across in his Hallam: –

'Quo desiderio veteres revocavit amores.'

And then he laughed to think he was about what he had been so certain he would never do – regretting his school-days. So, back in his room, from among a drawerful of odds and ends he pulled out and set in the place of honour on his writing-table the only photograph he had of the boy, one of a group taken with the ivy-covered west end of Chapel as a background. But mere contemplation of a likeness soon palled; he must somehow or other give expression to his emotions; and he cast about how best this object might be effected. For a while he caressed the notion of sending him a present; valuable of course it must be and anonymous: – though why this latter he could not tell. He saw himself making the purchase, proudly giving the shopkeeper directions where to send it, or perhaps himself fondly lingering over the address; he saw the parcel being brought into the dining-room by the butler at breakfast, the surprise it caused, and then, being opened, the delight. But here common-sense interposed and suggested the uselessness of making a present if he did not at the same time let it be known from whence it came. The thought gave him pause and presently it occurred to him that it would be cheaper, and better indeed on many grounds, to confine himself to making a will in Elsie's favour; so would his feelings have the vent they needed and yet he be put to no expense.

'I give and bequeath to Lancelot Charles Southwood, Viscount Tremlett . . . and of this I request his acceptance as a slight token – ' How should it run?

Then in the midst of these imaginings he heard that their object was soon actually to be at Tours. It appeared he was coming to learn French preparatory to going up for the army; and while he was to be at the same house as Orr, Nita was to stay with the Browns, who now for the first time he learnt were distant connections; Lady Adelaide would go on south to Royat to drink the waters. And for the next few weeks wherever he went – people were beginning to return – his talk was all of Elsie's charms and the close friendship that had knit them, boys, together.

# CHAPTER XXIV

But their first meeting in that green-hung dining-room of the Hôtel de l'Univers where Els was at breakfast left him strangely disappointed, falling so far short of what he had prefigured it. Not that the boy's welcome had wanted in heartiness; but there had presently ensued a pause in the conversation, and, happy in seeing him once more, he yet – nor was the discovery without surprise – had found that they neither had much to say. But he was sure they would have again become as great friends as ever if only it had not been for Orr, since while by themselves Els seemed quite content; sooner or later, however, his old enemy was certain to appear, and, with an air of possession vastly irritating, would take the boy's arm and so at once shove him as it were out into the cold. Such behaviour must be as odious to Els as to him, among whose faults, whatever they might be, this sort of self-confidence at least could not be reckoned. Nor was this all, for somehow Orr contrived that they should walk on footpaths too narrow for the three of them to go abreast, and that he should be the one outside and so prevented from taking his share in the conversation by having to keep looking to his steps. Yet indeed this hardly made any difference, since, no otherwise than off the pavement, was he elbowed out of their talk which never ran on aught but reminiscences he had no part in or subjects like hunting or shooting which he knew nothing about – really he had no time to attend to such things – he had other fish to fry. And although he would now and again attempt to assert himself, it was never with much result, and day by day his part in the conversation grew less until at last – so, bitterly, he thought – he might as well have been miles away. Presently from a chance allusion he discovered that already once they had gone together to the theatre, and to the café several times without having so much as asked him for his company, and, while at the moment he said nothing, from thenceforth, resigning Els to Orr, he was at no less pains to avoid going about with them than till then he had been to do so. He laughed aloud as he remembered the expectations he had indulged in; the lively pictures his fancy had painted and filled in with such nice detail of – 'Then I said,' 'Then he took my arm,' 'And then.' Luckily no one but he would ever know how great had been his folly. Still he could not conceal from himself that he had spoken in ridiculously high-flown terms of Els and of the friendship which had at school united them, and so, when the boy's name came up in conversation with any he thus had talked to, he could only hope that they on their part had forgotten what he had said. Once Lady Adelaide asked him to do his best to persuade Lance to work:

'You, who've so much influence over him!' she had said.

And he had had much ado to arrange his looks and reply in such fashion as, should she hereafter come to know how matters really stood between them, not to make her think that he had tried of purpose to deceive, and yet not to give her now an inkling of the truth.

Meanwhile, after his custom, he did his best to persuade himself the grapes were sour. Never, even at the height of his folly, had he thought Els clever; now, though still extraordinarily handsome, there was a something unpleasant about his good looks: not that he was in any wise set against the boy, but that this was so must be patent to all. No doubt his hair yet clustered over his smooth white forehead and about his ears; and no doubt but his eyelashes were as long and dark and curling as ever; but the eyes they shaded appeared to have lost the power of looking aught but love; surely there was something better to do in life than to make love. Was this a world to play with mammets in and tilt with lips? And yet even in affecting to despise him for thus having accepted the women who had flung themselves at his head, he knew that it was envy prompted his mood; and he would have given much had his own personal advantages put him in case to do the like. Besides, what mannerisms he had fallen into! Could anything be more ridiculous than the way he slipped his hand into your arm as you walked with him? Or the affectionate manner in which he leant over your shoulder when he wanted to see what you were reading? No – a spoon's manners should certainly not continue in after-life.

And these feelings were especially strong as one afternoon they sat in the Châlet garden, he and Els and Nita and Mabel and Orr and Mrs. Brown. And as he looked across to where the boy was leaning forward on his tilted chair and gazing up into Mabel's face as he talked, he thought what a pity it was they should have met again, for while he had certainly gained nothing, he had lost a pleasant memory. Of course you ought to keep the recollection of your divinity unspoilt by the present sight of the common piece of clay imagination once had fashioned it from; but such a height of philosophy he, no more than Teufelsdröckh, was capable of attaining to. Rather ought he to be pleased he took his disappointment so lightly; it was a gratifying proof of his advance in the conduct of his affections. And as he went away, and behind him the heavy iron gate clanged-to, he thought it symbolised the closing of the door of his heart that was never again to open.

The week after Lady Adelaide set off for Royat, Nita and her brother being left behind, the one at the Châlet, the other at Orr's tutor's; and the very next day, as Jaspar was sitting down after dinner to his work, he heard some one coming rushing upstairs and in burst Els. Would he go with him for a little to the Browns? Nor, when there, was it long before he perceived to what was due such unusual eagerness for his company on Elsie's part, who wanted some one to talk to his sister and Mrs. Brown and so leave him free to make love to Mabel. For a moment he was inclined to be angry that he should have been thought foolishly good-natured enough for an office which perhaps Els had not so much as ventured to propose to Orr; but soon the slight was forgotten in the amusement he found considering the two. Indeed so entertaining did he find the spectacle that when, the next evening about the same hour, Els came in, as up in his little room he sat by himself trying to fix his thoughts on his book, he was only too glad again to go with him.

And presently they had fallen into the habit of spending every evening at the Châlet. They would begin, the five of them, by playing cards, but by and by Mrs. Brown would get up and betake herself to her arm-chair; and so, leaving the great polished oval walnut-table they had been sitting round, they drew about the fire. Only Nita kept her place, and, with her right hand propping up her chin, with the left slowly turned the lamp-shade, considering its transparent pictures; Jaspar, piqued, would talk his best to the others. But at last she would laugh at something he said and rise and come towards them and so stand for a moment, her hand on the back of the empty chair by his side. So, while Mabel and Els were whispering together in their corner, and on the opposite side Mrs. Brown nodded in her arm-chair, Nita and he sat silent, looking straight before them into the fire which now and again crackled with a little crisp noise. Once or twice she set the musical-box a-playing; its tiny tinkle appeared somehow to fit both the curiously delicate lightness of his feelings towards her and her own tender young girl's body and shy soul that now and again, as he had stolen a sidelong glance at her and their eyes had met, he had caught peeping out with an air of the prettiest surprise and wonder. And so delighted was he with this look of hers, the like of which he had never before seen, that he was constantly trying to enjoy it again, and, failing, would long for the moment of separation when, as they said good-night, for an instant she would raise her eyes to his. Then through the close-curtained windows he would hear chime from the neighbouring church of St. Saturnin the hour he dreaded at once and desired, and Mrs. Brown would wake and Nita give a little yawn and rise.

So one fine day it struck him that he must surely be in love. He was delighted once more, after many years, again to enjoy the sensation, and at last in the full meaning of the term. And now, too, he conceived he was loved in return; nor since the early days of his friendship with Els at Rose Hill had he known the pleasure of such an assurance. Now and again indeed a doubt would cross his mind as to whether such a conviction was justified, and he had to build himself a bridge to retreat by in the event of his fears proving true, by repeating that of course he knew she was not in earnest; so would he be able to escape looking foolish in his own eyes at least, whatever he might have to appear in others'. And then he would think that great spirits kept out this weak passion; and though, wishing to example his digression by some mighty precedent, he would remind himself of all the various historic personages who had fallen victims to it; still he felt that, for his part, he inclined to Napoleon's view, who neither believed in friend-ship nor felt the necessity of loving. 'Leave sensibility,' he had said, 'to women: men should be firm of heart and purpose.'

Yet, despite these misgivings, he was now for ever at the Châlet, but each time carefully explained that he had only looked in as he was passing. Nor was it others merely that he tried to hoodwink, he did his best to deceive himself, and whenever he left his lodgings would begin by setting off in the opposite direction; while, as gradually he came round towards the house, at every step he would assure himself he was not going there. And when at last he was standing before the gate: 'Hullo!' he would say out loud with affected surprise; 'Well, I never! But, I suppose, as I *am* here, I may as well go in!'

He was careful, too, never to refer to Nita but in terms of disparagement. And assuming a critical air: 'To my thinking,' said he, 'she'll never be anything like so beautiful as her mother!' the while he knew he would not change her with that deliciously imperfect face for a wilderness of Lady Adelaides.

'And she's not quite tall enough!' he pronounced, and put his head on one side, considering her as she walked in front with her brother; then added condescendingly: 'However, I daresay she'll still grow a little!'

But he felt that Mabel was not taken in. Then one afternoon he called at the Châlet. As he stepped forward to shake hands with her, he threw one swift glance round the room in search of Nita, but she was not to be seen; and, as Mabel talked he had much ado to attend to what she said, though surely no one could have told that his attention was straying. At last he could refrain himself no longer.

'Nita's out, I suppose?' he observed. He was proud of the artful form into which he cast the question and of the tone of unconcern he put it in, and was proceeding to make some further remark of like indifference when he thought he heard the sound of footsteps outside and his heart beat violently and he stopped short so as the better to listen.

'Yes?' said Mabel with an air of polite inquiry.

'Er – oh – ' he began; and then, recalling with an effort his wandering thoughts, continued to talk, but all the time his ears were on the stretch, and every now and again, with a motion quick and half-involuntary, his head would veer round towards the door. As for the third or fourth time disappointed, once more he turned to Mabel, their eyes met, and he saw she knew all. There was a pause. At last:

'And so you're in love with my poor little Nita, are you?' she said.

Still for a while he remained uneasy as to the use she would put her knowledge to, but she allayed his fears and he found that now the only thing was his which had so far been wanting to his happiness – some one to talk to of it.

The next time he called he had been in the room but a little while when Mabel pretended some business and was for leaving them, but Nita jumped up and declared she would go too. So for a few moments they argued together at the door, while, affecting indifference, he looked out of window. He was annoyed at her thus trying to escape being left alone with him; but was it not rather a sign of love? And then he was delighted to see her coming back to her chair, on her lips the pout he was so fond of, and sitting down again with a petulant air she took the piece of work she had thrown aside and began to sew diligently. For a little neither spoke: he wondered to find himself so tongue-tied who, when anybody else was by, excited by her presence, always, he fancied, talked his best. Three or four times she gave a little murmur of impatience, and once, with a shake of her head and a pretty mowe, with the small sharp white teeth he remembered, viciously she bit her thread in two. At last – 'What's this?' he asked, and lifted the piece of work she was engaged upon. As he did so, just for an instant his hand touched hers, and he thrilled from head to foot. Then, though not without difficulty and with long pauses, they began to talk. Yet even as he spoke he did not so much think of what he said as how different it was from what he would have liked to say.

For the next few days whenever they met he would not even smile as, by way of greeting, he just touched the tips of her fingers nor did he pay her the least attention but addressed himself to Mabel; and so had too the amusement of obviously annoying Els. Then as one morning after a visit at the Châlet he was going down-stairs, from the opposite doorway she came floating radiant; round her neck and about her wrists there glittered something he took for gold embroidery. He stopped and looked up and she smiled down on him; it was like the balcony scene in *Romeo and Juliet*; through the arch he heard Mabel and Els talking in the drawing-room. She declared that he had behaved very unkindly; for the last week when any one had called while she had been out of the room, stealing forward on tiptoe, she had listened at the door, and, if it was his voice she heard, had gone away again; and he remembered how meanwhile upon the other side he had been venting the most bitter remarks and staying on and on in hopes of seeing her.

'Will you forgive me?' he pleaded in his most romantic tones. At first she would not even allow that there was anything to pardon, but he begged and begged; it would be much to get her to admit they were on terms in which there might be a question between them of forgiveness; and in the end she yielded.

## CHAPTER XXV

And now not a day passed but they met. Knowing that Mrs. Brown and Mabel and she walked every morning down the Rue Royale to Roche's, the *pâtissier's* – for Nita was very fond of little cakes – he would hang about close by in a fever of restlessness at the thought that at any moment she might appear. Often he would fancy she was just behind, and going more slowly and slowly, suddenly turn, making sure she was there. But at last she came:

'Hullo! How do you do? Er – It's you?' he would cry in a tone as if she was the last person in the world whom he had thought to see, and, smiling, he would shake her by the hand. He only wished he had known what afterwards to do with his own. She would look down.

Sometimes these meetings were of the briefest; yet even so, as he prepared his Dante, he thought he would gladly have purchased every minute of her company at the price Ser Brunetto was to pay for every one of the Divine Poet's. But their rencounters should rather be likened to that cup of cold water which saved the fainting traveller from falling by the roadside and gave him strength to stagger on a little farther.

When together for a longer time he would appear at first scarcely to notice her, affecting to absorb himself at once in lively conversation with Mabel or Mrs. Brown; but all his animation, all his wit were really intended for Nita; for from the moment he caught sight of her, every one else and everything faded away into a dim and shadowy background. Then by and by – but he could never tell how – he found himself walking at her side, and on the instant to his restlessness succeeded a feeling of repose so sudden and complete as to recall the way in which you changed from bustle and noise to a claustral peace when from the town you passed into the Place de l'Archêveché. Yet somehow it appeared to him as if he had been with her for hours; it was perhaps because as, while alone, his thoughts had been of her, so, when at last they met, it was merely as if these thoughts had become a little stronger. Still for a while neither spoke. For him, absorbed in feeling, he was content to say nothing. He fancied that in the silence

their souls embraced. Then suddenly it occurred to him that his happiness would be soon at an end, being at the best indeed so short he
was sometimes half-inclined to think it not worth the having, and that
he must at any rate secure a repetition of it; and often the first words
he uttered were to ask when he should see her again. So at last he
began to talk. Horses and dogs and boating, such were the subjects he
mostly chose, trying one after another as if seeking an entrance, now
here, now there to her heart; they were surely what best she liked
to hear about; for as for love, for that her mind was far too healthy.
Sometimes even he would despise himself for feeling it, and for what
too at Bonn he had heard contemptuously referred to as a 'Backfisch.'
On which reflection, he would begin to speak in those incisive accents
he always considered so appropriate to the bitter remarks he made in
them, that now however he chiefly used to pay her compliments in;
they served to leave him a means of escape in case she should laugh.
And then again, assuming an air of supplication, he would employ
that other voice of his which he regarded as so pathetically pleading.

And all the time he was aware he was talking nonsense; but he
could not stop; he seemed to have but little more control than in a
dream over what he was saying and doing. Her presence, not his will,
dictated both; while when he caught a glance from her bewildering
eyes he would become altogether confused. And so entirely, as they
conversed, did he forget all time, that the arrival of the moment for
parting never failed to surprise him.

'I know,' he would cry, 'that there was something I wanted to say,
but when I see you everything goes clean out of my head!'

'Why, that's just what happens to me!' she replied; whereat he was
almost as delighted as at an actual confession of love.

And as when they met out walking the moment of separation
always came on him as a surprise; so, when calling at the Châlet,
would Mabel or Mrs. Brown have to tell him he must really go. For
not only did the hours fly, but still, despite his happiness, he seemed
to be for ever on the point of reaching some greater height, and so
stopped on and on in the hope at last to attain it; or now and again
merely for the sake of outstaying Orr. Not that he was jealous; his
feeling was of pity rather at the uselessness of any attempt to supplant
him in Nita's affections, though it had been made by one as much his
superior as was Orr the contrary. And who could doubt but this was
so? Though he disliked having to change his first opinion of anybody

as arguing a want of that insight into character which was one of
the signs of a great man; but it was a thing he had so often had to do
that now he counted it fortunate to have kept his first impressions to
himself. Why, Orr's mere laugh, his great coarse laugh, was enough
to jar one's every nerve; while as for money, the poor devil hadn't a
penny piece. And he hugged himself on the thought of the fortune,
though but small, which would be his when he came of age. And then
he would veer about to wondering why everybody did not prefer Orr.
Who was *he* to contend with one so decided, so strong, so manly?

But however long his stay, no sooner was he gone than he had great
ado to keep from running back and begging to be allowed to remain
there altogether; if only he could be where he might see her, or even
hear her voice, there were no conditions, no, none, he would not joy-
fully subscribe to. For the most part he succeeded in beating down
such thoughts and driving on his body despite his heart's pleadings;
but times there were when this latter would prove too strong for him,
suggesting perhaps a good excuse for going back in the shape of a
book he had forgotten to bring away; and scarce had the notion struck
him than he grew wild to carry it out; the possibility of a release rendered the pain intolerable which before he had only just been able
to endure, and as fast as he could he hurried back. At the door of
the house he never failed to assume towards the servant an air of
haughty dignity; no doubt she knew the mind he was returning in,
but he would repel any familiarity she might attempt to make upon
that score. So suddenly he appeared in the room he had left but a few
minutes before; Mabel and Nita were standing up; they looked at him
in great surprise.

'Why, what ever brings you back?' the former cried. 'The prover-
bial bad halfpenny is nothing to you!'

Now was of course the moment to fling himself at Nita's feet,
and by some passionate apostrophe reveal his love in all its depth
and height and splendour of romance and sweep them both, as in a
torrent, away; but something – was it his ever-present fear of being
laughed at? – held his lips closed. Yet even though unable to heave his
heart into his mouth, surely he need not have been at pains to set so
false a construction on his return and lay stress on the fact of having
only come for his book: which he would search a while for nor cast so
much as a glance in Nita's direction. Then:

'Ah, here it is!' he cried and would go off.

And so completely, with her, was he taken out of himself that still for a little after they had parted his will had scarce anything to say to what his body did, which walked indeed, but in a dream. Then suddenly he would become vaguely aware that something had stopped his progress and would hear, faint as from a great depth below, a voice addressing him, and from the empyrean would return at length to earth.

'Woolgathering as usual, Rosy!' said Orr, whom he would try to get rid of as quickly as possible that he might essay once more to mount on high.

But though, if carried up into heaven, he could make shift to stop there, he could never succeed in ascending thither of himself. So he would turn to thinking of Nita in hopes – to change the figure – of shortening a way which otherwise had been tedious beyond all bearing; yet even then, so slowly did time pass in comparison of its swift flight when in her company, that he could only compare his life to a desert green-studded at long intervals with oases of exceeding smallness. And first he would look forward and make plans as to what he would do when next they met, and would even arrange little speeches for her ear:

'I wish I'd got a title and a fortune to lay at your feet!'

Or bethink him of something to quote, as –

'Give me one kiss, I ask no more!'

And lest, when the moment came he should forget, he would write them down on his cuffs. Yet nothing of all this ever happened. Once or twice he got so far as to begin one of his quotations, but while still not half-way through, becoming confused, he had perforce to stop; like one, he thought, who trying to manoeuvre a regiment in a few moments has it hopelessly clubbed. He might have had better luck, he fancied, could he but have got quite close to her, when it would almost have seemed as if still he had been talking to himself. For his eyes, them he was afraid to try and make do duty for his tongue, fearful lest he should not know how properly to manage them. He was greatly vexed at the way in which thus time after time the moment the action began all the plans of battle went clean out of his head that with such care he had been elaborating; he never even thought of them, so quickly was everything over. But with her he was all senses, no sense, nor was there any folly he would not at her bidding have committed; but was it really so?

Then, ceasing to think of what might happen, he gave himself up to recollection. He wished he could remember to observe her more closely when they were together so as to carry away with him when again he went forth into the desert – to crack the wind of the poor phrase – a better supply to quench his thirst. Yet he could almost have written an account of every slightest word and gesture and tone of her voice. For though even to himself he could not in set phrase have described, yet in a vision he saw everything as it had been; the room, its furniture, himself and her; he could even hear her talking though he could not make out what she said. And beginning from the beginning he tried with an – 'And then: – And then': – to go over everything in the exact order in which it had happened. Now and again however in the midst of these reflections his thoughts would stray off to his ambitions or his desires or even to some little trivial detail of his life, or his eye would be caught by his boots, and he would think how small they were and well-made. Then by and by he would begin to wonder what sort of impression he had left on her; and at one moment in the extreme of confidence, the next he would be almost as despondent. Perhaps when to-morrow he went as usual to the Châlet he would be met at the door with a 'Not at home.' How should he ever live till then to have his doubts resolved?

So having told himself all his tales he began to go over the long catalogue of graces that were concentered in her person. Her brown eyes were what he first and chiefly thought of, that rather gave than received light, sparkling so softly under their 'fringed crescents,' as he called their lashes; nor did he know whether the phrase was a reminiscence or inspired by his passion; but he no more minded his epithets of praise being old than he would have done offering her a carcanet of historic jewels; rather their having served before appeared to exalt his love at once and himself. For some little while indeed after parting from her he could think of scarce anything else, still almost physically dazzled. It was as though she had been all eyes. He recollected experiencing something of a like sensation when he and her brother, small boys together at Rose Hill, had amused themselves by trying to stare each other out of countenance. And so bewildered had he been in their light, he scarce could tell what had been their expression; one on the whole perhaps à demi-moqueur, à demi-tendre: – how French he was getting! Now and again he even dared to fancy he had caught a look in them as if a vision of some fair enchanted land were beginning to take shape before them; that first waking of love which, in a pair of bright young eyes, had been said to be more of a wonder than the dawn itself; and how much more so then for him, its cause! Was it too extravagant a conceit to ask with what feelings one would regard the rising sun if, beside the actual glory of the spectacle, one knew it to be rising for oneself? And after her eyes what chiefly he loved was the way in which, at each outer end, her eyebrows, growing sparse, lifted, as it were, a little; though how could he love less the delicious corners of her mouth? And then there was the hair she had such a mass of, dark-brown with streaks of a lighter shade; it reminded him – for he always thought of her under the most poetic tropes – of the different-tinted streams of the sea as many a lovely summer-day he had looked down on it from the white Sussex cliffs. For her smile, it was very like what he remembered had been Elsie's; and comic-pathetic was the best phrase he could think of to express it. But indeed with regard to some of her charms, he was even worse off for words to describe them. For the present, no doubt, while seeing her so often, this little mattered, but he must try and find some *memoria technica* to recall them by against the time when he would have to go away and when, in default of something of the kind, by and by they might escape his memory. As about her eyelids, to instance no more, there was a certain clear-cut grace, a sort of delicate transparency which reminded him of the Chinese-porcelain cups in the cabinet in the Rectory drawing-room; but he could hit on no collocation of words to fit it nicely.

Yet although there thus seemed nothing he did not dwell upon, and with delight, from the sheeny sweep of hair brushed up behind the tiny ear to the little shoe, the tip of which just peeped from beneath her skirt, to his great surprise he was always discovering some fresh object of admiration; and now it would be a curve in her lips that he had not noticed before and now the extraordinary softness of her throat, a softness he could see at least, if he might not feel. Even her freckles were each a beauty more as, had she been marked by a hundred moles, moles for him they never would have been but resplendent stars and moons. And with no other eyes did he regard what she wore, hats and gloves, skirts, jackets, boots and shoes; all which, not only pleasant in themselves to behold, gave him besides by their costly prettiness an impression that there was nothing she could not have; as was indeed but proper where a divinity of his came into question; so that money, in others vulgar, ostentatious, heavy, with her was turned into a thing of grace and lightness. Moreover, he liked to think it was all one day to be his. Nor had the life that animated it less charms; the way she smoothed her dress and the movements of her arms and head as she arranged the hair behind her ears; while he was specially fond of seeing her play with the buckle of her belt, the girdle his eager trembling hands would one day unclasp. Yet however intoxicating this thought of being admitted by a husband's right into that Holy of Holies, her bedroom, love would have still greater raptures if danger spiced it, and tears, and even perhaps death.

And as his eye was never satisfied with seeing, so neither was his ear filled with hearing. Not that he much attended to the sense of what she said; rather he listened as once to her brother's solos at evening-chapel at Bridwell, the melody of whose angel-voice had caused him quite to forget to ask what was meant by the words. She sang to his heart, he told himself, not spoke to his understanding –

'Her voice was music and her words a song.'

Nor again could he tell whether love was transforming him into a poet, or the line was merely one of the odds and ends which littered his memory and which, now catching his eye, he picked out to offer her. So for the most part not knowing what she said, he made the greater case of all he did remember, turning it over and over in his mind in an effort to discover, not only the signification she herself had wished to give it, but that it had borne unconsciously. And then he would laugh at himself as at a foolish deuteroscopist who sought to read two meanings into what most like had not even had one.

Yet now and again it would cross his mind that it was curious this goddess of his should have no other worshippers. Certainly she was not wise. Had she not more than once when he had been talking to Mabel and Els – and clearly interesting both of them – had she not persistently lagged behind, answering, when called on to 'come along,' that no doubt the conversation was very intellectual but she didn't understand it? And if there was one thing he could do it was to talk! But she wasn't even clever enough to see that he was so. And then he would start back in horror from such blasphemy, and could hardly believe that any one should care for a girl not her, or even look at another; though perhaps indeed – at such presumption should one laugh or cry? – there were of her age and sex who flattered themselves they also were pretty. Charms too she had for the mind's eye, who was of high birth and rank; and a beauty of noble race shone with far more splendour than that which was meanly born; while if Els should die unmarried, he would become, through her, master of Tremlett, and their son a peer of the realm. Besides, her innocence and youth had an ineffable seduction for one who affected to lament having lost the former so long ago he could scarce remember its ever having been his and who had so early been old. Yet while this contrast between them inflamed his passions, it purified them too. To kiss that wonder of softness, her cheek, would surely make him almost faint, setting to it his lips as to the sacramental cup. Yet even now he was afraid that in part he loved her for that she was half-woman, half-girl, as at Tremlett because half-girl, half-boy. Only this reflection bore with it its own antidote as showing him how constant he was of nature. He loved her now, and had loved her, a child, as Dante, Beatrice, and Swift, Stella, from their earliest years to the last.

And as he thus came to consider her after such a fashion that the mere repetition of her name was like the sudden sight of one of those way-side crosses that now and again he met with in his walks – the recall of the ideal in the midst of the real – so his opinion of himself as compared with her grew lower every day; and soon not only did he find it hard to conceive she would ever be his, but in the meantime he held himself scarce worthy to draw near her shrine, and thought he was rewarded far beyond his poor demerits by being allowed to stand and worship afar off. Who was he to ask more? Talents no doubt he had, and such as were going to enable him to surprise her, his wife, by the position he would raise her to, as Napoleon must have astonished Josephine when he set her on the throne of France. Yet so far he had done little, nothing rather, to prove his possession of such gifts; and he could scarcely expect to be taken on trust. Nor had he, to make up, any such personal gifts as might have won her heart. Not that he was ugly; indeed he had a singularly clear and fair complexion, white regular teeth, lips of an admirable curve, small well-shaped ears set close to the head, and beautifully fine hair; but of course beside her all was as nothing. And though still he dressed as well as he could, it was not in hopes to catch her eye, but as people put on their best things to go to church. Nor had he either money or rank to counterbalance such grave defects, he who longed to be Autocrat of All the Russias merely to lay a crown imperial at her feet, those pretty feet, and scarce could bear to think that she who was worthy to lie by an emperor's side should mate with one so lowly as himself.

So as he could not give he must be content to receive – perhaps the better part – and he dwelt with delight on the thought that not only would she bestow on him herself, but also the means of taking that first step in life which was ever the most difficult; and he would steal sidelong glances at her hand and fancy how it would be to that small soft and dimpled thing that he would owe success at once and happiness as his first marriage gave Napoleon both Josephine and the command of the Army of Italy. Then in the midst of these pleasing dreams he would be troubled by doubts as to whether she cared for him: and in search of better assurances upon this point, his gaze would plunge into her brown eyes which on their side, he thought, would draw back with shy delight. Or was she only amused? But surely those sparkling glances meant more now than when a child she had bent them on him; and that vivacity of movement and gesture was prompted by something more than exuberance of spirits. Besides, it was significant that once or twice when she had caught him looking at her, she had not asked him what he was doing as in old days at Tremlett. Yet – and so he was for ever changing his mind, for ever trying to see into her heart, and elated and depressed in turn by the interpretations he lent to all she did. But on the whole he inclined to the view that she loved him; and he would consider his reflection in the glass with quite a new interest; it was a strange sensation but a delightful to think there was some one beside himself who looked with affection at that hair, those eyes and lips, though only perhaps because *elle ne regardait qu'avec son cœur*. And then he would grow ashamed; unless he could be great in the eyes of the world, great he would be, he vowed, in none.

## CHAPTER XXVI

And now for some little while past he had been looking forward to an excursion they were all to make to Amboise, when one morning he received a letter from England to say that the date of the examination had been fixed and that he must start in a fortnight's time for

London. And full of pleasurable anticipations as before he had been, his eagerness for the day at Amboise now redoubled as for one which would, as it were, sum up in a few hours all the happiness of the past six weeks; and with such intentness did his mind fix on the event that he found it almost impossible to conceive of anything beyond; doubtless the world would go on, but how he could not imagine. The evening before his excitement reached the height, and when midnight chimed from the Cathedral towers, he was in bed indeed, but still awake. The notion however that now at last he was in the day itself appeared to soothe him, for he had presently fallen asleep. But at five he was awake again and at the window looking out to see what promise the morning gave of fine weather. Yet though thus early up he had strength of mind enough not to get too soon to the station, and when he arrived Mabel and Els were already pacing up and down the long low platform.

'But what have you gone and got yourself up like that for, my dear chap?' said Els, and pointed at his costume about which he had been at no small pains; and again and again he had recurred to the fine figure he would cut in the new suit he now for the first time was wearing.

'Oh,' cried Mabel, 'what a shame! Don't let him bully you, Mr. Tristram! I like it very much; except perhaps your hat!'

But it was just of this he was most proud. He said nothing, but his spirits fell. And then the others appeared; hearing them coming he turned, had a vague impression of saying how do you do, of seeing something blue and white, of feeling his hand pressed, and the meeting with Nita was over. In the railway-carriage he heard Mrs. Brown make some remark about Nita's dress being very pretty, but perhaps too delicate; and Lady Adelaide replied – she had only returned the day before:

'I wanted her to put on her old red one – you know the one I mean – which would have done much better, but she wouldn't hear of it. I can't think what has come to her. She's quite different from what she was when I went away!'

And from the corner where he sat he fell to considering the dress they were talking of. The skirt seemed made of nothing more substantial than flounces of white lace; in her belt, the diamond buckle of which sparkled and flashed with all sorts of rainbow hues, were a couple of pink roses; the jacket was of a very soft and delicate blue silk; and then he remembered how once he had told her that somehow sky-blue appeared to him to be the colour of her name, and he felt sure she had put on the dress for his sake. Yes: white and blue were certainly her proper colours, the latter, heaven's own tinct, signifying celestial things, the first, gladness, pleasure, rejoicing and delight.

Arrived at the castle they spent some time in going over its sights, but the more their guide discoursed of how under this five-aisled berceau of limes Catherine de' Medici had played at hide-and-seek with Francis the First; and how that same king had made the winding slope up the big tower in order to admit of Charles v. ascending in his litter; and how the deep cool shaded garden they were passing through once had been the castle-ditch, the more impatient he grew and angry: it was his last chance of having Nita to himself, and already several hours were gone and they had not been alone for a single moment. But at length Lady Adelaide and Mrs. Brown declared they had seen enough and sat down on a stone bench in the shade, and Els and Mabel and Nita and he went on together. The other two soon disappeared, and at last he and Nita were alone. For a few moments they remained where they were, sitting one on each side of a sort of raised fountain. Then presently she began slowly pulling her roses to pieces and dropping the petals into the water, and so, stooping, they began to puff them one against another. As she bent the light caught the tiny diamonds in her ears. They looked, he thought, not unlike the drops of water in some of the pink petals they were blowing. Then:

'Have you got a knife?' she asked, 'we'll cut our initials!'

And so he began to grave them into the stone, delighted to think that the letters of their names would thus go down to all time locked in an eternal embrace.

'J. T. – N. S.' –

he carved, and, underneath,

'19 June 1879.'

Presently she got up, as did he also after her, and they went and leaned together over the parapet of the castle-wall; the stone was hot to the touch. The sense of physical elevation, of enjoying at once an immense view and profound silence, made him feel as if he and she had somehow now ascended into a heaven of their own, far above the troubles that on earth below affected their lives and themselves. At their feet, so close they could have dropped stones into the courtyards, were the steep roofs and narrow streets of the little town; away in the direction of Tours the sun was sinking; you could just see the tops of the Cathedral towers; right and left wound the broad stream of the Loire, flashing silver here, there motionless, bottle-green, until at last it disappeared among the trees; on the other side came the Entreponts, and the horizon was bounded by a low line of wooded hills. And then they heard Els calling them, and Nita hurried away; still for an instant he remained looking at the scene, embracing it with as passionate a regard as that with which he imagined he would have looked into Nita's eyes had she been dying; and then he followed after. And as he ran to overtake her, his attention was caught by something white on the ground, and, stooping, he picked up her handkerchief – just such an one as she ought to have; a tiny delicate thing of cambric, all transparent, the edges scalloped, and with a narrow border of blue to match her bodice, and in one corner, embroidered in quaint letters, 'Thursday.' He showed it to her as he came up; she was delighted at its recovery, but he begged to be allowed to keep it, and she consented to let him do so – but only for a while.

And now it seemed as though he had already taken leave and was looking back upon his life at Tours from the opposite side of the gulf of parting; and now as if he had but to will hard enough, and he would find himself back at the day of Nita's arrival. But sometimes he would quite forget what was hanging over him and would begin to make plans. Then suddenly his heart would sink; what was the use? three more days and he would be gone. It was very hard the iron law of duty should thus force him to depart. And in that word how many deaths there were! And still as time went on, minute after minute falling away no otherwise than at Rottingdean, standing on some little sandbank, he had watched it crumbling away in front of him before the advancing tide; and as, almost with every hour, the weather grew more lovely, so did his melancholy become more profound. But this was only when alone; with them he laughed and talked incessantly; though what he said or the others replied, he knew not. Only he had a vague notion of hearing something about Orr's having come into a large fortune and of congratulating him with a warmth he could see he was surprised at. And then he had said good-bye and he and Els were in the railway-carriage. At every jerk the train gave as it moved out of the station, it seemed as if a fibre of his heart were being snapped. As long as he could he kept his eyes fixed on the twin towers of St. Gatien, but when they at length disappeared and nothing was to be seen but vineyards, on which, as now the sun was slowly sinking, the shadows of the tall poplars lengthened, he fell to considering Els sitting opposite, dwelling on those traits of his which most recalled Nita. And as once he had loved the sister for the brother's sake, so now he felt he loved the brother for the sister's. How he envied him to be sure, who would presently be back with her, while he would be far away! And his heart seemed wrung past bearing.

## CHAPTER XXVII

Three weeks later he was once again with the Binneys at Telscombe in the intention of remaining there till he should learn the result of the examination. He had lost no time in telling them that he was sure he had failed; such a philosophic preparation for the worst – if indeed the worst came true – could hardly miss of taking the edge off his own disappointment, or at least of saving him from the sarcastic remarks which in such an event he knew only too well that otherwise they all, his Guardian and Mrs. Binney, Rose and Violet and James, would be making at him and to him every hour of the day. But Hope, as he put it, altogether refused to accept suicide as a satisfactory mode of escape from the fear of death; and he was therefore very glad when a fortnight after he received an official announcement that he had come out first.

'Why,' cried Mrs. Binney, 'your fortune's made!'

And though, indeed, he affected to think but little of his success, his opinion in reality coincided with hers; only while in her view, as he felt, he was now provided for for life, in his own he had merely taken the first step on the road which eventually would lead so far. But not only did the fact of his having passed let him see a little ahead: it had in it also other good. Hitherto whenever he had ventured on snatching a few moments from his books, he had been haunted by the fear that he was losing his chance of learning some date or name or fact, on his knowledge or ignorance of which would turn his success in the examination – the examination which had to be passed before he could consider that he had really begun to live – but now, for a while at least, he might with an easy conscience spend as much time as he liked in amusement.

The next morning he went up to town, and as, from the top of the Duke of York's Steps, across the Parade, he first caught sight of the building where so often he had been in thought, for a moment he stopped. His heart swelled with pride at the reflection that at last he was a member of the august and mysterious body which behind the impassive walls of that huge grey sombre pile, sat issuing orders that for good or ill, in great things and small, affected men's lives in every part of the world. He would have liked to have struck an attitude and cried to the passers-by, 'Look, look at me and behold one of your rulers!'

But still in his fancy the present was as nothing to the future. And so he slowly descended that great flight of steps, feeling almost as if the wide white space he was going down to had been black with some vast crowd whose eyes were fixed on him as might have been those of his army on the Great Napoleon.

But there was still another advantage in his success; the possibility of once more enjoying the pleasure he had now for some three months past been obliged to forego, of thinking of Nita as often and for as long at a time as he liked. For the first few days after leaving Tours he had had no small ado to keep himself from rushing back; but he had fought against the impulse, and little by little it had grown weaker. And then he was being examined and had scarce leisure to do more than now and again murmur 'Nita' under his breath; though this was quite enough to make his surroundings, however prosaic, 'all soft,' as he expressed it, 'and beautiful.' But now the moment he was alone in thought he could be with her. And as he looked back upon the life he had led at Tours, so heavenly-happy in his eyes did it seem, that it appeared rather a dream than something which had really been. Indeed, he recalled it much after the same fashion as he did his dreams of sleep, of some scenes remembering only little scattered bits that stood out distinct against the dark background of forgetfulness in which all else had been swallowed up beyond recovery; while of others he could recollect each smallest incident with a vividness so intense as more than once to make him almost doubt which of the two, present or past, was real. More especially was this latter the case with regard to the last scene of all, when every one had been gathered in the hall of the Châlet to wish him and Els good-bye. Had he gone back he could, he was sure, have reconstructed the whole thing, not only setting each person in his or her proper place but telling them how to stand and look. Nor only so; but, had the room itself by any accident been destroyed, he could have rebuilt it again, putting here the door, and there the mantelpiece, against this wall the table, and, opposite, the sofa with its folded rugs. Yet even here there was one moment he was fond of dwelling on above the rest; a moment of which the recollection would never fade; when he and Nita had been as much alone as if in reality there had been no one by. It was that in which, as he had taken her hand, their eyes had met and his had said 'I love you! I love you!' the while into hers had come a look on whose meaning he had then indeed had no time to reflect but in which he now chose to see a half-shy, half-delighted acceptance of an avowal that, unexpressed in words, was yet the most outspoken he had ever dared. And always through these eidola of the past he could see, as he had read was the case with thin ghosts, whatever trees, houses, or room-walls, chanced to be the scenery of the present; while still in his ears there sounded, only faintly as if far away, the murmur of voices or the roar of the streets.

Nor did he ever find the least difficulty in calling up these visions; he had but to name her name or repeat some one or other of her favourite phrases, and, on the instant, not only did he see before him her look, her attitude, her dress, but he even heard the very tones of her voice. Not that material memorials were of no help; on the contrary, such of his belongings as had once been touched by her appeared to have become endowed with all sorts of wonder-working powers, as, from contact with the relics of a saint, scapulars, so Papists held, acquired a mystic property not theirs before. And of these his watch was the principal, that still he made keep Tours time: so, he conceived, he could the more easily figure to himself what she was doing, when, like a Mohammedan towards Mecca at the hours of prayer, he faced about in the direction of the city beside the murmuring Loire that, as containing her, was, in his thought, the most beautiful and the holiest in the world. But even more powerful in their effects were those few things which once had actually belonged to her – as the virtue inherent in the relics themselves is naturally greater than that of any object to which it is their contact alone that gives its value. Unluckily of these he had but two, the rose and the handkerchief he had got from her at Amboise. A petal of the former, shrunk now and dry and brown, he had enclosed in a tiny shell-shaped locket of blue enamel and gold and always carried, tied round his neck, for a charm that should save him in all dangers and give a successful issue to everything he attempted; the handkerchief laid up in a box of ivory and sandal-wood, he only allowed himself to look at now and again, when, lifting it reverently in his two hands from its bed of wadded silk, he would kiss it, and shutting his eyes, with worship and delight, inhale the delicate scent that still breathed from its diaphanous folds. Little by little however this perfume grew more faint, and, as it did so, it seemed to him as if his recollections of her and their life at Tours also began to fade. For a while indeed he still tried to believe himself mistaken: but presently he found it was becoming difficult even to see before him those eyes of hers in which he had, as it were, lived so long that at first their image had appeared rather to be stamped on the retina of his than from time to time by a distinct effort of his will recalled to sight: and then at last he was forced to confess that his memory was indeed no longer able to furnish the endless succession of pictures that in the beginning had given him almost as much pleasure as the scenes they brought back. Doubtless he had used it too much: it was evidently like one of those engraver's plates from which each successive print comes off less and less accurate in detail and less and less sharp in line.

So, while assuring herself that the fires he had lighted at her eyes were never going to die; that so long as the sun and moon endured, so long would his love do so too; he abandoned the used-up past, and turned, full of eagerness, to a future that he made sure was bringing delights of a like sort indeed to those he had already tasted but of an intensity to correspond to the way in which since then all his notions had grown. Nor was it one castle in the air that he built nor two nor three but half a hundred and each finished down to the smallest detail, to the last arch and moulding. Only, however widely they might differ from one another in design, they all had this in common, that they were planned as bowers for him and his love. Nor was any accident too trifling to set his fancy to work on the construction of what, in the jargon he flattered himself was poetical, he styled 'rainbow palaces': – which indeed he could raise to a prodigious height on the very smallest foundation of fact. He had but to look out of window and see a carriage at the door to think that such another, drawn by just such a pair of glossy bays, would one day wait for him with Nita – with Nita, his wife – and lovingly, lingeringly, proudly he repeated the words 'my wife': while whenever he went out for a walk he was sure to see at least one house he would delight to picture himself and her established in.

Often too he would take his way to the old family town-house. Even when he was still only in Oxford Street his heart would begin to beat faster. So, turning the corner into the square, he would cross the road and stand and gaze up at the wall behind which he conceived he was to spend so many happy hours. Nor was it long before he thought he could distinguish, as by an individuality of its own, each grimy brick and dirty pane of glass; and as he kept his eyes still fixed unblinking on the house with such intentness as to make everything else fade away on either hand into a sort of mist, it seemed as if some of the life he felt so full of were passing out of him and waking a sort of responsive consciousness in what before had been but lifeless matter; and as if that hitherto unmeaning screen wore now an air in which, had he had but skill, he could have read the whole history of the future. Then in a kind of vision he would see himself, with her as his bride upon his arm, descending those steps, now laid with crimson cloth, and coming down between the columns of the porch and under the striped triangle of the awning to the brougham that was to take them away. Or perhaps it would be better to be married at Tremlett; they would walk together down the path which led from the church to the house; children would strew roses before them as they went; from the tower the bells would be clashing and the sun would shine down brightly from out a sky of cloudless blue. He would still be debating within himself the relative merits of these two plans when suddenly he would awake to the consciousness of its being already long past the hour at which he should have been at work, and, calling a hansom, would tell the driver where to go in a voice he of purpose made loud to catch the attention of the passers-by. And as he went off at one moment he would look at the empty place beside him and, imagining it occupied by Nita, smile at the cushions as he thought he would have done at her had she been there; and the next would swell with pride to see himself, as he lolled at ease, catching up and passing, one after another, the omnibuses, wherein, in odious promiscuity, the base vulgar, his contempt for whom the sight increased, were slowly being jolted along.

Then at the Office he could talk, if not of Nita, at least of Els and Lady Adelaide: he found much the same pleasure in so doing as he had had at Tours when, unable actually to be with her he loved, it had at any rate been possible to be somewhere near. Or, when this could not be, slipping from the room, he would steal up to the Library and there for the hundredth time read the account of the family in the Peerage; or, opening the big map of England, put his head between his hands and so stare down at the little angular patch of green that represented Tremlett Chase till lines and names alike began to swim before his dazzled eyes.

Now and again no doubt his blood would run cold at the thought that by all these anticipations of love and happiness he might only be preparing for himself a disappointment, in comparison of which whatever he had suffered up to then would be but child's-play. For he was older now than when, as a boy, his affections had received their first wound, and the heart, like the body, grew stiff with age and, as time went on, suffered more and more from each accident it met with. Supposing for instance some great peer's son should fall in love with her. What could he hope when into the lists against him who had nothing but himself to offer, there should come a suitor with two coaches and six horses, twenty footmen and pages, a coat worth four score pound and a periwig down to his knees? But how indeed in any case could his unworthiness aspire to the enjoyment of such perfection? Yet on the whole he always felt that he gave entertainment to these sort of misgivings rather from a desire to be ready *en philosophe* for either fortune than from any real fear that they might one day come true. It was hard to conceive of her even as another's wife, and altogether impossible to suppose that she could ever cease to care for him. Nor could he realise that, when others took her hand with feelings like his or tried to look into her eyes, she might meet them otherwise than with the coldest rebuff. No: she was living for him alone as he for her.

In which security he did his utmost to render himself more worthy one whom indeed he put into the place religion would have had occupied by God. It pleased his vanity to think that, while the pious counted on obtaining a reward for what they did from their deity, being one no secrets were hidden from, the only recompense he asked was the assurance that every victory over his baser self was bringing him, at least in spirit, nearer his love. But while thus anxious to make himself morally less undeserving of her; the achievement of such qualities as name and money was no less the object of his desires. Of course he did not pretend but that in a certain measure he coveted such things for himself, but his chief reason for so doing lay, he was convinced, in the feeling that their possession would give him in his own eyes at any rate some sort of claim to possess her; and in the wish to be able to put at her feet a gift whose richness might supply whatever was lacking in himself of the sum necessary to purchase her love. If only now he had been a duke or earl! He could then have bestowed on her the coronet of some historic and high-sounding title, and as 'Nita Dorset, Pembroke and Montgomery' she would have reigned in half a dozen Tremletts in the country and in some great town-house of which the roof alone would have been visible above its blank court-yard-wall. The sight of one who would not only claim to be yielded to as a pretty child, but would besides command that profound respect which is always given to riches and exalted rank, would have been as delightful to his mind's eye as to his body's the contrast between her slight girlish beauty and the priceless and famous diamonds which would of course be hers.

But this unfortunately could never be, since of the two things, money and a good example, that parents could bequeath to their children, his, alas, had left him only that which, had he wanted, he could have always got from others. Nor ought he to waste his time in thinking of what might have been; he must make the best of what was and be content with such prizes as his profession afforded. He smiled so thinking, as he remembered how, a boy, he had had dreams of being a great conqueror and had even hoped to put his brows within a golden crown and call himself a king. Meanwhile it never failed to make him very impatient to hear of any one of his own age gaining distinction. Once, for instance, he had come across the picture of some Indian frontier skirmish an old schoolfellow had been engaged in and for days after he had hardly slept for thinking of the laurels wherewith a brow as young as his was already adorned. He tried indeed to console himself by the reflection that such a success was as nothing compared to what would one day be his, but do what he would there stared him in the face the dreadful fact that one who had started at the same time as he was now ahead. Why had it not been *his* fortune to do something that would have enabled him to present himself before Nita in all the glamour of one who had had his picture in the *Illustrated London News*? If by the time that she returned to England, he too had not gained some ground; was not, say, private secretary to some Cabinet Minister or another, he would – he would – he did not know what he would do. He had not been nearly so much annoyed when he had heard that Orr had come into a fortune of, it was said, ten thousand a year, though then the contemporary who had left him behind had been one whom ever since he had first gone to school he had always been finding in his path. For he had been able in the first place to reflect that chance alone was the cause of his being thus passed; and in the next to hope that, as Orr was some years his senior, he would by the time he was as old have attained a position which, while actually as good, would relatively be much better, as being due altogether to himself. And at each instance of the kind, with all the usual circumstances of lips pressed tight together and hands clenched till the nails bruised the palms, for the thousandth time he resolved he *would* achieve success; as moreover the fates, he was convinced, had decreed he should.

It was this assurance indeed which made him listen to his colleagues as they discussed their chances of promotion with something the like sort of pity as that wherewith in the pleasing consciousness of having private means of his own he was accustomed to look down on those unfortunates whose daily bread depended on their power to work. Only now and again, when they included him in their calculations, he could not help being irritated at seeing them thus count him one of themselves and had some ado to keep from telling them that what might be quite good enough for them was not by any means so for him. Why, the mere notion of some of them having high ambitions like his would make him laugh out loud in a manner he would have some difficulty in explaining. Yet could he never understand how one of any spirit might endure to live without ambitions. Were his to be violently done to death, or, starved for lack of food, gradually to fade away, he was certain he should not long survive them. More than once, however, it seemed to him as if his irritation took its rise in a feeling that after all the others might not be so wrong as he wished to think. Perhaps, while he was making sure he was a racer destined to run a course which history would be at pains to record, he was really a mill-horse just beginning the monotonous round he would continue in all the days of his life. And then he would dismiss all these idle and unpleasant fears and fall to wondering if he would succeed in a little intrigue he had just set on foot, and thinking how, if he did, he would drive off in a hansom to exhibit himself in his uniform to some of his friends.

Nor was he in a less pleasant frame of mind as regarded money. For the time being he had indeed, beside his pay, but a bare three hundred a year, yet not only did he feel certain that he would one day be rich – a conviction which saved him from ever being jealous of those who were so already – he even seemed to himself to be at that very moment a person of wealth who, only masquerading as a poor man, could whenever he so wished resume his own. Of course he would not mind making money if he could. How, he wondered, did people set about it? The only way he could see was to speculate in the City. But here some other subject would draw off his attention and he would turn from this with a half-belief that somehow or other it would settle itself. But still he wished he had had Orr's luck; then any difficulties would have disappeared which now there might be in the way of his marrying Nita.

For the rest, even when happy, he liked to think he had some one whom he loved and who loved him. Did not one enjoy travelling the more for knowing one had a pleasant home whither, if the fancy took one, one could always return? But it was when troubled in spirit that he most appreciated the being able at once to fly for sanctuary to the chapel he had built in his heart to Nita, as in the City he had seen people turn aside out of the noise and confusion of the streets to rest for a moment in the quiet of some old church. It was pleasant, too, when others seemed to hold him cheap, to reflect that there was one at least to whom he was everything that he thought himself. It was only unfortunate that this was not a fact which afforded him any very great consolation, since he was one who disdained to be great if he could not be so in the eyes of all. Even when a boy at school he had been the same, and the tendency, far from growing weaker, was now become so strong that he even disliked his dog looking up to him, since the attitude was one that so far the world had not thought fit to take up.

## CHAPTER XXVIII

He had been in his office about a year and a half when, at an evening-party, he first heard speak of the great ball by which young Lady Tremlett – for Els had married Mabel Brown – was going to celebrate her entrance and her husband's on the London stage. He was surprised to have been left to hear from others, not only of this intention of hers but even of her arrival in town, and he promised himself not

to forget to reproach her with such a piece of neglect. But as time
went on and still, though the cards had long been sent out, there came
nothing for him, he even began to fear he might not be asked. From
so heavy a blow recovery would be difficult. In any case his credit as a
person of fashion was concerned in being seen at a ball like hers; and
when, besides, he remembered the exaggerated terms in which so
often he had belauded her and Els, he could not choose but perceive
that not to be invited would render his position such as even he would
find hard to explain. Why, already many who had heard him talk – it
struck him now they must often have been hugely bored by all these
praises of people they did not know – were coming up with an, 'Of
course you're going!' He did his best with vague phrases about not
being quite sure, he might have to go out of town, to leave some loophole by which, if the worst came to the worst, he might escape, but
still he had an uneasy feeling that all the time they were quite aware
of the real state of the case. Nor could he find much consolation in
laughing in his sleeve at the airs of superiority put on by the lucky few
of his acquaintance asked – airs made only the more transparently
ridiculous, he thought, by their affectation of treating their going as a
matter of course – or at the various devices to which those who, like
himself, had been left out resorted to hide their chagrin, for Mabel's
position deprived them of all possibility of pretending that, even if
invited, they would stop away. But beside the alarm that his vanity
felt at the prospect of such a wound, he was hurt at having been so
quickly forgotten by Els and his wife. Such fickleness was enough to
make one renounce society and withdraw into oneself. Before, however, he took so extreme a step, it might be worth his while to see
whether leaving a card would produce the result he desired. And so
he did, abandoning his resolution to let the first advances come from
them. But then, though no doubt it was an act that must in any case
involve breaking his word and after all might humble him in vain,
of this none but Mabel and he would be aware, while that would be
known to him alone.

    But he need not have put himself about for he presently received,
though indeed at the very last, on the morning of the day itself, a note
from Mabel apologising in terms which even he allowed were handsome for not having asked him before and hoping that this once he
would forgive her and come. And 'P.S.,' she said, 'Nita will be here.'
Whereat his cheeks flushed, his eyelids lifted from their sulky droop

and his eyes themselves lighted up, and all that day he went about his business with a buoyancy of spirits which nothing could depress and which indeed was such as to extend its effects from mind to body and to make him feel as if, the laws of gravitation suspended, he were walking on air. He even forgot to regret that, his invitation not having reached him till late, he had been prevented running about and telling people he was going as on such occasions he always liked to do; since it was no longer the custom to publish lists of guests – at least of those to whom it was of consequence it should be known they had been asked – one had to do one's advertising oneself.

So evening come and dinner over – he could scarcely eat for excitement – he went up to dress. Nor did it prove an unnecessary precaution to take such ample time, for, so nervous was he, everything seemed to slip through his fingers and go tumbling about all over the room. And yet he could not realise that he was now within half an hour of what he had so long been looking forward to possessing the love of which even the shadows had been so rich in joy: within half an hour of an experience that would doubtless for the moment fill him top-full of all sorts of delightful emotions and for the future add another item to his collection of memories, the freshness of which too frequent use had a little impaired. He told himself that he was just setting his lips to one of those enchanted cups that made time and place and self itself disappear and turned one into a mere sensation. Only twice in his life had he tasted of this divine drink: once years ago at Bridwell, and once again when his eyes and Nita's had met as they had said good-bye at Tours; but both these draughts he could yet recall with a vividness which sometimes made him almost fancy that he still was drinking. Then, outwardly calm but really shivering with excitement, he was in the ballroom. Here, to the sense of content he would in any case have experienced in a place so large, so beautifully proportioned and so splendidly decorated, was added the pleasure, not only of knowing that he was now with people whose social position fitted the magnificence of the scene, but of recognising among them a number of his acquaintance. He had feared that the atmosphere would have been so rarified it would have been a relief to get away and sink, so to speak, once more into his native depths; that it would have been one of those parties – he had gone to several – where, oppressed with a sense that every one was wondering how he had got there, he would have had to move about from place to place to conceal the fact that of all the crowd he scarce knew a single soul: and that the only pleasure he would have had, apart of course from that of meeting Nita again, would have been the retrospective one of having gone. He noticed, too, several friends he had by no means looked to see, and resolved for the future to pay them more attention, raised as they were in his esteem – he hoped he was in theirs – by being met in such society. But soon he became absorbed in consideration of the fact that now at any moment he might actually behold in the flesh the goddess of whom for close on two years his heart had been so constantly talking. Why, even then her eyes might be upon him. And at this reflection he made haste to arrange on his face that grave air of preoccupation of which he was always so fond; it afforded, he thought, an effective contrast to his youthful looks and marked him out as something altogether differ- ent from the common run of young men.

Then suddenly, as the band in the music-gallery once more began to play, he saw her, this idol of his thought, advancing through the shifting crowd towards him. With what a grace did she float over the bright floor! No one but she could so have united the charms of age and youth, at once as dignified as her mother and as light of foot as, when a child, with blowing skirts and streaming hair, she had raced before him down the long Tremlett corridors. Yet as he looked his chief feeling was somehow one of disappointment: she was certainly not so pretty as his recollections had misled him to expect.

'Will you give me a dance?' he asked, and bent towards her as, not noticing him, she was going by. He felt himself putting on the submissive air by which, from the earliest days of his courtship of her brother, he had sought to win favour in the beloved's eyes, the while into his voice he could hear come the pleading note wherewith at such times it always thrilled.

'I'll give you this,' she said, 'if you like!'

And then his arm was round her waist, and they had struck into what he used to think of as the 'whirlpool' of dancers that with a curious undulatory movement had again begun swiftly to circle by. So was he at length at rest, his body being where for so long had been his soul, with her. The band was playing one of those dreamy waltzes in which he always found so much to provoke at once yearning and desire, and when presently they began to sing their voices so increased the sensuous pathos of which the music by itself seemed already full, that all at once his heart appeared to overflow with emotions he had no words to describe. He only knew that, with a force of aspiration such as he was sure that he had not felt since that time in Chapel at Bridwell when he had been so strangely moved by her brother's voice, he was longing to enjoy, as only could it be enjoyed, with her, a full perfect and simultaneous satisfaction of all those desires of heart and soul and body that hitherto he had been able very partially to content and then only one at a time. So with that little hand in his – still as of old was the small wrist clasped by its fragile bracelet of gold with the N of pearls – he went turning, turning, turning, the while his eyes, fascinated, again and again stole down to watch her tiny satin-slippered feet – how could she support herself on things so small? – as with dizzying regularity they came in and out alternately from beneath her skirt. He fell into a sort of trance: he fancied that he and she had already after some mystical fashion been made one and now, without any exertion of their own, were being carried along together on the smooth-rolling waves of the music. And over them, as from the spicy shores of Araby the Blest Sabæan odours blow out to sea, now and again would breathe the perfume of her hair; a few stray wisps loosened by the rapidity of their course even came floating against his cheek.

At last they stopped though still for an instant his hand lingered about her waist; he grudged to lose before he must the pleasure of feeling her young body alive under the stiff sheath of whalebone and silk in which it was laced, or the curious delight given to his sense of touch by the silver-spangled muslin with which her dress was covered. And then, raising her bouquet, delicately, as if to brush one of its flowers, with a delightful mowe she pouted out the lips to which, even as he looked, he applied the poet's epithets of 'moist' and 'ruby'; but something at that moment drew off her attention, and, parting them slightly, she glanced away across the room; and he knew what was meant by 'the grace of a startled fawn.' As for talking, the notion never occurred to him: he was too busy turning to what account the shortness of the time permitted this opportunity of correcting by a comparison with the flesh and blood original the image he had been worshipping so long in his heart. And this he did with eyes that, while, in the most curious way, as he thought, taking in at once details and whole, suddenly had become endowed with an acuteness of vision which showed him things as they really were. The dimpled elbows he well remembered; but how could he have forgotten so fascinating a detail as the soft bend of her arm? Other beauties too there were now for the first time visible: the rounded satin-smooth shoulders whose dazzling whiteness he had never seen anything to match, and the firm small breasts. Then the throat, which, while still she was a child, he had been so fond of spanning between his fingers – and at the mere recollection he could almost feel within their clasp its warm and yielding compass – now had a very different necklace: a row of tiny diamond flowers recalling those lines of Pastoral Phillips:

> 'Little neck so white and round,
> Little neck in brilliants bound.'

And for her hair which, at Tremlett, had in elf-locks tossed upon her shoulders and to touch which had been, at Tours, the object of many a long and craftily-calculated advance, now it was pinned, frizzed, plaited, curled with all the hairdresser's art and carried at top, twinkling and trembling, a diamond aigrette.

Then, as he would have talked, there appeared, on the arm of a gentleman evidently taking her down to supper, a hot red-faced dame who, stopping for an instant as she passed, exclaimed:

'Oh, my dear, do let me cool my hands on your shoulders! They must be white marble!'

And the two were once more alone. But the music of the next dance had already begun and a young man was coming towards them, obviously with the intention of claiming Nita's hand.

'You'll give me another, won't you?' he asked.

'Oh, I'm so sorry, but I'm engaged for the next two,' she said, 'and I'm rather afraid——'

All along he had had an uneasy suspicion that her manner was awkward and constrained, and now choosing to look on this reply as a confirmation of his fears:

'The next time we meet, then,' he interrupted, 'I shall hope to be more fortunate!'

And this he said in the chill tones he flattered himself he knew so well how to employ. He had only, he thought, to resort to them to place on the instant an immeasurable distance between himself and one to whom but the moment before he might have been speaking in the friendliest terms. And, bowing coldly, he turned on his heel and went off to the supper-room. Here, sitting down at one of the round

little tables, he pulled off his gloves with an air and called for cham-
pagne. The ceiling shook overhead.

'I suppose,' he observed to the friend next whom he had placed
himself, 'I suppose they're at the Kitchen Lancers!' And he assumed
an expression as if he had had some nasty taste in his mouth: it was
that he always put on when desirous of expressing scorn: 'In the
kitchen, you know, they're called Drawing-room Lancers!'

Then presently – 'If one did not know,' he said, 'that it was the fairy
feet of our loves flitting over the floor, one would have thought it a
herd of elephants!'

Again for a few moments he was silent; but when the person on his
other side – she could never have been pretty and was now no longer
young – turned to him with a –

'Mr. Tristram, you who have always such good taste, what do *you*
advise me to go as to a fancy-ball? Mr. Spicer here suggests a flower!'

He looked her up and down as if considering and in an accent into
which he tried to discharge all the disappointment and rage that were
consuming him, replied – 'Yes! a wallflower!' and so getting up without another word went out.

And that night as he undressed he set his lips in a stiff smile of
self-derision as he thought how happy he had been but a few short
hours before when putting on the very clothes that now, in a far different mood, he was laying aside. How he had desired to see that evening's face, and what a sight after all it had given him! He laughed out
loud as he remembered how, of the dozen different meetings his busy
fancy had imagined, not one had been like the reality.

The next morning however chanced to be fine, and with so bright a
sun overhead and so blue a sky, trees and grass so freshly green before
his eyes, and, in his ears, the cheerful busy twittering of the birds on
Duck Island, he could no more imagine as on his way to the office he
crossed St. James's Park, how he had yielded to such foolish misgivings, than, in broad daylight, he could understand how he had given
way to the ghostly terrors that, in the lonely darkness of the night,
so often made his flesh creep and his heart stand still. And taking the
incidents of the previous evening in order, from the moment when
first he had caught sight of Nita to that when he had turned on his
heel and walked away, he was soon so confirmed in this pleasanter
view that he grew impatient for their next meeting.

Nor had he long to wait. Two days after, as he walked in the Park by the Achilles Statue, he met her with her mother. He would have much preferred to have taken his place by *her* side and have talked to *her*, but the curious impulse that so often forced him to do and say just the opposite of what he would have liked, made him go – he felt its compulsion as of something outside him and beyond his control – next Lady Adelaide and address his conversation instead to her. But at all events she was gracious, and before they separated had told him he was to be sure to come and see them as soon as he could; while Nita, as he bowed and lifted his hat, bestowed on him one of those smiles in which his own consciousness and his perceptions of the surrounding scene were always for the moment lost.

So on the following afternoon he walked up to their house, but only to hear that they were 'not at home.' And this was what he still was told the next time he went and the next again. Yet was it to his own bad luck, not in the least to them, that he continued to attribute his disappointments till a young man of his acquaintance came, as to a friend of theirs, to inquire of him where they lived.

'What do you want to know for?' said he.

'Because,' the other replied, 'they've asked me to dinner, and as I've lost Lady Adelaide's note I don't know where to write to.'

And then he could think of nothing but how they had asked some one else to dinner before him. *Now* of course when they sent him an invitation, he would not dream of accepting it; and he even drafted his letter of refusal. But when none came his anger grew so hot against them that he was even glad of such relief as was afforded by putting his case under feigned names to friends:

'Not however that *I* care the least!' he would always conclude; 'only, you know, if that's the way they behave to others, they'll never get on!'

He was sorry that he had talked of them in such terms of enthusiasm; he felt sure that everybody was saying:

'But they don't seem to care much for him!'

He wondered what had changed them. What was his offence? Had any one been speaking ill of him behind his back? Perhaps after all it was merely a case of *souvent femme varie*. Only of one thing he was quite certain, that *he* would not be the first to try to restore to their former state the relations between them. But time went on, and still as they made no sign, unable to hold out any longer, he went off to call once more. He did his best indeed to persuade himself that he was solely moved by philosophic curiosity to observe how they would seek to excuse themselves; but in his heart he knew he was making the effort to see them in order that he might at least not be dismissed unheard; for, as when at school he had quarrelled with Els, he thought that if only he could plead in person he had won his cause. Then, as again he got the answer: 'Not at home,' and so turned away, his chief annoyance arose from his fear lest in his visit they should see but a proof of his extreme eagerness to keep friends. He would have liked to write a few lines on his card to explain that his one desire in coming had been to show them by a frigid and stiff manner that if they, upon their part, did not care for him, to him, on his, they were equally indifferent.

And that evening they met at dinner. His bow was cold, but it was in the friendliest possible way that across the room both Nita and Lady Adelaide nodded and smiled. Afterwards he was allowed to take a chair at this latter's side the while her daughter sat at her feet on a stool. It seemed to him as if they both were her children, he by adoption of marriage as Nita by birth. And presently from where it lay in the girl's lap he took her fan; with its soft fluffy pink feathers and delicate carved sticks it was somehow such an one as he would have expected her to have; and as he opened and shut it, he talked of old times, and chiefly of the summer they had spent together years ago at Tremlett: to speak familiarly of her as a child gave him a sort of lien on her now.

'We shall be there this autumn,' Lady Adelaide said, 'you must get Mabel to ask you too!'

'Oh, yes, do!' Nita chimed in, 'you will, won't you? And we'll go and see all the old places we went to when you were there before!'

Then, as at last they rose to take their leave, they asked him to come and see them on the following Thursday after the Drawing-Room; for Nita had not yet been presented and had only been allowed to go to the dance where they had met because it was her sister-in-law by whom it was given.

For the next few days he lived in an agony of apprehension lest something or other might prevent his going, and a dozen times he repeated to his fellow-clerks that, happen what would, on the Drawing-Room afternoon he must be away. And at last it came, this day so eagerly expected, and it was time to start, and he was driving off. By St. James's Palace he passed a troop of Blues; the officer who

was riding at their side was Els. His glossy-coated black charger was
tossing its head and, dancing sideways, stepped as if on eggshells, the
while he bent to its every movement with all that grace and ease which
long ago at Tremlett had seemed so charming. The gold and steel and
shiny leather of his accoutrements flashed in the sun; with his fair
boyish face he looked like Cherubin dressed for the part of Mars. And
so he reached the house. Nita was standing in the middle of the big
front-room, her train spread round her feet in sweeping and billowy
convolutions of soft white silk. There was something of the same
contrast between her child's beauty and the costly state and splendour
of her feathers and dress as that which had made him so fond of the
particular imagination of his which had represented her as a duchess.
Nor had he ever before realised how perfect a type she presented of
high-born girlhood. Yet even while he was thus admitting in her still
another claim to his worship, his manner grew momentarily more
constrained, and just touching the tips of her fingers with his own by
way of shaking hands, almost without a word, he went off into the
inner room where some of the company were already gathered at
tea. He was furious at thus again being forced to do the exact opposite
of what he wished; and his anger with himself and his world, already
great, was increased by the glimpses of her which he caught through
the crowd, bestowing on others those smiles and glances which might
well have been his and to have had but one of which he would, he
felt, almost have died. And the only means to his hand of gratifying
the rage he was consumed with was to do what he could to turn into
ridicule the ceremony she had just been taking part in; and that after
all was but a poor satisfaction, since, as at the ball, the bitterest utter-
ances to which he could frame his tongue were far from affording any
but the slightest relief to the fury that filled his heart.

No, he said, he had not been, not he; he had seen more than
enough as that morning he had passed through the Mall; really for a
moment he had thought it was Madame Tussaud's Chamber of Hor-
rors out for an airing.

But though it was torture thus to stay and see her physically so
near, the while, for all the good he had of her, they might still have
been separated by the Kentish woods and hop-gardens, the Channel
waves and the great plain of northern France, he could not bring himself to go. Nor did he succeed in so doing till he had been left alone in
a corner without a soul to speak to. Not that every one he knew was

gone, but to each in turn he had made some remark either personally so rude or such an outrage on some prejudice of the person addressed that one and all had refused to have anything more to say to him.

Yet scarce had he left the house than he began to count the hours that must elapse before he would see her again; as indeed his custom was, though each time they met he parted from her more unhappy than the last. For now having had a hundred fancies of the delights in the way of keen emotions, bitter or sweet he hardly cared, that their next rencontre would give, when at last it came, it would afford him absolutely no sensation at all; and now he would experience such a revulsion of feeling that for the moment love almost appeared hate. But whichever of these effects was produced, he always assumed an air either of surprise or indifference, as if she had been the last person in the world that he had cared or looked to see. He knew such conduct was unwise, but he could not help it: *c'était plus fort qut lui.*

And as it varied, the way these meetings affected him, so also did his behaviour towards her. At one time his cue would be humility; and then, his experience of her brother reminding him that, if you approached any one as a divinity, you would probably be used like a dog, suddenly he would become haughty and cold. Besides, since in love one always gave and the other received the kiss, he thought he would see whether, by displaying less eagerness, he could not arrive at playing the latter, instead of the former part, as hitherto had been his fate. He would however have been glad to hit on some other way of seeking to win her love than by begging for it like a slave, or trying to make believe it was a matter of perfect indifference whether or no he gained it. But he had never been of those who find that to heave their heart into their mouth is an easy task. Nor did the light in which he considered his position with regard to her remain always the same. At one moment it was a source of no small surprise that she did not seem honoured and delighted by his admiration; he had very little money, it was true, but that disadvantage should have been largely compensated by the triumph she ought to have felt in seeing him the clever, the amusing, the contemptuous, the proud, thus in submission at her feet; and then he would wonder how any one so poor, so insignificant as he could ever have hoped to get a girl like her to wife. A pleasant fancy forsooth for a fellow who hadn't a groat in his pocket to look for a yoke-mate above the clouds! A poor man should be contented with what he found, and not go seeking for truffles at the bottom of the sea. And while thus curiously he reflected on his own conduct, he tried and tried – thinking without ceasing till his head began to ache – to divine the reasons that dictated hers. To what was due the change that he could not help seeing had taken place? What had he done? But perhaps he was looking for facts, where there were only feelings. If so, all hope indeed was gone; for distance might have been traversed, difficulties surmounted, time lived through, but if the object of one's affections ceased to care for one, the possibility of satisfaction was cut off at its very source.

Sometimes, however, tired out with this perpetual see-saw, for a few days he would keep away. Then all at once, having up to the last moment been quite resolved not to go to the ball where he knew she would be, his courage would fail him, and he would hurry off, breathless with excitement lest after all she should not be there. It had been rightly said that to try and cure oneself of adoring a woman by leaving her, was like trying to get rid of one's thirst by refusing to drink.

## CHAPTER XXIX

On one occasion, full of anxiety to see her, his chief feeling as he went upstairs was yet only one of complacence at the fit of his shirt. Why did not others share his admiration? He made no attempt to dance, but, posting himself by the door, began to watch for her arrival. But time went on and when still she did not appear and now he was being 'silted up,' as he called it, by new comers, he set off to look for her. At one moment, edging, twisting, squeezing, he advanced a foot or two; the next, encountering a block, he would stamp with impatience and make faces of rage at the backs of those who thus stopped his way; and a dozen times his heart was in his mouth as he thought he recognised as hers a white shoulder or the back of a head. Yet, often disappointed, he had already begun to fear that she was not come, when suddenly in the distance he caught sight of her and turned sick and faint with desire. Even then however he would not make straight for where she was standing; and when at length by a roundabout way he got to the place, it was with an air of only just having found her out that he asked for a dance and in a tone of such indifference as must, he felt, draw an answer in the negative:

'I'm afraid,' she began, when he, not even letting her finish her sentence, broke in with:

'You've scratched yourself!' and pointed to a tiny red line on her shoulder.

Round her neck was a string of pearls; from between her breasts – a pair of maiden worlds unconquered – the lace edge of her handkerchief peeped out; it struck him that his glove was very dirty. But she appeared to resent his interest in her body as she would a touch, and at that moment her partner turning to her with a 'Come along!' she put her hand lightly upon his shoulder and without a word went floating off. So, making no further attempt to speak, he confined himself to acting at her. Once their eyes met and, though it was all he could do to sustain, unmoved, her glance, he did not change his air of impertinent indifference, but without an instant's stop continued to look slowly round the room; and once, as she was dancing with some one he knew, he actually went up to them, and, passing close in front without paying her more heed, he thought, than any piece of furniture – but he thrilled all through – talked for a moment to his friend with a semblance of great animation.

Presently she went dancing past him with Orr – Orr whom he had not seen since they had been together at Tours and whom he had not so much as known to be in town. He was always jealous of those whose society she took pleasure in, and the feeling was more intense than ever when he saw her with one he had so many reasons for disliking; and when besides, as the band was at the most pathetic bar of the waltz, smiling and blushing, with an airy lifting and falling of her skirt – he was so close it almost touched him in its rhythmical swing: – and with a waving grace of motion altogether indescribable, she went by upon this rival's arm, it seemed to him as if indeed a sword pierced through his heart. He could hold out no longer, but as, the dance now over, she was moving away, approached from behind, and:

'Will you give me the next?' he pleaded.

How pretty it was, the hair brushed up and back so as to show the tiny shell of the ear and the lines of the neck and shoulders as they swept down under the inverted curve of the bodice! But she either did not or would not hear, and as, making no reply, she passed on, with a laugh he dropped back. He tried to feel glad that his dignity, if not in his own, still in others' eyes at least, was safe.

And then he fell to dancing; in violent and ceaseless exercise lay his sole chance of delaying the moment when he would have to think. It was the Hungarian band that was playing; the dominant note of all their airs was that of the table-like instrument whose wires a gipsy-faced fellow with a movement at once rapid and considered was striking here and there with a hammer; and each appeared to breathe a savage harsh despair much more in accord with his mood than would have been the voluptuous melancholy of such a waltz as he had danced to with her the first night they had met. The wild strains challenged him to keep up with their storm and rush, and faster and faster flew his feet over the polished floor, as he felt himself and his partner swept along on the torrent of sound, now up, now down according as it sank and rose. And still he looked about for Nita; but so fast did he revolve that the faces of those standing round all ran one into another and everything became a confused and confusing haze of light. He only hoped that she for her part could see him, and that, while she would be piqued by observing how little what she did and said affected him, she would at the same time feel sorry that she was not dancing with one who danced so well.

In the intervals he talked; but, far from seeking to please, his one desire was to make the bitterest remarks he could on as many subjects as possible. He spoke in the clear-cut tones which he always liked to think gave an added sting to what he said, and felt the same strange swelling sense of command which, when dancing, made him fancy he was dominating the tumult of sound: but yet he had to recognise that his words were without effect; the only powers of satire which would have contented him, would have been such as would there and then have dashed the objects of his animadversion into ten thousand pieces.

'Just look at that fellow over there!' he said. 'Did you ever see a better specimen of that sexless horror, Society's pet fool?'

And presently he went on: 'They're all very smartly dressed, aren't they? Woman is different from meat, for though being well-dressed makes her more appetising, she's also very good partially dressed, as is the case here; or even you know undressed altogether – like the schinken I used to get in Germany.'

It was quite as much her obvious happiness as any general sense of anger against her that forced him to such talk. Though how if after all, like him, she were merely affecting a gaiety she did not feel? And now with eyes cast down and, hovering about her lips, the amused shy smile he knew so well, he saw her standing listening to her partner, now, with the prettiest twistings of her head and neck, rearranging her sleeves; and every pose increased his rage against the small face that with an air of such unconsciousness was troubling him so deeply. He could scarce keep from rushing forward and forcibly carrying her off. It made him mad to think there was a danger of all that proud delicate grace for him meaning nothing. Yet the time had been, and not so long ago either, when he had had reason to hope it would be his. But since then, while he on his part had been travelling one way, she upon hers had gone quite another, and the small distance which had separated them at Tours was now a great gulf. Why had he not seized his opportunity and placed it out of her power to look down on him by gaining the right of doing so on her? But he had been a fool, and so now all he had was the memory of the innocently familiar terms on which once they had lived together. Perhaps it was not yet too late. Why should he not at least make the attempt? He would do himself a pleasure, since he still desired her, though surely now not out of the lust love sublimated, but with that to which hate lent an added zest; and it would be fine sport to win her affections and when she had given him all that a girl can, to turn upon her and vow that he had never cared for her and cast her off, her heart broken and her body shamed. So would he recover, and more, that relative superiority of position which he had all along been thinking was his, but which now, to the no small hurt of his vanity, he was beginning to see was really hers. It was a blow he could never forgive, never – and then he laughed. Why, what an ass he was! In a very short time he would have forgotten even her name! Meanwhile, if he intended to execute this plan, the first thing was to keep his temper; which it was as necessary for him to do as for a fisherman. Up to then, instead of bringing her to love him by making her, for instance, laugh, as did Orr, his only notion had been to show her how much he loved. All that must now be changed. He was only sorry that he could not, as with her brother at school, have recourse to gifts to aid him in winning back her wanton heart; but certainly the plan had not in that instance been a success.

The thought of Els recalled the curious pleasure he had always taken in the fact that the sister had succeeded to the love whose first-fruits had been the brother's: while, as Orr had ousted him from the affections of the boy, so now he was doing, had perhaps done, from the girl's. The coincidence was strange and inclined him to think that very likely after all his life at school had been as real as that he had lived since. And then he caught sight of him leaning against the wall further down, and talking to Nita. He wondered what he thought of him and if he knew that they were once more rivals. For himself, he was surprised and angry to find that the sentiments he had entertained for the boy, so far from being dead as he imagined, even then were struggling within him to burst the bands of what had been no more than slumber and live again towards the man. And as he recognised the same air of authority he had so often admired in him at Scarisbrick and found himself involuntarily admiring it in the same way now, he turned to a friend:

'Look at that chap down there!' he said; 'don't the baggy knees of his trousers give him the appearance of one of those broken-down old cab-horses one sees in the ranks?'

But here the band struck up for the next dance and his friend went off. A sudden gust of fury swept over him to see himself thus left, and he had in an instant comprehended in his rage and hate him for whom but a moment before his feelings had been almost kindly as for the confidante of the expression of those sentiments towards the rest of the world. Why was he not great so that people would have to treat him with respect? And a sour smile fixed itself at once on his lips, and still was there when, passing through the entrance-hall on his way out, he saw Nita sitting in the recess under the stairs. She was alone amidst the roses, but he went by with an affectation he was at pains to make transparent of not even noticing that she was there. Then once outside he began to hum a snatch of a waltz: 'Damn her!' he said, and hummed again.

Then by and by he thought he perceived that Orr was a suitor for Nita's hand, and favoured by Lady Adelaide; but he maintained that he bore this latter no grudge for her preference. It was merely a question of money. As well fall foul of a City friend for leaving you to attend to business! His rival was wealthy, a fact patent to all; while he had as yet but talents and even in them could not expect others to share his own lively faith, since his very vanity forced him to acknowledge that, so far, he had done nothing to prove the claim he laid to their possession. Nor was there any need to be angry with the girl herself. While she had loved him, he had loved her: she had desisted; and on both sides the obligation was void. He ought never to have expected that the hours of bliss in which they had met so often would last for ever; and now that they were gone, while of course free to regret the present, he should at any rate be grateful for the past. But though he would nourish no feelings of ill-will towards either, he was equally resolute not to let himself be used as a second string to their bow. And while regard for that personal dignity of which he flattered himself he had always been so careful, forbade him further to press his attentions on one to whom they were so obviously indifferent, if no more: it needed no great powers of perception to see how much truth was contained in Priscilla Lammeter's remarks as to the folly of continuing to sit on an addled egg. Only, while waiting till more effectually he could get rid of the old infection by taking some new one to his eye, he might as well do what he could by refusing to think of her. But hardly had he formulated this resolution than he found his thoughts once more in their accustomed track. They had acquired as strong a habit of running in her direction as had at Tours his footsteps of going to the Châlet.

And when he had three times repeated his vow never again to waste on her so much as a single thought, and three times had broken it in scarcely more than that number of minutes, he resolved to see if a surfeit would produce the same effect as he had looked to have from abstinence. Were not drunkards cured by never letting them taste of anything that had not spirit in it? Besides, now that he was no longer under the spell, it would be very entertaining to submit her to a critical examination. It would be as if a priest, after implicitly believing for years in the wonder-working powers of some image, should one fine day get up from his knees, and proceed with an amused curiosity to investigate what for so long he had held a shape of heaven. The Nita of his fond imagination was dead, and that being so, he would now at last be able to see what the real one was like. And, considering, he marvelled how he could ever have complained of fancy and memory as being both alike unequal to the calls he had made on them for poetic epithets and synonyms wherewith fitly to describe her. Why, except just when her face lighted up, she was scarce even pretty! And that this was indeed the case, and that his beloved was after all no more than another beloved, he was certified by the fact that, with one solitary exception, he had worshipped alone. There could then be no doubt that her beauty had in greater part been his, her lover's, gift. Yet he could not but confess that still she moved him as did no other girl though a hundred times more charming. But this was only a proof of the theory which had been suggested by his relations with Els long ago at school and first had taught him to know them for what they were: that, while for friendship there must be reasons, love could not only exist without any seeming-adequate cause, but even draw life from what appeared as if it much rather should have been its death: so the skilful chemist distilled scents that were the more exquisite as the substances from which he compounded them were the more repulsive. He could not of course deny that loving her had given him sensations such as he had got from nothing else: but in this she had been merely, the instrument from which his own exquisite skill had drawn the ravishing melodies whose echoes even then still murmured, inexpressibly charming, in his heart; and no doubt but that, as he went through life, he would find lots of others to serve him in this respect every bit as well as she. A lovely air will always please, change as one may the piano or violin that it is played upon. But even as the assertion that she was not pretty crossed his lips, in his heart he knew that there was no sight in the world which he preferred to her, while for the stupidity he also accused her of, he felt that he would have counted all the wisdom of the earth but a sorry exchange.

Yet still, grounding his belief on the fact that once or twice for quite an hour at a time he had forgotten her, he made sure that he was fast outgrowing, if he had not already outgrown, his foolish passion. It was therefore not without pleasure that one afternoon he found himself by chance in the Row about the hour at which, as he remembered, usually she took her ride, and so like to have an opportunity of proving to himself how complete was his cure. Yet what if, after all, in thus wilfully running into danger, he were only acting as he had often done when, a small boy, he had cut his finger and had pulled at the plaster to see whether the place were well? And he had already turned to go home when suddenly he caught sight of her on horseback. For a moment their eyes met and it seemed to him as if his heart had stopped beating and as if, so far from being cured, he had never loved her as he loved her then. But he only bowed coldly, the while his feet, as though moved by a will of their own, continued to bear him away and he even gave a hearty laugh at some small joke of a companion's.

That evening he heard that Orr and she were engaged. At first he could think of nothing but vengeance. He would have such revenges on them both that all the world should – he would do such things –

what he knew not, but they should be the terrors of the earth; and would follow the advice that Spendius gave to Matho and, since he could not satisfy his love, at least would glut his hate. Yet was it not very ill-becoming one who prided himself on his power to remain unmoved by mere externals, this display of what was really a like spirit to that which leads a bully to break the windows of his light o' love? And he was the sooner led to abandon all schemes of active retaliation by considering that luckily there was a way in which, while still fully asserting his own loftier dignity of mind, he could revenge his injuries far more effectually than by any of the thousand and one plans he at first had thought of: a way that not only would leave his own wounds to heal instead of keeping them green, but enable him to rise superior to his enemies with whom the utmost vengeance within his power would at best but have made him even: and that was to treat them with silent disdain.

'The robbed who smiles steals something from the thief!'

And he repeated the line with a delight caused partly by finding that the view he now inclined to had already been put in the metaphorical way he was so fond of, and in part by the gratifying discovery that his reading was able to supply him with so apt a quotation. He recognised indeed that it was not philosophy so much as incapacity of action that was the cause of his change of mind. He could not even wring her heart by letting her see that he did not care for her any longer, or rather had never done so at all. If only the village of Tremlett had been a place where one could go and stay! He would have walked about till he had met her, and then shown her by his demeanour how absolutely indifferent she was become to him. But though the consciousness of how matters really stood might disturb his own self-content, he hoped that to others at any rate his conduct would seem dictated by the higher motive.

And then, if he had not her herself, he still if he liked could have his illusions about her, as would certainly not have been the case had she become his wife. Or, if he preferred so doing, he could imagine himself married now to this kind of girl and now to that, instead of being tied for life to one hard material fact. It was easy enough to strip her shrine of all the decorations his fancy had adorned it with and carry them bodily off to ornament that of some other saint. There were quite as good fish in the sea as ever came out of it, and when one could get *a* woman, to go hankering after one in particular, was as foolish as to wish for some special leg of mutton and refuse to satisfy one's hunger with any other. Besides, since Fate had been so far good to him as to remove both his father and mother while still he was young enough to enjoy the money which they would have otherwise absorbed, it would be doing but greenly to make so much kindness of none effect by voluntarily saddling himself with a wife. Parents were a misfortune, but a wife a fault.

But there was still another reason for not being moved by the news of her engagement in the proof of her unworthiness, which was furnished by the very fact of her jilting him. Doubtless in a previous state of existence she had been just such another boy as her brother; and he laughed to think how apposite in both the affections of his life he had found that aphorism of Plato's, now in its original, as once in an inverted form. And while her preference of another argued her morally undeserving of him; the fact of that other being Orr was enough to show her mentally so as well. And with her folly she must certainly have infected him: it was impossible otherwise to account for his having been so stupid as to waste so much time and emotion over one who was too dull to see that he was clever and who, like Æsop's fabled cock, was better pleased with such a barley-corn as Orr than with a gem like him: but he had to make excuses to himself for the vanity of this comparison. Nor ought he to feel surprise at such an one dispensing her favours after the fashion of her kind, which was always widely different from that of those mares of whom Xenophon tells, who, while in their beauty, would never admit the embraces of an ass. And yet – and yet – as he knew himself to be worth far more than any one else suspected, how could he say but that this might not also be the case with his rival?

Yet the pleasure he obtained from these reflections was but another form of that he was always so fond of – blaspheming the idol he adored. For he was almost beside himself at the mere imagination of any one so much as kissing her, so much as setting profane lips to those ears, that mouth, those cheeks, the thought of which was by itself enough to turn his blood. And this in spite of all his efforts to convince himself of the unreasonableness of such jealousy: her features – Lord warrant us, what features! – were not joints of meat from which each bite taken would have diminished the portion remaining over for him, or even grapes with a bloom that any touch rubbed off. And if such had been his state of mind when merely obliged to admit as a general proposition that she might be kissed by another, what were now his feelings when forced to think, as of something going to happen almost immediately, of her surrendering, not alone those lips which his had never dared to touch, but the whole of her sweet young body, and that to one whom of all others he had reason to hate. However, he tried to believe that he ought rather to be glad she had not died, for a husband one may always hope to get the better of, but never death.

He had vowed never if he could help it to see her, certainly never to speak to her, again; but the Foreign Office party was now near at hand and his resolutions all melted away as he remembered that, since she was leaving town, it would be his last chance of meeting her for a whole twelvemonth. And while, resolved to go, he yet pretended that his mind was not made up, or that, if he went, it would only be to show her his love was dead; he was busy considering in what words to take his final leave. They must be such as she could never forgive, so that there might be fixed between them a gulf no weak craving on his part for reconciliation could ever bridge; and such too as to give him the sole pleasure, that of making her miserable, which, since he could not make her happy, was all he had left. For anything was better than to have to think that he had entirely passed out of her life. And as this meeting must needs be their last – for once he had spoken he could not expect her to afford him another chance of wounding her or of throwing himself at her feet and passionately entreating still, on any terms, to be allowed to keep a corner in her heart – so must he choose his phrases with all possible care. Yet though he thought and thought, he could only settle on the concluding words:

'I can but regret, Miss Southwood, that I should ever have been so misjudged as to take a very ordinary rocket for one of those stars by which a whole life can be guided and cheered!'

This, followed by a frigid bow and a turning on his heel, should be effective enough. He would take, too, the famous Amboise handkerchief and tear it in two before her. Knowing, however, by previous experience that, admirable strategist on paper, in the heat of battle he was apt to forget his plans and act on the spur of the moment, he was afraid that this might happen now, and to guard against such a danger, not content with repeating this peroration over and over again till his head ached, suddenly, as he read or walked, he would stop and go through it once more.

'Of course,' said a lady of his acquaintance a few days before, 'of course you'll go in your uniform!' And to his own cynical amusement – for he did not possess one – he found himself saying, 'Oh, of course!'

Indeed to be able to go at all, he had to borrow one from a friend. Yet even so, he wished he had been dining out that night in order to have had a chance of showing-off. As it was, all he could do was to walk a little way to a cab and lean over the doors as he drove along, thus enabling passers-by to wonder who he was and himself to admire the fit of his gloves and the smallness of his hands as he put them out. Then all at once he was horrified at the effect mere clothes were producing on one who flattered himself he was a philosopher. Once or twice, too, the rolling of the cab, the keen evening air as it came in puffs against his face and the noise of the wheels nearly sent him to sleep. Arrived at the door, he was quite astonished at the crowd he found going in. It had never occurred to him that there would be any one there beside themselves.

Then, as slowly with the crowd he went upstairs a step at a time, he kept making, to an acquaintance he found next to him, remarks of the same sort as he had done at the ball where he and Nita had last met.

'Don't you think,' he said, 'they ought to supply one with catalogues of all the prize-beasts with their stars? At least on foreign diplomats they tell one the different posts they have been at, like the labels on a portmanteau.'

Presently there was a general movement, the band in the hall struck up 'God save the Queen' and down the lane suddenly formed through the room, over the heads of the people, bending, as he thought, like corn before the wind, he saw the royal guests advancing. They passed, and as the crowd closed up behind, he found himself suddenly face to face with Nita. Haughty and unsmiling he bowed ceremoniously, wishing to signify that by the laws of society they were acquainted, but that he had no desire to be friends. For a moment he made as if he would have passed on his way, but scarce had he gone a step when he stopped short, hesitated, took another step, and at last came up to her with a set face in which he fancied she must surely be able to read his determination to have a battle. And, 'What an awful crowd!' he said, 'how hot it is! Are you going on anywhere?'

And as he uttered these commonplaces, his clear-cut tones appeared to him to have acquired a power of stabbing quite independent of what they meant, while his eyes were ablaze with scorn. He could never remember what more either he or she had said till at last he had heard her asking: 'What's that you've got?' as she pointed to a handkerchief he held in his hand.

'Oh, that?' he cried, and looked at it; 'I found it the other day when I was turning over some old drawers. I rather think it's what they call a *gage d'amour*, but I've forgotten whose it was. You don't happen to know by any chance?' and he held it out.

'Oh,' she exclaimed, 'why——' and stopped.

'I beg your pardon?' he said with elaborate politeness. 'What did you say?'

But she answered never a word. For a moment he hesitated, and then with a gesture of sudden fury tore it in two; the sound of the tear seemed to him to symbolise the breaking of his heart; and, turning, he disappeared in the crowd.

# CHAPTER XXX

The next morning as he dressed, he kept on repeating to himself, 'Well, it's a mercy that's at an end!'

Though, even as he uttered the words, he knew that he did not in the least believe what he was saying and that, had he done so, he would have been, not glad, but more unhappy than he was. Still, if it indeed were true that everything was over between them; if at last he could apply to something real that 'O, and is all forgot?' of Helena's, which he had never read in the tone he believed so pathetic without half fancying it a cry wrung from his heart by no mere imaginary sorrow; then at any rate he might console himself with the reflection that he had come nearer than ever before to the experience of one of those great griefs he had long considered the only tolerable alternative to a perfect felicity. Yet if he now were actually in the midst of one of these same terrible delights of which he had formed such high notions – well, they were very tame. But perhaps, even if the end had come in the shape of such a Paolo and Francesca tragedy as would have been the climax most to his taste, that too would have proved equally poor in emotions.

Meanwhile, he must lose no time in resolving on what to do. Once before he had decided against attempting revenge; while a critical examination of his idol had proved nothing to his purpose: it only remained then to forget or to fall in love with some one else. Of this latter or homœopathic mode of treatment by which Romeo had been so quickly cured of his passion for Rosaline, he had twice already made trial. Fruitlessly once when, as a boy at Bridwell, he had thought to expel Els from his affections by installing young Clavering in the place; and once with complete success, when he had been more than consoled for his disappointment in the brother by the love he had little by little come to feel for her from whom now in her turn he was so anxious to divert his thoughts. But it was a remedy which had one great disadvantage, that of not being within one's own control, and his pride preferring something for which there would be no need to depend on any one beside himself, it was the former of the two methods of cure that he finally decided on trying. So only would he be able to retire once more into the refuge he was always so ready to fly to, himself, and there, secure from the outer world, sing his favourite song:

'I care for nobody, no, not I,
And nobody cares for me!'

Of course there were difficulties in the way. If he went out he would recollect how he had met her driving here or walking there, or riding in the Row; and indoors it was the same. A hundred times a day he would be reminded of what was gone from his life, now by some poetry once learnt to be quoted to her, and now by a book he remembered to have been reading just before going to a party where he knew they would meet. And sometimes through the open windows from the neighbouring barracks would float the faint strains of a waltz, and he would feel that vague yearning which, now that she was never to be his, was only pain as being without a hope of satisfaction. Even if, retreating within the very last of his defences, he shut his eyes, he could not blot hers, those charms, forth of his heart, nor indeed prevent himself seeing that smile he had never yet found words to describe. He told himself again and again that, as he had had the courage to quit her with his body, he could surely do the like with his mind; and yet the very act of trying to forget recalled her:

'En songeant qu'il faut qu'on oublie,
On s'en souvient!'

It was obvious that his only chance was to discover something to fill
the void that she till then had occupied. For she had been to him, as
once her brother, what God ought to be to all, and everything that he
had done, he had done with reference to her. Now of consequence he
had as much time on his hands as one day he would when, after the
appointed number of years, he took his pension.

This something should of course have been Ambition, in satisfying
which he ought by rights to have found a more than sufficient solace
for the disappointment of its twin-passion, Love. No doubt he had
thought that only in the gratification of the two at once could he ever
have found a resting content; and had maintained that he who had
gone nearer than any other to enjoying in one supreme hour all that
the world can give, had been Napoleon when, at the height of his
fame and power, he had gone out to Compiègne to welcome as his
bride the Cæsar's daughter. But he had never had a moment's hesitation as to which of the two he would abandon if he could not have
both. Indeed he had always held this to be no world in which to play
with mammets or tilt with lips. Nor ought Love to dwell with one
whose every thought should be of schemes of ambition, whom lust
of power would age before his time, and for whom happiness itself
must never be expected to do more than just for a moment allow of
unstringing the bow in order that it might presently again be bent
with even greater strength than before. Was he not one of those who,
still like the Corsican Upstart, cannot spare the time to amuse themselves with feelings or regrets? To whom everything, hate and revenge
no less than love, that comes under the head of mere personal action
is altogether unworthy concern. And though he had often tried to
justify his sighing by the example of all the great men that had done
so likewise; he had found his best comfort in pretending that he loved
but for pastime while unable to pursue the real object of his desires.
He ought the rather to be glad that, not having himself had courage
enough to cease from so wasting his energies, Fate had come to his
assistance and made it impossible for him to do so any longer. And the
rather as this same Jack-o'-Lantern chase was one he had been consistently unlucky in from the first days of his devotion to Els to those
when it was to the boy's sister that he had offered his heart. But what

if his ill-success in the satisfaction of this passion was a forewarning
of that which would attend him in his efforts to gratify the other?
At school everything had – how ran his favourite phrase? – yes, had
'broken under his hand.' Was it to be the same in real life?

And he would gladly have bidden his soul aspire to higher things,
and have found a way to utilise the whole forces of his mind, as well
those which had always been affected to the service of ambition as
those hitherto engaged in that of his heart, that were now set free;
thus would he have obtained ample relief for the pangs of disprized
love, and the higher he climbed the more deeply wounded her who
had rejected his affection, by showing her how much she had lost in
losing him.

But up to then he had made not one step on the road that was to
lead so far. No doubt he had gained his clerkship; true, he frequented a
society much better than any his birth or means could justly have pretended to, and had even won within its narrow limits a name for being
clever and amusing; while of his moral progress he had surely reason
to be proud. Yet, though without these things he would have thought
that he was still more hardly used, he scarce marked their possession.
It gave him no more pleasure than to use forks and spoons of silver
rather than of steel and electroplate. What was it after all to be what
Lady Hester Stanhope had called 'a dirty clerk'? For though doubtless
the position was one which for years he had aimed at reaching, it was
as a means he had looked forward to it, not as an end. And what was
it to go about to parties, and even to be considered as of some weight
in a certain set? Had rumour spoken truly, the fact would rather have
been a source of shame than pride; but he could never see what was
meant when it was said that every one had some influence, however
difficult it might for the moment be to recognise. As for his moral
progress, well, no doubt it was considerable, but it was not a thing
you could demonstrate to others; and much as he liked reality, he liked
show no less, and must seem as well as be. Besides he knew that, great
or little, he would have been neither envied for it nor admired. Many
of course would have been content, and rightly too, with what he had,
or, having so much, would at least have found patience to wait for the
more coming; but then he burnt with that desire to be distinguished
above the rest of mankind, which, according to the old man in *Paul et
Virginie*, was so unnatural, but without which he for his part would not
have cared to live. Content he scorned; content was base; his whole

nature revolted at the bare notion of resting satisfied with merely doing the duty that lay next before him. While still his examination was to pass, he had never taken an hour's rest without reproaching himself for halting before he had reached, not indeed his journey's end, but a point whence he could start; and now he felt the profoundest contempt for any one who could think of ease or pleasure while fame was still to achieve. As for being thankful – and to whom? – that he was no worse off, the very notion made him laugh aloud.

Nor was it only that he had not advanced, that he was nothing, who desired to be all, but for the life of him he could not perceive how the first step was to be taken. At Bridwell he had seen others make friends and achieve all sorts of successes, while he could do neither, and now on a larger scale it was the same. Round him on every side were contemporaries happy in the satisfaction of their love or their ambition, while he was still hedged in by that impalpable something he could never break through. The world was a weltering mass of drift, or at any rate unlike that smaller one of school, which yet he had not understood; nor could he recognise in it those traits the concentrated action of books had taught him to look for. He must not wonder then if he could not discern what place in it ought to be taken by the individual, or what that individual should do when, like himself, he wished to get on. For he could nowhere obtain a satisfactory reply to the questions he was always asking himself upon this point. As for books, they only told what had been the successive stages on the path of glory that their heroes had trodden, while what he wanted was processes and not results. One might as well think to learn how to play cricket or football from a manual of games as from the lives of the great how to grow great oneself. In former times one could be sure of achieving success, if only by the simple plan of having no scruples; and a few days ago he had come across a striking proof of the truth of this contention in the story of Chief-Justice Scroggs. But now there would be hundreds, not only ready but eager, to sell far more at a much smaller price. Besides he doubted whether, even if such things could still have been, he would have had any better success. For though surely capable of any wickedness, it must be wickedness on an heroic scale; his pride would never stoop to the thousand-and-one petty meannesses it was necessary to condescend to before one had a chance of committing the crime which would so raise one that all future misdeeds would be matters of history. In short, to put it in one of those figures under which he was always so fond of representing himself and his life, he would not hesitate to dye in blood his soul's robe of spotless white, but could by no means away with the notion of draggling it in the mire. Nor was it only his pride that here stood in his way, it was absolute incapacity, to judge at least from the bad fortune that had attended his efforts to curry favour with the authorities. He had tried at first to win their regard by just the same little artifices, just the same inflections of voice, with which he had in succession essayed to gain the hearts of Els and Nita, but none of his attempts had had any result, and he had soon given up, not them alone, but those besides he had made to intrigue. Nature had obviously designed him for an honest man.

Meanwhile he remained undecided what to think of this state of inactivity in which he appeared to be kept against his will. At one moment he would reflect that it was not *by* but *in* time that changes were wrought, and that the fatalism he inclined to consider a pledge of future success was, on the contrary, nothing but a device by which he sought to justify himself in his own eyes for sitting still; and at another that Fortune might any day come to his aid, and with some extraordinary event – a revolution perhaps, who could tell? – give him that lift-up on to the first rung of the ladder, which was all he needed to enable him, another Jack-o'-the-Beanstalk, to climb into the very clouds. And yet – and yet – since so far he had not succeeded, he found it hard to imagine how he would ever do so. But on the whole it was to the fatalistic theory he leaned as to the easier. If Chance would have him king, why Chance might crown him without his stir.

And while unable to find in books an answer to his questionings, it was equally impossible to do so from observing those he was brought into contact with. Why, for instance, had he failed to advance a single step while Orr was already well on the way? He was the cleverer of the two, and yet, whenever they had come into conflict it had been he who had gone to the wall. Yet with all the force of will that people talked so much of, what had his rival done? Look, too, at Lord Augustus! And how many other governors, who did not come up to the sole of his shoe, were called your lordship and ate their victuals off plate! And Els! what could he not have done with *his* advantages, who, for all one could see, was quite content to remain where Fortune first had set him down.

Which things being so, it only remained, by affecting content, to preserve his dignity in the eyes of the world until such time as he could appear, coming in a glory all the greater as the means he had achieved it by had been unseen. For as he was careful never to go where he would run a risk of being insulted, or even having violent hands profaning with their rude rough touch that temple of his own divinity, his person, so must he avoid the least appearance of trying for anything he was not sure of getting. Only he should not o'erleap his selle and, falling into the opposite extreme of protesting over-much as to his indifference, expose himself to the danger of having it said it was a case with him of sour grapes. And though he recognised that the brave ambitions he had had as a boy already by steps and slow degrees were descended into those of his present self, which by comparison were poor, he did not fear their suffering further diminu-tion, strong in the belief that, however to others he might seem sunk in the disgraceful sloth of contentment, still in his brain the tide of life was at the flood, swelled by that which but a little while before his heart had absorbed. Indeed he had made up his mind that the first signs of satisfaction which he discovered should be a signal for killing himself, and so escaping a life that in his own view would be one of intolerable unforgettable shame, as so different from that he once had hoped would be his.

And then again he began to long for the day when not only in his own eyes would he be justified in having feelings and opinions, but when the world would be all agog to know what they were. Indeed the frenzy to achieve success scarce left him a moment's peace. It made him mad to think that the sands of youth at least, if not of life, were even then running out, and that so far he had done nothing towards making himself a glorious name. What had not Napoleon already accomplished when but little older than he? Though it was true that Cromwell at fifty – at fifty, was it not? – had been still obscure. And he had only to read of Henry iv. of France having been famous at thirty-three; of some trait of the Great Emperor's iron will and endurance of fatigue, or even of any one being ambitious and forming resolves, to be filled with disgust of himself, of his way of life and of those he had to live with, and to long to be up and doing. He felt as if, sustained by his unconquerable will, he was sure of making himself an everlasting name; as if he could have commanded animate and inanimate nature and have created worlds. And then he would seem to be exhausted by these efforts of resolution, always without result, and would, as he

called it, fall back, only presently once more to spur his tired resolves
and so go through the same phases over again. As for the calamities
endured by so many of the great historical characters he thus loved
to compare himself with, for them he had scant sympathy. He for his
part would have been content to forego all the pleasures they had had,
and to have his life filled from beginning to end with misfortunes, so
long as they were sufficiently great and tragic and of a kind to draw
all eyes upon him. It was *la tourbe des menus maux* that was so hard
to bear. Only they must be misfortunes that were really great, for if
there was one thing more than another which he had in abhorrence,
it was that vulgar ape of greatness, notoriety; he could no more away
with it than with anything else, jewellery, plate, furniture, what not,
which tried to be taken for something better than it really was.

And while his reading thus a dozen times a day inflamed that impatience of privateness from which he already suffered so much; a like
effect followed each small success that from time to time was gained
by any one of his own standing or age. Never, indeed, as he listened
to the tale, did he forget to smile, but there was death in his heart, and
his only comfort was the thought that at least there were none whose
tender jealousy would have pressed him with questions as to why such
an one, and not he, had done this or that, to whom he would have had
to pretend that the news had not put him beside himself with rage.
And again he fell to wondering why others succeeded where he failed.
What was the use of his talents? For certainly, so far as he could judge
from their respective powers of conversation, he was far cleverer than
any of those, of those at least whom he knew, who thus outstripped
him in the race. Besides, he had that mysterious power of seeing into
things which was as much greater than any tangible achievement as
was potentiality than actuality. Moreover, such triumphs as appeared
to fill them with pride would have by no means been enough for him;
and the very inordinateness of his desires had this much, at any rate,
of good, that, if it prevented him from ever for a moment being content with what he had, it saved him from feeling jealous of others'
successes. For indeed he flattered himself that he was never nearer
such a sentiment than was implied in the fact of being in a hurry to do
something which should make him an object of envy and respect and
give him that right to criticise which he had already indeed assumed,
but dangerously and indefensibly. He only hoped that he was not
deceiving himself, and that it was not after all mere vulgar jealousy

this feeling which he liked to think compact of the noblest pride and emulation. For people often sought to hide, not alone from others but from themselves, their extreme unwillingness to bow the knee before any idol whatsoever, by constantly and vehemently asserting that no one could be readier to give ungrudging love and admiration if they could but find a worthy object, thus at once satisfying their envy and setting up as persons of superior taste to the general.

Nor was it only for thinking of the laurels of one particular person that he could not sleep. So long as he himself was kept at a standstill, the mere fact of some one else advancing, even though on a road he had no thought of journeying by, was enough to drive him almost mad with impatience. And he began to fear that nothing would ever satisfy him but being great in fifty different ways, and enjoying at once the reverence which is paid to a saint, the fear a Mephistopheles inspires, the ready service money and power dispose of, and the enthusiasm called forth by a conqueror in his hour of triumph. Even the little popularity of an amusing man was not too small a thing for his desires. He would have liked to be at once the Maréchal de Luxembourg in all his splendour of immense wealth and exalted rank and Rousseau at the Hermitage, owing to charity the roof that covered him and in such intervals as he could snatch from that labour of copying music by which he tried to support himself, composing the writings that were to shake the whole fabric of society to its foundations.

And while he grieved himself at everybody whose way prospered, he was quite as bitter against such as had merely inherited those advantages of money and position which, had they but been his, he could have turned to such good account. And as he looked askance at them, he thought how ridiculous and unjust it was that such creatures, incapable alike of sentiment and reflection, should, as a matter of course, be seeing and doing things which for him would have been rich in emotions he now could never hope to enjoy. He felt ashamed that by his very nature he must always remain unable to make bricks without straw, and that, however much effects might be in his own hands, causes must come from without. Really it was almost worth while to be a Christian, to be able to believe the Parable of Dives and Lazarus, and to think that, while oneself would be in Abraham's bosom, those who had now their good things would be in hell in torment. A short while since and he had found no hardship in his poverty; but that was when he had felt as if at any moment he chose he could cease to be poor, and was only playing at being so for the moment, as at the Petit Trianon Marie Antoinette had played at being a peasant; or as Haroun Alraschid had pretended to be all sorts of different people when wandering of nights with Mesrour through the streets of Bagdad. But now he knew that it was not his star to be wealthy; at the best he was only one of those who, ignorant how to acquire, can hope for nothing more than to be neither ridiculous nor base. He tried indeed to persuade himself that his character was too lofty and noble to find favour with that vulgar sovereign of the vulgar, Queen Money, and to raise himself to a height whence he might be able to look down as on things of no account on her gifts. But all the same he would have liked to be in the position of the old Greek philosopher he had somewhere read of, who made a fortune just to show that even on their own low ground he could beat the rabble. Meanwhile, as it was apparently beyond his power to make money for himself, he ought to be glad that a little was his by inheritance. Surely one was never sufficiently thankful it was not property, but people that died. Fancy, if the reverse had been the case, and, instead of having one's relations' money for oneself, one had to support them on one's own! Nothing in a person's life became him so much as what he left.

And as he envied every one's success, of whatever kind, and thought that, in their place, their fortune too would have been his, he began to wonder whether his choice of a career had been well made. He should have gone into an office where his interest would have been enough to give him that start which was all he needed; for could he but have walked he could have soared. And every part of the landscape becoming greener than that he stood on, he was certain that he would have been more content as anything but what he was; and, seized by a sudden passion for the far-away and unknown, he felt sure he would have been happier if he had gone into the Foreign Office or the Diplomatic Service, or even become a consul like one or two of his old schoolfellows. Only if he wished to change, he must be quick about it, since every moment necessarily made the doing so more difficult; the longer he stuck in his Slough of Despond, the harder would it be to get out. Yet surely even now he might have done some good, could he but have limited his ambition to one particular kind of success and bent up all his energies to win that: with talents far inferior to his, a fixed determination to succeed in some one special line had often achieved wonders. But while he could not bring himself to resign one single desire, fixing his eyes on the perfect result, he forgot that there was nothing he did but what, how unimportant soever at the moment it seemed, might have helped him to his end and for that reason was worth doing well.

So far he had always firmly believed his talents to be superior to those of others, and the only question he had ever asked himself was why, this being so, he did not, like them, succeed: what if, after all these years of being happy in so comfortable a conviction, he should have to acknowledge that it had no foundation in fact? How if the power had been right in the way in which, as at school, so now consistently, it had left him as he was? Why then, since this was a view to which he felt certain he would never succeed in bringing himself, he had not even that faculty of seeing things as they were, in the fancied possession of which he had now for so long taken pride?

Perhaps had these same talents of his been as great as he had thought for, he could have raised himself to a height where even his ambition would have been satisfied. He had always been fond of sarcastically praising the form of government that still obtained in England, as one which overrode the unjust saying, 'Unto him that hath shall be given,' and very wisely prevented any superabundance in one person of claims to consideration by hardly ever allowing anybody to be great at once really and in the eyes of the world; and he had often maintained that one reason for supporting it was that it afforded you a chance of attributing your failure in life to favouritism and so of preserving your self-esteem. Perhaps his fondness for saying smart things had led him unconsciously to fix on that very quality in the constitution he lived under which ought, in his eyes at any rate, to have redeemed all its other defects. And yet if he were nothing, and was not to be more, why those dreams of glory that ever since he could remember had filled his imagination? Why that confidence of success which till then he had enjoyed unshaken? But others doubtless had had the like, and yet had lived to prove that the world was right, which all along had held such a different opinion of them from that they had entertained of themselves. Such premonitions resembled those Bible prophecies the precocious irreverence of his boyhood had so often laughed at, of which the one that comes true is remembered out of the hundreds that, proving false, are forgotten. Though even were this not the case, what anticipations could he found on a presentiment that he would one day be great, when he had one as strong that he was to spend the whole of his life in waiting for something which would never come, and that, as he had failed at school, so was he destined to fail in after-life? At first he had been proud of his inability to do at all what others did well, considering an incapacity in trifles as strong presumptive evidence that one would succeed in matters of weight; and when, in his performance of some ordinary little official task, he would meet with no praise but even perhaps blame, he had consoled himself with the reflection that he was evidently one of those who, unnoticed in the second rank, shine in the first; now he began to doubt whether even in his own case – in that of others, of course, it was nothing of the kind – failure was indeed a proof of being above success. Very likely not: any more than it necessarily followed that whoever got ahead in the race of life did so by trickery and not for the simple reason that he had better legs and lungs than others; or that wickedness was always implied in the fact of being rich. But then, if this were not the case, he would have to admit that there might be people to whom this world and the next would be a place of delight; and with such a thought as that he felt he could never away.

These doubts of himself could not really have been set at rest but by his receiving from others some such obvious proof of their not being shared as admiration, fame, or envy; and even then his pride would have considered that, though indeed none did so well, he still was far from doing all he ought. But now he was quite at sea as to his value. Failing to get his way, he would wonder whether he had really cared to have it, or whether he lacked that force of character on which he had always so prided himself; and when his remarks did not meet with the appreciation he considered their due, he would think, now that it was because they were not worth being listened to, and now that it was owing to their being above the heads of those to whom they had been addressed. And he would in turn believe himself capable of anything and nothing, genius and fool; at one moment feel sure that he would have made an excellent Secretary of State, and the next doubt his ability to be a passable clerk.

And as his estimate of himself thus varied, so too did the way he behaved. At one time thinking that, as a person without consequence and therefore a care to none, he was unworthy of being so to himself; he would fall into one of those fits of apathy to which even in his schoolboy days he had been subject: he could still remember that which had succeeded his final quarrel with Els. And with his face, as he could feel, heavy and clouded over and all life departed from his eyes, he would go about his work, scarce uttering a word from the moment when, in the morning, he left the house to that when, in the evening, he went back; and this absolute silence of his tongue was no more than a true index of the dull vacantness which had descended on his brain, preventing it formulating so much as one clear thought. And when work was over for the day and once more he was in his rooms, for hours together without so much as stirring he would remain in the position he first had chanced to assume. Even if he presently found it uncomfortable, he could never summon up enough energy to move, but would stay as he was, and go on reading whatever book he had picked up on coming in. He could scarce have told you its title, content if its pages were not so silly as to irritate and wake his mind which it was all his care still to keep in a kind of torpor. And he would read far on into the night in order that, when at length he went to bed, he might at once drop off to sleep, and so avoid what he most disliked, the interval that otherwise came between awake and asleep.

Then all at once the forces of his energy, now rested, would spring again into life, and he would feel that, no matter at what cost, some outlet for them must be found. If it could not be in rearing the lofty structure of his own fortune, why then he must seek it in pulling down that of others. And while the fact of possessing all this idle strength – of knowing himself capable of moving Heaven and yet being nothing – made him long to be up and doing; he burnt besides with a sense of intolerable wrong at seeing those only great whom he scorned. He would have liked to pour the sweet milk of concord into hell, uproar the universal peace, and confound all unity on earth; to trample the people in his fury and stain all his raiment with their blood. And reckless what he did to spite a world which had given him such vile blows and buffets, so long as he could see his lust of his enemies, he would have consented, like Samson, to be crushed to death along with them in the ruin he himself would pull down. In life perhaps he might be obliged to remain obscure, but at least he would not perish without any regarding it. Heaven and Earth and Hell, out-done in cruelty, should know by his death that he had lived; and in imitating, he would surpass Erostratus, by as much as the splendid edifice of the British Empire surpassed the temple made with hands which the old Greek had fired. What more splendid monument could even he hope for whose proud and ambitious heart had always beat so high for glory and greatness? And in the paroxysms of his rage, when with a violence that jarred every nerve he stamped his foot on the ground, he would feel as if it did not matter there being none to help; his own arm would be strong enough, not only to bring salvation to him; his fury would suffice, not only to uphold him, but to call from Heaven on to the place of his abode such fires as once had descended on the Cities of the Plain.

But presently when he began to seek for means to give effect to all this passion – though now and again, for a few brief moments, he would have hopes of some wild project, such as trying to cut those cords of imagination which made one man obey another, and so at a single stroke dissolving society – for the most part he recognised how far anything of the kind was beyond his powers. Sometimes this consciousness of his impotence would nearly choke him with fury, and sometimes make him all but cry for spite; but the very violence of the storm rendered it short, and soon with a laugh, such as Mephistopheles himself, he thought, would scarce have disowned – and then he laughed again at this conceit – he would be mocking at himself as at one whose so magnificent dreams ended in the refusing of some trifling favour he had by chance been asked, or in wishing that Napoleon had conquered at Waterloo. Now again, as so often before, it was the weapon that failed him, not the will to use it. It had been just the same with Nita when, unable to make her happy, he could not even make her wretched.

## CHAPTER XXXI

He was at this comparison as, late one afternoon, walking across the Park, he met an acquaintance, who was also one of Lady Adelaide's, and they stopped for a moment to talk.

'I suppose,' the other said, 'you're going to the funeral to-morrow?'

Nita was dead. As he continued on his way he was surprised to find how immeasurably futile in comparison of his grief suddenly all else was become. Nor was this the case merely with his own thoughts and words and deeds; but Society, ambition, pleasure, beauty, everything he had ever desired for himself or known as being coveted by others, all alike had in one instant together faded away like ghosts at the voice of the morning. Yet while her death had turned all else into a shadowy and unsubstantial dream, do what he would he could hardly realise that she was dead, and that so hope was even more hopelessly cut off than if she had ceased to care for him. And though for the last few months he had been trying his hardest to persuade himself – to use a favourite phrase – that this same hope of his had by suicide escaped the shame of being violently done to death, now he plainly saw that it had only been gagged; and this its final and absolute extinction was as much of a shock as though he had never tried to anticipate the worst. But death was to be preferred to a long separation; the forgetfulness which would so change the very nature of the former as to turn what was at first a grief into a pleasure, was far better than the disappointment in which the latter would have ended – to judge, that was, from his own feelings with regard to Els who, met again as a young man at Tours, had proved so different from the boy-hero of his waking dreams. It might be of course that the mere fact of dying opened the eyes to what before had not even been suspected; and that the dead could clearly discern what those they had left behind really were and had been: so while in the hearts of those who remained on earth every hour replaced some actual trait of theirs by one of ideal beauty, they on their part would from the first look down on their former equals as now immeasurably their inferiors. But should one not rather think that since they knew what was, they also understood the wherefore of its being, and, understanding, forgave?

Nor could he quite repress a feeling of satisfaction that now at last he was really enjoying that sort of romantic misery which at first he had thought he had found in his final parting from her at the Foreign Office party. But still, as he proceeded to turn this mortal maid into a goddess, he was aware not only that she could not have undergone such an apotheosis without first dying, but that, much as she had occupied his thoughts, she had never been anything like so dear to him as his desire to feel now made him wish to believe. But after all, there was some good in this consciousness of how much was factitious in his sensations, since it prevented his giving utterance to any such rash vows of life-long constancy as had made a certain relative of the Binneys so ridiculous. Many a time had he heard them, with a spiteful laugh, recount how, when his first wife had died Uncle Robert had passionately proclaimed that now his only hope was to meet dear

Jane in heaven, and how then within a year, a little year, he had married again!

And presently he was writing to the head of his department to say
that he could not be at the office on the following day. Nor in so doing
was he without a certain sensation of pride at the thought that at last
some one he really knew well had been singled out by death; and that
the obligation of attending the funeral placed him for a few hours at
least above all official orders and ties. And then he laughed.

The next morning early he set off. Even now – and the discovery
brought to his lips their accustomed smile of amused contempt – he
found himself as pleased as ever at travelling first-class: so, at any
rate while the journey lasted, he could feel that, for all passengers, or
guards, or porters knew, he might be some one of the greatest consequence. Presently the outskirts of London had been left behind and
they were in the open country. Fields and cottages and trees flitted
by; it was as if some gigantic and unending roll were being unwound
before him; the smoke from the engine, streaming away at an ever-
widening angle, floated over ploughland and meadow and trailed, like
a long torn lace-scarf, through the hedges; and the telegraph wires
rose and rose, just as they got on a level with the top of the window
were suddenly snatched down by their poles and then at once began
again to rise. And while his eyes were as much fascinated by these
sights as when he had fixed them on the huge dizzily-revolving wheel
at Bower's Mill, his ears were lulled by the full rhythmical rush of the
train as it went on. Meanwhile, anxious to let the spell work, he kept
himself statue-still; only from time to time he had rapidly to blink
his eyes whose gaze had grown fixed and unseeing. Nor did he wake
from his trance till at last they stopped at the little wayside station he
was bound for. How many years ago was it that, top-full of hope, he
had set out from that same platform to which now in very different
mood he came back, and so completed as it were one lap of the race
he then had started to run? So with an air befitting the occasion, he
walked across the platform to the fly that was waiting on the other
side of the low white-painted wooden palings.

By and by the extraordinary fineness of the day – it was surely
too fine to last! – reminded him of those on which long ago she who
now was dead, a woman, had, a child, gone off to ramble with him
through the Chase. Then, their exceeding beauty had caused his heart
to ache with a foreboding of some calamity of he knew not what sort

or provenance that had in some curious way intensified the pleasure they always gave him: now, it made a real woe more dark. Meanwhile, as they went along, he tried to believe that he remembered the various landmarks and that the sight of each added yet another drop to his already brimming cup of sorrow. At last, unable to keep still any longer, he stood up, and, leaning forward against the box, began to talk to the driver of the places and people of the countryside.

'I was very happy here long ago,' he said. 'And now they're all dead!'

It was an exaggeration, of course, but then one must always allow for one's statements being discounted.

'Ah,' the old man replied, 'and so are all them as I've known!'

He dropped back without a word into his seat The idea of a thing like that – and he darted a look of the most intense contempt at the old fellow's doubled-up back – imagining he could have anything in common with him! But the man, half turning round, was talking again, explaining how it was they had not taken the ordinary Tremlett road. They had all then been wasted, the fine poetic emotions he had been trying so hard to feel! So, his chin sunk upon his breast, from under his bent brows he scowled darkly at the tall hedges which shut in the view on either side and thought what a fool he had been. But here at any rate, in the shape of Stoke Fleming Church, was something he recollected without any need to make believe. In another minute they would be round the corner and in sight of ground holy as not having been seen since he had been with her; and, sitting up, with a gulp he prepared himself for the emotions that he doubted not he would presently be feeling. Then, as they began to go down hill, the horse broke into a trot, and, once more standing up, he looked eagerly about from side to side to see if anything was changed since he had been there last.

He still was gazing up the valley that now had opened on the right, its stately hanging-woods asleep in the noontide sun – 'Did they know,' he wondered, 'that their child was dead?' – when the fly stopped at the bottom of a cottage-garden. Surely he remembered those tiny lattice-windows peeping out from among the flowers which hid the low walls, and the steep thatched roof pegged out at the edges into patterns like those of a smock-frock. Of course! It was Prickett's Hatch, where once he and Nita had had tea. So, bidding the driver meet him later at the church, he got out; it would be pleasant to walk up through the woods. But first he thought he would see the room they had sat in, and unlatching the small wooden gate he went up the narrow path towards the rustic porch; against one of its rough-hewn pillars, lichen-grey and split with long exposure to the weather, hung, catching the eye with its brilliant colour, a great loose bunch of some violet-hued flower of whose name he was ignorant. And, as he went, he stooped to pick for remembrance one of the ox-eyed daisies growing just inside the square-clipped edge of box, but in the very act, catching sight of some heartsease, instead took that. So, coming to the door, he rapped upon it with his stick. It was opened by a woman he did not know, but on his explaining that having come there once years ago he wanted to look round, she showed him indoors. And would he not please to sit down, she asked. But he refused, and, going forward, conscious the while her eyes were on him, gazed for a moment at the valanced chimney-corner under whose capacious sooty hood he and Nita had sat side by side and eaten off one plate and drunk of the same cup.

'Perhaps you knew Miss Southwood?' she said.

And then, as still with his back toward her, he nodded:

'Oh, I'm sorry!' she cried.

And the phrase sounded so poor, he almost laughed. Then, as he was going, one of the children, a girl about ten years old, came running in, and he, wishing to repay the mother's civility, pulled out half-a-crown and was giving it to the child when by a sudden impulse which, even in the act he knew not whether to call real or affected, he bent and kissed her little smudgy face and so went off without a word. He heard the woman saying something he did not catch and was aware of the child herself gazing after him with round-eyed astonishment. As for the mother, she followed him out on to the doorstep and thence cried directions after him as to the way up to the House. But he went on down the path merely, without turning, calling back:

'Oh, I know it, thanks, I know it!' And as he walked slowly forward, he gazed about. Surely the pony over there which, in the shade of the clump of elms by the paddock-gate, with head hung down was lazily flicking his tail from side to side, was that on which from the steps of the hall he had so often watched Nita riding away with Els down the Long Walk. Why should that, or indeed the trees and flowers, have life, and she no breath at all? Why——

'But that's the wrong turning, sir! It's to the right!' the woman cried from the porch, whence all this time she had been watching him. He stopped, looked round, saw that he had made a mistake, and took the direction she had pointed out.

Now, out of sight, he was more at ease, and presently began to croon the song of which when there before he had been so fond – the 'Wenn sich lau' from *Faust*. He remembered – and as he did so, there flitted over his lips the smile he always thought of as melancholy-bitter – he remembered how he had brought the book with him when he had come and had been so proud of the reputation for superior learning and taste which he had fancied it got him. Now the air, like an incantation, called back to a ghostly life the dead and the dead past, and slower and slower grew his pace; for rarely did he get a chance of such emotions, and he wished to taste every drop in the cup, not drain it off at a gulp. Yet was his behaviour not altogether due to the connoisseur's anxiety to make the most in an artistic sense of a grief, but even more to his reluctance to admit that grief to be the result as much of deliberate cultivation as of the circumstance of Nita's death, and to his desire to turn it into one that should be real: a desire to which, as he saw, he tried to give effect in the same way as those who, assailed by religious doubts, will endeavour to maintain their ground by efforts at belief which grow more intense as they feel the faith within them becoming weaker.

And what place could he hope would aid him more in so doing than that in which he was, wherein, as in a church of God, there was nothing but what spoke of her? So, delicately and in awe, he walked on. When last his eyes had rested on that scene and his feet trod that ground, her small brown hand had been in his. He could almost fancy that he saw her footfalls, air-drawn as those of the child in the story of the Haunters and the Haunted, printing themselves silent and light – but indeed scarce more light and silent than in life – in the thick white dust of the road; and, forgetting her as she had been at Tours and in London, he tried to conjure up a vision of her as he had known her then. Yes, he could see the very dress she had worn – a soft cream-coloured stuff, with a border of flowers worked in silk. They should have been forget-me-nots. He almost fancied that he could see himself and her and hear the music of her voice and laugh: the double charm which – only scarce in so high a degree, or was it that already he had been growing harder to move? – she had possessed in common with her brother. It was curious, too, but at one and the same time he felt as if it all had never been real, or at the least had happened years and years ago, and as if at any moment he might be back in that time and what he had gone through since turn out to have been as brief and unsubstantial as a dream that, while one dreams it, appears so long and real. Now and again he even fancied that with Nita as his wife by his side, he would presently be walking along that very path, the lighter-hearted for having once dreamt that she had died. And now he would believe that he had done what he had not, and now that he had not done what he had.

But in this attempt to make his dead love and his dead self live again, the sight of a spot he could definitely associate with them would be of no small help; and so, when he came to the path that winds away down to the bridge over Bartley Water, he thought he would like to take it. Only was there time? He stopped, pulled out his watch, saw that he had still over an hour before he need be up at the House, and turned down to the left. Arrived at the bridge, he hitched himself up on to the parapet; in the interstices of its sharp edgeways-set grey stones were some of those wildflowers growing – crane's-bill and toad-flax and ground-ivy – of which she had taught him the names. He remembered how her knowledge in such matters had seemed to make her more than ever a portion of that countryside, his love for which had grown with equal pace with that he had had for her.

And so, half-standing, half-sitting, he waited as he had waited years before while, bare-legged, she had paddled in the water below. And so much was everything the same, he found himself actually growing impatient because she would not come. Still, over its brown pebbles, tinkling and gurgling, ran the little stream; and still the firs on the knoll upon the other side murmured as they had murmured then; the faint soughing of the wind in their tops filled him with a tender melancholy longing after a something he knew not what, towards which his soul, with a sudden passionate impulse, threw out its arms, but which appeared as impalpable and far away as the sound itself that was so strangely moving. How curious that the same cause should, at two different times, produce two such different effects! But when before he had listened to the sound, it had been the complement of what else had so pleased heart and eye. And now, besides, it had a note of mockery. With what an air too of absolute indifference the sun and sky were for their part regarding his grief! But why should he expect it to be otherwise? To do so would be to appear as ridiculous as that Grub Street elegist who was so surprised when he saw the sun rising and going to bed again just as if Partridge had not died. And what a common thing it was, this Death! And how absurd to make such a fuss over one his love for whom had died while she yet lived and had only come back to life since she was dead. Once her name had held within the narrow compass of its two short syllables whole worlds of meaning; now, as he repeated it, it left him equally unable to realise that she had ever lived and that she now was dead; that she was dead and would come no more – never, never, never, never. Was, and is not; such was the sum of all.

And then his attention was caught by the blue sky overhead, and once more he tried to think she was there. But no! That was too foolish! It was deep, perhaps, but quite, quite empty, and it was useless to lift one's hands to it, whether to pray or curse. Not long ago he had thought it almost worth while believing in God if only to indulge the soothing reflection that those whose success here below so offended him would presently be in hell in torments while he was in Abraham's bosom; now he would have liked to do so merely to have some one to revile for what in his life had gone amiss. Indeed he was not far from considering that the very fact of his ill-success was proof enough of the existence of a deity. It was impossible he could so have failed in everything his heart had most been set upon unless there were a supernatural Power to whom he was an object of especial dislike and to contend with whom was beyond his strength. It was really a wonder he had been allowed to win such a wretched little triumph as getting into the Office. Perhaps at the moment his foe in heaven had been talking or pursuing or on a journey or asleep.

So, what with the gentle touch of the wind on his forehead, the ceaseless ripple of the stream and the rustling of the trees, now swelling and now sinking again away almost into silence, he fell, as in the railway-carriage, into a kind of trance. Yet he knew that he was regretting, not so much the Nita, as the Jaspar of the past. What brave ambitions he had had when he had last been there! Then confidence and hope had been his companions; now they were shame and discontent and doubt. In those happy days he had thought it was already much to be ambitious; now he knew that ambition no more implied success than did hunger food. He could have found it in his heart to wish that this passion too had, like its twin, gone down to the pit. After all, Nita's death had in it at least this much of good, that here it had brought him peace of mind. For had she continued still in life, he knew it would have been long before he could have ceased devising all sorts of elaborate plans for showing her she was nothing to him.

So at last he got up and began to climb the hill. More than once he stopped and turned and looked back. He wished he had had time to go a little way up the stream whose waters he could see here and there through the trees, sparkling in the sun. But never more to eternal ages would he tread its banks. And at every step another portion of the landscape was taken away. On the crest of the hill he paused and for a while stood gazing back. It was hard to go. It seemed as if to do so were to part from her. Who could tell, indeed, but that something of her spirit had passed into the valley she had been so fond of? Perhaps even then she was looking down on him. Perhaps, when the time for him too to die should come, his spirit would fly to that beloved spot which thenceforth he and she would haunt together. But now he must be getting on his way. What should he kiss in sign of everlasting farewell? He knelt and pressed his lips passionately to the earth – how different it felt from her little soft warm cheek! – and so, rising, went forward. The last scrap of the scene was hid from his eyes. Perhaps when next he saw it he would be dead.

## CHAPTER XXXII

A few moments more and the house was in sight. How tranquil it rose from its trim-shaven lawns! How smooth every angle was worn! To what a mellow red and orange had its bricks been turned by all the springs and summers, autumns and winters, whose winds and snows and rains and suns it had endured! And now for the first time, as he saw people moving about, he remembered there were others beside himself whose claim to take part in the funeral he could hardly dispute. Had he been free to do as he liked, he would have had no mourners but himself, and alone with his thoughts have followed her to the grave.

Once indoors he made for the Schoolroom by way of the Matted Gallery which to his surprise he found much smaller than it had been in his recollection. But this discrepancy between fact and memory was forgotten as he gazed about at the portraits that still covered the walls. Even when as a boy he had been there before, they had impressed him with a vague notion that the house was of more importance than he who for the moment chanced to be its possessor. Now the same reflection occurred to him, but, to his thinking, with as much more force as his man's understanding was superior to that he had had then. *Eripitur persona, manet res.* The house remained for ever; the dwelling-place endured from one generation to another and even the land was still called after his name who had held it centuries ago, but the owners themselves disappeared. So far from being lords and masters of this everlasting habitation, they were there as at an inn in which each, on his road to the churchyard, tarried his appointed hour, and which, as one after another, feet foremost, they were carried out, became on the instant ready for another guest, while the life of the fabric itself was by entail as well protected as that of any human being, though of course, like them, it might be injured or destroyed.

But even this objection did not hold as against the claims of the dead, who, being but an incorporal memory, could take no harm from anything a mortal might do; and indeed their influence was far more felt than that of the living present. The originals of all those painted eyes had looked on the very scene his now were resting on. Within those walls successive generations had, like him, been filled alternately with despondency and hope, love and lust, sorrow and joy and spleen; and this reflection and the thought of what scenes they might witness in the future, these same walls that, dumb though they might be, yet to his fancy had as much a physiognomy of their own as he himself; of what voices they would echo to when he and his contemporaries had passed in their turn away and were now as forgotten as those whose likenesses surrounded him, made him, as he had done before, lose all sense of identity, and consider, not only the Jaspar of the past, but even himself as he was then, as but one more among the hundred other figures his imagination represented as having strutted and fretted their brief hour on that gorgeous stage. And as he thus dreamt the whole place became alive and he could almost believe he heard the sound of the voices and movements of those who had long been still and silent. But no portrait of him would ever hang there, before which others, as now he in front of these, might come and dream, try from a consideration of his features to discover what thoughts had occupied the brain behind, and wonder if in life his lips had met any of those depicted, now for ever out of reach on other of the canvasses, or his eyes gazed into any of those the expression of whose painted images was now fixed once for all. He was sorry, for if it were true that only in the fancy of the living can ghosts revisit the earth, then it followed that, unlike those whose pictures he saw around, once dead he would never be able to enjoy among the scenes he had, alive, been so fond of, the spirit-existence which, if not so full as that he had led in the flesh, would be at least of eternal duration. He wondered whether he should find a picture of Nita there; and, if so, whether it would be in the sprightfulness of youth or with the fair cheeks and full eyes of childhood, as he would have much preferred, that he must look to see, blooming in some great painter's colours, the flower of that beauty which had proved so frail; so would it still be unfaded when the original, long the heritage of worms and ser-pents, rottenness and cold dishonour, had been sleeping many years in that charnel-house whither even then she was being carried out to make one more in that numerous company of ladies whose portraits crowded the walls.

So at last he reached the Schoolroom. But he had barely time to glance at all the dear old familiar things he remembered so well, the paper with its daisies and its motto; *Si douce est la marguerite*, and the shabby little mahogany bookcase with its rows of 'Illustrateds,' when he heard voices in the bedroom beyond and the sound of something heavy being moved. So, stepping quickly away, he returned down-stairs, and had presently followed the rest in to lunch. But he could eat nothing and, his plate untouched before him, sat silent, now gazing out into the garden, now looking round at the others. Els was not to be seen; it appeared that he and Mabel were away yachting and it was even doubtful whether they had so much as heard of Nita's death. The head of the table had been therefore taken by Lady Adelaide's elder brother, the Duke. His presence seemed to be the human com-plement of all the stately surroundings that so dignified as almost to change in nature those common necessities of the flesh to which it always irked him to think that he with the great, equally with the meanest, was subject. Close to him two old gentlemen were talking.

'Dreadful!' said one, and helped himself to another slice of brawn. Certainly, if one might judge from the way they were all behaving, there was little fear of the poor child's ghost being disturbed by their deep sorrows; and the reflection intensified his feeling that he was in some sort in a communion with her in which no one else had any share. But at length even he took a sip of claret and was just proceed-ing further to eat a biscuit, when he remembered it was one of the sort they had used to take with them when they went out in the boat and at the same instant he caught a glimpse of the coffin as it was carried past outside. Involuntarily he rose, and then everybody was in the hall, forming confusedly into a kind of procession. Then, as they all stood waiting, suddenly the bell began to toll. At the first stroke it seemed as if his very soul were shaken and as it went on, slowly and sullenly, allowing to every clang its full effect, he thought it was somehow vibrating within him.

So they began to move forward, while he, seeing that no one else wore gloves, was hurriedly pulling off and shuffling away into his pocket the new black pair he had bought for the occasion. And as they went he looked about. On that bank, overgrown with ivy and St. John's-wort, once, as they had been on their way to the river, she had let fall the wraps she was carrying; on the bench under that tree she had been sitting as he and Lady Adelaide had come back from the village; there on the lawn she had lain one afternoon trying to mend her old red parasol; over those flower-beds they had often jumped. And under the influence of these recollections he almost forgot what he was doing. Besides, the weather was so lovely such a ceremony as that he was taking part in seemed not only an unreality, but an unreality so out of place that he was nearly crying, 'Oh, let's get it over and return to something more suited to the time!' Now and again he would try to recall himself to a sense of what he was about by glancing at the coffin which he could just see over he heads of those in front; its brass and polished oak flashed in the sun as, with a dumb and helpless pathos inexpressibly moving, it swayed in cadence to the walk of the men on whose shoulders it was being borne. Then he would think that the tender grace of that autumn day, so far from being out of tune, was rather appropriate, not only to death, but to such grief as it became him to feel for her loss. And then again there recurred to him the notion which had in various shapes so dominated his mind ever since that morning he had set foot within the Tremlett bounds: that he himself was but one more among the unsubstantial figures which haunted every nook and corner of park and garden and house. Their little troop – they were scarce more than a score – was surrounded and accompanied by the shadowy host of all who at different times since the house had been built, had issued from the great gates they too had just come through and, with every variety of feeling, from the deepest grief through indifference to satisfaction scarce hidden under the decent mask of regret, had followed coffins down that path to the lych-gate they were even then approaching.

There, in white surplice and red hood, he saw the clergyman awaiting them, who was presently going before to the church.

'*I am the resurrection and the life!*' he heard; and there fell a few drops of rain, and the thunder rumbled in the distance. As they went slowly up the narrow path they passed a rough heap of earth cast up against its side and a shiver ran through him to the very soles of his feet; it was the natural shrinking of his flesh at sight of the hole:

'*And though after my skin worms destroy this body,*'

Yes, the hole into which it would one day descend to be destroyed by worms; and he tried to peer down to see how deep it was. He was glad that they were not going to lay her in the vault, for now, while the green turfs and brambles of their dear summer would bind her grave, he could think of her immortal part as living with angels, and not as shut down for ever with her body beneath the great stone he remembered, in the company of all those ancestors who, on their backs, motionless and silent, peopled the awful chamber of death whither his imagination had in old times so often strayed but which he never yet had seen.

In church he took a seat as little in view as he could manage always with the notion that he must not put himself forward, and, after kneeling for a moment, stood up. The coffin was at the altar-steps and he grew sick at the thought of finding himself so close to the dead. But had not death come so near him as to fetch a portion from his very heart? Perhaps one night from her bed of darkness she might call and draw him against his will – no, surely willing – to: – And here Lady Adelaide entered and for the first time in his life he saw overwhelming grief. His impulse was to turn away but resolutely he forced himself to look; only he could not see her face which was hidden by a long thick black veil. He wondered vaguely how she had contrived to have her mourning ready. So with his eyes he followed her, as, half-led, half-supported by two other women – who they were he did not know – slowly she moved towards her place.

And then the service began. For an instant he grew dizzy with his emotions, and staggered and only saved himself from falling by clutching the trefoil headed bench-end of his seat; but recollecting how unseemly it would be for him to faint while others were unmoved who by the laws of society had far more reason for so doing, with an effort he regained his composure, and, firm and upright, addressed himself to listening.

'Now is Christ risen from the dead and become the first-fruits of them that slept.' The words appeared to have a charm independent of any meaning or intrinsic beauty; a charm, he fancied, due to the thought of all the generations who had heard them read over what they held dearest on earth, knowing that they by and by would in like manner be read over themselves. Just so did the house close by, in the memory of all who had suffered and been happy and lived and loved within its walls, speak to the heart as could have done no modern building, how splendid soever.

Then, as the service went on, the clergyman's monotonous tones began, as in the old days, to lull him to sleep. Here and there his attention was aroused by some particular sentence: 'Let us eat and drink, for to-morrow we die'; and again: 'There is one glory of the sun and another glory of the moon and another glory of the stars.'

But for the most part he was lost in fancying that he was once more back in those times. There was the pew he had so often sat in; those books on the ledge were surely hers; while just above was the board:

'To the Pious and Beloved Memory of Anita Southwood, whose Body lies interred in the Vault Below, while her Soule lives in the Felicities of Heaven and her Honoured Memorie in the Register of Fame.'

And there were the monuments with which the dead child's race, their vain ashes still followed by pomp to the grave, had so filled the church as to remind him now of what he had read of that at Rimini which the Malatesta had erected, nominally indeed, as this, to God, but in reality to the Divine Isotta. And there was the window through which, as then, he could see little scraps of blue sky between the trees; the light struck through the leaves and showed them translucent yellow-green against the diamond-panes; the sun was evidently shining only by fits and starts, for they were at one moment flickering and wavering and the next gone altogether, the shadows that fell upon her trailing silver and white pall instead of on that sea of her hair whose waves had in curls been broken. Yes, it was true indeed; her body, ceremoniously washed, was to be laid in the lap of its kindred earth, there to dwell with dust; the beauty he had so loved would consume in the sepulchre. Yet perhaps, could he but wish hard enough, even now he might raise her from the dead. If – but here he was suddenly awakened from his dreaming by a cry that like a trumpet-call thrilled through the church:

'*O death, where is thy sting? O grave, where is thy victory?*'

The words were no longer a sentence coldly read from a book, but a defiance hurled at some actually present foe, and fearfully he looked round, almost expecting to see, shrinking back into some dark corner, some such awful shrouded figure as that which in Watts' picture bears down the struggling Amor. Yes, the poor relic of clay was in a few moments to be given back to its native earth and for ever hid from his eyes, but the gracious soul that had informed it, that surely had never stained the whiteness of its baptismal robe, but passed from the font unspotted to the grave, had already winged its flight to heaven. And while for the rest of his life he would keep the divine essence of his dead love, he would hope for the day when he might mingle his bones with that beloved dust and have at last some satisfaction for his unsatisfied affections by being neighbours in the grave, by lying urn by urn and touching, as at Tours, in their names.

Suddenly there was a rushing noise and the rain came down. Falling straight and steadily, it served for a dreary accompaniment to the Vicar's monotonous tones. But by and by these ceased, there was a pause, and then the bearers advanced, and to the incessant pattering of the rain that had for a moment been the only sound to break the silence was added the trampling of their feet as they raised the coffin and turned it round. Then, as it was carried down the church and passed the end of the bench where he was sitting so close he could have touched the pall, he bent his head. 'Adieu,' he murmured, 'adieu, adieu!' It was her spirit to which in Lady Holt he had said good-bye; now it was of her body that he was taking farewell. Then, looking up, he saw the men disappear with their load into the porch and Lady Adelaide make a groping movement with her hands which struck him as infinitely pathetic. Somebody half-pushed the old duke towards her, who vaguely dropping his hat and stumbling forward gave her his arm.

'I suppose,' he heard one standing by observe, 'I suppose she feels he ought to be with her as her nearest relative!'

But now there appeared to be some hitch, for the bearers were stopping; he could still even catch a glimpse of the coffin. Nothing was to be heard but the ceaseless pouring of the rain. His emotions, for a moment raised to the height, began to drop and he found him-self wondering what was the cause of the delay in a spirit as indiffer-ent as though it had been simply a question of a block on the road. They were waiting, he presently gathered, in the hope that the rain would cease. After a while however, when still it showed no sign of abating, they began once more to move slowly forward. He followed among the rest. At his side was an old gentleman who in an agitated manner was talking to himself.

'Oh, it's impossible,' he heard him say, 'quite impossible! I shall wait until it's over!' And now he looked up at the sky and fumbled with his umbrella and ruefully considered his hat, much scratched already and rumpled.

He for his part set down his on the stone bench of the porch, and, stepping by, put up his umbrella and began as well as he could to pick his way after the rest of the company who, plunging about among the tombstones and mounds and plashing over the soppy grass and muddy paths, were making for the farther corner of the churchyard. So, after all, the grave they had passed was not that Nita was to be buried in, and the feelings its contemplation had excited had been excited in vain.

So, with their umbrellas spread, they all stood round and listened to the concluding part of the service. Thus far the coffin had been still above ground, but now the men again advanced and began to let it down into the grave; it descended slowly. Up to the very last moment that it remained in sight he watched it with a gaze into which it seemed that his whole soul passed, and then, as it disappeared below the edge and the cords ran on, his mind took up the task and followed it with so lively an imagination, he almost fancied that it still was vis-ible to his bodily sight. But as his ears were struck by the sound it made as it reached the bottom, as if now that he knew it to be where it would never again be moved, he needed not further to concern himself with it and what it held; his thoughts flew off to her soul that must surely be but a little way above their heads. But now the rain had stopped and a small patch of bright blue sky appeared; a tiny puff of wind stirred the ivy the sides of the grave had been lined with and the sexton with a mechanical gesture threw in a little earth. He had seen him stoop to take it and then scatter it lightly down, but had not at first realised the significance of the act. And then there came the final words: '. . . be with us all evermore. Amen.'

For a moment everybody still kept their places and then, putting on their hats, began to break up and move slowly and confusedly away. He was already following when, hearing a bustle behind, he turned round and, as he did so, saw Lady Adelaide totter, slip from between the hands stretched out to save her and without a cry fall forward, a mere huddle of black in all the piteous abandonment of grief, on to the heap of clay at the edge of the grave. A few minutes after, having fetched his hat from the porch, he was going away down the path when he had to stand aside to let go-by a couple of men who were carrying her between them in their arms. Her veil, thrown back, showed her face a lifeless white – scarcely less white perhaps than her daughter's who was lying in her coffin a few yards away – her head dangled pitifully, her eyes were shut. Just however as she was being borne past him, she appeared to wake to the consciousness that she was being taken away. She made a feeble struggle:

'Oh, don't, don't!' she cried; 'I won't go back! I don't want to go back any more!'

'Ah,' he heard some one just behind observe, 'Ah, I saw her face working from the other side of the grave!'

As he reached the lych-gate, the sun came out, a bird began to sing, and a man said:

'Look sharp with those trestles there! I want to catch my train!'


THE END

www.ingramcontent.com/pod-product-compliance
Lightning Source LLC
Chambersburg PA
CBHW031111030726
47496CB00002BA/498